Wealth, Sorrow, Redemption

The Adventurous Life of a Countess

A Biographical Novel
by
Kathleen Ambro

First Edition published by Positive Waves Publishing
Positive Waves Publishing
225 Crossroads Blvd. Suite 332
Carmel, CA 93923

Library of Congress Cataloging-in-Publication Data
Ambro, Kathleen. Wealth, Sorrow, Redemption – *The Adventurous Life of a Countess*

Library of Congress Control Number: 2017946116

ISBN (978-0-9991391-0-3
1. Biographical novel 2. Countess Kinnoull 3. Photojournalist
4. Artist 5. Spy 6. Racecar driver 7. Pilot 8. Catholicism
9. African Missions 10. SPCA 11. Society of Saint Pius X

Printed in USA

Cover Design by John Ambro

DEDICATION

To my husband, John – for whom I could not have done this nine-year journey without. Thank you for your love and support and for your vast knowledge of war, weapons and cars, and for your artistic abilities in designing the cover of this book, but most of all, for believing in me.

K.A.

PROLOGUE
The Last Rites

The phone rang, echoing through the lobby of the St. Aloysius Retreat in Campbell, California. A young priest rushed to the phone hoping it had not disrupted the early morning prayers.

"Hello? Yes, this is the St. Aloysius Retreat." He sensed uneasiness in the woman's faint, almost inaudible voice. "One moment, please." The priest's hand trembled as he fumbled through the desk drawer, frantically searching for a notepad and pencil. Surely he had not heard her correctly.

On the other end of the phone, Nancy Welch felt her voice quiver as the sharp pain of arthritis in her hips flared up. She slowly lowered herself into the chair by the phone. She was apprehensive, wondering if she was doing the right thing. She hoped they wouldn't think she was an old busybody, but somebody had to tell him. He must know. It was a matter of life and death.

"We seem to have a bad connection, could you please repeat that?" He tried to keep up with everything the woman was saying. "And how much time did you say? Yes, I'll see he gets this immediately. He'll be most grateful that you called. Thank you, Ms. Welch." He hung up the phone, tore the message from the notepad and headed down the hall to the chapel.

Archbishop Lefebvre stood at the dark mahogany podium at the end of the gothic chapel. His eyes sparkled with enthusiasm. The natural upturn at the corners of his mouth and the touch of grey along his receding hairline gave him a welcoming allure in the warm light emanating from the stained glass window behind him. He had just finished prayers when the young priest handed him the note. Upon reading it, he closed his eyes for a moment then looked out at the acolyte students in front of him.

"May I have your attention? I am sorry to say that I will not be able to meet with all of you tonight as we had planned. A most urgent matter has been brought to my attention that needs my attendance and I'll be leaving shortly." He dismissed the acolytes then headed to his room with the young priest in tow.

"You must call and arrange for a car to be ready to go. I'd like to leave immediately. Please inform Fathers Laisney and Finnegan of the situation and that I'd like them to accompany me."

"I'll get right on it, Your Grace." As the priest left the room, he turned to close the door and saw the elderly Archbishop drop to his knees and begin to pray.

A black sedan was waiting with the motor running. A young Father Finnegan was at the wheel, adjusting the radio and the temperature in the car. Father Francois Laisney soon approached with the Archbishop and they were on their way.

God's providential timing brought a smile to Father Laisney's face. He had planned the Archbishop's whole 1985 Confirmation Trip with quite a heavy schedule: each day in a different place, with only one day a week for a little rest in a priory.

It was after Sunday mass that the two young priests were told of Archbishop Lefebvre's desire to visit a sick friend living in Carmel-by-the-Sea, and he asked that they accompany him. They, of course, put themselves at his service.

The month of May was quite pleasant and they had all looked forward to a day of relaxation, a reprise from their busy schedule. The unexpected trip to Carmel was seventy miles away and would take at least an hour and thirty minutes to drive. Father Finnegan was familiar with the Monterey Peninsula, so he was appointed driver. Father Laisney would keep an eye on the road signs. The Archbishop fingered his rosary while he contemplated the circumstances of this visit with his old friend.

The sun had just broken through the clouds when they drove away from the priory. They followed a two-lane road winding over the lush green hillsides. The farmlands were bursting forth with an abundant harvest, evident by the numerous trucks piled high with fresh produce, their pungent aromas wafting through the air. Acres and acres of precisely placed rows of vegetables and fruits in a palette of deep rich colors appeared like a patchwork quilt covering the hillsides.

They had been traveling almost an hour when the farmlands faded into the distance. A few miles further the Pacific Ocean appeared on their right. The sea was frothed with whitecaps and a fog bank grew on the horizon. The sun that had followed them the whole trip now disappeared behind menacing clouds.

Traffic had been light and the Archbishop seemed to know exactly where they were, instructing them to take the Ocean Avenue exit. They drove down a steep hill toward the village of Carmel. Just before they reached the beginning of the town, the Archbishop told them to turn left on Torres and continue on. Father Finnegan cautiously drove along the narrow winding road through the forest. At the end of the road was a large wooden gate. Father Laisney got out and unlatched it, allowing their car to pass. A thick fog drifted through the tops of stately pines and delicate fingers of moss dangled from numerous oak trees oozing droplets of water onto their car. Dampness crept in from the ocean, nourishing the lush green vegetation with clumps of stately white Calla lilies scattering across the property. A short drive from the gate, the roadway curved to the left and ascended a slight hill to the front of the estate. It was a two-story sand colored stucco house with a red tile roof reminiscent of the Spanish style so prevalent in California. A tiered stone fountain stood in the courtyard and an intricate pebble mosaic pathway led to the front door.

Helen Dunn, the housekeeper, greeted the gentlemen. She explained that the priory had called to inform them of the Archbishop's visit, and that the Countess was waiting to receive them in the living room.

Helen led them through the entry and into a large rectangular room with French doors leading to a veranda where terra cotta pots over-flowed with cascading geraniums in a blending of various shades of pinks and reds. The lofty ceiling accommodated the numerous portrait paintings hanging throughout the room.

An over-stuffed armchair dwarfed its frail occupant. Her large standard size poodle stayed obediently at her side and an oxygen tank with a ventilating mask was at arms reach. Her short stylish auburn hair had only a few flecks of grey with not a strand out of place. She ran her hand down the right sleeve of her royal blue silk dress and straightened the white lace cuff that had caught on her watch. Although the fashion had faded from years gone by, she always felt a certain elegance and dignity whenever she wore it. And today of all days called for just such a dress. As she lifted herself from the chair to greet the visitors, she winched from a sharp burning pain in her lungs. Archbishop Lefebvre rushed to her side insisting she remain seated. He then introduced Countess Claude Kinnoull to the young priests who had been admiring the mosaic above the stone fireplace.

Although her body was failing, her intellect was very much intact and she was delighted to explain to her guests that she had titled the eight by eight foot mural mosaic *The Tree of Life*. She had created it with pebbles from places as far away as Spain and Africa and also used forged iron, brass, seashells and obsidian. Her artistic abilities went further than mosaics. She had studied portrait painting with the famous Ignacio Zuloaga y Zabaleta while in Spain and his realistic influence was evident in the portraits she had painted which hung on the walls

Both Father Finnegan and Father Laisney knew that the Countess Kinnoull was a great benefactress for the cause of the Traditional Catholic Mass and that it was through her funding that the Society of Saint Pius X, which Archbishop Lefebvre founded, was able to thrive.

But it was most unusual for an archbishop to pay a personal visit to a benefactor's home. No, there was more than just her wealth that bound her to the Archbishop. There was much, much more to be discovered about the Countess, for she was truly a woman of substance.

Several times, she had to use the oxygen apparatus to calm her labored breathing. The Archbishop sat on the chair next to her, and the young priests listened, conscious of being in front of two *elders*. They talked about her health and reminisced about their first meeting and how important that was to the Society. He thanked her in the name of all the members; telling her that she could in a certain way consider all the young priests of the Society of Saint Pius X as her children, since without her help at the beginning, he would not have been able to realize this priestly work.

After he listened to her confession of sins, Lady Kinnoull asked for a blessing, which Archbishop Lefebvre happily gave her and then blessed them all. The whole visit was not more than an hour.

Father Laisney realized that Archbishop Lefebvre and Countess Kinnoull were both very much aware that this was their last meeting on earth.

PART 1

Enid

INTRODUCTION

*T*o *understand the importance of Countess Claude Kinnoull, one must start at the beginning of her life. It is only then that one can truly appreciate the full extent of the decisions she made in her later years. Her stage was the world and she played many roles. She was the adored grandchild of Sir Frederick and Annie Wills of England's Imperial Tobacco Dynasty, but became a confused little girl at the age of six when her parents divorced. She was a rebellious teenager; a racecar driver; a pilot and a countess at the age of twenty. She endured a sad rocky marriage with the young Earl of Kinnoull, which finally led to joy with the birth of her son, only to be grieved by the child's tragic death. A conversion to Catholicism set her life in a new direction, in which she brought medical supplies to 112 Catholic missions in Africa and set up a hospice outside of Paris. Her role as an actress in a spy movie turned to reality when she became a spy for the British and French governments. As a photojournalist with Franco's Army in Spain during the Spanish Civil War, she spied on communists while studying portrait painting with Spain's renowned artist, Ignacio Zuloaga y Zabaleta. Fleeing France to the United States when Hitler had placed a price on her head and the Germans entered Paris, she ended up in Carmel-by-the-Sea, a quaint little California village where writers and artist gathered and lived a bohemian lifestyle. It was here that she continued painting, writing books and became a champion for animal rights and welfare. She supported the Society of Saint Pius X for the much loved Traditional Latin Mass with her generous financial backing, and her legacy lives on in the many contributions to various charities that are still financed by her estate today. And so her story begins with the Wills Family . . .*

Chapter 1

A Noble Heritage – The Wills Family

Mrs. Ethel Leach shivered from the dampness of the early morning fog. She adjusted a few stray wisps of salt and pepper hair, which had managed to fall from the neat French knot on the top of her head, and pulled the collar of her tweed coat tighter across her neck. She only had a block to walk and quickened her step. It was a crisp morning on October 20, 1904. A strong breeze sent a pile of brown leathery leaves of the London Plane trees, swirling over her shoes. She stopped and stared at the imposing structure across the street and grinned.

The Imperial Tobacco Company's brick building encompassed almost the entire block. It was thought to be one of the largest factories built in London at the time and would surely take a lifetime to fill. The fast growth of the company surpassed everyone's expectations. Except for Ethel, of course. She knew from the day she started working for the company back in 1870, under the part ownership of Henry Overton Wills II, that she was working not at a factory, but for a very remarkable family.

The Wills Family's Non-Conformist Congregational beliefs fortified their sense of accountability to those less fortunate. This played out in their work ethic by always showing genuine concern for their employees. At first employees were skeptical that their employer had overstepped his boundaries by interfering in their personal lives, for this was unheard of. But the Wills Family's sincere Christian love toward their fellow workers soon won out and the employees welcomed the fair and honest treatment that they received.

As the business grew so did the benefits to the employees. In 1889 wages were increased by 10% and because the business was doing so well, a percentage of the profits was given as a bonus to each employee in proportion to his or her earnings during the year. Amazingly, that bonus grew from 10% in 1889 to 40% in 1900.

Ethel took a deep breath and closed her eyes, remembering that glorious afternoon in England on March 27th, 1886, at the historic high tea commemorating the new factory on East Street in Bedminster. Why, she could almost smell the delicious aromas that wafted through the factory on that day. Over nine hundred employees and their families had filled the enormous Cigar Room. Swags of purple and white fabric with detailed lace had draped the walls and colorful banners flowed from the ceiling illuminated by electric lamps. Portraits of past employees were proudly displayed on the walls accompanied by the many medals and honors bestowed upon its employees and employers for their generous contributions and volunteer hours to local charities. Samples of tobacco from all over the world had been on display. But it was the posted menu that had amazed Ethel. It listed: Roast Sirloins of Beef, Corn Beef, Veal and Ham Pies, Pigeon Pies, Fillets of Veal, York Hams, Ox Tongues, Rhubarb Tarts, Apple Tarts, Cheese Cakes, Tea Cakes, Buns, Bread and Butter; there were platters of artfully arranged food, enough to satisfy even the most finicky of diners.

Ethel opened her eyes, grabbed her purse closer to her chest, walked across the street and entered a side door of the Imperial Tobacco building. She removed her coat and hung it on a peg in the employee lounge. Even though it was early in the morning, the factory was always quite warm. She was grateful for the lad they had hired to keep the fires going during the night. Ethel made it a habit to arrive a little early each morning to enjoy a warm biscuit and cup of tea before the morning rush.

She glanced at the clock on the wall; it was almost time. Putting on a freshly laundered white apron, Ethel headed to the Leaf Room.

Each year as business increased more employees were needed, so it was with the highest esteem that Mrs. Leach was appointed in 1888 to see to the wellbeing of the girls and women employed by the firm. She became one of the first female factory welfare officers in England, a duty she accepted with gratitude and honor. It was not often that there was an opening for a new employee, but when there was a new hire, it was Ethel's job to acquaint the new girl with the procedures at the factory. Today was one of those days and Ethel was delighted to share the incredible history of The Imperial Tobacco Company once again.

Mrs. Leach entered the Leaf Room and began to sift through the mounds of tobacco leaves next to several massive baskets flanked with stools on either side. A young girl of about eighteen poked her head into the room and nervously looked around.

"Why, you must be Lizzie," said Ethel.

"Yes, Ma'am."

"Don't be shy, my dear. Come sit next to me." Ethel patted the stool to her right and Lizzie sat down.

"Are you Mrs. Leach?"

"Yes, and I'll be showing you the ropes, so to speak."

It didn't take long before women of varying ages filed into the room each pulling up a stool next to a basket of tobacco leaves. Mrs. Leach introduced young Lizzie to the other women, then proceeded to demonstrate to her the proper way to sort the tobacco leaves.

"Now Lizzie, the leaves are sorted according to color . . . from light brown to dark brown. Each shade represents a different strength of tobacco, so it's important not to mix them."

Loud voices emanated from the hall. The women all looked up. Sir Frederick Wills himself entered the sorting room.

"Good morning, good morning, and how are my drawing room ladies today?" he asked.

"Good morning, Sir Wills," the women sang out in unison.

"A wonderful morning, indeed," said Sir Wills, "for today is a very special day. I'm the proud grandfather of a precious baby girl, born in the wee hours this morning." All the women applauded. "Come, William, pass out the chocolates." He was referring to a young lad who had followed him into the room carrying a rather cumbersome basket filled with truffles.

Sir Frederick Wills, like his father and grandfather before him, sported a white beard and mustache with silver gray highlights. His was a kind face, which was a reflection of his life. He was a generous and God-fearing man.

Sir Wills stopped and chatted with each of the women, asking about their families. He stopped in front of Mrs. Leach. "And this must be Lizzie Murphy." He handed each woman a truffle.

"Yes, sir," Lizzie replied.

"Welcome, Miss Murphy, you're in good hands with Mrs. Leach. See to it that you listen to all she tells you and you will do fine. And I expect to see you in Sunday School."

"Yes, sir, thank you," said Lizzie lowering her eyes.

Ethel smiled, "Now, Mr. Wills, please tell us the name of the baby."

"She is Enid Margaret Hamilton-Fellows. Quite a long name for such a little one, but mark my words, she is bound to do great things. Good day, ladies." Sir Frederick Wills smiled then continued on throughout the factory delivering the good news of his granddaughter's birth.

"You're quite fortunate to be hired by this company, Lizzie. Not a finer employer than Sir Frederick Wills."

"He seems quite nice, ma'am, but what did he mean by I'll see you in Sunday School?"

"All the Wills Family members are righteous God-fearing people, Lizzie. Their family has always been known for their generosity in the building and repair of churches throughout England. Why, if a church needs an organ you can best be assured that a Wills would promptly take care of it."

"But why Sunday School?" asked Lizzie.

"Their Non-Conformist Congregationalist beliefs require them to pay special attention to instilling moral and religious truths into the minds of children, giving them view of their situation and sound practical rules for their conduct."

"What happens if someone does not attend church?" asked Lizzie.

"You would more than likely be invited to theirs. Why, ever since The Bristol Union Society for the Promotion of Sunday Schools was founded in 1813, anyone who applies for employment in the Wills tobacco business is required to be a Sunday School member."

Lizzie helped Ethel move the large basket of sorted tobacco leaves over to the cutting machines. "Tell me more, Mrs. Leach." They had to raise their voices over the noise of the machines.

"Well, this company began back in 1804 when Henry Overton Wills I, the great-grandson of Anthony Wills, a small shopkeeper, went to Bristol and founded a tobacco business. By 1901, what began as a family partnership had grown to the largest and most prosperous tobacco manufacturer in the United Kingdom," said Ethel.

"What's been their secret?" asked Lizzie as she continued to sort tobacco leaves.

"Well, child, I do believe it's their fundamental belief in God that has given them a sense of responsibility to those less fortunate. Why, even when their wealth grew, they were always concerned with the welfare of their employees."

A loud bell rang, echoing throughout the factory.

"Good heavens, what's that?" asked Lizzie, dropping several leaves.

"It's time for lunch." Ethel smiled, placing her handful of leaves back into the basket. "Come, you'll dine with me."

"Oh, I've just brought an apple for my break. You go on ahead," said Lizzie.

"Nonsense, an apple will never do. You need a hot meal on a cold day like today. Why, for less then what it costs to make a cold lunch from home, you can have a hot meal in our dinning room here. Besides, it's my treat today."

Mrs. Leach ushered Lizzie out into the hallway where they followed the other employees to the dinning room. The smell of freshly baked meat pies and vegetables, bacon and plum cake wafted throughout the building. Tea, coffee, cocoa and lemonade were served at the end of the line, much to Lizzie's delight. The two women sat down at a table by a window.

"This is wonderful," said Lizzie, tasting a spoonful of beef and carrots.

Mrs. Leach smiled as she spread soft butter on a thick, warm slice of bread. "Much better than an apple, hey?"

"Tell me about yourself, Mrs. Leach. Did you meet your husband here?" asked Lizzie, cupping a hot cup of tea to warm her hands.

"Oh, my Henry was the dearest man, God rest his soul. On my first day at the factory, it was Henry who took me on a tour of the place. Now, Henry had worked for the company a good two years and after a spell we decided to marry. Well, Sir Frederick Wills sat my Henry down and figured out that he needed to work one more year in order to make enough money to provide for a wife and family."

"And you allowed that?" Lizzie waited as Mrs. Leach took a few bites of meat pie.

"At first we thought it was none of his business, but than my Henry said we would wait because Sir Wills had our best interest at heart."

"And did he?" asked Lizzie.

"It turned out that it was the best thing we ever did. After another year the company started a new policy that when an employee worked at least one year, they would receive a one week paid holiday."

"A whole week!" Lizzie almost spilled her tea.

"Yes, and that was unheard of at that time. Plus we were to receive new benefits."

"What benefits?" Lizzie could hardly contain herself.

"They now provide a company doctor, a sickness pay and a matron to deal with minor illnesses or injury at work. It was in the 1880's that the company started providing subsidized meals. When they finished this factory they made sure every department included a large dinning room and kitchen. And it was just four years ago that they introduced a savings benefit where we place a third of our annual gift in the Wills Saving Plan, which would build interest. And when we retire we get a lump sum equal to twelve years pay."

"I'm so glad to be working here," said Lizzie. "Why, at the last place I worked, I got yelled at for taking a ten minute lunch."

"Child, you're not just working at a factory here. You're part of a family."

Chapter 2

The Early Years

The family home of Sir Frederick and Annie Wills was always a beehive of activity with six children. Margaret Hamilton Wills, their third child, who preferred to be called Margie, was married at the late age of twenty-nine. On June 10th, 1903 she married Ernest Gaddesden Fellows. Ernest was a major with the 1st Suffolk Regiment and lived near Guilford; and this is where he took his bride to begin their new life together. The following year on October 20th, 1904, they were blessed with the birth of their daughter, Enid Margaret Hamlyn Fellows.

Enid's Childhood Home in Tangley Park in Worplesdon, Surrey, near Guilford
Bought by Margaret Hamilton-Fellows in 1917.

During her young years, Enid looked forward to visits at her grandmother and grandfather's country estate and summers at their seashore home where she learned to swim in the cold ocean. She seldom lacked for attention from her numerous aunts and uncles and especially enjoyed playing with her cousin Irene, who was eight years older.

Sir Frederick believed that children should be brought up in the country and taught to work the land. Enid often sat with her grandfather on a bench overlooking the rolling hills of the estate, listening wide eyed as her grandfather told stories of the importance of working the land and protecting the animals, except for when needed as food for survival.

Enid saw something shiny in the walkway and jumped down to pick it up. "Look what I've found, Grandfather." He took the object from her and dusted it off.

"Why, you have found a magic half penny."

"Why is it magic?" asked Enid.

"It is magic because of what you do with it." He handed the half penny back to Enid. "It is something to think about."

Although he was wealthy, Sir Frederick Wills used his 1500 acres of country estate at Northmour, near Dulverton, to teach his children that although education from books was good, it was the traditions of working the land where one learns life's real lessons. Teaching survival techniques, especially to his sons, was the utmost on his mind. Studying the nature surrounding them, be it fish, fowl, wild animals or weather, his children and grandchildren would be prepared to face any dilemmas, sorrows or perils with bravery and good spirits; he knew that one day his sons might be going off to war. Little did he know that one day that would include his granddaughter.

Above all, glory was given to God for their blessings, which they generously shared in assisting those in need. All members of the Northmour household, including the servants, were expected to attend the daily family prayers.

The Wills Family practiced the Nonconformist Congregationalist principles of hard work, prudent endeavors and honorable agreements. These virtues grew the Imperial Tobacco Company tenfold over the years and endeared the Will's employees with their kindness, which was evident when over 1,000 people attended the funeral of Sir Frederick in February 1909. A year later, his wife Annie passed away from a long illness, but many thought it was from a broken heart. This was indeed a sad time for little Enid, but things were about to get worse. In most marriages the good years seem to cancel out the bad years, but unfortunately in the Fellows household that was not to be.

Ever since her grandfather died, Enid had been shuffled between her home and the Wills estate, where nanny Bardie would take charge of Enid and her cousin Irene. At home, she found herself being told to go to the nursery where she would pass the time preparing tea parties with her doll. She often found her mother short tempered and seldom saw her smile anymore.

In 1910, six-year-old Enid was alone in the nursery dressing her favorite doll for a tea party. The doll was almost as tall as Enid. She struggled to button the doll's brown felt shoes, and then sat it down on a small-upholstered chair, straightening the delicate ivory lace dress and fluffing the matching bloomers. Enid pulled up a chair for herself and pretended to pour tea into the miniature teacups on the table when loud voices could be heard down the hall.

"I don't care what you say, Ernest. You will not drag my good family's name through the gutter. I will not allow you to enter another gambling hall and foolhardily send us into ruin by throwing away hard-earned money," yelled Margie, slamming a book down on the table.

"Well I've got news for you, woman. You don't tell me what to do. And another thing . . . when a man puts his life on the line for his country, he can do what he damn well pleases. You can keep your family's reputation and money . . . I've had enough!"

Enid put the teapot down and stared at the nursery door. Heavy footsteps were coming closer. She jumped up and grabbed her doll, not taking her eyes off the door. There was silence, and then the doorknob began to turn. Enid squeezed her doll and closed her eyes.

She felt a presence in the room and slowly looked up. Her father knelt down in front of her and they gazed into each other's eyes. He reached over, caressing her tiny face in his hands, and gently kissed her forehead. He stood, took one last look at his daughter, then without saying a word, walked out of the room and out of her life forever.

Enid's Childhood Doll

Confused and frustrated by her mother not answering questions regarding her father, Enid spent a good deal of her time with her various aunts and uncles. Her cousin Irene, whose father died when she was only eight, knew the pain that Enid suffered. The two girls formed a special bond comforting each other with the loss of their fathers at such a young age. Enid's mother, Margie, consoled the sorrow of her divorce by traveling.

It had been almost a year since Enid's father had left when the little girl watched her mother hand clothes to the maid that she wanted packed for a trip to London.

Enid sniffled and blinked back tears. "Don't go, Mommy." Clutching her doll, she ran down the hall to the nursery and slammed the door.

Her mother quickly followed, finding her daughter sobbing into her pillow. She gathered Enid in her arms, held her tight and began to stroke her hair.

"Now, now, little one. I'm only going on a short trip. I promise you that I'll be back real soon." Little Enid tightened her grip around her mother's arm. "But Enid, you get to go on a trip, too," her mother continued. "You will be staying with Irene and Auntie Kath. Nanny Bardie will be teaching you your numbers and letters along with some music and art. You are going to have so much fun that the time will pass quickly and I will be home before you know it. Now let's pack your suitcase." Enid squirmed off her mother's lap and ran to her closet. Together they assembled the outfits that Enid would need for her visit to Cousin Irene's home.

Jack Newbury, the household chauffeur, loaded the last of the baggage into the car and waited for his passengers. Enid ran out with her doll under her arm and scampered onto the back seat. Mrs. Fellows followed, pulling up her gloves, then slid onto the seat next to her daughter.

"Let us be off, Jack," she said, patting her daughter's knee.

They dropped Enid off at Auntie Kath's and before her suitcase was unloaded from the car, Irene had wrapped her arm around her young cousin and led her toward the house, all the while telling her the wonderful, fun things they were going to do.

Margie handed her sister a paper with her contact information and thanked her profusely for attending to Enid while she was away.

"Come, Jack," she said, "I want to reach London before dark." The chauffeur held the car door open for Mrs. Fellows. She blew kisses to her daughter, who was waving from the top of the steps, and then they were off to London.

It was known in those days that if you were in search of a traveling companion, London was the place. Housemaids always informed other housemaids which ladies were available for housework, traveling companions or nannies. Mrs. Fellows heard of one particular young lady that was in need of a position in a household, and immediately sent word of her desire to interview the girl.

They arrived at the Hyde Park Hotel just before dusk. The doorman took Margie's suitcase into the lobby. Jack was instructed to return in five days and headed back to Tangley Park.

Well known in the society circles of London, Mrs. Fellows was invited to several parties while in town, including a visit with her friend, Queen Alexandra. Margie was proud to wear the diamond necklace that the queen had given to her as a gift. It was a strand of diamonds with a pendent of smaller diamonds in the shape of a crown hanging from it. It resembled the necklaces worn by the Queen's Maids of Honor at her Coronation.

On the last morning in London, Mrs. Fellows had crumpets and tea brought to the drawing room in her suite anticipating the arrival of the young lady she hoped would be her new travel companion and lady's maid.

Florence Saffrey had never been to London before. In fact, she had never traveled outside her hometown of Liverpool until now. Growing up on a farm with her brothers and sisters, she was accustomed to long hours and rigorous work ethics. But with the sudden death of her father, and her mother unable to handle the situation, Florence, being the eldest, was sent to London to find service as a maid.

The Hyde Park Hotel was an impressive structure. Florence had never seen such elegance and tried to capture to memory all the details as she made her way to Mrs. Fellows' suite. She stopped to scrutinize her reflection in a massive gold-framed mirror hanging in the hall, ran her fingers through her short wavy brown hair and pinched her cheeks to verify rosy good health. Taking a deep breath Florence turned and with much self-assurance, knocked on the door that upon entering could very well determine her future.

Mrs. Fellows was impressed with the young, slender girl standing in front of her. She was a breath of fresh air and would not only make a worthy traveling companion, but her experience with her younger siblings would be put to good use with young Enid. Florence was excited to learn that she would be more than a maid. She had dreamed of traveling and now she had the opportunity to travel in style.

Not only had Florence impressed Mrs. Fellows, but she had also caught the eye of Jack Newbury when he returned to pick them up. Eventually they married. As a couple they continued to faithfully serve Mrs. Fellowes and Miss Enid for many years.

Chapter 3

The Right of Passage

By the 1920s Enid had become a typical spirited teenager looking for fun and adventure. While visiting her aunts and uncles she became a student of the latest dance steps. Not just the dances one must learn for the annual Debutante Ball, but with the arrival of the Roaring Twenties' era, Enid became proficient in all the new dance craze styles such as the Charleston, the Bunny Hug, the Black Bottom, and the Shimmy.

With the onset of the Roaring Twenties, a new woman emerged, the Flapper. Enid fit the style perfectly. The flapper dress with its straight and loose styling, the waistline resting snuggly on her hips, silhouetted Enid's petite figure.

It was all the rage for the young girls to shear off their childhood ringlets into the fashionable boyish hairstyles of the straight bob with bangs or the more stylish shingle bob with finger waving technique. The upper class flappers were given the nickname of *The Bright Young Things* and they often possessed a wig or two that they could plop on at a moment's notice, to always be available for a good time. Ditching their chaperones for two-seated sports cars and smoking cigarettes with long holders in public became part of their game, and with that came headlines.

Enid Fellows during the 1920's
(Graciously provided by the Anita Roy Family)

With the onset of spring close at hand, Mrs. Fellows knew it was time to submit Enid's application for the Debutante Ball, a right of passage for young socialites of marital age. Applications had to be filled out by a former debutante. If her application was accepted, the young lady would receive a royal summons to attend the presentation.

Florence Saffrey brought a tea tray into the drawing room for Miss Enid and her mother along with the afternoon mail.

Mrs. Fellows glanced through the mail, stopping at an official looking envelope. "Enid, my dear, it's here, it's finally here." She handed her daughter an envelope marked with the seal from the Sovereign Queen. "Hurry child, open the letter."

Enid put the envelope down and poured herself some tea. "Mother, would you like me to pour you a cup?" she asked.

"Don't torment me like this, dear. Just open the letter."

Enid slowly tore the end off the envelope. "It appears that it is a royal summons for me to attend and be presented at the Debutante Ball."

"This is something I've been grooming you for since you were little." Her mother grabbed the letter from Enid and read the enclosed proclamation for herself. "My little girl will be presented by the Sovereign Queen herself, and introduced to society; at last my dream comes true."

"But Mother, some of my friends have decided not to attend the ball. They think it pretentious and old fashioned."

"I won't hear another word, young lady. Why, all the most respected and eligible bachelors will be at the ball."

"I know who they are, Mother, and I would not presume to be the least bit interested in any of them."

"Such obstinate from my own daughter will not be had. Need I remind you of the aristocratic background from which you were born?"

"I'm fully aware, Mother, of the privileges your family name provides me."

"Then you are aware of the importance of tradition and you will abide by our family tradition of being presented by the Queen to society. After all, dear, money can be lost, but keep this in mind; a title can open doors for you that money cannot buy."

"I'll respect your wishes and abide by tradition, Mother, if you will allow me to have the best dance band in town for my coming-out party."

"I know you young things like your dance bands and there is nothing too good for my little girl. So now that we've agreed on something, let's plan our shopping adventure for your new wardrobe."

The traditional dress for such an important occasion was a floor length white evening gown worn with long white gloves. Jewelry consisted of family jewels or pearls. After being presented to the reigning monarch, the young debutante was officially launched into society and was expected to attend the full social season with ladylike manners. The Season was the debutante's launch into society as a young lady, and always correlated with Parliament and hunting. Months of activities were planned and each young lady was expected to attend every function starting with the Royal Ascot horse races. Proper attire was required at each of the numerous balls, tea parties and sport matches.

Many debutantes made plans for their own coming-out party before the London Season ended on August 12th. The "Glorious Twelfth of August" as it was called, marked the beginning of the Hunting Season when families headed back to their country estates.

Mrs. Fellows had planned just such a coming-out party for Enid that was announced in the *London Evening News*:

Mrs. Hamilton-Fellows is giving a dance for the coming out of her only child, Miss Enid Hamlyn-Fellows, at the Hyde Park Hotel, on Tuesday, May 29. Mrs. Hamilton-Fellows is the daughter of the late Sir Frederick Wills and sister of Sir Gilbert Wills.

Chapter 4

High Society and The Mysterious Mr. Hay

George Harley Hay was known in London as a young, handsome member of nobility who had a way with the women and a compulsive appetite for gambling.

Born into nobility on March 30, 1902, he was the son of Edmund Alfred Rollo George Hay-Drummond (Viscount Dupplin) and Gladys Luz Bacon. Harley, as his friends called him, never had the opportunity to know his father, who died a year after Harley was born. His grandfather, Archibald FitzRoy George Hay-Drummond, 13th Earl of Kinnoull, was to become his father/mentor.

Gambling was a favorite pastime of the rich and famous. When one attended a dance, you could be sure that there would be a card game going on in another room.

Baccarat was a popular card game along with the dice game of Hazard. Exclusive clubs seduced many of the upper class into high wage betting. Numerous aristocrats, including royalty, had such a thirst for this type of betting that it soon became an addiction, which led to the ruin of many fortunes and loss of substantial estates. The Kinnoull peerage was no exception.

There was a time in 1860 that the Kinnoull estate was in excess of 100,000 acres, which included the whole area of Perth in Scotland. From Kinnoull Hill one could look down upon miles of lush green rolling hills and forests where the River Tay serpentines its way across the vast valley below. It has been said that the estate was reduced to only 12,500 acres after poor management and gambling debts.

In March 1886, Harley's great uncle, George Robert Hay-Drummond, Viscount Dupplin, died at Monte Carlo, the gambling resort of the rich and famous in Monaco. He was only thirty-seven years old and it was rumored that he had committed suicide because of major losses at the gambling tables. It would seem that his suicide correlated with the estate's loss, valued at 87,500 acres.

When his grandfather, Archibald F. G. Hay, 13th Earl of Kinnoull, died in 1916, Harley became the 14th Earl of Kinnoull at the young age of fourteen. He was sent off to the Eton College boarding school near Windsor to finish his education.

Harley Hay was a product of the post-war generation, which boasted that nothing in life was worthwhile unless if it was *pour le sport* (for the sport). With his new title, Harley soon gained a reputation as quite the ladies' man, a playboy flaunting his money about at the various Mayfair nightclubs.

In 1922 the Earl's reputation caught the eye of the widow Mrs. Esther Dulcie Trewartha Surle. Although not as young as Harley, she knew that her maturity could work to her advantage and that if she played her hand well, she might soon become the next Countess of Kinnoull. Instead of waiting to be pursued by the charming young royal, she plotted to seduce him. As they played the gambling tables, she ordered the drinks, which kept her youthful conquest coming back for more. Twenty-year-old Harley could not hold his liquor as Mrs. Surle could. She started to refer to him as her lover and he played right into her hand.

One night in particular when Harley was especially inebriated, the widow Surle suggested they should marry. Upon his supposed agreement, she left him in his room while she made all the arrangements.

Word of mouth spreads fast in the gambling world and when Harley's mother heard what was about to happen she immediately informed the English registrar's office to put a stop to the marriage because her son was under age. His mother sent a cousin to rescue Harley by booking them passage aboard the *Edinburgh Castle* heading to South Africa, and with word that she would meet them there. After Harley had sobered up, his cousin explained why they were at sea. Harley insisted that he was so drunk that he didn't remember the widow Surle's proposal and that it must have been a prank.

When Mrs. Surle arrived the next day to pick up her groom, she was told that he had considered her proposal just a lark and was on his way to South Africa. Furious, she insisted that the joke would be on him. She would take the next ship to meet him in Madeira and then they would be married. But it was not to happen, for Harley's mother, being of the highest social standing, had definitely put a stop to that marriage.

Upon his return from South Africa, Harley continued to be a regular customer at the Mayfair clubs at night, but during the day he pursued his passion for fast cars by entering races at the Brooklands' Racing Club near Weybridge in Surrey.

About a year later, he was asked by a friend to join him and his brothers at a seaside resort. On the drive up the coast, Harley stopped at a lodge to hear a popular dance band and that is when two lives intertwined their destinies.

At the end of July, with the "Glorious Twelfth of August" fast approaching, Enid and her mother had headed for some sunshine on the coast. Their favorite vacation spot included a scattering of bungalows interspersed among the towering pines at the water's edge.

After dinner at the lodge, Mrs. Fellows excused herself and returned to their seaside bungalow for much needed rest. Enid remained behind waiting for the dance band to begin. As soon as the music started, several young men eager to dance approached her. Enid surprised them with her proficient knowledge of all the popular dances.

Harley sat at the bar observing this attractive young girl dressed in a shimmery, silver blue, sleeveless frock, showing off her mastery of the latest dance steps. She appeared to glide across the dance floor, arms flying through the air to the rhythm of the music, like a bird freed from its cage. When the band took a break he picked up his drink and approached her table.

"Mighty impressive footwork. You're a girl after my own heart."

"Do you enjoy dancing, too?" she asked the rather short gentleman with slicked back, dark brown hair and mesmerizing hazel eyes.

"One of my favorite pastimes." He offered his hand, "I'm Harley Hay. And who do I have the pleasure of meeting?"

"I'm Enid Fellows. Would you care to join me, Mr. Hay?"

"I was hoping you would ask, but please call me Harley." He waved for the waiter. "I'll have another scotch on the rocks. And another drink for the lady?"

"A cola, please," she replied. The waiter went to get their drinks.

"How long will you be visiting here?" asked Harley.

"My mother and I will be here till Friday. I'm enjoying the last week of my first London Season before returning to the countryside. And you, are you staying here?"

"No, I'm afraid I'm just passing through. I'm meeting some friends at the next resort up the coast for a week's vacation. I stopped off just to hear the band. Say, while you're in the countryside, you must visit Balhousie Castle in Scotland."

"And why do you recommend it?"

"Because I live there and would like to see you again."

"You live in a castle? What are you, a king?"

"Not quite. I'm the 14th Earl of Kinnoull and inherited it."

Enid laughed and took a sip of her cola. "I insist you meet my mother. She won't believe that I've been dancing with an Earl."

"I could stop by for a tennis match tomorrow, if you play."

"No, I don't play tennis. But I do enjoy golf, although I'm not very good at it. I'm quite good at swimming. When I was little, my grandfather taught me how to swim at the seaside. But I'd have to say that my favorite pastime is dancing."

"Then we shall dance," said Harley. The band had returned from their break and Enid and Harley danced until closing time. After the dance they walked over to Mrs. Fellows' bungalow.

Enid's mother was delighted to hear of Harley's royal connection and was excited to tell him of her friendship with Queen Alexandra. He, on the other hand, was impressed to learn that Mrs. Fellows was the daughter of Sir Frederick Wills of the Imperial Tobacco Empire.

Although Harley stayed with his friends, he spent most of his days with Enid. She introduced the Earl to another favorite pastime of hers, writing poetry. She spent a great deal of time reading her creations to him.

By the end of the week they had agreed to meet again in August when she would be visiting her "Auntie Kath" at Clifford Manor, in Warwickshire.

Chapter 5

The Rumor

Harley Hay was true to his word. He arrived on a late afternoon in August at the planned rendezvous. The revving engine of his two-seater, forest green roadster announced his arrival as it came to a stop in front of Clifford Manor.

"Are you expecting anyone?" asked Auntie Kath when she heard the car's engine.

"No, but I'll go see who it is," replied Enid, jumping up from their afternoon tea. "Maybe somebody is lost."

"We'll both go see who it is," replied her Aunt, following Enid outside.

"Oh, just look at that car. Have you ever seen anything so dreamy?" Enid ran down the steps and winked at Harley.

"Can we help you, young man?" asked the aunt.

Harley took off his driving gloves and got out of the car.

"Why, Auntie Kath, this is the gentleman I met last month, when mother and I spent a week on the coast. Mother must have told him where I was. Earl of Kinnoull, I'd like you to meet my Aunt, Mrs. Kathleen Douty."

"It's a pleasure to meet you, but please call me Harley. All my friends do."

Enid loved fast cars. She gently ran her hand over the warm metal bonnet. "She looks new."

"Just got her two weeks ago. Isn't she a beauty? Would you like to see how she feels on the road?"

"Would I?" Enid glanced over to her Aunt.

"I don't think that would be a good idea, dear."

"I can assure you, Mrs. Douty, its quite safe. I'm a certified racecar driver. Enid would be in good hands."

"Besides," Enid interrupted, "Mother would approve . . . she met Harley."

"Well, if you think she wouldn't mind . . . but take a sweater, it's starting to get a bit chilly."

"Oh, thank you Auntie Kath." Enid gave her a hug and ran into the entry for her sweater.

"I'll take good care of your niece," said Harley. He revved the engine and they were off.

Auntie Kath was a stickler for keeping an eye on her young niece during her visits and felt a little uncomfortable allowing her to go un-chaperoned. But what's an aunt to do when a gentleman shows up in a two-seater automobile, she thought.

Enid's natural curiosity of racecars impressed the Earl, who was more than happy to demonstrate his driving abilities. They took turns racing throughout the countryside, finally stopping at a pub for a bite to eat.

"I must say, Enid, you surprised me with your enthusiasm for car racing. I'd say you're a natural."

"There's just something about the thrill of it that excites me," said Enid as they entered the pub.

"Wait a minute," said Harley. He ran back to the car to fetch her sweater. "We can't have you catching a chill. Your aunt would never forgive me." They both laughed.

A waitress showed them to a cozy booth away from the bar and handed them a menu. They both chose fish and chips with a cola.

"I didn't realize that racing cars could make one so hungry," said Enid after they had ordered.

"It could be the time." Harley pointed to the clock on the wall.

"Oh, please tell me that clock is wrong."

The waitress arrived with their order.

"Miss, do you know if that clock is correct?" asked Enid.

"Yes, it is exactly eight o'clock. Enjoy your meal."

"Harley, what are we going to do? My Aunt will be furious."

"Well, I say let's enjoy our supper. Surely we can put our heads together and come up with some excuse."

"I've got it," said Enid. "We'll say there was a flat tire or the radiator overheated."

"That won't work," said Harley. "Your aunt knows it was a new car with a spare tire. And as far as the radiator goes, the weather was getting cool when we left."

"You're right, Harley. We need to concoct a story that will squash any rebuke from Auntie Kath."

"Well, there is one story that just might work." Harley leaned closer and whispered his idea. They both laughingly agreed that Enid would say that they had become engaged, and then in the morning they would call it off.

It was dark when they pulled up in front of Clifford Manor. "Wish me luck," said Enid. Harley reached over and pulled her closer.

"We need to make this look real, just in case your aunt is watching." He held her face in his hands and gently kissed her lips.

Enid felt a fluttering in her stomach. She wasn't sure if it was the fear of her aunt or that she might be falling in love. She wondered if she was stumbling into a dangerous game.

Enid quietly closed the front door, but could feel her aunt's presence.

"Well, young lady, I knew I went against my better judgment by letting you drive off without a chaperone. What will your mother think of my letting you traipse around the countryside until dark? Think of your reputation, Enid. For that matter, think of your family's reputation. And then to see you two kissing is totally inappropriate."

"But Auntie Kath, let me explain."

"I don't think you can explain your way out of this one."

"But I can, if you give me a chance. The reason he kissed me is because we are engaged."

"Engaged?"

"Yes, I'm engaged to the 14th Earl of Kinnoull."

"Darling, that means you're going to be a countess. My niece is going to be Countess Kinnoull? Wait until your mother hears this news."

"Auntie Kath, I'm a bit overwhelmed by it all. Let's talk about it in the morning."

"Of course, dear. You get a good night's sleep and then tell me all about it tomorrow." She gave her niece a hug and kiss.

With the announcement of her engagement, all seemed to be forgiven and an exhausted Enid headed straight for bed, knowing that in the morning she would be able to explain that it was all just a practical joke.

However, as a typical teenager, Enid overslept the next morning. By the time she awoke, her aunt had spread the news of the engagement. The first person Kath telephoned was her sister.

Upon hearing of her Enid's engagement, Margie Fellows was excited that her daughter would be marrying into such a noble, time-honored lineage. She immediately called the Earl's mother to express her excitement.

Harley's mother, on the other hand, was thrilled that her son would be marrying someone closer to his age and out of the grasp of the persistent widow, Mrs. Surle. As a bonus, she was extremely pleased by the fact that Enid Fellows came from the Imperial Tobacco Family dynasty; being well aware of Harley's gambling addiction, she hoped that this suitable marriage would finally rein in her son.

By early afternoon, Margie bounded through the door of her sister's house, bubbling with excitement. "Where is my Enid? Where is my darling daughter?"

"Margie, I'm afraid there has been a terrible mistake."

"Kath, what are you talking about?"

"Go into the drawing room. I think it's best to let Enid explain. I'll have a tea tray brought in."

Enid was staring out the window when her mother entered the room.

"Would somebody please explain what is going on?"

"Oh Mother, I tried to explain to Auntie Kath that it was all a joke, there is no engagement. I just went for a drive with the Earl. He was showing me his new sports car and one thing led to another, which turned into a race through the countryside and time got away from us. I was afraid Auntie Kath would be furious so we came up with the story that we were engaged. Now I hear she has told a lot of people of the engagement while I was asleep."

"Enid, this is no joking matter. The rumor is out and it's too late to withdraw honorably. Not only is your reputation at stake, but also your entire family's honor is at risk of being compromised. I assure you that marrying an Earl and having the title of Countess will allow you access to numerous things that money cannot buy. Money may not always be there, but a title is forever. I can assure you that if it wasn't for my inheritance from my father we would have been in deep trouble after your father left."

After much discussion, both families agreed that the engagement should be properly announced and a wedding planned. The *London Evening News* was contacted and a representative was sent to interview the young couple. The next day's issue read, *Lord Kinnoull and His Betrothal – Girl Who Writes Poetry.* The article went on to tell how they met at a seaside hotel in July.

"She dances beautifully," stated the young Earl. "She also writes poetry and has read a great deal of it to me."

Enid replied, "I do not play tennis, but I dance a great deal. That was a great link between us. My fiancé dances quite beautifully. I am very happy."

Nine days later an engagement picture of Enid Margaret Fellows and the 14th Earl of Kinnoull appeared in *The Sketch* society pages.

Enid Margaret Fellows and Harley Hay, 14th Earl of Kinnoull
Engagement photo (August 29, 1923 in *The Sketch* society page)

Caught up in a whirlwind of engagement parties and teas, young Enid had no time to rationalize if they were doing the right thing. And Harley knew that marrying into money would allow him to continue to live the life of fast cars and gambling clubs, which he had become accustom to. So the word spread about their engagement and a winter wedding date was chosen.

Margie, who enjoyed writing music, set about composing the departure Salutation for the ceremony.

Enid Margaret Fellows in 1923 Vogue Magazine Before Her Marriage

Chapter 6

The Wedding

In search of the perfect wedding gown, Mrs. Fellows wanted only the best for her daughter. They shopped at the most fashionable stores in London, finally deciding on a gown they could agree on.

"Now that is stunning," said Margie when Enid appeared from the dressing room in a sleeveless, creamy white satin gown adorned with crystal and silver beads. "Lots and lots of satin. Now that is what you need to be proper, my dear. I should know, for I've been to many a wedding in my day and believe me, people will talk if there is not enough satin."

"Don't you think that the beads are a bit excessive?" asked Enid, gazing at her image in the three-way mirror.

"Nonsense. It's the crystal and silver beads that will turn heads. Enid, you are after all going to be a countess. It is time you started dressing and acting like one."

The flowing train was made of two white satin panels stitched together with an interlacing of the same beads. A wide embroidered band of silver ribbon held the tulle veil with tiny myrtle flowers, securing the folds of tulle over the ears. Myrtle flowers were associated with love and affection and also signified joy and happiness, the two things that would soon elude Enid within this marriage of convenience.

On December 15, 1923, the weather was clear, but dark ominous clouds were commencing to form. Friends and family of the couple were arriving at St. Paul's Church in Knightsbridge to witness this joyous occasion of the marriage of ancient lineage with recent riches, which the families felt would be beneficial to both sides.

St. Paul's church in Knightsbridge
(Photo graciously provided by Elisabeth Karr)

St. Paul's Church was ornately decorated with abundant displays of yellow and bronze colored chrysanthemums cascading from tall gold wicker baskets. Guests being escorted to their seats were greeted with rich Christian imagery in tiled panels on the walls that depicted scenes of the life of Jesus Christ. In between each tile were exquisite paintings of the *14 Stations of the Cross,* showing detailed scenes of the Crucifixion story. After following the images of the life of Jesus depicted on the panels and paintings, one's eyes came to rest on the High Altar where today a young couple would see their love sanctified by the sacrament of marriage.

When the guests were all seated, six bridesmaids stood on either side of the aisle awaiting the bride. They consisted of two children, Miss Alexandra and Miss Cynthia Fraser, in gold lace knee length dresses bordered with fur. Golden ribbons were in their hair. The four adult bridesmaids, Georgia Doble, Nancy Stallibras, Rosemary Wills and Lady Elizabeth Townshend, were stunning in their orange-red, long-waisted satin gowns with headbands of pink and gold satin ribbons. Each of the bridesmaids carried a gold staff topped with orange-brown chrysanthemums and gold satin ribbons.

While waiting in the narthex, Margie adjusted Enid's headpiece and looked into her daughter's blue eyes. "I've dreamed of this day for you, my dear. I am so honored to be giving my only daughter away to a family of such distinction."

"I know, Mother. There have been times when we have had our differences, but you have always been the one there for me and I know I don't say it enough, but that has meant the world to me."

Margie kissed her daughter on the cheek and rushed back to her seat as the music began to play.

Miss Enid Fellows carried a bouquet of white carnations and white heather (the badge of the Hay family) and was assisted down the aisle by her trainbearers, cousins Michael and David Wills. Both boys wore matching velvety short pantsuits in dark tangerine with paler silk shirts.

Enid's maid of honor was Miss Dorothy Royde-Smith who wore a similar gown as the other bridesmaids, but trimmed in sable with a matching hat. The Earl of Kinnoull's best man was Mr. Reginald Palgrave.

Wedding Picture of the Countess and Earl of Kinnoull
(December 16, 1923 *The Sketch* society page)

Enid's uncle, Sir Gilbert Wills, contributed the chant for the doxology, *Deus Misereatur*, and Enid's mother wrote the Salutation, *Lord, to Thee be all the Glory*, which was sung at the end of the ceremony.

After the ceremony, Mrs. Hamilton-Fellows gave a reception at the Hyde Park Hotel with a very impressive guest list.

Enid's mother, wearing a rust-colored silk dress with an embroidered velvet coat and gold hat with rusty-red feathers, presented the first toast to the Countess and 14th Earl of Kinnoull.

"To my darling daughter and her handsome husband: Starting life as a new married couple can be complicated when two young lives merge as one. So to ease that adjustment as you start on this new journey, I give as my wedding gift to you a completely furnished new house in the fashionable Princes Gardens." Loud applause sounded across the reception hall. Harley and Enid stood to thank her mother, and then Harley took the mike.

"Not to outshine my mother-in-law with her most gracious gift, but to appeal to my wife's wild side," he reached into his jacket pocket clutching something in his hand, "I, the 14th Earl of Kinnoull, present to my gorgeous bride, Countess Enid Margaret Kinnoull, a brand new racing motorcar which we will use on our honeymoon in the South of France." He handed the keys to his wife.

Enid was stunned. Her voice rose in surprise when she took the microphone.

"A new husband, a new house, a new car, what a great way to start a new life!" She took the keys and dangled them so everyone could see, and then gave Harley a warm embrace.

For their honeymoon, the young couple crossed to France on the ferry and then drove from Boulogne to southern France. Upon the return from their honeymoon, Enid and Harley divided their time between the Earl's residence at the Balhousie Castle in Scotland, his apartment in Paris, and their new home at Princes Gardens in London.

The Kinnoull's Apartment in The Fashionable Princes Gardens in Hyde Park
(Photo by Elisabeth Karr)

Chapter 7

Every Girl's Dream

Having returned from her honeymoon, Enid settled into the life of every girl's dream. She and Harley occupied the Balhousie Castle during the hunting season, which varied according to the animals hunted. Most families headed for their country estates on the 12th of August, and by spring the women were more than ready for the move back to the fun and excitement of London with its various parties and nightclubs to attend.

On one occasion during her first visit to Scotland, the young Enid practiced her speeding when she drove through a town at twenty-five miles per hour in a ten-mile per hour zone. It was reported in *The Scotsman*: *Exceeded The Speed Limit, Countess of Kinnoull Fined*. This was to be the beginning of many speeding tickets and fines to come, for indeed, Countess Kinnoull had the thrill of the race in her blood.

Often bored by being left alone, while the men hunted, Enid unbeknownst to Harley had taken her sports car and secretly practiced high-speed and quick navigation of sharp turns on their property.

"Now that we're settled as a married couple," said Harley, "we should have our first hunting party."

"How many were you thinking of inviting?" asked Enid, a bit apprehensive of her expected duties.

"I prefer smaller, more intimate parties. What do you say I invite three of my fellow classmates from Eton College and they can bring their wives?"

"Including us that makes a nice, doable size of eight. Yes, I think I can manage that," said Enid. "What exactly is expected of me at a hunting party?"

"Well, you will plan the meals with the cook. The staff will prepare three guest rooms and while the men are out hunting, you, my dear, will entertain the women. Lavish afternoon teas will satisfy their hunger while they hone their skills and strategy practicing the most popular games such as Mahjong or Rummy until the men return with their wild kills to be prepared by the staff for the evening dinner. Conversations will meld into hysterical laughter as the men make fools of themselves by trying to out perform each other with their hunting exploits, hoping to capture the attention of the ladies. Which I find a bit trite considering that we are all now married."

"Sounds like you've been a participant in many a hunting season."

"You might say it is the young men's coming-out party, but at a much younger age than the women. As soon as we learn to handle a gun and clean the kill we transverse our *Right of Passage* into adulthood."

"My, we are such fascinating creatures of habit." Enid smiled and Harley poured them both a cocktail as they planned the entertainment for their guests during their three-day hunt.

Everything had gone along as planned for the Kinnoull's first hunt party, except when the evening meal was finished. These bright young wives wouldn't hear of being sent to another room while the men stayed and enjoyed a good cigar and brandy after dinner, as their parents' generation was accustomed to.

"I'm sure you lovely ladies would be much happier partaking of sherry in the drawing room with Enid, discussing the latest gossip, than bored with us men bantering about our preferences in the political arena," said Harley.

"No," replied one of the wives. "We emancipated young women of the 1920's era prefer to join our men, and learn about the latest political situations."

"What on earth for?" asked Harley. "Why, you know that since 1918 only women over the age of thirty are granted the right to vote."

"We all know that, Harley. But things are changing. We need to be prepared. It's only a matter of time before all woman will be able to vote with equal voting rights as the men," said another of the young wives.

"I have to agree with Harley on this matter," replied one of the men. "How utterly absurd it is to even imagine that a women's brain is equal to that of a man's before she has reached the age of thirty."

"Hear, hear," chorused the other men jokingly.

"Then I trust you gentlemen who are expressing your superior knowledge and skill over that of a woman are up to the challenge of a fair game of Mahjong?" asked Enid with a mischievous smile.

"We men prefer the similar game of Rummy," said Harley.

"Are you suggesting that you men do not have the skills to play Mahjong?" asked another wife.

"I do believe, Harley old chap, that the gauntlet has been dropped," said one of the men.

Many a man has been put in his place by losing to the fairer sex at various social gatherings, proving that not all men are of superior intellect. It wasn't until 1928 in Britain that women twenty-one and older finally received the right to vote.

At the onset of spring, the aristocrats return to their residences in London to start the much-anticipated social parties. The Countess and Earl of Kinnoull were no exception, having sent ahead a few servants to air out their apartment in London.

Countess Enid Margaret Kinnoull with the 14th Earl of Kinnoull at their
Balhousie Castle in Scotland in 1924.

The Balhousie Castle in Scotland

Chapter 8

Return to London

"I can't wait to get back to the city," said Enid. "This countryside, though beautiful, can be a bit dreary when one is accustomed to the fun nightlife of the clubs."

"It has been a while since we've been dancing," replied Harley. "Sometimes I forget how lonely it must be for you when I'm out hunting."

"Well, now that I've met some of our neighbors in the other country estates, perhaps next hunting season won't be so lonely," said Enid.

"I'm going to make it up to you, Enid. How would you like to try your hand at car racing?"

"You mean on the track?" Her face brightened at the suggestion.

"Definitely on the track. I think it might be the only way to restrain you from racing through the villages and collecting tickets and fines."

"Do you think I could qualify?"

"Absolutely. You've shown such a keen interest in all aspects of automobile racing that I think it is high time that I teach you the fundamental rules and maneuvers of the race track."

"Harley, this means so much to me!" She flung her arms around his neck. As they kissed, she had no doubt that she truly loved this man.

Upon settling into their apartment, one of the first places they visited was the Brooklands Race Track twenty miles southwest of London.

They parked next to the red brick two-storied clubhouse that stretched a half a block.

"What is that for?" asked Enid pointing to a green roofed cupola perched atop part of the building. It was surrounded by a white picket fence resembling a widow's walk.

"It allows officials or special guests to get a birds eye view of the races," he said.

Bang! Bang! She jumped and turned to see an automobile backfire again, giving off a whiff of grease and gasoline as two soot-faced mechanics drove by. Harley laughed holding open the door to the clubhouse.

They poked their heads into a dark paneled rectangular room. At the far end were two round gambling tables with red leather lounge chairs. Several men were nursing drinks at a bar, but much commotion was centered on the billiard table with its intricate carved legs and green felt top. A crashing of balls and an echoing of ahhh . . . could be heard. A cloud of stale cigar smoke hung in the air seeping into the dark green velvet draperies of the floor to ceiling paneled windows.

"Let me guess," said Enid as they continued on to the registers office. "That was the Old Boys Club."

"Most of us are in our twenties . . . if you consider that old! It's a darn good place to calm our nerves between races and to celebrate afterwards. Besides, women are not allowed!"

"Oh? Where do we meet?" she asked looking around the area.

"You'll have to ask after you sign up," said Harley as they entered the main office.

It was a good-size room in the center of the building. Floor to ceiling fixed wooden lattice windows surrounded the office allowing the attendant full view of the comings and goings of the club.

Knowing Harley's reputation as a well-respected member, they took his word that his wife could handle the car and the stress of competition.

Enid anxiously signed her signature on the registration form for the Women's Junior Car Club.

"Welcome to the elite organization of women racecar competitors," said the group's president. "I'm very pleased to present to you, Countess Kinnoull, your new member badge for the radiator cap of your racecar."

She was handed a chromium-plated, rectangular badge with a black background. Embossed J.C.C. lettering shined brightly at the top. Silver wings spread across the middle of the badge as if in flight, and attached to the wings was a black diamond-shaped box framed in silver and white with the words *Junior Car Club* in red enamel centered on the black background. The badge was soldered to a highly polished, chromium-plated radiator cap.

Enid ran her fingers over every aspect of the badge. "Thank you so much. It's an honor to be a member of such a prominent and highly respected organization."

"We are happy to have you." The president handed a current 1924 Brooklands Race Track booklet to Enid. "You'll need to familiarize yourself with the clubhouse rules and the track protocol. You are now registered for your first race, to be held this Saturday, May 3rd. I'm afraid that the track will be closed until the morning of the race, but if you arrive a few hours before the first race you should be able to get in a few practice runs. Best of luck to you."

"Thank you," said Enid. "But, where do the women meet while waiting to race?"

"We have a lovely place called the Ladies Reading Room. You can take a look, it's right around the corner next to the lounge where you can change clothes."

The Reading Room was painted in a shocking pink. Varnished mahogany bookshelves lined the walls with popular books and magazines. A teacart provided a variety of teas and pastries. Satin brocaded armchairs with footrests were clustered in small groupings near marble end tables with Tiffany reading lamps.

"Now, let me guess," said Harley. "They must call this the Old Ladies Brothel!"

"Okay, I think we're even now," she smiled. They both laughed.

On the day of the race the weather was not cooperating. The fluctuating temperatures brought threatening clouds, an ominous omen of things to come. Harley and Enid arrived at Brooklands a few hours before the ticket booth opened, when the track would still be vacant.

Enid pulled her Salmson racecar up to the starting line for the first of two practice runs. She half heartily listened to Harley as he offered her tips from his experiences on the track, for she already knew how she would handle the runs. The first round would be taken slow just to get a feel of the track, then she would open it up, surprising the Earl.

"Now just remember what I told you and you'll do fine," said Harley, having checked off everything on his clipboard. "Looks like you're all set to go."

Enid adjusted the leather helmet then tightened the strap on her goggles. She revved the engine, waved to Harley, and then took off.

Viewing the racetrack from a spectator's point of view was totally different than actually driving on the track. This was the first 2.75-mile oval-shaped track built in England. To some spectators the repetitive oval run was boring, but not to the driver. The challenge of the one hundred-foot wide track was anything but smooth. It was built with thin concrete that had not been allowed to cure properly, and the bumps formed from the concrete sections restricted the speed. A bisecting straight finish was recently added, increasing the length of the track to 3.25 miles, of which 1.25 miles were banked.

Enid was approaching the most daunting obstacle, the thirty-foot Weybridge bank. It was so steep that a person could not climb it, even on all fours.

The first run was slow as she inched her way up the bank, only making it half way before reaching the final straight stretch of track. On the second round, Enid floored it and made it to the outer bank, much to the surprise of Harley. She kept up that speed, testing not only the car's mettle, but also her own fearlessness on the rest of the rough track. She eased up on the last stretch, finally bringing the car to a stop a few feet from Harley.

"What the hell were you thinking?" Harley hurled the clipboard to the ground. "Did you not listen to a word I said?"

"I don't understand. I thought you would be pleased that I made it to the top of the Weybridge bank."

"Pleased?" Harley yelled. "Do you see any other cars out there to race? No! This was a practice run to get a feel for the conditions of the track. But oh no, you foolhardily pushed the car to its max; your stupidity may have driven the car into the ground."

Enid cringed at his outburst. Her hands began to shake. This was a side of Harley that she had never witnessed before.

As other drivers began to arrive for the *Annual Members' Spring Race Meeting,* the young Countess looked around to see if anyone was within earshot of her husband's continued fury.

"Damn it Enid! You never listen to a thing I say!"

"I'm sorry, Harley. I don't know what came over me. Once on the track I just wanted to see what the car would do . . . it was such a thrill."

"If you expect to be in the racing circuit you have to show discipline, patience, and above all, you must listen to the one in charge. that would be me!"

A young couple, they had met at a party, came over to wish then well in the races. Just as quickly as the mean spirited words had spewed from Harley's mouth, they had now ceased. Enid watched as her husband greeted his friends with levity as if he had no care in the world. Harley looked at his watch, and then excused himself to prepare for the 3-mile *Novice Handicap Race* starting at one o'clock. Enid, feeling a bit nauseous, headed to the clubhouse to watch her husband race and have a cup of tea. Her race wouldn't start until 3:20 p.m.

Harley, driving his own Salmson racecar, was the eighth car in a field of nine. His entire attitude changed for the better when his Salmson won second place. Even though he participated in four more events, he did not make the top three in those races, but was still happy with his second place win.

Harley drove into the mechanic's pit. "Hi Max! It needs a good overhaul . . . ran a bit sluggish in the last four races."

"Congrats on the second place win, Harley. I'll give it a good maintenance check. Say, I heard that Enid will be in the *Ladies' Handicap*, can't wait to see that."

"I've scratched her from that race . . . axle problems . . . can't be too careful."

"But Harley, her car was in great shape. I checked it myself," said Max. "I'll check it again and have it up and running for the race."

"No, Max . . . too late for changes . . . I'll let you tell her the news."

"Enid, doesn't know?"

"She needs to learn that not everything can go her way. Racing is a tough business, with tough breaks. Maybe next time she'll listen to me. See you later, Max."

Enid zipped up the tan jumpsuit and tied a brown and white polka-dotted silk scarf around her neck. She took a deep breath and slowly exhaled. She lifted her head high and placed her hands on her hips. The reflection in the mirror showed a woman of confidence and determination. She put her personal items in a wire basket, and then handed it to the woman at the counter in the ladies lounge.

"Here you go," said the woman, handing Enid a pin with the basket number painted on it. "Give them hell, luv."

Enid laughed. "Thank you, I needed that today." As she headed to the mechanics pit, even her walk had a sunny cheerfulness.

"Hi Max . . . what do you think?" She twirled around showing off her new jumpsuit.

"You look lovely as always," he replied. "But Enid, I've got some bad news."

"What is it? Is Harley all right?"

"Yes, Harley is fine, but you've been scratched from the starting list. It appears that something has happened to the axle of your car."

She listened with bewilderment. "Max . . . could I have damaged the axle on the practice run? I hit it full speed to make it up the steep grade."

"No, Enid. I don't see how that could have caused any damage, but Harley thinks there's a problem with the axle."

"He just wants to get even with me . . . he didn't like the way I drove at practice."

"No, I don't think that's it at all, Enid. He's just looking out for your safety."

Enid felt screams of frustration trying to get out. Her throat began to tighten as she fought back tears. Not wanting to show defeat, she rushed back to the ladies lounge to change.

Event No. 7 was the *Ladies' Handicap* with a distance of 5.5 miles. There were only four participants, Countess of Kinnoull being the fourth car . . . but she never showed.

Immediately following the last race, all members of the club were invited to a dinner dance at the Burford Bridge Hotel. It was noted in the program that the dance would conclude at 10 p.m. so that members returning to London would have ample time to get home fairly early.

When they entered the Burford Hotel Harley pulled Enid to the side. "I know you're upset with me, darling, but I really did feel that there was something wrong with the axle . . . I couldn't live with myself if anything happened to you. That's why it is so important that you listen to me when it comes to racing cars. You do understand my concern, don't you?"

"I suppose . . . perhaps I was being a bit foolish. I was just trying to impress you."

"There, that's better." He held her face in his hands and gently kissed her. "After all we can't be mad at each other . . . we're toasting my second place win."

Harley, in a celebrative mood, spent the rest of the evening dining and dancing with his young wife. Enid was happy to have her fun-loving husband back in his good spirits. Their mutual love of dancing always brought them closer together. He seemed to have forgotten his earlier words spoken in haste.

The victory celebrations were brought to an end when the 10 p.m. deadline was announced. This was far too early for the winners.

"Let us adjourn to the Silver Slipper," said Harley. "They usually have a fabulous dance band."

"I prefer the gambling rooms, don't you, Harley?" asked one of the men.

"The Silver Slipper will cover both requirements," replied the Earl. "If you get there before us, just tell them Harley sent you." They all headed to their cars for the drive to London.

"They know you on a first name basis at this club?" asked Enid.

"There are benefits to having a title before your name, darling, as you will soon discover. The clubs in London welcome those with titles; it brings a certain prestige to their establishments."

The group of aristocrats, and upper middle class adventurers, embraced the life of partying. Society considered them a lost generation, whose fathers or brothers had fought in World War I and now had no war to fight. So instead, they would celebrate life and good times.

The new Licensing Act allowing alcohol to be served after 12:30 a.m., as long as it was served with food, gave rise to the nightclub scene. The most famous of these was the exclusive Silver Slipper on Regent Street, a favorite of the rich, famous, and nobility.

Mrs. Kate Meyrick owned the popular club and spared no expense in the lavish decorations. Walls were painted with scenes of Italy and impressive lighting lulled, or stimulated, according to the mood of the music. Only the finest bands performed at the Silver Slipper, where dancing couples glided across the dance floor made of glass. Kate Meyrick started the club to provide a means of support for her three daughters' education. But there was an alternative motive, for she desired that all her daughters marry into aristocratic society. Kate's strategy was simple: her daughters were instructed to get to know the aristocratic patrons of the club very well and ply them with drinks so they would continue to gamble away their fortunes. Then mother Kate would eliminate all their bad debts if they would marry one of her daughters.

Harley was still in a celebrative mood when they arrived at their apartment to change clothes before meeting up with their friends at the club. The incident at Brooklands' track was never brought up again. Enid tried to forget the whole matter, but a twinge of disappointment tore at her heart.

"Harley, I've been thinking. Now that we are back in London we should really start going to church as a couple. Sundays were always such a special day with my grandparents. I do so miss them."

"You can do what you want on Sundays, Enid. Just leave me out of your plans. I never said you were marrying a saint; best to leave me out of it."

When they arrived at the Silver Slipper, Harley was shown to a reserved table next to the dance floor, and was told that the others in his party had arrived but were in the gambling rooms. They had just sat down when the band returned from a break. The George Fisher Kit-Cat Band was renown for its powerful rhythmic section, which defied anyone to remain seated. Harley and Enid came to do what they did best; they captured the respect of all those watching as they held a commanding presence in their mastery of all the popular dance steps.

When the band took a break, Harley went to the bar to order drinks. Enid felt a nauseous feeling return and welcomed the chance to sit. From her chair, Enid could see into the other room and watched the double deep row of young men vying for the attention of the bartenders. She also noticed a vivacious dark-haired woman clinging to Harley's arm and gently kissing his cheek.

May Meyrick had been eyeing the smooth dancer from afar and asked the people standing near her if they knew him. When she heard that he was Harley Hay, the 14th Earl of Kinnoull she knew what she had to do.

May asked Harley what he was ordering then went behind the bar and returned with the drinks so he would not have to wait. He offered her money, but she pushed it back into his pocket. She kissed his cheek and whispered that she was May, the proprietor's daughter, and that there were more free drinks in the gambling rooms if he asked for her.

Harley returned to his table with their drinks, knowing that Enid had been watching him the whole time.

"Looks like you were having a good time." She took the drink from her husband.

"Enid, the most extraordinary thing just happened. You see that dark-haired girl over there at the bar? Well, she just happens to be the proprietor's daughter. She had heard that I had come in second place at the Brooklands' race and congratulated me with free drinks. Can you believe that? This has certainly been my lucky day."

Extraordinary indeed, thought Enid. But before she could say anything, their friends returned from the gambling rooms to join them for a last round of spirits before heading home.

The conversation centered on the excitement of the Paris Olympics and *The Flying Scotsman,* Eric Liddell. He was the son of missionaries blessed with an amazing gift of speed. His commitment to the sport of track racing was empowered by his total devotion to his Christian beliefs.

"I have a great idea," said Harley. "Why don't we all fly over to Paris for the start of the tract meet competition during the second week of July and cheer on our fellow Scotsman?"

"If we're going to be there in July, we might as well stay for the closing ceremony on July 27th," suggested Enid.

"Hear, hear!" They all seemed up for the challenge. Those that had their own aeroplanes were always excited for new ventures in flight and those without decided to charter their own. The chatter of their conversation in anticipation of being together at the Olympics overflowed into the street as they found their cars and headed home.

The next morning, Enid felt better and was delighted to see the end of dreary days. She quickly dressed and joined Harley for breakfast.

"I think I'll work in the garden this morning. It would be a shame to not take advantage of this beautiful day. What about you, darling? Should I have the cook prepare a picnic basket for our lunch?"

"It's nice to see you feeling so chipper. I'm afraid I have business to attend to this afternoon at the racetrack . . . but I do have a present for you. One that I hope will make you happy." He handed her a large envelope.

"What have you been up to, my dear Earl?" She opened the envelope and poured out a brochure and a thick paperback book onto the table. Her mouth dropped open. "Oh, Harley . . . the De Havilland School of Flying." She looked up at him. The tenderness in his expression brought her to tears.

"I thought it best that you learn how to fly, if you are going to be my copilot when we travel to Paris for the Olympics." He handed her the *Pilot Operating Handbook* for a De Havilland double-winged aeroplane. "Now it's important to familiarize yourself with every aspect of this aircraft. Your instructor, C.D. Barnard, is a tough old-schooled pilot, but the very best."

"When do I start my lessons?" asked Enid as she eagerly flipped through the handbook.

"Next week, so start reading the book. I'll go over the chapters with you each night." Harley kissed his wife on her cheek. "I have repairs to do on the cars. I'll probably eat with the mechanics at the club, so I'll be home late."

"And I have a lot of reading to keep me company. I think my gardening has just been placed on hold." She walked with her husband to the door and gave him a hug. "It was a wonderful present," she said, surprised again by this unpredictable man she had married.

Before she started studying about aeroplanes, Enid picked up the morning paper to read with her coffee.

In the sports section of *The Scotsman,* it was reported that the Countess of Kinnoull entered her Salmson in the 5.5 mile *Ladies Handicap Race*, but was unable to be ready in time for the start.

"How could they print that . . . it makes me sound lazy and that's not true at all. I was dressed and ready to go way ahead of time," she said out loud.

However, the second newspaper, *The Autocar* reported that the reason the Countess was not ready in time for the race was because her car had developed axle trouble.

Could it be, she wondered? Perhaps the car problem was a result of my pushing the speed in the practice run; could Harley have been right, after all?

Enid had a hard time concentrating on anything when her mind was wandering with the excitement of her first flight. She had so admired the American pilot Amelia Earhart, who on October 22, 1922, had set a world record for the first female pilot to fly to an altitude of 14,000 feet. Now she, too, would be a woman in flight.

For several days Enid felt a nagging uneasiness that left her stomach in knots, but she wasn't going to let anything interrupt her flying lessons.

"I've noticed you've been complaining about your upset stomach for a few days now," said Harley. "I want you to call the doctor if you're not feeling better by tomorrow."

"I'm sure it's just the excitement about my first flight," Enid insisted. "I only need some rest and I'll be fine."

When Enid retired for the evening, Harley decided to take up May Meyrick's offer for free drinks while using the gambling rooms at the Silver Slipper. He enjoyed the thrill and competition that the club offered; it didn't matter if it was a card game or dice, Harley was hooked. At first he only spent a few evenings a week at the club, unfortunately loosing more than he won. But soon the gambling addiction got hold of him . . . sneaking out every evening after Enid had fallen asleep. By the end of the month Harley's argumentative state confused and frustrated Enid. Little did she know that Harley was slowly gambling away their fortune and his addiction was sending him into a spiraling decline.

Chapter 9

The Freedom of Flight

The 20th of May 1924 finally arrived and the prospect of her first flight after several weeks of classroom instruction produced a radiate smile that had long forsaken Enid's countenance. Her cheerfulness and excitement pleased Harley and he was looking forward to seeing his old flight instructor, Captain C.D. Barnard.

"Well, today is the big day, Enid. Are you nervous?"

"I think I'm more excited than nervous . . . but my stomach is in knots."

"We all feel that way on our first flight. I think you will handle it quite well. I've been impressed by how quickly you acclimated to my drilling you on the various emergencies scenarios that might transpire during a long trip."

Enid smiled. She had spent the last few weeks memorizing every aspect of the detailed illustrations of the aircraft in the pilot's handbook. She wanted so much to prove to her husband that she was quite capable of flying a biplane and would be prepared for any emergency that they might encounter during their cross-country flight.

It was a brisk, foggy morning when they drove off toward the De Havilland Aerodrome in Hendon, approximately nine miles from their apartment.

"Harley, they won't cancel the flight because of this fog, will they?"

"I was a bit concerned, but the fog is beginning to dissipate. Looks like some blue sky is breaking through. Not to worry, you'll be up in the air in no time," he reassured her.

Harley was delighted that his friend had been available for Enid's flight instructor. Although Captain Barnard had an unorthodox way of instruction almost to the point of being perverse, Harley felt it was the best way to ensure Enid would be capable of dealing with any situation that they may encounter while on a long distant flight. Captain Barnard had been known to take new students for their first flight, and then cut the engines to see how they would react to an emergency. Or he would unexpectedly fly upside down. Harley of course did not inform his wife of this tidbit of information.

Captain Barnard greeted them when they entered the hanger of the De Havilland School of Flight. "How's my favorite student?"

"Excited about my first flight," replied Enid.

"Now, wait a minute, Barnard . . . I thought I was your favorite student," said Harley.

"Back in the heydays, Harley, you were right up there, but I have to say that with this new era of female insurgence into the world of flight, a beautiful women trumps all from your gender."

"With that, I shall leave you two so you can do your preflight checklist, while I commiserate with the last bastion of my fellow male chauvinistic pilots over by the coffee pot."

"Well, let's get started, Enid. The heavy fog has saturated the soil, so we need to review the procedure for a soft-field takeoff."

"If I recall," said Enid, "the run-up series of last minute checks before takeoff will now be done prior to taxiing to the runway, so we won't need to stop and take the chance of getting stuck in the mud. And when returning, we should keep in mind that the landing could be slippery."

"I see that you've been doing your homework. I'm confident that you are going to make an excellent pilot, Enid." She followed Captain Barnard out to the aircraft parked just outside the hanger.

The De Havilland DH37's painted white body glistened from the morning dew. It was an open cockpit biplane that had been modified to seat two . . . one in the front and back. A cold breeze swirled around them. Enid turned the collar up on her leather jacket, allowing the sheepskin lining to cover her ears.

"Now that the fog has dissipated, let's get started on the pre-flight checklist." Captain Barnard handed her the clipboard.

Although she had memorized the pre-flight procedures, Enid was glad to have a step-by-step checklist to follow. She first secured the wheel chocks, noticing that the two triangular pieces of wood connected by a piece of rope were not wedged properly in front and behind each wheel . . . undoubtedly left that way by her instructor. She next untied the ropes on each wing and one on the tail. Standing on the foothold in the fuselage, Enid looked into the cockpit making sure that the magnetos switch was off. She remembered that the magnetos kept the ignition independent of the rest of the electrical system to ensure the engine would continue running in the event of alternator or battery failure. She then jumped down and went over to the front of the plane. Enid reached up to the cold wooden propeller blade, trying to recall what the pilot's handbook had instructed about pulling the prop through. She remembered that the illustrations showed cylinders radiating out from the center of the engine, like the numbers on a clock. The six o'clock position was considered upside down. If left in this position, the oil would leak down through and past the pistons causing a liquid lock, preventing the pistons from going their full length. If the propeller cannot be pulled through, then there could be an oil leak. Enid held her breath as she yanked down on the propeller . . . praying that she would not feel it stop at the six o'clock position. She was surprised and relieved with the ease that the propeller moved through its complete cycle. Even though there was no oil leak, Enid still checked the oil quantity located in front of the engine.

One particular warning sign in the handbook stood out in her mind with its bold lettering: DO NOT RELY ON THE GAS GAUGE! Many a pilot has not heeded this warning and ended up crash landing their aircraft. This was not going to happen to Enid. Not trusting the accuracy of the gas tanks while racing cars, she had made her own gauge by using a painters' stir stick . . . marking off each five gallons of gas she added to the gas tank. This time, Enid checked the plane's gas level using a similar devise. With the outside checklist done, it was now time to get a feel for the cockpit.

Placing her left boot in the foothold in the fuselage, Enid grabbed the handle on the edge of the wing. The tape of fabric covering the wings was pulled taut by large stitching, resembling the skin of a drum. She stepped onto the seat then slid down into the back cockpit. It was a snug fit even though the exposed wooden ribs, running the length of the fuselage, made the interior of the aircraft seem huge.

After familiarizing herself with the instrument panel and the map showing the route they would be taking, Enid folded the flight plan and put it in her jacket pocket. Captain Barnard helped adjust her leather flight helmet and made sure the speaking tube was audible and clear. Enid strapped herself into the seat, then calibrated the altimeter dial on the instrument panel to the correct altitude of the airport above sea level. Testing the ailerons by moving the stick sideways, she watched the hinged surface on the edge of the wing move up and down . . . this would control the angle of the bank during a turn. Moving the column fore and aft directed the elevators to cause the nose of the plane to go higher or lower. Pushing on the pedal board under her feet controlled the rudder. Enid was glad she had consumed an extra cup of coffee for breakfast, knowing full well that she would need all her senses trying to maneuver three controls simultaneously during the flight.

After tightly fastening the goggles' strap, Enid said a quick prayer. She then pulled the primer knob out about three inches, creating a suction that allowed fuel to be injected into the primer. Her stomach churned with anxiety. She shoved the knob forward, sending gasoline into the cylinders.

"Clear prop," she yelled out to Captain Barnard, letting him know that the magnetos were live.

"Clear prop," he replied.

She shouted, "Switch on."

And he confirmed, "Switch on."

The live magnetos were now ready to send the spark that ignites the fuel in the cylinders to start the engine.

Captain Barnard pulled the prop down as hard as he could . . . with a putt-putt-putt the engine sprang to life, increasing in noise. Within ten seconds all cylinders were running, sending white smoke bellowing from the engine until it began to run smoothly.

The nauseous fumes of gasoline and burnt oil wafted through the cockpit. Enid's stomach began to churn. Smoke blew past the breather tube and vented out the bottom of the engine, coating the underside of the plane with greasy soot.

Captain Barnard yanked on the rope of the wheel chocks, allowing the plane to slowly move forward. He climbed into the front cockpit, strapped himself in and adjusted his goggles. He then signaled Enid to do a run-up to ensure that the engine would run smoothly on only one magneto. Enid located a four-position switch: (1) *Off*, (2) *L (left)*, (3) *R (right)*, and (4) *Both*. She pushed the switch to #4 and throttled up to 1500 rpms, then switched over to the *L position* dropping the rpms to 100. Doing the same procedure with the *R position* assured Enid that all magnetos were running smooth. She turned the switch back to the *#4* position and again increased the rpms to 1500. Enid gave a thumb up to her instructor and began to taxi toward the runway. The plane bumped along the rutted field. Enid looked around for any incoming or outgoing aircraft. She kept reminding herself not to stop or they could end up stuck in the wet grass. Seeing no other traffic she checked the windsock near the end of the runway to determine the direction of the air current, then accessed the runway heading into the wind. Her heart throbbed madly. The muscles in her arms tensed when she punched the throttle increasing the speed of the plane 25, 30, 35, 38, 40, 41, 42 miles per hour. The plane caught the cross winds and began to rise. She used the in ground effect of keeping the plane level just above the grass to increase the plane's speed. When Enid got the thumb up from her instructor, she pulled back on the stick, causing the nose to lift. They began to gain altitude.

A newly awakened sense of freedom washed over her. Enid was amazed at this new perspective. From up here she had no cares in the world.

Captain Barnard yelled into the speaking tube attached to Enid's leather helmet. "You need to make a ninety degree turn to the left to avoid the mass of clouds up ahead."

"Roger that." Enid turned the stick to the left and followed through with the rudder, making a coordinated move. The plane began to turn, but the tip of the wing grazed the dark billowing clouds. The different atmospheric conditions caused the plane to shudder from the turbulence, jarring Enid back and forth in the cockpit. Her knee hit the side of the stick . . . the speed indicator needle fluctuated radically from 5,000 rpms up to 5,000 rpms down. Her experience of split second decision making while racing cars, gave her the confidence to calmly bring the aircraft back under control.

Looking over the side of the cockpit, Enid searched for familiar landmarks below that would lead to the turnaround point of their flight. She fixed her sight on the Great Western Railway, following the tracks as they serpentined across the vast English countryside. They left the tracks at Wokingham and headed north to the town of Reading . . . onto Henley-on-Thames and then turned northwest to Didcot, a village directly south of Oxford. From Didcot they headed due west to their destination, the *White Horse* on a hill . . . five miles west of Wantage and five miles south of Faringdon.

Enid had only heard stories about the great *White Horse* on the hill, but now she was about to see it for herself. The strange, almost mystical creature emerged from miles away. Its elongated figure stretched out in full gallop across the hills in the parish of Uffington in Berkshire. Nobody seems to know who created the rather large four hundred foot *White Horse,* although it resembled similar creatures rendered on coins from first century BC.

Enid decreased the plane's altitude while soaring from the horse's tail to its head. This closer look revealed deep trenches filled with the crumbled white chalk of the Berkshire Downs. Legend says the horse figure was created to protect the knob of Dragon Hill protruding below the *White Horse* . . . believed to be the area where Saint George slew the dragon.

Having reached their turnaround point, Enid headed the plane in an easterly direction, glad for the increased tailwind. After reaching Henley-on-Thames, Captain Barnard instructed her to follow the Thames River back to London.

They made good time with the 10-knot tailwind and soon the Hendon Aerodrome came into view.

"Enid," yelled the Captain into the speaking tube, "there is one more area you need to be tested on."

"What's that?" Enid yelled back.

Captain pulled back the throttle to idle. The roar of the engine stopped.

Enid smiled. Rather than panic, she welcomed the silence. She felt the power of being in control as the plane glided toward the Aerodrome. She looked around for any incoming planes. With no air traffic, Enid kept the altitude up and began to lower the flaps with a manual handle, making her approach heading into the wind. Flying level above the runway she gently pulled back on the stick and the nose of the plane came up ever so slightly. This slowed their speed from 60 mph to 55, 50, 45 . . . when the speedometer needle hit 42 the two main wheels touched down with a thud, followed by the tail wheel. She worked the rudder pedal pumping it back and forth while simultaneously moving the tail wheel lever left and right.

"Well done, Enid," remarked her instructor when she finally brought the aircraft to a stop near the hanger.

Harley ran up to greet them. "Bravo! Marvelous landing."

Enid was all smiles, beaming from Harley's approval. Now she would be able to get her license in time for the July flight to Paris.

Captain Barnard got out of the cockpit with his clipboard. "I must say, Enid, I was impressed with how calm you remained when I cut the engines. And your landing was flawless."

"I surprised myself," said Enid. "The silence of the engine had a calming effect, which allowed me to concentrate on the landing."

"Before you two head off, let's schedule several more hours of airtime, then you'll have no problem getting your license," said the Captain.

"I knew you would be a fearless pilot," said Harley as they drove home. "So, old Barnard cut the engine on you. He let you off easy. He flipped the bloody plane upside down on me." They both laughed. "What say we go to the club to celebrate?"

"Harley, that sounds wonderful . . . but to be honest with you, the constant mental exertion while in flight was exhausting. Every muscle in my body aches. Right now all I long for is a hot bath and a nap."

"I'll tell you what," said Harley, "you take a long nap and we'll go out to celebrate this evening."

But it was never to happen. When Enid awoke from her nap the queasiness that had plagued her for the last few weeks had returned. Harley insisted that she see a doctor and this time Enid agreed that she would call the doctor the next morning. She then turned over and drifted back to sleep. But Harley wasn't tired and quietly slipped out to the Silver Slipper for a couple of those free drinks that May, the owner's daughter, had offered.

Captain C.D. Barnard (Instructor), Countess Enid Kinnoull, greeted by her husband, George Harley Hay, the 14th Earl of Kinnoull after Enid's first training flight. (Copyright photo provided by The Image Works)

Chapter 10

The Kingdom Falls

The next morning when Enid could not keep any food down Harley called the doctor. Upon hearing of her condition for the last few weeks the doctor told Harley to bring her to his clinic for some lab work.

Enid sat in the doctor's office after the lab tests were taken.

"Lady Kinnoull, the results of your tests won't be available for a week," said the doctor. "In the mean time, I want you to curtail your extracurricular activities such as racecar driving and flying. I recommend complete bed rest until I drop by at the end of the week with the results. I'm also giving you some medication that will calm your stomach and allow you to eat."

"But it's important that I continue with my flying lessons."

"That is out of the question until I can read the lab report."

By the time they got home, Enid was in tears. The day before was so exciting with her first flight, but now she was grounded for at least a week. She immediately called her mother to complain of her situation.

The days and nights soon began to meld together. That was fine with Enid, for all she wanted to do was sleep. Harley on the other hand took advantage of the clear weather and headed for the racetrack during the day and to the Silver Slipper in the evenings.

Enid's mother agreed to daily visits with her daughter hoping to cheer her up. After breakfast they enjoyed playing the latest game craze called a Word-Cross puzzle. At the end of the week while they were engaged in the morning's puzzle, the doctor arrived to inquire of his patient.

"Well, ladies, the lab report finally came in and I'm happy to announce that Enid's stomach problems are not serious and that the lab tests have confirmed my suspicions. Lady Kinnoull, you are indeed pregnant."

"Did you hear that, Mother? I'm going to have a baby." She patted her stomach.

"What wonderful news you bring us, doctor. To think that I'll soon be a grandmother."

"I'm glad to be the bearer of such good news. Now, Lady Kinnoull, I want you to take it easy but you are no longer on complete bed rest. You'll need to call my office and make an appointment for next month. Good day, ladies."

Margie was ecstatic to learn of her daughter's new circumstance and couldn't wait to tell her friends.

"Darling, I'll pick you up after breakfast tomorrow so we can shop for baby furniture." She gave her daughter a hug and was out the door.

Enid was glad her mother was leaving so she would be alone with Harley to announce this joyous occasion. Knowing he wouldn't be home from the track until late afternoon, she was determined to be dressed and ready to go out and celebrate upon his return.

When Enid heard Harley's car roar up the driveway, she quickly took one last look in the mirror and adjusted the blue satin ribbon in her hair. Harley closed the front door and threw his keys on the entry table.

"Enid, I'm home," he yelled and then turned to watch his wife descend the stairs wearing the same silver blue dress that she had worn on the night they first met at the seaside hotel.

"Now that is one dress that brings back some good memories. I'm glad to see you are more chipper this evening."

"I feel like dancing tonight. Let's go out," said Enid.

"Isn't that against doctor's orders? What about complete bed rest?"

"The doctor came by this morning."

"And what were the test results?"

"Well," said Enid. She could not contain herself, knowing this joyous news would bind them closer . . . "the report said that you are going to be a father."

For a fleeting moment he was speechless, then with an unexpected tenderness he wrapped her in his arms, showering her with kisses.

"But of course this calls for a celebration, we're going to be parents."

"I'm in the mood to go dancing," said Enid. "The Silver Slipper has a wonderful dance band." She felt his body suddenly stiffen and the tender moment vanished.

"Our lives will change forever. I feel that a quiet dinner for two where we can discuss our future with a child is the more prudent thing to do."

Enid had never known Harley to be so sensible and silently admired his change of attitude at the prospect of becoming a father.

"Very well, you go freshen up and I'll think of a quiet restaurant." Enid wondered how she could feel both excited and annoyed at the same time.

About forty-five minutes later, they were seated at a secluded table next to a fireplace in a quaint French restaurant near the Thames River. During their meal, the young couple amused each other with a varied selection of names for the baby.

"Now, you realize my dear, that it's customary for women of your stature to remain at their country estates during their confinement. Once you start showing your condition, I'll have the servants prepare for your return to Balhousie. I also think it would be a comfort to you to have your mother move in during your confinement."

Suddenly Enid had lost her appetite for dessert. "Harley, you can't be serious. I can't think of anything worse for my health than being isolated in a damp, cold castle. If you won't think of my health, than at least consider the baby's health."

There was an uncomfortable silence between them as Harley sipped his wine. A pianist started playing the popular song by Marion Harris, *Who's Sorry Now?* She looked at her husband who silently stared at the flames in the fireplace and wondered if someday she, too, would be sorry.

After much deliberation they arrived at a compromise. Enid would remain in London. But socializing at the clubs was no place for a pregnant woman although she could entertain her friends with afternoon tea if she so desired.

Over the months as her physical appearance began to change and her mood swings became unpredictable, Harley chose to spend less and less time at home and more time at the clubs.

"Harley, you're never here anymore. I need you to be home with me," said Enid when Harley arrived late one night with alcohol on his breath.

"Since it seems that I can never do anything right by you, why would I want to be around your irritable mood changes?"

"The doctor told us that there would be some difficult times, but we just laughed. We were going to be different. We were growing a family together. Please give me your hand. I think I felt the baby kicking." She reached out for his hand, but he shoved her arm away, knocking her off balance. Enid fell back into a chair.

"And another thing, my dear wife . . . you don't tell me what to do. I'm the head of this household and what I say goes. And you might as well know it now that you will not be flying with me to the Paris Olympics."

"But Harley, why not? The doctor said I should be able to fly in July."

"I say no. I'm just looking out for my son or daughter. You wouldn't even be able to use a seatbelt. You don't want to harm the baby, do you? Now, I'm going back to the club where they appreciate me." He grabbed his coat and slammed the door on the way out.

The harder she tried to ignore the truth, the more it tormented her. Could it be possible that this child she felt would bind them closer together was actually tearing them apart. She wondered.

As the summer months lingered on so did Enid's thoughts. With Harley away at the Olympics, she began to blame herself for his aloof behavior. She would strive once again to be the carefree, adventuress girl that had captured his heart less than a year ago. Enid started reading as many newspaper accounts of the Olympics she could get her hands on in hopes of conversing intelligently with her husband about the games.

When Harley returned he was pleasantly surprised to be greeted by a cheerful smiling wife.

"I hope you took a lot of pictures," said Enid. "The stories in the papers about the Olympics have been marvelous. I'm so anxious to hear all about the trip."

"Here I thought you'd still be mad at me," said Harley. "It really was a good thing you weren't there, darling. There was a lot of walking and standing in long lines for food and drink. At times the heat was a bit much even for me. But you would have enjoyed the thrill and excitement of the competition among the athletes from the various nations. The camaraderie of all the athletes at the closing ceremony was so uplifting. It felt good to see the world at peace."

Enid was pleased when Harley never mentioned going to the clubs and began to spend more time at home. And for a while peacefulness enveloped them, or so it seemed.

Unfortunately Harley's decision to spend more time with his wife had an alternative motive; it was brought on by his running up debt and loss of credit at the major clubs.

Near the end of her pregnancy, Enid found it hard to sleep. The arrival of the cold winter months brought an ominous premonition that tore at her dreams. Her lack of sleep brought emotional outbursts that she didn't understand.

"This crying all the time has got to stop," said Harley. "We both need a break. I'm going to the club to have a good cigar and a drink with the men."

"Please don't leave, I need you." She reached out to her husband.

"What you need is some sleep. Go back to bed, Enid." He gave her a quick shove and stormed out the door. Enid's shoe caught the edge of the rug. She slipped, hitting the floor on her side. A maid heard a thud and ran to her aid.

"Should I call the doctor, Milady?"

"No, no . . . just help me to bed. It was clumsy of me to slip like that." A fear came over her, not only for her unborn child, but also for her marriage.

Harley had not known that Enid had fallen. As he drove to the Silver Slipper, his mind was focused on other things, especially a cute brunette with a tray of free drinks and a sympathetic shoulder.

Finally the end of November arrived along with labor pains. Enid gave birth to a son, who they named Henry George Adam Hay, at their home at 44 Princes Gardens on Sunday, November 24, 1924.

Two months later, a choral christening service was officiated by Prebendary Leith Boyd and sponsored by The Duke of Atholl, Sir Hugh Fraser, Mr. F.P. M. Schiller, and Mrs. Hamilton-Fellows (maternal grandmother). The child was given the Christian name Atholl James Adam, Baron Hay of Kinfauns, and wore a family christening robe of

Flemish lace with a white fur trimmed bonnet and an embroidered Indian shawl as a wrap.

Enid began withdrawing from any social events, spending every waking moment with the baby. She had never felt needed before but now a little person that she had created was dependent on her. Enid enjoyed this new role and although a nanny was there to offer assistance, she, unlike her friends or her mother, wanted to be a bigger part of her child's life. Enid finally felt in control of something greater than herself.

Margie worried about her daughter's health. One day she pulled Harley aside.

"You've got to do something, Harley. She won't listen to me and she can't keep going on like this."

"I don't know what you expect me to do."

"You know how much she enjoys flying. Take her away for a few weeks and let her do most of the flying. Concentrating on something other than the baby will do her good."

Harley looked over at his wife. "Darling, I think it is time you and I had a fresh start. I promise things will be different. What say we fly over to Algiers for a few weeks? It'll do us both good."

Enid laid the infant in his crib. "But I worry about the baby, there's a rash on the inside of his leg."

"Let me see," said Harley. He pushed the blanket aside and lifted his son out of the crib. "I see a few little red bumps . . . what do you think, Margie?"

"Not to worry about a thing," she replied. "Babies get heat rashes all the time. Between the nanny and myself, the child will be in good hands. You need to get away for a while, Enid it will do you good."

All of a sudden the baby stiffened his arms and legs and pushed hard against his father's stomach. His body arched as he threw his head backward.

"Whoa! Henry, you're a mighty strong little fellow," said Harley. They all laughed.

"Perhaps you're right . . . I could use a short holiday," said Enid.

"Then it's settled," said Harley. "I'll make all the arrangements."

A few days later Enid and Harley kissed their son good-bye and began their flight to Algiers.

The Earl had arranged accommodations at the most popular resort and one with the best dance bands around. They spent their days lounging by the pool and their evenings dancing away the nights.

"Hasn't the weather been marvelous, darling?"

"Compared to cold, foggy London, I must admit that the sun and warm weather was just what I needed," said Enid. "This has been like a second honeymoon."

A waiter arrived with two cocktails. "Here are the drinks you ordered, sir. I have a Rickey made with gin, lime juice and seltzer for you and the popular Mary Pickford made with white rum, pineapple juice and grenadine for the lady. Will there be anything else, sir?"

"Yes, I'd like to make reservations for two at a table near the dance floor around eight tonight."

"Very good, sir. I'll see to that right away."

Their joy, however, was short lived when two weeks later they received the news that their son was quite ill and had been stricken with meningitis at three and a half months of age.

"I never should have listened to you, Harley! What was I thinking, to be gone so long from my son?" Enid began to weep.

"He's my son, too! And another thing . . . it was your mother's idea to take you on this trip. Pack your bags! We'll leave immediately. I'll call ahead to the hanger." He also called down to the front desk informing them of the emergency situation and they would need a picnic basket with sandwiches and fruit along with two Thermoses filled with hot coffee.

Devastated, they headed for the airport where Harley's aeroplane was gassed and waiting.

"If we take turns we can fly all night and should be home by morning. I'll take the first shift, which will get us over the water and along Spain's eastern coast" he said.

"Harley, I don't think I can sleep. I just want to hold our baby in my arms."

"I know how you feel, but you need to try to doze off. We both need to keep our wits about us if we are to get home by morning."

Enid closed her eyes remembering the excitement of holding her son for the first time . . . the continuous humming noise of the engine finally lulled her to sleep. About two hours later, Harley hit some turbulence, which jolted Enid awake.

"What happened?" she asked, rubbing the back of her neck.

"Sorry to wake you, just ran into some heavy clouds. Looks like we're out of it now. Think you can handle it for an hour?"

"Let me eat and get some coffee down me, first. Do you want something?"

"I'll take a sandwich and some water, then I'll try for an hour nap. We've had a good tail wind. Made up some time. We should be home in six hours with only a stop at le Bourget Airfield outside of Paris to refuel and stretch our legs."

After they ate, Enid took over the controls. Now she needed to focus on the instrument panel in front of her. Her instincts from her first flight lesson clicked in. The weather seemed to be cooperating still giving them a strong tailwind. At this rate we might be able to cut another hour off our time, she thought. She glanced over at her husband . . . he began to snore. She smiled. Even though it had been a few weeks, we had needed this time alone together, she thought. And soon we'll be home with our son.

Two hours later, Harley woke and took over the flying. It wasn't long before the lighted runway of the le Bourget Airfield came into view. They stayed only thirty minutes to refuel, and then they were back in the air.

Harley radioed ahead to the Hendon Aerodrome near London to have a taxi waiting when they arrived. They both smiled when the wheels finally touched down and they taxied to the hanger.

The waiting taxi driver helped load their luggage and they were off to their apartment where Enid's mother and a nanny were taking care of the baby.

Once home, Enid rushed through the front door, not even stopping to say hello to her mother before running upstairs to the baby's room.

"We left as soon as the telegram arrived," said Harley. "I think we made great time . . . how's Henry?"

"Oh dear!" Margie put her hand across her mouth. "I'm afraid you're too late."

Enid came running down the stairs. "Where's my baby?" she yelled.

"What do you mean, too late?" asked Harley.

"I need to sit down. Let's go into the parlor," said Margie. She walked into the next room and they followed.

"I don't want to sit down, Mother. Where is my baby?"

"Harley, take her hand . . . please." He pulled Enid down on the sofa next to him.

"The baby seemed to be improving. But last night he took a turn for the worst and we rushed him to the hospital."

"Then we must go to the hospital, Harley! We can't let our son be there alone!"

"You don't understand, Enid. Henry will not be coming home from the hospital. There was nothing the doctors could do. He died late last night." Margie put her head in her hands and cried.

"No! No! This can't be true! You told me he would be fine. I trusted you, Mother!" Enid jumped up from the sofa. Harley grabbed his wife and held her tight.

"It's not your mother's fault. It was the meningitis that took our son's life." Enid sobbed uncontrollably on his shoulder. Harley looked down at Margie. "We'll want to see our son before the funeral."

"The funeral home is preparing his body for viewing tomorrow. I'll take you there."

"Margie, I think this is something that Enid and I need to do on our own."

"I understand," she said. "Harley, the doctor has given me several tranquilizers." She pulled a pillbox from the pocket of her sweater. "He said to be sure to give one to Enid . . . it will help her sleep tonight."

Twenty-one year old Enid was growing up faster than her young years could cope. She and Harley, both dressed in black, walked arm in arm into the viewing room at the funeral home. They wanted nobody else around as they looked upon the face of their son for the last time.

The dark mahogany paneled walls and deep red carpet made the room eerily quiet. Several rows of chairs faced the built-up platform where a tiny opened casket stood under the warm glow of two candelabras. Enid felt her heart pounding . . . her throat constricting . . . trembling, she gripped Harley's arm tighter as they made their way up the center aisle and onto the platform. A large stained glass cross covered the entire wall behind the white marble casket. Enid looked up at the cross.

"Why him, Lord? You could have taken me . . . why a precious innocent child? What have I done to deserve this? You call yourself a loving God . . . then take a baby's life?" She closed her tear filled eyes, afraid of what she was about to see.

"He looks very peaceful," said Harley looking down upon his son in the blue satin lined coffin.

Enid opened her eyes and gazed upon her child for the last time. "Oh Harley, he looks like a baby doll dressed in his christening robe and fur trimmed bonnet. I think the day Henry was born was the happiest day of our lives."

"I'll always remember that sweet little smile of his." Harley put his arm around his wife.

"But why are there pennies on his eyes?" she asked.

"I believe it's to keep the eyes closed," he said.

"I remember my grandfather telling me that they were magic pennies. It was what you did with them . . . that made a difference."

"What an odd saying," said Harley.

Enid bent over her baby and gently kissed his forehead. "Goodnight, my sweet little angel . . . may you rest in peace." She reached into her purse and pulled out Henry's favorite toy. It was a small stuffed lion with a silky mane. She placed it in the casket at her baby's feet.

Harley reached down and moved the lion up next to his son's face. "Leo the Lion will look after you, Henry. He will protect you on this next journey you are about to take." He bend down and kissed his child's check. "Be brave . . . my son."

That afternoon at the funeral, a pain seared Enid's heart as she watched her son's tiny coffin being lowered into the ground, leaving her with a distressing feeling of emptiness. Her pain soon turned to anger aimed at her mother for not taking better care of the baby; at her husband for taking her away; and especially at herself for being so selfish as to leave her child for such a long time. An inner anguish began to torment her.

After arriving home from the funeral, Harley fixed himself a drink while Enid grabbed a stack of mail on the entry table. She mindlessly flipped through the letters, but stopped when she noticed that several had return addresses from attorneys. She tore open the envelopes and was shocked to discover that during her pregnancy Harley had been foolishly gambling their fortune away at the Silver Slipper and that now the matter would be sent to collections. The other letters were from moneylenders demanding their payments. Harley came over to see what she was looking at.

"That's quite a stack of mail there. Anything important?" He asked.

"Important! I thought we were important! How could you promise me that things would be different? That things would get better between us . . . when all along you've been putting us into financial ruin? You're sick, Harley! You are addicted to gambling just like your grandfather and your cousin." Enid flung the letters in his face and stormed out of the room.

Slamming the bedroom door shut, she threw herself on the bed; a feeling of despair swept over her. She heard the rev of Harley's sports car as it sped down the driveway. This nightmare was slowly dragging her down like quicksand, suffocating the life out of her.

Her bedroom became her sanctuary. She fingered the delicate yellow, satin ribbon tied around the neck of Henry's teddy bear. She talked to it in whispers, of the wonderful plans for the day. Yet, she never got out of bed. Food trays were brought in, but left untouched. A concerned maid tried to speak to the Earl, but he consoled his sorrow by drinking and staying away from the house.

Several days later, when the effects of the tranquilizers finally dissipated, Enid asked the maid to fix a breakfast tray and to run a bath for her. After she ate and dressed, Enid went downstairs. She went into every room, looking around their home that at one time had brought her happiness, yet now was filled with nothing but heartache. She decided that the sensible thing to do would be to sell it.

Once word spread that their house was up for sale several private offers came in. On April 20, 1925, the Earl and Lady Kinnoull sold their home at No. 44 Princes Gardens before it came under the hammer of solicitors; hoping that the money from the sale and its furniture would pay off any debts. They moved into a smaller apartment at 47 Portman Square in London, but the gambling addiction had its firm grasp on Harley and continued to put a strain on their marriage.

The tension between Harley and Enid played out in an accumulation of several traffic tickets between the two of them. Both had the propensity to jump into their sports cars, taking out their frustrations in the form of acceleration, not on the racetrack but through the streets of London.

Remembering the tranquil feeling of her first flight, Enid decided it was time to continue her solo flying lessons. Once again soaring above the clouds and leaving her troubles below brought the serenity she had been seeking; for a while a truce coexisted between Enid and Harley.

In June 1925, after receiving her pilot's license Enid was eager for a trip.

"Harley, I've been thinking. It's been awhile since we've checked on your apartment in Paris . . . what say we fly over there next week?"

"Want to try your skills on a longer flight, I see. Are you sure you want to try flying over the English Channel so soon?"

"I think I'm up to the challenge. Besides, I have an ace as my co-pilot."

"Then Paris it is," said Harley. "I'll check on the weather forecast for next week."

The forecast predicted the entire month of June would be one of the sunniest and mildest months in recorded history. Harley submitted their flight plan for June 9th.

"Have the cook fix us a light meal. I should be home by four from the Palace of Westminster. I've scheduled our takeoff at six."

"Harley, couldn't you forgo the meeting this time?"

"Enid, you know how much this means to me. My membership into the House of Lords goes into effect next year. This entitlement is my hereditary right as the Earl of Kinnoull. It is important that I accustom myself to all procedures and that others recognize my faithful presence and see me as a most worthy member to be."

"Very well, I'll see you after the meeting."

Enid was too excited to eat much and was glad that the cook had made a potato soup with a garden salad. She silently prayed for a safe trip.

When they arrived at the Hendon Aerodrome Harley's aeroplane was waiting by the runway. Enid checked and double checked the pre-flight procedures, and then gave Harley a thumb up that they were cleared to go. It was a smooth take off and Harley settled back in his seat watching his wife glow with confidence.

"Wake me when we get to Paris."

"What?"

"Only kidding. It's your first flight over a large body of water. It's crucial to keep your bearings. That's why you have me as your copilot."

Enid watched the White Cliffs of Dover disappear and saw the choppy English Chanel spread out below them. After one hour of flight time she had run into only minor turbulence.

"Only about thirty minutes left," reported Harley. "How about giving me the wheel for the final landing?"

"Sounds good to me," said Enid. "My shoulders are beginning to ache."

But when Harley took over the controls an ensuing cloudbank engulfed them. The plane shuddered from the unsteady movement of air, causing sudden drops in altitude as they approached Le Bourget Airfield outside of Paris. It was 9 p.m. and the sun was just beginning to set when Harley tried to control the plane as it went into a steep descent.

"Brace yourself for a rough landing," yelled Harley.

Enid watched the ground come barreling toward them. She covered her face with her arm.

"Looks like we're going to make it after all," said Harley. But just as the front wheels were about to touch down, a severe crosswind shot across the runway flipping the plane, tail over nose. The plane landed on its top wing and tail with a thud.

An ambulance siren could be heard coming closer. Several men from the hanger went running to the crash site to help the occupants.

"Miss, are you alright?"

"Please, check my husband, he's bleeding," yelled Enid.

The ambulance arrived and the medics rushed to Harley's aid while another man was cutting the seatbelt from Enid. With his help, she was able to crawl out of the cockpit. Harley's unconscious body was put on a stretcher and they both were whisked off to the hospital.

The accident caused only slight injury to Lady Kinnoull, but put the Earl in the hospital for several days.

While Harley was recuperating in the hospital, Enid stayed in their Paris apartment at 48 Rue de la Bienfaisance. She had been away too long and missed the Parisian *laissez-faire* approach to living. Her afternoons were spent visiting the places that gave her the most pleasure. She was drawn to the colorful mosaic designs of the windows adorning the majestic Notre Dame Cathedral, or could it have been the stories of Jesus' life depicted in the windows that was tugging at her heart?

She walked along the cobblestone courtyard in front of Notre Dame, which was bustling with activity. Several artisans were selling their crafts; her favorite was the booth selling delicate Belgium lace doilies. She purchased two for her mother, hoping it would cheer her up, for she had been ill for a while. A visit to Paris was not complete without a stroll along the River Seine, where Enid stopped to admire the plein-air artists of French Impressionism. At home she had tried her hand at painting, which leaned toward realism, but Harley had teased her about her earlier attempts. Perhaps a tinge of impressionism is what was lacking . . . she wondered.

After a few days of observation Harley was released from the hospital and the young couple headed back to London.

Ever since their marriage at such a young age, the society pages of the local newspapers had labeled them the *Baby Countess and the Boy Earl,* a nickname that continued to follow them. Gossip began to spread of the young couple's growing estrangement, but to her friends Enid appeared carefree and happy. If there was any truth in the gossip, she concealed it. Enid and Harley were seen golfing, flying, dancing, and driving their racing cars around the countryside. On one occasion Enid was ticketed for speeding and because of her previous tickets was given a summons date to appear in a London traffic court.

They had hardly been home a month, from Paris, when Enid found out about additional gambling bills piling up and Harley's constant visits to the Silver Slipper.

With the letters in hand, Enid confronted him. "Harley, do you really want these gambling bills to tear us apart?"

"Darling, I knew you would come around."

"What are you talking about?"

"I know now that I have a sickness and with your help we can work through this together. With your money, you can pay off my debts. I'll be forever grateful and I know that I can make you proud of me once again."

"If you are serious, then I insist that we leave immediately to spend some time at the Balhousie Castle to avoid any further humiliation. We need time alone without any outside interference." Harley agreed to try to reconcile their growing indifference.

They had been in Perth for only a few days when Enid started sorting through the mail and paying bills. An official looking envelope slipped off the table. Enid noticed it was addressed to her. She quickly opened it and let out a gasp.

"Harley!" she yelled. "Today is my court appearance for my traffic ticket and there is no way I can drive from here to London in time. Do you know of anyone around here that has an aeroplane you could use to fly me?"

"Well, I certainly can't have my wife in contempt of court when I'll soon be assuming my seat in the House of the Lords," replied Harley.

They drove to the nearest airport where the Earl of Kinnoull's flying record was well known. He was able to command an aeroplane and flew with Enid to London in time for her court appearance, where she was fined and warned to watch her speed.

Enid was grateful to Harley and during their time together in Scotland she tried to work things out between them.

"Harley, these last few months, being here alone with you has made me stop and think that perhaps I've been too quick to judge you. I see now that your financial situation has not been entirely your fault."

Harley reached out and took both of Enid's hands in his. "If only my father had not died at such a young age, perhaps he would have given me better foresight into the financial matters of running a large estate. Instead I was weaned on my grandfather's insatiable addiction to gambling. Your paying off my debts will give us a fresh start."

Enid wasn't so sure, however for a time there was a civil peace between them. But Harley missed the excitement of London. The isolation of the countryside was beginning to wear on him.

"Darling, you must read this article in the sports section of today's paper. Brooklands is about to start their car-racing season. We don't want to miss that now, do we?" Enid had always enjoyed the thrill of the racetrack.

"It would be nice to get in a few races. But if we go back to London, you must promise me that you will contact a financial solicitor and no more gambling."

"You are a dear," Harley smiled. "Then it's settled, we'll leave tomorrow."

Chapter 11

The Auctioneer's Hammer

London in July was bustling with end of summer parties. The Brooklands' boisterous racing enthusiasts made their appearance at the usual clubs, always ending the evening at the Silver Slipper with their lively dance band. Once the couples from the Brooklands Race Club ordered their drinks they all headed for the dance floor.

"Come on, Harley, let's dance," said Enid, expecting Harley to follow.

"I see a few of my buddies at the bar that I haven't seen in a while. You go ahead, don't let me stop you. You've never lacked for dance partners."

"Are you sure?"

"Absolutely. Have fun."

While Enid swirled around the dance floor she tried to take an occasional glance to see where her husband had wandered; she abruptly stopped dancing when she saw him enter the gambling room. Excusing herself from her dance partner she returned to her table. While slowly sipping her cocktail Enid tried to calm her anger and disappointment over broken promises. She finally realized that her husband's ancestral blood ran very thick indeed, apparently thicker than his promises to her.

"Tired of dancing already?" asked Harley when he returned to their table with the others.

"I saw you go into the gambling room, Harley. How could you? You promised."

"Just because I was in the room doesn't mean I was gambling."

"Really? Then what's in your hand?"

Harley put a stack of gambling chips down on the table. "These were given to me by some friends. You don't expect me to insult them by not using them, do you?"

"Let's go home, Harley," said Enid. "It's been a long evening."

"Are you joking? The night is young. Why don't you go home where you can dilly-dally with your so called art and let me be?" He threw his car keys down on the table. "And don't wait up. My evening is just beginning. To the bar, men, drinks are on me." All the men followed Harley, leaving the women with their mouths open.

"As you all can see my husband has had a few too many drinks. Would you please have one of the men get him home safely?" She picked up the keys and stormed out of the club with tears streaming down her face.

Seeing her world spin out of control, Enid was overwhelmed and turned to the one constant in her life, her mother. Margie was shocked by the lack of discipline that the Earl displayed in his financial affairs.

"Mother, I didn't know who to turn to but you. I hate to burden you with my problems when you are so ill."

"You did the right thing by coming to me, Enid. I've been through the same thing. I don't understand why men get so addicted to gambling. If the Earl isn't stopped now . . . you'll only end up ruined. The humiliation of dragging the family name through the courts would be devastating to both families and must be stopped. Tomorrow I will elicit the services of my solicitor to protect not only your inheritance, but also the family name. Before I die of this nasty lung infection, I'll make sure that your foolhardy husband does not receive a penny of your money."

With fearful apprehension, Enid informed her husband of her mother's decision to protect her inheritance against him. Furious, Harley retaliated on August 1, by moving into his own apartment at 94

Cheyne Walk in Chelsea. However, without his wife's money, nine months later he was forced to declare bankruptcy, which automatically barred him from assuming his seat in the House of Lords.

Enid sought solace in isolation at the Balhousie Castle. But the Earl had other plans for his family's ancient estate.

One morning Enid had overslept and woke to a commotion coming from the first floor. She threw on a bathrobe and cautiously made her way down the stairs. The front door was wide open. She saw two burly men struggling to load one of the heavy burgundy, velvet sofas into a moving van along with several of her favorite upholstered armchairs. A number of paintings in lustrous, mahogany frames flecked with gold leaf were scattered randomly about on the lawn. Rolled and tied tapestries depicting hunting scenes of long ago, now leaned precariously by the front door, leaving faded shadows where they once hung in the great entry hall.

"What on earth is going on?" asked Enid. Not knowing whether to be scared or mad.

"I'm sorry, Miss, didn't know anyone was still living here." A man who appeared to be directing the movers handed her a paper with a solicitor's letterhead describing the furnishings that were being put under the auctioneer's hammer.

"But there must be some mistake," said Enid. She walked through the main level of the estate, shocked to see no furniture or carpets remaining.

"Miss, I was told it was a bankruptcy. We didn't mean to frighten you."

"Well, I need some time to dress and pack."

"I can see that this is upsetting to you. I'll take my men to a local pub and give you about two hours to pack."

"I would appreciate that." Enid looked over the list in her hand as she went back upstairs to her room. At the bottom of the paper was the

Earl's signature allowing for all the contents of the estate, except the family portraits, to be auctioned off for payment due lenders.

Enid was outraged that Harley would do something so humiliating, knowing full well that she was staying at the castle. Her eyes welled with tears. She pulled two suitcases from a closet and began packing. When the suitcases bulged with as many clothes, shoes and jewelry that could be squeezed into them, she sat on them in order to close the latches. She dragged them to the top of the stairs, but returned to the bedroom to take one last look around. Her hand grabbed an antique crystal vase that she and the Earl had purchased during their honeymoon.

"This is one item that will not be auctioned off, my dear husband!" she yelled and hurled it across the room, watching it shatter to pieces when it hit the wall. She grabbed the two suitcases, struggling to get them down the sweeping staircase.

A loud knock on the door startled her. It was too soon for the movers to return. She slowly opened the door. Two men stood before her with notebooks in hand.

"We're sorry to bother you, Miss, but we are here to inspect the estate."

"I don't understand. Why do you need to inspect the residence?"

"Perhaps this will explain everything." The larger of the two men removed some paperwork from his notebook and handed it to Enid.

"This looks like a lease for this property." She turned to the second page and recognized the signature.

"That's right, it's the lease we signed with the 14th Earl of Kinnoull. We are deacons from the local church, here to inspect the property to see how best to set up the Balhousie Castle as a rest home."

"A rest home! Why, this drafty old castle should be put to rest instead. I'm afraid my husband has neglected to inform me of this new arrangement, but since I was about to leave anyway, if you gentlemen would be so kind to load these suitcases into my car over there, I'll be on my way."

The two deacons were happy to oblige. Enid took one last look at the Balhousie Castle, where she and the Earl had entertained many young couples during the hunting seasons, then tossed the keys to one of the deacons.

"By the way, there are some movers returning from the pub soon and they'll be packing up the remainder of the furnishings," said Enid. She got into her sports car, revved the engine and sped out of the driveway, leaving a swirl of dust in her wake. She headed back to her ailing mother in Tangley Park where they both came to the same conclusion that the marriage was a complete failure.

Enid was shocked to see her mother so pale and thin. "Can't the doctors do anything?" She sat on the edge of the bed and held her mother's hand.

"I'm afraid, my child, that the infection has spread. I've been told to get my house in order."

"But this can't be! We need to get a second opinion."

"No, Enid. It is too late. It's just my time, and we have to accept that."

"I don't know what to do, Mother. My world is falling apart and you've always been there for me. Even when I blamed you for my son's death and I knew it wasn't your fault, you stood by me. Can you ever forgive me? I'm so sorry." Tears began to stream down her face.

"Oh . . . my dear child. There is nothing to forgive. We were all mourning the death of little Henry." Margie put her arms around her daughter and let her cry on her shoulder. "Enid you need not worry, you will be well taken care of. When the time comes, you will find an envelope addressed to you in my desk drawer. It is a copy of my will and I leave everything to you. There's also the card of my solicitor. I've instructed him to stay by your side during this whole turmoil with the Earl. He is a trusted friend and you can count on him for sound advice."

Margie rang a bell on her nightstand and a maid arrived. "Florence, we would like a pot of tea and scones. Miss Enid is looking a bit peaked."

"Right away, Milady."

Enid's London society friends showed her great sympathy during these trying times, especially when they read that the Earl had declared bankruptcy and emptied out Balhousie Castle without informing his wife. But three months later on August 3rd, when her mother passed away and Enid inherited over 5 million pounds, her friends admonished her.

Now that she was wealthy and held the purse strings, her friends expected her to not only buy back the Earl's castle and its furnishings, but to have a reconciliation with her husband. Many tried to convince her that Harley was a really good chap, but foolish when it came to finances.

A group of reporters had been hounding the *Baby Countess* for answers. She finally turned to them, shook her head and said, "There will be NO reconciliation, NO spending of my good money on the Kinnoull estate." Her statement shocked even those who sympathized with her. They felt it was a slap not only at high society, but also at her native land.

"I don't care about the title," she told some friends. "Life, I am quite sure, would be much happier without it. I have made no plans except that I shall leave England as soon as possible, and live here as little as I possibly can. What a pity that titles cannot go to those who esteem them."

Now she could be financially independent from Harley. Having become aware of her husband's philandering, the Countess of Kinnoull, on Wednesday March 2, 1927, sued in the Scottish courts for divorce against him, for infidelity.

In May, the Earl offered a counter action against the Countess but asked for a continuance since she was abroad. The action was continued until June 7th.

In order to protect her family name and estate, Enid agreed to pay a percentage of the Earl's debt owed to his creditors if the courts would drop the bankruptcy charge. Harley agreed to this arrangement, but unbeknownst to Enid, he continued with his extravagant living and borrowing money from moneylenders. When his case came to court Harley tried to work out a similar solution with the courts that Enid had offered him. Her attorney opposed it on the ground that Lady Kinnoull entered into an agreement with the debtor whereby she was to provide the money for the purpose of obtaining an annulment of his bankruptcy. It was alleged that the debtor was not carrying out the terms of that agreement. A writ had been issued on behalf of Lady Kinnoull to obtain specific performance of it and for an injunction against any disposition of property in breach of its terms.

His Honor adjourned the application and held that if the court found the debtor had wrongfully repudiated the agreement with Lady Kinnoull it would be open to counsel to urge that the scheme ought not to be approved by the Court by reason of the conduct of the debtor.

By July 30th, the London Bankruptcy Court formally approved the arrangement of the affairs of the Earl of Kinnoull. Harley attributed his failure to his having lived beyond his means, and to heavy interest on money borrowed from and commission charged for introductions to moneylenders. This arrangement allowed the Earl to regain his seat in the House of Lords.

The bankruptcy matter was over, but the divorce battle raged on. The Earl of Kinnoull lodged a minute of abandonment in his action against the Countess, and Enid proceeded with her action against the Earl.

Finally, in November of 1927, the whole matter was over. A degree of divorce was granted to the Countess of Kinnoull in her action in the

Court of Session against the Earl of Kinnoull. The ground of action, which was undefended, was infidelity.

The Earl immediately announced his engagement to Mary (May) Ethel Isobel, daughter of Kate Meyrick, the nightclub queen. They married on June 6, 1928.

The indignation of this humiliation was a slap in the face to Enid. She sought solace in speed, returning to the racetrack, letting her frustrations run wild. Unfortunately her racing overflowed onto the public roads, running up so many tickets that her license was suspended for three years.

Now she was a young woman facing the grim reality of loneliness, but rather than give up her passion for driving, she was determined to build a new life for herself in Paris.

Chapter 12

A Troubled Soul

The move to Paris was not difficult for Enid. She moved into the apartment at 48 Rue de la Bienfaisanes Street, once owned by Harley, but now granted to her as part of the divorce agreement. She immediately immersed herself into the Parisian lifestyle, which included purchasing a pedigreed champion French poodle puppy she named Ali Baba. Jack and Florence Newbury had been kind enough to follow her to Paris and to attend to her needs as they had done for her mother.

It has been said that in England one tinkers with the arts, but if one is truly serious about writing and painting, it is in Paris where one should live. Enid, inspired by her new environment, applied pen to paper, writing poetic prose and a few short stories that were later published. It was hard for her not to be drawn in by the creative atmosphere and the inherent encouraging nature of the local artists displaying their talents throughout Paris.

Enid's artistic talents began to emerge while taking lessons in oil painting, enamel, mosaics and sculpture at the Academie Ranson, but in 1927 at the young age of twenty-three, Enid could not shake the debilitative criticism she had received from Harley in the past and was now reluctant to have her work openly reviewed. She preferred to work entirely on her own. For several years she was freely and gloriously "modern" and experimental in her artwork, no doubt a release of much pent-up anger. She was encouraged by her fellow art students to join them in membership in the *Societé des Artistes Independents*. The motto

of this organization was *Sans jury ni recompense* (No jury no awards).
For Enid this was the perfect solution. She now had an opportunity to be
in exhibitions throughout Paris and not worry about bad reviews.

Although her artistic endeavors helped to close the curtain on her
tragic past, the deceptive calmness could not mask the inner turmoil of
her heart. The constant reminder of her mother's family and how
generous they were to those less fortunate and her grandfather's lessons
haunted her mind: *" . . . It's what you do with the penny that counts."*

What had she done with her pennies?   She had squandered her
fortune on fancy clothes, cars, apartments and fun times, seldom
considering those less fortunate. Pangs of remorse overwhelmed her
senses as she reached out for a new life, one that would make a
difference.

Enid awoke one morning with a determination to turn her life
around. She had noticed that Saint Augustine Church down the street
from her apartment would occasionally setup tables with piles of clothes
for the needy. She decided that was something she could help with.
When she arrived at the church, Enid began folding the children's
clothing and stacking them in piles according to size.

One of the Catholic nuns had been watching her out of the corner of
her eye.

"Hello, my name is Sister Margaret. May I be of assistance?"

"Actually I was hoping that I might be of assistance to you," said
Enid. "I find myself with extra time on my hands and wondered if you
might need some help once a week."

"My dear, you are an answer to prayer. Several of the sisters have
come down with the flu and I've been short of help. I see you have a
knack for color coordinating the clothing. I have several more bags of
donated clothes that need to be sized."

"Then I'll start there," said Enid with a smile.

After several weeks, Sister Margaret approached Enid to invite her to mass.

"My child, why is it that I have not seen you at any mass?"

"I'm not Catholic," replied Enid.

"But my child, you don't have to be Catholic to enjoy the service. The music alone has freed many a troubled soul. I'll look for you next Sunday; you will sit with me. Then after, you will tell me what you think of our service." Before Enid could reply, the nun turned and briskly walked back into the church.

Glad he had been blessed with a strong athletic physic and height over six feet, Monsignor Vincent de Moor found no need for a ladder while stacking new Bibles on the top library shelf in his office. He smiled when he heard a familiar voice calling.

"Father de Moor, Father de Moor." A stout rosy-cheeked nun appeared at his doorway.

"Hello Sister Margaret, what can I do for you?"

"Oh my dear Father, we must pray diligently," she said half out of breath.

"Please have a seat. I just have this last box of books to take care of." He motioned to the chair in front of the desk as he kept on shelving.

She took a deep breath then continued. "Several weeks ago a young English girl asked if she might be of service to our charity for the needy. Naturally we are always happy to have volunteers."

"Naturally." Father de Moor smiled.

"So we put her to work sorting and sizing all the donated clothing. And what a wonderful volunteer she has been. Always shows up on time and is so accommodating to the people needing clothes for their children."

"So should we pray that she continues to show up?" asked Father de Moor.

"Oh Father, I fear she has a troubled soul. I can see it in her eyes. That's when I asked her why I hadn't seen her at mass."

"And . . .?"

"She said she wasn't Catholic."

"Well, there's your answer."

"No, there's more. That's when I invited her to one of our services."

"And is she coming?"

"I don't know. I didn't give her a chance to answer. I ran right back into the church to find you."

Father de Moor put the last of the Bibles on the shelf and dusted his hands off. "Well, let's go talk to your young troubled soul."

"Oh no, not now, Father. We don't want to scare her away. I was hoping that if she comes to the Sunday service, that I would be able to introduce her to you. You are such a terrific teacher, and upon observing this young lady, I'm of the opinion that she would make a remarkable student for you."

"Well, I do have a new convert class starting soon, but to put ourselves on good footing we should turn to the Almighty and trust in Him. For as the Lord says in Mathew 18:19: *If two of you agree on earth concerning anything that they ask, it will be done for them by My Father in heaven.*" Father de Moor sat down with Sister Margaret and they began to pray.

Enid stood at the corner of Rue De La Bienfaisance and Cesar Caire, captivated by the magnificence of the Saint Augustine Cathedral. The majestic dome towering eighty meters above was capped with an ornate bell tower, which began to toll, calling its people to the first Sunday service. Enid crossed the street and proceeded down the block to the front of the church. At the base of the stairs leading to the entrance stood a lifelike statue of Joan of Arc dressed in battle armor, sitting astride her mighty steed with her eyes gazing upon the heavens. Her raised sword glistened in the morning sun, poised always at the ready to do battle at the Lord's calling. The stone statues looking down upon her from the front façade of the cathedral were the four evangelists and above them stood the twelve apostles and a stained glass rosette window.

Saint Augustine Cathedral in Paris

An unexpected serenity enveloped Enid when she stepped over the threshold and entered the church. Sister Margaret immediately rushed over to greet her.

"Oh my child, I'm so glad you were able to make it. Just follow me. The best seats are up front and you are in for a treat. We have two well-known organists performing today. We are the only cathedral that I know of that has two organs built by Charles Barker. He built the first organs to be powered by electricity." Sister Margaret led her to their seats and handed Enid a missal.

"What's this?"

"Our service is in Latin. The missal shows both the Latin and French so you can follow along." The bell tolling had stopped and the first sounds of the two organs heralded the arrival of the choir boys followed by the priest and his server. The entire Latin Mass was performed in haunting chants that reverberated throughout the cathedral.

Enid tried to follow along with the French translation, but closed the missal and became transfixed instead on the rituals and reverence with which the priest performed the Latin Mass. After the ceremonial rites, the priest turned to the parishioners and spoke about the Apostle Peter and how God gives grace to believers, particularly in the midst of suffering and difficulty. It was a message that resonated with Enid. The final benediction was said, and then the boy's choir performed a cappella a rendition of *Ave Maria*. After two verses the choir proceeded down the main aisle while the double organs joined in with the accompaniment. When they passed by Enid, she noticed their very young angelic faces. Her eyes filled with the unspoken painful visions of the past.

Sister Margaret sensed that there was something amiss. "Come dear, let's go out the side entrance, there is someone I would like you to meet."

Monsignor de Moor was sending the last of the choirboys off to their parents.

"Father de Moor, Father de Moor," said the Sister.

He turned around, "Good morning, Sister Margaret."

"I would like to introduce you to my new friend, Enid."

"Hello, I'm Monsignor Vincent de Moor." He reached out to shake her hand. "It is a pleasure to meet you, Enid. Did you enjoy the service?"

"Very much, it was quite inspiring. It was a new experience for me. I'm not Catholic, but I felt like I belonged here, it was very comforting." Shaking his hand, Enid felt a kindness behind the priest's inquisitive hazel eyes. His light brown hair showed strands of grey at the temples. A fatherly type, she thought.

"Well, if you are interested in learning more about our faith, you have come to the right person. I teach a new convert class and there is a beginning session starting on Wednesday at 7 p.m. if you would like to join us."

"I'll certainly keep it in mind," said Enid. "It was a pleasure meeting you, sir, and thank you Sister Margaret for inviting me to the service. I'm afraid I must leave now for I have another engagement to attend this afternoon."

Once Enid was out of earshot, Father de Moor and Sister Margaret continued discussing her. "She seemed like a very pleasant young lady," said Father de Moor.

"Oh, yes indeed. And a very hard worker, too, I might add. She seemed to enjoy the service and I noticed her wiping her eyes a few times."

"Perhaps that is the troubled soul part." Father de Moor smiled and put his arm around Sister Margaret's shoulder. "I know, I know, we must pray with diligence!"

Enid had acquired a few eccentric literary friends since her move to Paris and they agreed to meet every Sunday afternoon at a local coffee shop to encourage each other in their writing endeavors. Many an afternoon they pondered over the hidden messages in each other's work. This circle of intellectuals strived to unearth the writing styles of each other, and decided that Enid possessed the uncanny ability to convey a sense of deep melancholy and yearning through most of her poetry. Their misplaced good intentions haunted Enid. Is this what she had become, a self-pitying lonely introvert?

Chapter 13

A New Beginning

Monsignor Vincent de Moor arrived at Saint Augustine Cathedral on Wednesday at 6:45 p.m. to ready his classroom for his evening New Convert Class. Last year he had filled the room with thirty students and was anticipating about the same this year. He attached the sign-up sheet to a clipboard and straightened a stack of folders he had prepared with the answers to the most frequently asked questions regarding the church. He checked his watch with the clock on the wall. It was now 6:55 p.m., but where were the students? He started to pick-up the folders.

"Excuse me, Father de Moor. Do I have the right night for the New Convert Class?" asked Enid as she entered the room.

"Why Miss Enid, I'm so glad you are able to join us, or should I say join me. It appears that it will be a class of one tonight."

"Are you sure you don't want to cancel the class? I could come another time."

"Perhaps this is meant to be." He motioned her to a desk. "Please have a seat. Private classes are often more productive and can cut the class session in half." He handed her the clipboard. "Please fill out your full name, address, and phone number. I don't believe I caught your last name?"

Enid smiled, quietly filled out the form and handed it back.

Father de Moor read the name on the form out loud. "Countess Enid Margaret Hamlyn-Fellows Kinnoull. My, that is a long name for such a petite young lady."

To her surprise he had shown no reaction. His kind quiet voice reminded her of her grandfather. Had she finally met a man she could trust?

"Tell me, Countess, what has drawn you to our church?" he asked.

"I can't really say for sure," she replied. "My life has been an emotional ebb and flow . . . like a sailor lost at sea with no compass for direction."

"Perhaps it is a higher entity that you seek for guidance." he replied.

"If you mean God . . . well, I always went to church when I was little. Grandfather insisted that we attend Sunday School, so I heard about God, Jesus and the Holy Spirit. I just never paid that much attention . . . didn't think it applied to me."

"Well that is what this class is all about. It will help to answer all those questions for you."

The weeks turned to months and during the classes Enid had grown to appreciate her new Catholic religion and to respect the man who was now her spiritual mentor. She acknowledged the Lord's calling in her life and desired to belong to something bigger than herself by helping those less fortunate.

Enid also learned that Father Vincent de Moor was actually Lt. Marcel, a Belgian priest and spy who had been a national hero during the First World War. He in turn had learned not only of her tragic marriage and divorce and the death of her son, but that Enid was a very independent, capable young woman with a passion for fast cars, planes, art, journalism, photography and now Catholicism.

Countess Kinnoull's apartment in Paris at 48 Rue de La Bienfaisance
It had royal blue doors. (Photo graciously provided by Wayne Chapman)

PART 2

Claude

Chapter 14

Where Jesus Walked

Upon her conversion to Catholicism in 1928, Enid wanted a fresh new beginning and changed her Christian name to Claude. She had always liked the name Claude and felt that this new name would help fulfill the transformation to her new life.

One day she approached her godfather with a perplexing yearning.

"Father de Moor," said Claude. "I don't quite know how to explain this, but lately I've had this uncanny desire to walk where Jesus walked."

"What you are experiencing is not uncommon when one acknowledges the Lord's calling. Only a pilgrimage to Jerusalem will quench that desire. If that is your intention, then I'll contact the Seminary of St. Anne's Church in Jerusalem."

"I'll want to take my time and fully assimilate what life was like during the Lord's walk on earth," she said.

"You'll be welcomed there as long as necessary. The good sisters will be happy to show you the areas that we have been studying in the Bible," replied Father de Moor.

About a week later, she was on her way to Israel.

Claude tightened her seatbelt and watched the runway appear closer and closer; she felt the tires bump on the tarmac as the aeroplane landed at the Tel Aviv Airport. In the arrival waiting room stood a young man dressed in a long white robe holding a sign that read *Chauffeur for Countess Kinnoull* in large bold letters.

Claude approached the man, "I'm Countess Kinnoull," she said.

"I'm Father Paul, sent to escort you back to our Seminary at Saint Anne's. Do you have any bags?"

"Just this small suitcase I was able to carry onboard," replied Claude. The young priest picked up her suitcase and she followed him to the waiting car.

"How far is the church from the airport?" she asked.

"It will take about an hour to get there," replied Father Paul. "In the meantime, I'll tell you a bit of history about our church. What many find surprising is that the church and the property surrounding it was given as a gift to the French government for their aide during the Crimean War in 1856."

"Does France still own it?"

"Indeed. Since the church had been partially destroyed during that war, France undertook extensive restoration, returning Saint Anne's Church as closely as possible to the original basilica. It was built to honor Anne, the mother of Mary, and the grandmother of Jesus. There are ancient ruins on the property dating back from the time of Christ to the fourth Century. The church itself is located next to what is believed to be the pools of Bethesda."

"Isn't that where Jesus healed the crippled man?" asked Claude.

"That's correct, as stated in the Bible in John, Chapter 5."

The hour passed quickly. When they entered the ancient city of Jerusalem they went directly to the Seminary of St Anne's Church. A nun came out to greet them.

"Lady Kinnoull, I'd like you to meet our Mother Superior."

"I do hope you will be comfortable during your stay with us, Lady Kinnoull. I'll walk you to your room. I know you'll probably need time to freshen up. Then please join us for lunch."

"Reverend Mother, I was wondering if I might ask a favor of you?"

"But of course, my child."

"While I'm here, I do not want to draw attention to myself. I would prefer not to be called by my title, but by the name Claude. I'm here to give reverence to my Lord and to walk where He walked. I don't want my title to be a distraction to others."

"I fully understand. I'll send Sister Angela up in about thirty minutes. She will show you to our dining room."

The thirty minutes passed too quickly for Claude. She had just finished changing when there was a knock on the door. "Come in," she replied.

"Hello miss, I'm Sister Angela. If you are ready, it will be my pleasure to escort you to the dining room."

"Lead the way," said Claude. "I'm rather hungry from all the traveling."

The dining room was a simply decorated room. Dark, rough-hewn planked floors had a hand-polished luster. A massive, rectangular, distressed oak table had seating for twelve. The beige stucco walls with their candled sconces showcased several religious paintings and a rustic wrought iron chandelier was centered above the table. The aroma of freshly baked bread and homemade soup wafted through the air. Prayers were said and then the meal was served.

"We understand that it is your desire to walk the path that Jesus walked," said Sister Angela. "Every Friday, a guide takes groups of tourists along the Via Dolorosa, stopping at each of the fourteen Stations of the Cross for explanations and prayers. But we sisters prefer to walk the path during the week when it is less crowded, and we can linger however long we want for reflection."

"I would certainly prefer walking the path with my beloved Sisters in Christ," said Claude.

"We were hoping you would say that," replied Mother Superior. "I understand that Father Paul has told you a bit about St Anne's Church, but I was wondering if you might like a tour of the church and grounds after lunch."

"That would be lovely," said Claude. "I would also like to see the work your charitable group is doing, if possible."

"Why, we would be delighted to acquaint you with our numerous causes," said Sister Angela.

After lunch Claude was introduced to the Fathers of Cardinal la Vigerie, the Reverend Fathers of the Assumption, and the Benedictine Fathers. She was shown the many and varied charitable causes in which the Seminary of St. Anne's was involved. That evening Claude attended a service in St. Anne's Church.

"This twelfth century church has the honor of being one of the finest examples of Crusader architecture in Israel," said Sister Angela.

"The simplicity of its décor is refreshing," replied Claude as her eyes followed the tall stately columns to the high exquisitely arched ceilings.

"Its simple design gives this church a most unusual acoustic sound," said Sister Angela. "Just wait until you hear us sing."

Although there were just the sisters in attendance, when they began to sing *Ave Marie* with no musical accompaniment, Claude felt shivers go up her spine. She looked around to see where all the voices were coming from, for the church had filled with echoes of what seemed like the voices of a million angels.

After the service the sisters took Claude to an adjacent chapel. They descended a stairway leading to the site where Jesus miraculously healed a crippled man at the Bethesda Pool.

"It is believed that the Bethesda Pool contains miraculous healing powers," said one of the sisters. "You may touch it if you like."

Claude kneeled at the edge of the pool. Dipping her cupped hand into the cool refreshing water, she noticed it had a slight sweet smell of roses. They continued down a narrow rocky stairway to their right, ending up in front of an altar with candles and a picture of Mary.

"This is believed to be the birthplace of the Virgin Mary," said Mother Superior. Claude lit a candle, made the sign of the cross, knelt down and prayed.

The next day, after early morning prayers, Claude and the sisters set out along the Via Dolorosa; *The Sorrowful Way*. At last Claude would realize her dream, to walk where Jesus walked. The fourteen Stations of the Cross, symbolizing the journey of Jesus from when He was condemned to die to when He was laid in the tomb, were set up at intervals along the winding road. Nine of the Stations were outside and the last five Stations were located inside of the church of the Holy Sepulcher. Claude reverently made her way to each Station, stopping to make the sign of the cross and expressing penitence through prayer and serious reflection. When they turned to go to the ninth Station, Claude tripped on the edge of a stone throwing her off balance and she started to fall. Sister Angela grabbed Claude's arm and pulled her to safety.

"Thank you, sister, for stopping my fall." Claude looked up at the plaque describing the ninth Station of The Cross. It was here where Jesus fell for the third time.

"I would be the first to admit that I have also fallen several times in my life, but the Lord never gave up on me. He reached out and grabbed me just in time."

"And for that we are truly grateful," replied Sister Angela.

They entered the Church of the Holy Sepulchre to view the last five Stations. The simple Romanesque architectural style did not distract from the hallowed site venerated as Golgotha, the Hill of Calvary, where Jesus was crucified and the sepulchre where Jesus was buried.

Claude knelt down in front of the last Station, the rock-cut tomb of Jesus. She made the sign of the cross, closed her eyes and began to pray, but she could not control her emotions when her eyes filled with tears and she wept.

Sister Angela knelt down next to Claude and put her arm around her. She reached into a pocket in her habit and pulled out a white handkerchief. "We always need plenty of these by the time we get to the last Station." She placed the handkerchief into Claude's hand.

They waited outside for Claude, then they strolled back to St. Anne's Church in silence, each meditating on their own walk with Jesus.

That evening after supper, the sisters were joined by the fathers at the Seminary for lively discussion on the various historical sites that they thought Claude should visit during her stay.

Not knowing when she would be able to visit Jerusalem again and with such eager guides, Claude decided to stay several weeks to see all the sites and to participate in their various charitable causes.

At the end of her visit, Claude was so impressed with their hard work and faithfulness to the many charities that she later bestowed upon them monetary gifts of such magnitude that word got back to the Vatican.

After arriving back in Paris, Claude took several days to reflect on her pilgrimage to Jerusalem and how differently she now looked at her life. She had inherited a fortune and this time she didn't want to waste it on frivolous material things. Claude needed direction on the best course of action and turned to the one person she trusted the most: her mentor, Monsignor Vincent de Moor.

"I appreciate you coming to me with your dilemma," he said. "And of course I do know of several causes that could use your financial assistance. However, it is not up to me to make that decision."

"But Father de Moor, I really could use some direction in this matter."

"I suggest we request an audience with the Pope."

"The Pope! Do you really think that he would see a new convert?"

"With your title, influence and fortune he is the one who would be most knowledgeable as to where your help would be most needed. I'll immediately prepare a letter and we will wait for the reply. But in the meantime there is someone I'd like you to meet."

She followed Father de Moor from his office back into the Cathedral. They stopped in front of an alcove. A simply framed picture of a middle aged man hung before them. His mousey brown hair was cut close to the scalp, and he sported a neatly trimmed mustache and beard. He wore a white robe and centered on a long bib, embroidered in blood red, was a cross atop a heart. Claude shivered as a chill run up her spine. She felt a strange connection when she stared at the image becoming transfixed by the pensive hazel eyes grabbing at her very soul with their gaze.

"Charles de Foucauld born in 1858, died in 1916," she read aloud the name on the frame.

"Yes, this man's life and yours have a very similar link that might interest you," said Father de Moor. "He was born into a wealthy French family; you were born into a wealthy English family. He was orphaned as a child; your father left you when you were only six. He received a large inheritance, as did you when your mother died. Charles became an aristocratic playboy; you married an Earl and lived the fast-paced life of an aristocratic countess. Charles gradually lost his faith and joined the French Army seeking direction in his life; you lost a child and a husband, then resumed racing cars and finally moved to Paris seeking a better life. When Charles returned to Paris he felt a need to renew his own religious commitments here at St. Augustine's Church; and with you, a small seed of faith planted when you were just a child tugged at your heart, bringing you to St. Augustine's with a conversion to the Catholic faith. Charles was inspired to live the "hidden life" of Jesus of Nazareth, a life of silence, obscurity, humble work, domestic charity, and simple joys. He lived this life in the African desert among the poorest of the poor. And now, we are waiting in great anticipation to see how the Lord will use you."

"I know the Lord does work in mysterious ways, but I do not see how I could be of much significance to Him," said Claude.

"You must have patience, for the Lord's timing is not like ours," he replied.

Several months later in 1929, Father de Moor approached Claude with an exciting letter from the Pope's staff.

"It appears that news of your most generous gift to the Seminary at St. Anne's Church has fallen upon the ears of the Pope and that you have been granted a personal audience with him."

"When I gave that financial gift to Saint Anne's Church, I gave with no expectation of anything in return," said Claude

"And you can be assured that the Pope realizes the full intentions of your heart," said Father de Moor.

With blessings and prayers from her new church, she packed her bags and headed to Rome, Italy.

Claude had always been interested in the arts, but nothing could prepare her for the overwhelming magnificence and splendor of visiting Vatican City for the first time. Nowhere in the world could be found such awe-inspiring art and architecture in one place. It was as if her earthly existence was transported to a spiritual realm where other people and exterior noises didn't exist.

St. Peter's Square was impressive with its massive colonnade on top of which stood 140 statues of saints, each seemingly to beckon one to enter the most spiritual center of Vatican City, St. Peter's Basilica.

Upon entering through the central doors, Claude was struck by the immense expanse of the interior stretching out over five acres. The most exceptional Renaissance monuments, in all their intricate details created by the finest talents such as Michelangelo and Bernini, filled the Basilica. But it was the statue immediately to the right of the entrance that caught Claude's eye. She was transfixed by Michelangelo's beautiful Pieta depicting the Virgin Mary cradling the dead Jesus after his crucifixion.

Claude closed her eyes remembering cradling her own son with a devastating hopelessness that seared her heart. She opened her eyes and studied the Virgin Mary's face, feature by feature. There were no tears or anguish on Mary's face. There was tenderness in her expression, a hope in her eyes. The shock of this discovery hit Lady Kinnoull full force . . . Mary knew that she would see her son again. Claude smiled at the Virgin Mary and a joy filled her heart with the hopefulness that she too, would one day see little Henry again, in eternity.

It was early the next morning that Countess Kinnoull had a private audience with the Pope in his sitting room. She felt his powerful presence, but his eyes revealed a kindness and concern that calmed her nerves. She was impressed by his strong stance against Communism and Nazism, which he considered demeaning and a violation of basic human rights. He also felt that social and economic issues were vital to the Church in terms of moral obligations involved. Ethical considerations included the nature of private property in terms of its functions for society and the development of the individual.

"I understand that you are seeking my council on the financial gifts that God has bestowed upon you. Have you given this much thought?" the Pope asked.

"Yes, your Holiness. It keeps me awake at night. While in Jerusalem, I saw what little money it takes to feed and clothe the less fortunate. I felt ashamed of all the money that the Earl and I spent on frivolous things. It opened my eyes."

"I understand that you are a new convert to Catholicism. Can you tell me what brought you to this decision?" he asked.

"It's a bit hard to explain," she said. "When I was little, I enjoyed the music and the picture stories that were read to us in Sunday School class. But when I became a teenager . . . well, I was a bit rebellious."

"Weren't we all," he interrupted with a smile.

"As a teenager, I often stayed with my aunt. She was Catholic and insisted that I accompany her to church. I noticed right a way the stark difference between our Non-conformist Congregational services and that of her church. It may have been the more structured traditions that stayed in my memory."

"Yes, we can be a bit of a stuffed shirt as the teenagers would say," replied His Holiness. They both laughed, easing the tension.

Claude wiped her sweaty palms on her skirt and continued. "When I married the Earl, my life became a whirlwind of new adventures. There was no room for spiritual matters. Little did I know that it would soon spiral out of control. Starting over in Paris and accepting the Lord's plan for my life has freed me from a crushing burden of guilt that has been eating away at me for a long time. I'll be forever in the Lord's service." She brushed away a tear running down her cheek.

Lady Kinnoull's young age and enthusiasm for her new–found religion and her determination to turn her life around pleased the Pope. He pulled his chair closer to hers and took both of her hands in his.

"I can see that you truly want to make a difference for good. There is an urgent financial need for medical and educational supplies for the Catholic missionaries in Africa."

"Like Charles de Foucauld!"

"You know of him?"

"You might say we have both lived a similar aristocratic lifestyle before we converted to Catholicism."

"Definitely a courageous man to be admired, but few can emulate. There is however, another area that could use financial backing. It is the highly regarded *Catholic Herald* newspaper out of London, which has proved to be an excellent way of drawing in new converts."

"Your Holiness, I want to be involved in a meaningful way. I can't just put a check in the mail . . . I need to see the money in action. I want to report on the needs of these warriors for the Lord. Let me take the supplies to the African missionaries, directly where it is most needed. I can write about my experiences to the *Catholic Herald,* increasing donations."

He stood up and walked over to his desk. "I can see that you are not going to be a sideline benefactress, Countess Kinnoull. Africa can be a dangerous place for a young, single woman. I'll write to Father de Moor. He is an experienced traveler. I'll have him accompany you to Africa."

"Oh, he is not going to like that idea," said the Countess.

"I'm afraid he has no choice in the matter." The Pope signed the letter and sealed the envelope with his official wax stamp.

After a blessing from the Pope, she left Vatican City with a new direction for her life and a determination that nothing and no one could deter her from God's calling.

Upon her return to Paris, Claude was excited to relate her visit with the Pope to Father de Moor. She found him in his office knee-deep among various stacks of pamphlets and workbooks scattered across the floor.

"Isn't it a bit early for spring-cleaning?" she asked.

"I was wondering if you would soon be gracing our doorstep, or if the beauty of Vatican City would draw you away," said Father de Moor. "Please come in and tell me all about your journey. Don't mind the mess. Just getting things organized for my next convert class." He emptied two chairs so they could sit and talk.

"I have to tell you, Father de Moor, when I left here it was impossible for me to convey how lost I felt. But when I met with the Pope, he sat me down and held my trembling hands in his, then looked directly into my eyes as if he could see into my very soul. He spoke the most kind, sincere words, which immediately eased my aching heart. I knew then that you had been right and very wise for sending me to meet with his Holiness. I just wanted to thank you."

"May I ask what advise he gave you?"

"He felt that the White Father African missionaries have the most financial needs and that the *Catholic Herald* in London would be better able to spread the message of the Catholic Church if it had more financial assistance. Do you know why they are called White Fathers?" she asked.

"Yes. The name comes from their habit of a white gown, called a gandoura and a white hooded cloak, known as a burnous. I can understand why the Pope suggested the African Catholic missionaries, for they are always in need of medical supplies and educational materials."

"And we will be doing just that," said Claude.

"What do you mean by we?" asked Father de Moor. "I've classes to consider."

"Well, it seems that you have been relieved of your obligations." Claude handed him an envelope with the Vatican seal on it. "It's addressed to you."

He slowly opened the envelope. "It says I'm to accompany you on this humanitarian journey through Africa and since I am your mentor, I've been told to further your immersion in the Catholic religion along the way. And we are to report about each mission that we visit."

"I'm looking forward to continuing my education." Claude smiled, "Since you have been on mission trips before, if you would write down a list of supplies we will need and the cost, I will write you a check."

"It may take a few months to gather all the supplies. You do realize that this is a very treacherous journey that we are about to embark on?" asked Father de Moor.

"Well," said Claude as she stood to leave. "I know now that with you beside me and the Lord behind me, I'm up for any challenge."

Chapter 15

A Woman with a Mission

Claude arranged for Jack and Florence to take care of her poodle and the apartment during her mission to Africa.

"Florence, while I'm out buying supplies, I'd like you to pack a suitcase for me, with several light weight skirts, trousers and cotton tops I can layer with sweaters."

"I'll throw in sturdy walking shoes and a pair of boots along with a warm jacket for the cooler evenings," replied Florence.

"You might add one of my racing jumpsuits . . . I'm bound to be working on the truck's engine from time to time."

"I'll get right on it," she replied.

While Florence had the task of putting together an appropriate wardrobe for Lady Kinnoull, Jack chauffeured Father de Moor and the Countess around Paris looking for the most reliable vehicle for their journey. Their final choice was a 12-horse power, six-cylinder, six-wheeler Citroen truck. Because of the diverse road conditions that they would be experiencing across Africa, they were assured that the six-cylinder pickup would do the job. Although an older model, this particular truck had proven its durability on previous trips across the Sahara Desert. Claude's experience as a racecar driver gave her the confidence that she could handle any road problems. However, she was totally unaware of, and perhaps a bit naive, about the many setbacks and disappointments that would soon befall them.

Jack insisted that they take him along as a back-up driver, but both Lady Kinnoull and Father de Moor were resolute to put their faith in Divine Providence. To prove this to themselves, they would depart unaccompanied by others.

After the purchase of the truck, their next task was to obtain enough medical and relief supplies that could be stored in the massive Citroen, since there would be no backup vehicle. They started with 300 liters of gasoline and 100 liters of water, (which they would replenish at specific times and places marked on their map,) along with a variety of canned foods, cooking supplies and utensils, tents, sleeping bags, and mosquito netting. Father de Moor had traveled to missions before and was accustom to using every nook and cranny in a vehicle. In no time he had found a secure place for everything.

"Now there is one more item we need to purchase," said Claude. "Knowing that you were at one time a spy, what would be your weapon of choice for big game hunting in Africa? Not that we will be big game hunting, mind you. But I am not so naive to think that we might not run into a lion or two that may want us for their next meal."

"I've heard that the Holland & Holland .600 double barrel is the gun for big game. However, it is on the pricey side," said Father de Moor.

"Price is no consideration," said Claude. "After all, I am dragging you along on this mission and you shall have the best of equipment." She turned to her chauffeur.

"Jack, drop me off at my apartment and then take Father de Moor to the best gun store in Paris. He is to have whatever he needs for this journey." She then made arrangements with her bank to have money wired to her if needed during their trip.

When they picked up their truck, it had been painted the royal blue that Claude had requested. The vehicle was baptized *La Croisiere Bleue* (The Blue Cruise), the color of the Virgin, reminding them that this mission trip was entrusted with the protection of the Queen of Heaven.

Lady Kinnoull and Monsignor Vincent de Moor had become a team, and with the blessings from Pope Puis XI they were about to embark on a treacherous journey across the great continent of Africa to aid and assist the poorest of the Catholic missionary posts.

On April 4, 1929, leaving the comforts of home and with the blessings and prayers from their local church, Lady Kinnoull and Father de Moor began the eight-hour drive from Paris to the seaport of Marseille. They stopped at their halfway point in Burgundy at the Paray-le-Monial Basilica. The next morning was Easter Sunday and the Countess and the Monsignor were delighted to be included in the Basilica's most celebrated of Christian holidays. The Easter service was a blessed beginning to their journey and they were pleased with the addition of many more prayer warriors.

After attending the High Mass Easter Service Lady Kinnoull and Father de Moor continued south on their pilgrimage to Our Lady of the Guard, in the port city of Marseille. This impressive basilica overlooked the city atop the highest natural point in Marseille at about five hundred feet. A square bell tower topped by a belfry supported a monumental twenty-seven foot statue of the Madonna and Child made of copper, gilded with gold leaf. It was often referred to as *la bonne mere* (the good mother) and as the protector not only of the city, but also to all who traveled the seas.

On April 8th, a mass was celebrated with communion. Then trusting in Divine Providence, Countess Claude Kinnoull and Monsignor Vincent de Moor boarded the ship *Pierre Loti* along with their one-ton truck, *The Blue Cruise*, to begin their five-day voyage to Alexandria, Egypt.

So many conflicting thoughts went through Claude's head . . . fear of the unknown, then again, excitement in the anticipation of this dangerous but most worthy journey she was about to embark on. They stood at the railing waving to the priests and nuns who had come to wish them a *Bon Voyage* as the ship pulled away from the dock.

"What's the matter, Lady Kinnoull? You look like you want to say something," said Father de Moor.

"I was just thinking," she replied. "Since we will be traveling together for such a long time, I'd prefer that you drop the titles and just call me Claude when we are by ourselves."

"And you may call me, Vincent," he replied. "Now that the formalities are over, let's enjoy our trip.

The Countess Kinnoull receiving a blessing before boarding the *Pierre Loti*
(Photo from *La Croisiere Bleue et les Misiions D'Afrique* book)

After an uneventful but relaxing voyage, the *Pierre Loti* finally docked on April 13th in Alexandria, the largest seaport in Egypt, known as *the Pearl of the Mediterranean* because it has a more Mediterranean-like climate than Middle Eastern.

The squawking of seagulls rose above the sounds of men shouting directions for the offloading of cargo. Women filled their woven baskets with fresh fruits and vegetables, then balancing the heavy baskets on their heads they moved along paved streets to their sidewalk stalls. Donkey driven carts with the fresh catch of the day headed to hotels and restaurants, where merchants hoped to get top prices.

Once their vehicle was on the dock, they made sure all their supplies were still strapped down and were about to get into the truck when two young priests approached them. They wore the traditional ankle-length white cotton cassock with a matching four-inch sash cinched at the waist.

"Good afternoon, I'm Father David and this is Father Joseph. We couldn't help but notice your heavily packed truck. Are you planning a long trip?"

Vincent laughed. "We are planning to visit at least 112 missions."

"A long trip indeed, perhaps thousands and thousands of miles," said Father Joseph.

"We are up for the challenge," said Claude. "Are you from around here?"

"No, we were attending classes at Saint Francis Xavier here in Alexandria."

"You mean to say that there is a Catholic college in the midst of this Muslim civilization?" she asked.

"Yes, there are a growing number of young people that are attracted to the Jesuits; and in Egypt there are currently about thirty Christian boarding schools totaling nearly nine thousand students," replied Father David.

"We are Verona missionaries near the village of Juba. We were wondering if you might be headed that way, and if we could hitch a ride?" asked Father Joseph.

"But we are forgetting our manners. Gentlemen, I'm Father Vincent de Moor and this is Countess Claude Kinnoull."

Claude reached into the glove compartment and pulled out a map of Africa. "Well, I see that Juba is indeed one of the posts we will be visiting. We would be more than happy to have such knowledgeable and friendly guides accompany us there."

"I must warn you that it will be very tight seating," said Vincent. "I've packed every inch of the truck with supplies for the missions."

"Not to worry about us. We are used to small quarters and are most grateful for the ride," said Father Joseph.

"We won't be leaving until tomorrow . . . we're staying at the Hotel Cecil," said Claude.

"Then tomorrow it shall be. We'll meet you in front of the hotel in the morning," said Father Joseph. "By the way, since you will be here the rest of the day, may I suggest you visit the oldest Christian church in Egypt? It was established by Saint Mark during his journey as an apostle and evangelist."

"Sounds like something we should definitely visit," said Father de Moor. "Until tomorrow."

The two young priests walked off in the opposite direction and *The Blue Cruise* headed to the luxury Hotel Cecil.

"I thought we should have one day at a nice hotel before we embark into lands unknown," said Claude. "I hope you don't mind my booking rooms at the Cecil . . . a friend suggested it."

"It will be a fine start to a long journey," replied Vincent.

Once the luggage was put in their rooms, they had lunch at the hotel's restaurant.

They were enjoying a fresh fruit pie when the waiter refilled their iced-tea glasses.

"This is a delicious tea," remarked Claude.

"Well, you best enjoy the ice while you can. It will be a difficult commodity to come by once we are in the Bushland," said Vincent.

After lunch, they followed the directions the waiter gave them to the St. Mark Coptic Orthodox Church. While admiring the arched ceilings of the massive cathedral and its stained glass windows, a priest came over to explain their history.

"Over the centuries this church has been rebuilt several times, but it still stands on the grounds where St. Mark established the first Christian church in Alexandria in approximately 48 AD. However, when St. Mark's life was threatened, he left Alexandria to continue his journey evangelizing which brought many to the Christian faith. He returned twenty years later and was amazed at the growth of Christianity in Alexandria. Unfortunately, this was also the time of the pagan Serapis celebration honoring the Greek Egyptian god, Serapion-Abbis. Infuriated that the Apostle Mark arrived during their celebration, several pagans plotted and successfully kidnaped Mark during the night. They tied a rope around his neck, attached it to a tail of a horse and dragged him through the streets until he passed out. They then threw him in prison."

"Was there nobody who tried to stop this?" asked Claude.

"Everyone was afraid because the streets were filled with pagans celebrating their god, so the Christians hid in their homes not even aware of what was occurring outside. It has been said that while in jail, an angel appeared to Mark telling him that he was a good servant and that his name had been added to *The Book of Life* and that he was counted as one of the saints. But the pagans were not finished with Mark. They returned the next morning, again tied a rope around his neck and again dragged him through graveled streets . . . until his body was shredded and bleeding. This is when his soul left his body and he had been crowned a martyr."

"I don't recall that the Bible actually tells us how all the apostles die," said Vincent.

"You are quite right," said the priest. "Alexandria has an impressive library with an expansive collection of papyrus papers from witnesses of the days. It is the study of these papers that Biblical scholars have used to surmise how Apostle Mark died."

"The horror of the account is so real to me . . . I don't think that I'll be able to get those images out of my mind," said Claude as she sat down in one of the pews.

"Oh, but there is more to the account," said the priest. "You see, those drunken pagans were not satisfied with just the death of the Apostle Mark. They wanted his body burned to ashes. They gathered enough firewood for a huge flaming fire and were about to throw the body onto the flames when a severe storm struck bringing torrential rains and wind. The fire smoldered from the rain and the frightened pagans ran in fear. This gave the Christians a chance to retrieve the body of Mark taking it to the church to be wrapped and prayed over. They placed the Apostle Mark's body in a coffin and hid it in a secret crypt in the church. It laid there for many years until in 828 AD, some Italian sailors discovered the body. They left the severed head but took the remaining body to Venice, Italy. The Apostle Mark's head is preserved to this day and is shown each year in May, on the celebration of the martyrdom of Saint Mark."

"That must be quite a celebration," said Vincent. "Unfortunately, we are leaving tomorrow."

"I'll pray for your safe journey," said the priest.

"Thank you for that fascinating story of the Apostle Mark. I'm really glad we came. It makes me curious to learn about the other saints," said Claude. They said goodbye and headed back to the hotel.

Early the next morning they found their two missionary friends from Verona waiting in front of the hotel.

"What a beautiful day to start our journey," said Claude as she climbed into the driver's seat of their truck.

"You are the one driving?" asked one of the priests.

"Don't women drive in Africa?" she asked.

"I have yet to see a woman as petite as you driving such a large truck," replied Father David.

"Not to worry, gentlemen," said Vincent. "Don't let her size fool you. When it comes to driving, she is a force to be reckoned with."

The priests squeezed into the back of the truck and they departed on the four-hour trip from Alexandria to Cairo.

"In the few years that we have been in Africa, there are some things we have learned that never seem to change," said Father Joseph. "It's imperative to be on the alert for sudden and unpredictable geographical and climate changes that can occur while traveling throughout this country. One minute you're driving on a paved road, the next minute you're dodging potholes or the whole road may seem to disappear into a muddy pathway. The weather here is most unpredictable . . . one day it can be hot and humid, the next day might bring a torrential rain causing dangerous flash flooding."

"It sounds like we are in for an amazing adventure," said Vincent.

Though yearning for speed when behind the wheel of a vehicle, Claude quickly learned to acclimate to a slower pace while trying to maneuver along the most treacherous road conditions. Having been informed by the Verona missionaries of what to expect, she and Vincent decided to exercise prudence when it came to their money, the engine and especially the drivetrain with its many gears and shafts that connect the engine to the wheels, which was most on their minds considering the length and importance of the trip ahead.

They arrived in Cairo, another bustling city with the honking of cars and trucks.

"Let's have lunch where the regular African people eat," said Claude excitedly. "I want to soak up every aspect of what life is really like for the inhabitants of this unique country.

The missionaries directed them to the older part of Cairo. They passed flatbed carts being pulled by donkeys; its occupants were women in long black robes and veils, their children sat next to them. There was less traffic in this part of the city.

They parked their truck next to a portable restaurant for lunch. These restaurants moved wherever crowds of people congregated. The occupants of *The Blue Cruise* sat down on makeshift benches, assembled with a plank of wood resting on two upside down metal buckets. A square, rusted table with wobbly legs held stacks of warm flatbread. A kettle simmering with a substance that resembled stew, but with a much stronger aroma of mouth watering exotic spices, was served in wooden bowls. A young boy in white pants and shirt, wearing a red scull cap carefully poured a thick black liquid into small tin cups for his customers. Claude picked up the cup, which she thought was chocolate, but got a strong whiff of burnt coffee beans instead.

"Do you have cream?" she asked.

"I don't think you should use the cream. There is no refrigeration out here," whispered Vincent. He asked for sugar. The boy brought over a can of brown sugar. They all added several scoops to their drinks.

Claude looked around for spoons to eat the stew with. Vincent nudged her arm and pointed to the young priests. They were pulling apart the flatbread and using it to scoop up the stew.

Claude laughed and started pulling her bread apart. "Nothing like learning the native ways." When she tasted the stew she was surprised how tender the meat was and how the spices brought out the flavors of the vegetables.

After lunch the young priests decided to stay with the truck while Claude and Vincent visited the street bazaar. They meandered through narrow cobblestone streets. Tiny den-like shacks were packed together so tight that there was barely any room for the proprietor and his merchandize, let alone a customer. They stopped to watch a shoemaker cut and sew red leather slippers with upturned toes that were the usual native footwear. At another stall, Claude bought two cotton scarfs, one white to shield herself from the hot sun, the other a multi-colored jungle scene, a souvenir of her African adventure. Vincent had a sweet tooth and bought a bag of candy to share with his traveling companions. Claude insisted they stop to watch a snake charmer before leaving.

A man with sun-withered skin sat cross-legged on a grass mat. His grey shoulder length hair was topped with a white turban. When they approached his stall, the man removed the top of the large wicker basket in front of him. Holding a flute-like instrument made from a gourd, the snake charmer started playing a hypnotic tune. The large head of a brown and white cobra rose from the basket. Its head moved back and forth as if mesmerized by the music. When the music stopped, the snake recoiled back into the basket and the snake charmer replaced the lid. Claude put a few bills on top of the basket and they returned to their truck.

They left Cairo, with its over four hundred mosques, and headed thirteen miles southwest to the ancient city of Giza on the Nile. *The Blue Cruise* stopped by the broad river, where its occupants enjoyed a cool breeze blowing off the water. The temperature had increased from the mid 60 degrees of Alexandria to the high 70's of the spring desert. Soon the hot and sometimes unbearable summer temperatures would be upon them.

"Countess Kinnoull, if you look off in the distance past the palm trees, you'll see three pyramids. They are considered one of the great Seven Wonders of the World. Although Father Joseph and I have been there several times, it would be a shame for you to be so close and not visit the pyramids."

"Oh, you must go see them, they are magnificent," said Father Joseph. "And it's only five miles from Giza."

"I may never be this close to them again. Let's go!" said Claude.

She parked the truck as close to the pyramids as allowed, then grabbed her camera. Appearing to guard the three pyramids was the Great Sphinx. "I've seen pictures of it before, but it's even more impressive in person." While she took pictures, Vincent read the plaque.

"It says here that the Great Sphinx towers sixty-six feet high, twenty feet wide and two hundred and forty feet long, making it the world's largest monolith statue depicting the mysterious creature that is half-lion, half-human."

"The magnitude of the task to build these pyramids must have been overwhelming," said Claude. "The stones are waist high. I can't imagine how they built them without modern tools."

"According to the sign, the largest pyramid is the resting place of the Egyptian Pharaoh Khufu," said Vincent. "The smaller pyramids hold the Pharaohs of Khafre and Menkaure."

"I feel as if we have just crossed over centuries," she said. "From the bustling cosmopolitan city of Cairo, to the sound of the grinding sand underfoot . . . sands of ancient Egypt where pharaohs had once walked." She reached down and picked up several small rocks in various shades of tan and slipped them into her pocket.

Cognizant of the hundreds of miles they needed to travel before reaching the first mission station, *The Blue Cruise* and its passengers paused only a short time to admire the incredible workmanship of the ancient Egyptians.

"Claude, I've noticed that you've been picking up pebbles from wherever we stop. What are you planning to do with them?" asked Vincent as they walked back to the truck.

Claude blushed. "I look for specific colors and shapes that remind me of the area. I plan someday to put them into a mosaic piece."

"With the amount of traveling that we will be doing, that is going to be one large art piece," said Vincent. They both laughed, then got back into the truck.

They continued their journey south, driving along the riverbank of the Nile, known as the oldest road in Egypt. Several families could be seen along the river's edge. The women washing clothes, children chasing each other through the tall grass and men known as water carriers filling the large kidney-shaped skin bags that hung from canvas shoulder straps. These were the men who filled the people's water jugs as they traveled throughout Africa.

Traversing the rough road conditions made progress annoyingly slow, causing them to stop several times to stretch their legs. With the scorching sun beating down on them, and the annoying buzzing of mosquitoes, the group decided to continue on to Luxor, on the east bank of the Nile River. The four hundred mile trek was exhausting and they looked forward to a full day respite once there.

During their stay, Claude and Vincent took the time one evening to visit the Luxor Temple. It was impressive at night with the up lighting illuminating the massive structure of the Colonnade. The pair were dwarfed by the fourteen imposing concrete pillars standing sixty-two feet high in two rows, impressing on all who strolled the full length of the three hundred foot Colonnade that they were about to enter a temple of greatness.

"It would have been a grand entrance to the temple," remarked Vincent, a Biblical scholar of religious history. "During most of the Pharaonic period, Luxor, once known as Thebes, was the religious capital of this area."

"Yes, I can see that the massive structures would have been an impressive sight," she said. "But look around you . . . there is nothing but crumbling ruins. If this was their religious center, what happened to it? I think of our religious center, Vatican City, but there is no comparison. In Vatican City I felt a Divine presence everywhere I looked, through everything I touched . . . but here I smell death and destruction." Her mind searched for a plausible explanation. "Could it possibly be that their religion is crumbling, too?"

She suddenly felt anxious to leave such a disturbing place. "I feel an urgency to reach the missions, we must not dally any longer."

They packed up *The Blue Cruise* and left in the early morning of April 25th, continuing south. They had traveled over a hundred miles when a whirlwind of dust headed their way. With zero visibility, Claude pulled to the side of the dirt road.

"What on earth is that horrible smell?" she asked, covering her mouth and nose with her hand. "It smells like a neglected barn, only worse."

The young priests laughed. "You'll get use to the odor after a while. What you smell is Africa's largest animal market," said Father David. "People come from all over Africa to purchase camels, sheep, goats, cows, water buffalo, oxen, donkeys and poultry. You should stop. It's quite a sight, something to write home about."

"Very well . . . as long as I don't gag," said Claude.

Once the dust had settled they continued up the road to the entrance of the animal market and parked the truck. Claude grabbed her camera and began taking pictures of the menagerie before her. It was like a circus atmosphere; harmonizing chants kept time with the tempo of the rhythmic beat of drums, donkeys hew-hawed, camels growled and spit, while water buffalo flapped their ears and tails to ward off the aggressive bites of tsetse flies.

Auctioneers sounded the beginning of bidding with their forceful, shrill voices, trying to be heard over the babel of various dialects and languages. The Sudanese stood out in their distinctive high white turbans and tan or white robes. The Bedouin camel traders wore various colors of robes and long head coverings of red and white, or black and white, checkered scarves held down with twisted ropes across their foreheads.

"I feel sorry for the women dressed in all black robes and veils. The heat must be unbearable," said Claude.

"They have always lived in this area . . . they become use to the heat," replied Father Joseph.

"Look at those colorful characters standing by the oxen," said Vincent.

"I've got to get a picture of them," said Claude.

Two bare-chested native men wearing long striped skirts, tied at the waist with twisted cloth, stood proud, happy to have their picture taken. What caught Claude's eye were their sharp distended earlobes touching their shoulders, appearing to be tied down under their arms by strings of beads. The rest of their arms were covered in various sizes of metal bands.

After picture taking they started to head back to their truck, when Vincent noticed a stand selling fly swatters, whips and harness bits. "I see something we need," he said. He purchased a fly swatter for each of them. "Now we can rage war against those nasty flies."

Twenty-two miles later they arrived in the town of Aswan, the surprising opposite of the area they had left. Mature trees provided much needed shade and gardens bloomed with pink and white oleander bushes. Frangipani shrubs with their clusters of fragrant white, pink and yellow flowers brought forth an aromatic scent like that of an *eau de cologne* from a perfumery.

"If we continue down to the Nile River, you will see what has made this town so fertile," said Father David.

Claude stopped their vehicle at the water's edge and they all got out. Before them stood the town's major sight, a huge dam that stretched over a mile in length.

"This impressive dam regulates the water flow of the Nile," said Father Joseph. "Located in the middle of the dam is an island of 1001 dreams. This island called Philae was once considered to be the jewel of the Nile, but now is covered with the ruins of magnificent temples and palaces."

"Philae will soon disappear forever under the water of this great, but necessary dam," added Father David.

The Blue Cruise didn't linger for long, because despite the first six hundred miles that registered on the odometer, they had not yet reached a single mission. Claude and Vincent began to reassess the amount of time they had been spending on viewing the sites of ancient history.

Traveling south toward Khartoum the temperature rose dramatically, almost to the point that one could smell the burning desert of Libya. They hugged the shoreline of the Nile with their cumbersome truck, hoping to capture a slight wind. The glare of the sun reflecting off the windshield made driving extremely difficult. They spotted a patch of shade under a grouping of palm trees and stopped to check the condition of their vehicle. It was a stifling 127 degrees Fahrenheit in the shade. They added water to the radiator, nourishment for themselves, a prayer for a continued safe journey, and then they were back on the road. It wasn't until the evening of April 30th, seventeen days after their landing at Alexandria, that they finally reached Khartoum at the confluence of the Blue Nile and White Nile rivers.

Their missionary passengers were delighted to share their knowledge of the great Nile.

"It is the heartbeat of Egypt," explained Father Joseph. "The river is over four thousand miles long and floods once a year spreading rich silt over the land, which in turn nourishes the soil, producing the most delicious fruits and vegetables."

"But why the two different names for the same river?" asked Claude.

"The Blue Nile begins in the mountains of Ethiopia starting out in a bright blue color. As it passes through Sudan, however, it picks up black sediment that gives it a darker shade of blue. The White Nile, which begins in the forests of Rwanda and flows through Lake Victoria, is a whitish gray color, due to the light gray sediment it carries."

"But," interrupted the other missionary, "although the White Nile is longer than the Blue Nile, it is the latter that carries about two-thirds of the Nile's water supply. And it is here in Khartoum where the two rivers with the same name join each other."

"Fascinating," said Vincent. "We will replenish our food supply with some of their fresh produce while we are here in Khartoum."

On the morning of May 2nd, *The Blue Cruise* was loaded onboard a ship traveling up the White Nile River. It is a desolate land that this great river flows through, and both the Countess and Father de Moor were thankful for the respite not only for themselves, but also for their vehicle.

"When Verona Fathers first arrived in this region," explained Father Joseph, "the Muslim population offered little hope for any future conversions. The task seemed too difficult, yet we persevered in the sweltering heat of the long summers. Now the Congregation of the Sacred Heart of Verona has recorded results of over twenty thousand new Catholic members."

"How do you account for that?" she asked.

"We find that educating the natives while they are at the clinics is the most effective way to reach the population," replied Father Joseph.

On May 16th they had a stopover in Malek, a small settlement about twelve miles south of Bor in the Upper Nile Region.

"Malek is where the first Christian mission was established," said Father David. "It's considered a missionary stronghold, but we discovered that throughout this region there is a lack of knowledge; the natives think an education is a wasted effort. The students appear to have no desire to be elevated from the stature of their circumstances."

"I can now understand why health clinics are the best way to reach new converts," said Vincent.

The ship finally arrived in Juba on the evening of May 18th. It was a muggy seventy degrees when they stepped onto the dock and waited for their truck to be unloaded. Wet grasslands stretched out before them bordered by tropical forests. Claude watched as several large birds with eight-foot wingspans swarmed overhead, then landed in the grassy wetlands.

"What kind of birds are they?" she asked one of the priests.

"Those are the beautiful saddle-billed storks," said Father Joseph. "They stand almost five feet high. They are looking for their dinner of frogs in the swampy water."

"Their long black and red striped bills and feet are so striking against their glossy black and white body feathers," said Claude.

"Yes, the size and colors of the birds, animals and even the insects of Africa are most remarkable," he replied.

"But these birds don't seem to make any noise," she said.

"Once their bills are filled with their latest catch and they settle down in their nests high in the trees, an amusing beak clattering sound begins. Other than that, these storks are quiet, which is amazing considering their wingspan. The South Sudan is home to over 400 species of migrating birds. Now that's enough to provide quite a variety of bird sounds during the daylight hours," he replied. "The birds won't bother you other than their chirping and cackling choir. But there are two animals that lurk in the shallow waters that are extremely dangerous . . . the crocodile and the hippopotamus."

"I've always been leery of crocodiles knowing how fast they can move from water to land. But hippos I've only seen in the largest of rivers; they've always seemed quite playful, not a threat," said Claude.

"You must never underestimate the danger of a hippo," said Father Joseph, "I can't stress it enough. Although they are in the water most of the day, they come on land during the night foraging for food. Their massive 3,000 to 9,000 pound bodies require about eighty pounds of grass and fruit each night and they will travel several miles to get their fill. They use their sharp teeth and tusks to ward off anything standing in their way, including humans."

"I had no idea that they came up on the land at night," said Claude. "I'll certainly keep that warning in mind."

She snapped several pictures of the storks and then met up with Vincent, who was signing the release papers for their truck. They were then introduced to the Verona Fathers who came to the landing to pick up their fellow missionary travelers.

The Blue Cruise followed them to the Verona Mission where a cordial reception awaited them. While Vincent collected the reports on the everyday workings of the mission, Claude photographed the area and seized the moment to ensure that their vehicle was still in good working order before continuing their journey.

"Excuse me, Countess Kinnoull," said Father David as he and Father Joseph approached *The Blue Cruise* truck. "We were hoping to get a picture of you and Monsignor de Moor by your vehicle before you leave. We are so grateful that you allowed us a ride to Juba." Vincent joined them by the truck.

"I have a better idea," said Claude. "Why don't we have someone take a picture of the four of us by *The Blue Cruise*?"

"Wonderful idea," said Father Joseph. "And as a token of our thanks we would like to give you a gift from Africa." He handed them each an intricately designed covered basket.

"The colors are so vibrant," said Claude. "Who made them?"

"The Nubian weavers from Kenya are known for their black, orange and yellow dyes. These baskets are made from papyrus stalks on the inside and palm leaves around the outside, which produces a tightly woven basket with thick walls. The domed lids are called *kutas* a cultural requirement to protect food from insects and dirt."

"Now, that is certainly something we will use a lot of during our travels," replied Vincent.

Chapter 16

The Congo

On May 19th they left Juba, heading west by way of Faradje and Dungou. The cooler 80-degree temperature of the Congo Basin was a welcomed relief for the weary travelers, despite the high humidity. The road started out as a two lane red dirt road, allowing them to make good time. They passed several small villages with thatched-roof huts. Many looking more like giant umbrellas, with no walls at all, to allow for air circulation. As they traveled further into the Congo, the road narrowed to one lane and the dirt was less compacted, causing a billowing dust storm in their wake. After several miles the open fields began to shrink in size as thick tropical forests encroached on the land.

Tired from the high humidity and dust, they decided to set up camp for two days and visit a few of the smaller missions in the area. With the sun beginning to set, they found a level spot where the Dungu and Kibali rivers run into the much larger Uele River.

While Vincent extended the awning from the side of the truck and brought out the table and chairs, Claude headed to the river's edge with a bucket.

"I'll fetch the water," she said. "Can't wait to wash off this annoying red clay dust."

"Watch out for the water snakes," he yelled. "Want to take my knife?"

"I'll scream if I need help," she yelled back.

Vincent brought out his cooking utensils, a set of knifes, and a basket of fruits and vegetables and set them on the table. He went to the back of the truck looking for a can of cooking oil and a bag of rice. He then dug a firepit to hold a metal basin for the wood and assembled a spit above it.

Claude took off her shoes and socks, hiked up her skirt and walked into the water that lapped at the river's edge.

"Ah . . ." She wiggled her toes enjoying the cool water rushing over her feet. Claude walked a bit further into the river where she could fill the bucket, all the while glancing around for any water snakes. When the bucket was almost full, she noticed a dark shadow in the water moving closer toward her. She turned to run but the bucket was too heavy. Suddenly a large head of a hippo emerged from the river with it's mouth wide open, water dripping from its sharp teeth . . . emitting a thunderous growling sound that could be heard miles away.

"HELP!" she screamed. "HIPPO! HIPPO!

Vincent grabbed his gun and ran toward the screams.

Claude dropped the heavy bucket, almost loosing her balance and ran ashore. Vincent aimed the Holland and Holland .600, ready to fire. The hippo appeared confused by the commotion and slowly sank back into the murky water, joining its family floating up the river.

"Are you okay?" Vincent asked.

"Scared to death . . . I just can't stop shaking . . . that horrible growl was unnerving."

"I've never heard anything like that," said Vincent. "I think your scream startled the hippo." He refilled the bucket and they walked back to camp.

Vincent lit the firepit and placed a cooking grate over it, then put on a pan of water to boil. "Looks like the fruits and vegetables are beginning to wilt from the heat of the day. I'll cook them all so they won't spoil."

"Vincent, don't make any sudden moves," Claude whispered. "There is a rather large snake that is sneaking its way down that tree by the canopy and I think it wants to join us for dinner."

Vincent reached for his chopping knife, looked toward the tree, then with a quick flick of his wrist . . . thud . . . the snake and the knife fell to the ground.

"Are you sure its dead?" she asked.

"Of course it's dead, and it's just in time for dinner. Nothing like fresh meat." He chopped off the snake's head, and then prepared the snake for the evening's meal.

"How did you learn to throw a knife like that?"

"It was a skill I picked up during World War I. It came in handy a few times. You'd be amazed at what you can do when your life depends on it. Perhaps you should learn that skill."

"Maybe, but I don't think it would have helped against the hippo."

"You're right, your scream was the ultimate weapon in that case."

Vincent tied the snake to the spit and put a skillet of chopped okra, eggplant and onions along with oranges, mangoes and papayas on the grill, then added a cup of rice to the boiling water. He crushed several chili peppers to add to the skillet along with curry, nutmeg and cumin. He then cut up the seared snake and added it to the pot. Covering the fruits and vegetables with water, he let it simmered for thirty minutes to thicken the sauce, then poured the meal over mounds of rice.

"This is delicious," said Claude. The cooked fruit gives it a Mediterranean flavor."

"All compliments are welcomed," he replied.

"Tell me, Vincent . . . are you ever afraid?"

"I'd be a fool to say no. But if you let the fear eat away at you, then you truly are a fool."

"Is that where your faith comes in?"

"I'd say that is where my faith makes me stronger. I believe that in whatever situation I may find myself, that the Lord has placed me there for a reason."

"And how do you determine what His reason was?"

"It's all in the outcome of your situation; did you help somebody or learn something new?"

"Ah . . . I think I understand. I remember when my father walked out on us. I was so angry and later as a teenager, I became rebellious. But now, looking back, I can see where that painful experience actually made me a stronger person."

"Exactly! And look at you now, a brave young lady driving a truck across Africa bringing much needed help to missionaries."

"It's really quite amazing when I think about it. When I accepted the Lord as my savior, all my fears seemed to disappear. I know that no matter what happens, I will one day see you in heaven along with my child."

"When your belief is strong, nothing else seems to matter," said Vincent. "But this does not mean that you throw caution to the wind. The Lord has given us a brain after all and he expects us to use it."

"As my grandfather would say, *'There is nothing wrong with being prepared and learning survival techniques.'*"

"A very wise man indeed." They both laughed as they cleaned up the campsite.

That evening they decided to sleep in the truck in case the hippo returned. After an uneventful and restful night, they made an early morning visit to the relatively new Catholic mission in Dungu.

"I was wondering if you have a place where we can do some laundry?" asked Claude of one of the sisters.

"Of course, I'll show you the laundry hut. I'm afraid we have no modern conveniences, but one of the sisters in there will be glad to help you."

Claude and Vincent followed the nun; each carried their own bag of laundry.

They were introduced to Sister Ann, who was happy to have visitors and eager to help.

"I'm afraid this red dirt has gotten all over our clothes," said Claude.

The young nun laughed. "Yes, that clay dirt is hard to get out. We use a good strong bar soap and some bleach with a lot of scrubbing, that usually does the job. Just leave your bags on the counter and I'll get on it right away."

"We wouldn't think of burdening you with our dirty clothes, just show us where we can hang them to dry," said Vincent.

"There's a clothes line behind this hut. With the heat of the day, they should be dry within an hour," said Sister Ann.

After washing and hanging their clothes to dry, they joined the others for lunch. An hour later they went to retrieve their clothes, but they were missing. Looking in the laundry hut, they saw Sister Ann ironing each piece of underwear with an old rusted charcoal heated iron.

"It's not necessary to iron my underwear," said Claude, looking a bit embarrassed.

"Oh, but it's the only way to kill the larva that the flies deposit on wet laundry hanging outside," she said.

"Does that happen throughout Africa?" Claude asked.

"I believe so," she replied.

"Well, in that case I'm very happy to have you iron my underwear." They all laughed.

Sister Ann pulled back on the wooden handle of the iron, opening the metal box. Using a pair of tongs, she carefully picked up several pieces of hot grey-ash charcoal from a kettle on the floor, cautiously placing them in the bottom of the iron. Closing the top again, she gently blew into the holes on the sides to keep the embers burning.

Once the ironing was done, Claude and Vincent thanked their hosts and left a box of medical supplies for the mission. *The Blue Cruise* headed back on the road to continue its journey.

They arrived in Niangara on May 21st with the rumbling of thunder close by. They were grateful to be spending the night in the mission.

Father de Moor being a Belgian was particularly pleased to meet the apostolic vicar of this Belgian Dominicans mission, Monsignor Lagae, who provided an update on its progress. With over a half a million inhabitants of Niangara, there were currently ten thousand Catholics ministered by only twenty-two hard working missionaries. Vincent handed the report to Claude for review.

"These statistics must be wrong," she said. "It says here that out of all the elementary schools, there are over three thousand boys in attendance but only ninety-seven girls. And look, in the three high schools there are only forty-nine students and not a single girl. Where are the girls?"

"It's difficult for the local natives to adapt to our moral standards. They have become accustomed to what is acceptable in their local social life, which dictates that young girls be sold," replied Monsignor Lagae.

"Sold! Why, that's barbaric!" Claude stood and started pacing back and forth. "Something needs to be done . . . why would the parents allow such a thing to happen? None of these children should be sold as slaves!"

One of the missionaries spoke up. "It is a slow and painstaking process with only twenty-two of us trying to visit thousands of families in their homes. In our visits, we are finding that the young girls are often sold so that the rest of their family will be provided for. These families often live in deplorable conditions and it is their only way to survive. We try to visit the highest-ranking natives first because they are the most influential in the area. We pray that their hearts will be open to the error of their ways and that they will put a stop to this horrendous situation."

"How can we help?" asked Vincent.

"The parents need to be educated in the harm that is being done," replied Monsignor Lagae. "Most natives understand and speak the

French language. However we lack the Bibles and educational materials."

"We have brought with us boxes of French Bibles and thousands of brochures explaining our Catholic religion, and we will provide more at your request when we return to Paris," said Claude.

"Your help is most appreciated and desperately needed," replied Monsignor Lagae.

They were shown the rest of the mission, and then after a hearty meal everyone retired for the evening.

The next morning a tropical downpour did not deter *The Blue Cruise* from its scheduled early hour departure. They set off traveling south heading toward the missions Rungu and Wamba. The rainy season was finally upon them and roads were often impassable. The red dirt became slippery, sending their truck sliding into foot deep potholes or entirely off the path. Several river bridges became a lesson in patience and endurance. This was no small task considering the weight of their one-ton truck and the load it was carrying. Driving alongside the river they passed numerous bridges, but none appeared wide enough or strong enough to support their vehicle. After several miles, a concrete reinforced bridge came into sight and *The Blue Cruise* finally crossed.

The rain slowly dissipated and the forest with its towering trees loomed over the cascading Liana plants, creating a thick curtain of greenery. To the weary travelers, the road leading to Mission Rungu seemed sent from heaven, providing shade from the sun's glare reflecting off their windshield. This mission on the tributary was a refreshing respite for Claude, who enjoyed a long walk in the evening and delightful conversations with the missionaries. The constant buzzing of a variety of insects was something they learned to ignore, and often lulled them to sleep.

Tall grasses surrounded the mission and dense forest closed in on its boundaries. The black faced and black haired chimpanzees known as bonobos hung from trees, observing the activities of the mission below.

Occasionally they would let out a loud grunting, hooting and screaming sound.

"Listen to that racket those chimps are making," said Claude.

"Look over at the edge of the forest by the tall grass," said Vincent. "The chimpanzees are excited because a hyena is stalking that water buffalo who is trying to find its injured calf."

The hyena let out several hackling high-pitched laughs, which set the chimpanzees into a screaming fit. When two more hyenas arrived, the buffalo ran off toward the river. The three hyenas let out a chorus of laughs, and then tore strips of flesh off of the injured calf.

"That's awful! You can actually hear the crunching of bones." Claude turned away from the sight of the carnage.

She and Vincent walked back to the chapel where they had been asked to talk about *The Blue Cruise*. They spent a full day at Rungu then drove to Mission Wamba, delivering medical supplies and Bibles. After which they pressed on toward Mission Avakubi, arriving on the eve of Pentecost (a celebration of a direct personal experience with God akin to the descent of the Holy Spirit upon the Apostles).

The following day as they were ushered to their seats for the morning Mass, Claude whispered to Vincent. "Just look around us. These people gathered here represent all the nations of Europe, yet despite this diversity they all understand the Latin mass and are truly bound in one heart and one mind in their devotion to God."

"It fills my heart with joy to see the work that the Lord is doing here," replied Vincent.

After visiting the Avakubi post, *The Blue Cruise* retraced their path back to Rungu before venturing more to the west. With over a hundred missions to visit, Claude and Vincent tried to visit several of the posts in one day, if in close proximity. The mission posts of Dingha, Bairbill, and Titoule were heartened by the arrival of *The Blue Cruise* bringing the much-needed supplies. They then continued west to Buta.

"I don't know how this can be considered a road," said Claude as they bumped along. "This is a mud and rock ditch!" The 178 miles they needed to travel to Buta became an exercise in patience. Just when they were about to leave the ditch, a family of five elephants ambled across in front of them without a care in the world. Two baby elephants had wrapped their long trunks around the tails of the older elephants, slipping and sliding up the side of the ditch.

"You have to laugh at this sight," said Vincent. "The elephants don't see us; we're all covered in caked-on red dirt."

They watched as the last of the elephants made it to the other side. Claude looked at her watch. "I sure hope we get to Buta before nightfall."

"Looks like the road up ahead is two lanes with a flat surface," said Vincent. "The kind of road you like."

"We'll fly like a gazelle . . . hold on to your hat," she said.

They finally arrived in Buta as the sun was setting. Vincent read the directions to the Chamoines Mission where they would be spending the night.

They were greeted by a nun and a priest and were shown to their rooms, and were told that supper would be served in about an hour in the cafeteria building.

Claude was glad to have time to wash away the smelly red dust covering her from head to toe and was also glad to have a comfortable bed for the night.

After delightful conversation with their hosts and a mouth watering meal of chicken and vegetable pies and hot bread, topped off with a dessert of fresh berries and lemon cookies with Earl Grey tea, it was time to review the progress reports of the mission.

"As you will see from these reports, our mission has been quite successful in a short period of time," said the head bishop.

Vincent read the reports. "It seems that in this territorial jurisdiction of the Roman Catholic Church, this mission has established forty-eight schools from elementary to college, furthering the education of two thousand boys and over three hundred girls," he said.

"I'm pleased to see that the number of girls being educated is beginning to increase," remarked Claude.

"Ah, yes, patience is a virtue when it comes to these matters," remarked the bishop.

"But mark my word," said Vincent, "with Providence as your guide, you will one day be triumphant in convincing the leaders of the tribes that educating all their children, both male and female, should be their top priority."

"My heart aches for the young girls in this continent," said Claude. "I fear that their survival most assuredly depends on their being educated."

"Prayer is a remarkable tool that too few people avail themselves of," said one of the sisters.

"And we must always remember, the Lord delights in rewarding those who soldier on His behalf," said Vincent.

"It is definitely a battle winning souls to Christ," replied Claude. "Now if you'll excuse me, it has been a most tiring day. I know we'll need an early start in the morning if we are to reach Stanleyville at a decent hour. It was delightful meeting all of you and sharing a meal together."

Returning to her room, Claude laid out an outfit of tan trousers and a red blouse, hoping to blend in with the dirt that was caked on their truck. Now all she could think of was a comfortable bed with clean sheets. The minute her head hit the feather pillow, Claude's eyes closed and didn't open again until there was a knock on her door.

She grabbed her light cotton robe and rushed to the door. "Did I oversleep?"

"No, Miss . . . Father de Moor requested we wake you at 7 a.m. sharp. I hope you slept well," said Sister Ann.

"The best sleep I've had in months."

"I've fixed you a breakfast tray with an omelet, fresh fruit, a biscuit and a pot of English Breakfast Tea."

"Have the others already eaten?" she asked.

"I'm afraid so, we get up before the sun," Sister Ann replied.

"Well, everything looks wonderful. Thank you so much. Please tell Father de Moor that I'll be ready by eight."

"I'll prepare a picnic basket for you to take along," said Sister Ann.

While eating her breakfast, Claude wrote in her journal about their visit at the Chamoines Mission. Precisely at eight, she was packed and ready to go. She heard the truck approach and was surprised to see the mud was gone and the windshield sparkling clean . . . even the inside of the truck had been wiped down.

"What a wonderful surprise. It even smells clean!" she shouted.

They gave the missionaries some medical supplies and several boxes of Bibles, then *The Blue Cruise* was on the road again, heading south to Stanleyville.

"This road, although still made out of dirt, appears to be well traveled," said Vincent.

"If it stays this way, then we should make good time," said Claude. "We only have about 250 miles to Stanleyville."

An important inland port for river and land transportation, Stanleyville was referred to as *The City on the Island*. It is located at the northern tip of the Congo River, at the junction of the Tshopo and Lindi rivers. The surrounding tributaries separate Stanleyville from the mainland.

The Blue Cruise arrived at the port around noon on the 26th of May. They drove just south of the city to view the seven arched falls, with their combined drop of two hundred feet. Claude grabbed the picnic basket and Vincent laid a blanket on the shore above the Wagenia Falls. While enjoying their lunch of chicken salad, fresh fruit, lemon cookies and tea, they watched the local fishermen drop their cornucopia shaped nets into the churning waters, filling their nets with a variety of fish that they would sell at the town's market.

"Even though Stanleyville is slightly north of the Equator and the humidity is high, the cool breezes from the Congo River make the eighty-eight degree temperature quite enjoyable," said Claude as they packed up their picnic basket and headed back to the truck.

"I'm looking forward to spending a few days with the Fathers of the Sacred Heart of Saint Quentin," said Vincent. "It's a much larger mission. In this vicariate, their activity of evangelism is scattered throughout a vast area, serving a population of over a million inhabitants."

"Yes, it will be interesting to see how they manage that," said Claude.

They arrived at the Mission of Saint Quentin in time for dinner.

"Something smells wonderful," said Claude.

"It's our version of porcupine stew," said one of the sisters. "If you like it, I'll give you the recipe."

Claude tasted the stew. "The sauce is quite flavorful. I can taste green peppers, onions, corn and carrots and the meat is very tender, almost like duck, but with a more gamey beef flavor to it. It really is delicious."

"You'll have to tell me the recipe," said Vincent. "I'm the designated chef on our journey."

The sister laughed. "The key to a good porcupine stew is to simmer the meat in a tasty sauce for four to five hours, until the meat falls off the bones."

"I'm afraid we don't have enough time to watch the stew cook," said Vincent. "I would have to wait until we return to France and I think a porcupine will be hard to find in Paris."

After the meal they met with the head bishop to read the progress reports of the mission.

"I see that this mission's fruit of evangelization has grown to thirty thousand converts and the establishment of almost two hundred schools to accommodate eight thousand boys and seven hundred girls," remarked Claude after perusing the reports. She handed the report to Vincent.

"I can conclude from reading this," he said, "that the success of this mission in covering such a large area has been dependent on the concerted effort of the priests and nuns from various countries as well as the Marist Brothers."

"I'm not familiar with the Marist Brothers. How do they fit in with the missions?" she asked.

"They are a Catholic religious order of brothers who live simple lives forsaking personal wealth to follow Jesus," he said. "Their primary work is the Christian education of the young and the neglected. They strive to teach and guide the young toward a future rich in knowledge, service to others, and strong spiritual values. Their motto is taken from the Bible in John 10:10 – *'I have come that you may have life, and have it in abundance.'*"

"I am impressed by the growth of schools that we have seen in Stanleyville," replied Claude. "I'm a firm believer in Proverbs 22:6 – *'Train up a child in the way he should go; and when he is old, he will not depart from it.'*"

"We try to speak with the elders in a family; the young ones will follow their parents' beliefs. Then we try to get the acceptance of the village with much needed clinics," said the head bishop.

"Amen," replied Vincent. "I also see from this report that there are not enough clinics to cover those that seek medical help. Now that is an area where we can help by multiplying the number of medical clinics to help relieve the misery as much as possible."

"I'll speak with the Franciscan Missionaries of Mary who run the hospitals to see where the best location would be for new clinics," said Claude. "Within a few days we could have several clinics up and running."

The excitement of opening several new clinics was so appreciated by the nuns and priests that they worked tirelessly to see the project come to fruition. Although the clinics were often one large hut with only a few beds for those severely ill, it was a start. It allowed natives access to clinics in their villages, rather than traveling sometimes hundreds of miles for aid. For the missionary, it allowed them to work with individual natives, training them in the works of the clinic and introducing them to the Bible.

The Blue Cruise left Stanleyville for Ponthierville, which was only ninety-five miles south. This allowed them time to visit several small missions along the way. Once at Ponthierville, they were offered a ride on a 150-ton steam wheeler traveling up the Lualaba River (part of the grand Congo River) toward Kindou. River travel was often the only way to traverse the thick jungles of the Congo.

The natives not able to pay for travel on a large ship make their own flat-bottom dugout canoes out of the rot-resistant wood of the Pirogue tree. When roads flood during the rainy season it is these dugout canoes that are often the only means of transportation.

Claude and Vincent were given cabins on the upper deck of the steam ship, usually reserved for government officials. The native passengers brought their own food and had no cabins in which to sleep. Although the Congo River is considered one of the deepest rivers in the world, it is a dark muddy brown and fraught with many sandbars. Navigating the river at night is extremely dangerous, so each evening at dusk all ships and canoes pull over to the banks of the river. Those without cabins go ashore and sleep on the sand until morning.

The occupants of *The Blue Cruise* were invited to eat with the captain in a small dining area. Their meals consisted of goat, chicken or fowl with rice. Fresh fruit was bountiful with pineapples, grapefruit, oranges, bananas and pei pei, a fruit tasting like cantaloupe.

"Captain, the other morning I was out on the deck and noticed several mounds of dirt next to a village. Some of these mounds were as tall as a hut. Do you know what they are?" asked Claude.

The captain laughed. "Run in the opposite direction if you come across one of those mounds . . . it's an ant nest."

"That big?" she asked.

"I've seen them as high as forty feet."

"What type of ants do you have here?" asked Vincent.

"There are hundreds of varieties," said the captain, "but the three most common are the white ant, the ones that build the towering mounds and are famous for destroying property. They love to eat wood and leather, so don't leave your shoes out at night; pack everything in metal boxes. The red ants have a horrible sting and the driver ants, which travel in armies, have been known to take over a house driving out the humans, but eating all the vermin in sight. Then they move on as quickly as they came."

"Thank you for that bit of information," said Vincent.

"I know we have an early start in the morning," said Claude. "It was a delicious meal and we enjoyed your company. Goodnight, Captain."

Claude and Vincent stood on the top deck looking out at the passengers from the ship sleeping with their blankets on the sandy shore, like a large family commune. In the darkness of the night millions of stars covered the sky above and the subdued sounds of the jungle could be heard in the distance as animal predators began their nightly rituals.

"It's amazing the variety of animals and insects that live in this area," said Claude. "It gives me a real appreciation for them."

"Every turn in our journey brings us new wonders," said Vincent. "Have a good rest . . . I'll see you in the morning."

After three days of sailing, they docked at Kindou, feeling nourished and refreshed, but their vehicle on the other hand was beginning to feel the wear and tear. The truck chugged along, occasionally emitting a muffled explosive sound with a cough and a sputter as it journeyed toward Kongolo and the Mission of the Fathers of the Holy Spirit, where they had planed to stay a few days. This was a beautiful area with a variety of brightly colored birds flocking to the numerous lakes that dotted the landscape. They stopped for a break by one of the lakes. Tall papyrus plants growing six to ten feet high anchored their roots at the lake's edge often spreading into the water.

"After looking at these plants, I don't see how they can turn them into thin writing sheets," said Claude.

"The process is quite interesting," replied Vincent. "The long papyrus stalks are cut down and soaked in water until they get a bit mushy . . . then several of these stalks are laid next to one another. Next you take more of these water soaked stalks and lay them crosswise to the first group. You then pound them together into a creamy pulp. Once dried it resembles parchment paper. But now we must be off, they will be expecting us at the mission."

The Mission of the Fathers of the Holy Spirit had only twenty missionaries to serve seventeen churches and almost two hundred chapels. In a large city, where transportation was not a problem, this would be plausible; however, in a population scattered over forty-three thousand square miles, reaching all the posts was daunting.

The missionaries were pleased that the Countess and Father de Moor would be staying long enough to participate in their Feast of Corpus Christi (celebrating the belief in the body and blood of Jesus Christ's Real Presence in the Eucharist).

After their noon meal, Claude was approached by one of the missionary sisters. "Pardon me, Lady Kinnoull, but if you have the time I would like to show you another area of our mission that is seldom talked about."

"But of course," replied Claude, "that is why I'm here, to report on the progress of the missions and to learn of any needs that you may have. What is this area you talk about?"

"Please follow me." The missionary led her down a grassy overgrown path and up a hill invaded by tall prickly thistle. Ahead of them stood Acacia Thorn trees in various heights, tipping their umbrella shaped tops and offering a bit of shade from the unbearable heat. Claude paused to take a picture.

"I do believe that wood from this type of tree was used to make the Biblical Ark of the Covenant," she said.

"That is so, according to tradition," replied the missionary. As they passed by the towering trees, there appeared a grouping of several circular thatched-roofed huts.

"Who lives here?" Claude asked.

"These huts are run by the *Girls Cross,* a group of nuns who care for sick women and children. Such affection and inspiration that they have shown to these poor disinherited, have earned them a very sweet name: we call them *Mothers.* It is a valuable auxiliary for the Fathers of Holy Ghost, who are themselves extremely zealous workers," replied the missionary.

They visited each of the huts and were shown how the *Mothers* not only attended to the sick women and children's physical needs, but also to their spiritual needs.

"I'm afraid we are a bit overwhelmed today," said one of the nuns. "A few of our fellow sisters were needed for the preparations of the celebration."

Claude rolled up the sleeves on her blouse. "I'm here to help. What would you have me do?"

"Oh, the babies, they need so much attention. Sometimes they just need to be held," said the nun.

Claude immediately started changing and bathing babies. One little boy about two years old caught her eye. He had been quiet the whole time she was in the room. She noticed that now tears were rolling down his face, yet he didn't say a word. Perhaps he was used to being left alone. She walked over to his crib and picked him up. He threw his arms around her neck and began to sob. She started to sing softly into his ear, allowing the subconscious thoughts of her own son to resurface. Her eyes clouded over with visions of the past. Could this be the reason the Lord had brought her here, to take care of these babies? The child in her arms had finally fallen asleep and she gently laid him back in his crib. She pulled her drifting thoughts together; they still had a long journey ahead through this vast and unpredictable nation of Africa.

The next morning was bustling with excitement as the mission prepared for the Feast of Corpus Christi. This wonderful event of faith had arrived at the most opportune time for Claude. She needed to refocus her thoughts away from herself to a more spiritual level with the Lord.

She saw the Mother Superior making her way through rows of chairs toward her. "My dear Countess, we have reserved two seats up front with us, for you and Father de Moor."

"Reverend Mother," she began, "we are so honored to have arrived in time to be part of this special celebration with you and this mission. Why, just yesterday I was telling Father de Moor that if we had not been blessed with the opportunity to share a ride on a ship up the river, we would not have been here today for this wonderful occasion."

"But my dear, God's timing is always perfect, even though at the time we may not think so. One must have faith that the good Lord will always put us in the right place at the right time. Why, our faith is the backbone of our beliefs. We must never forget that."

The canopied area where the Holy Mass was to be performed was beginning to fill with the faithful. Streams of colorfully dressed natives swarmed down the hillsides and through the grasslands balancing large baskets on their heads full of food for the celebration. The religious zeal of the natives confirmed to Claude that the sincerity of their beliefs was unquestionable. After the Holy Mass, the procession that followed was a triumphant parade attended by over twelve hundred.

On June 8th, *The Blue Cruise* set off with exuberant renewal in the unforgettable memory of the Corpus Christi celebration. However, this exuberance was to be short-lived when they discovered that the area they were passing through had sudden and severe flooding rains. They were forced to park their truck on higher ground under a cluster of trees for the evening. The river below them became precariously close to overflowing its banks, sending an onslaught of frogs leaping from its shores into the underbrush surrounding the trees. They joined *The Blue Cruise* for the evening in a shirring chorus of raspy croaks of which the frogs never seemed to tire.

When the rains had subsided to a light shower, Vincent attached a canvas awning to the side of the truck, then dropped its mosquito netting, while Claude set up a small table and two canvas chairs. Vincent, the chef during this pilgrimage across Africa, was reprieved of his duties for the evening. Their meal tonight would consist of leftovers from the delicious array of native African food from the celebration the day before.

"What a treat to again savor the many delectable flavors of true African cooking," said Claude, looking at the abundance of colorful fare set before her.

"It is definitely a joy to the senses. The colors of the food are like an artist palette, the aroma tickles the taste buds and the savory, mouth-watering textures are a kaleidoscope to the tongue," he said.

"Spoken as a true chef would." She laughed.

As the evening wore on, several hundred crickets decided to join the frog choir, filling the night with raspy croaks and high-pitched chirps. Later the incessant buzzing of Tsetse flies and mosquitoes joined the choir.

"I do believe that we should definitely say a special prayer for the inventor of mosquito netting," said Claude.

"Wait a minute," said Vincent, "I do have something that might help." He pulled out a large black gun case.

"Oh, I see, you want me to use the mosquitoes for target practice," laughed Claude.

"No, I have something that may help you sleep." He opened the case and took out two small packages of beeswax earplugs and handed one to her. "At least it will help block out the animal choir."

A clap of thunder sounded in the distance and the drizzle that had been with them all evening turned into a heavy downpour. The treetop canopy acted as a natural umbrella, protecting them from the rain. Vincent loaded the double barrels of the Holland & Holland .600 just in case some other creatures might seek shelter from the rain among the trees.

After an evening prayer for safe protection through the night, Claude put in her earplugs and made herself a bed in the back of the truck. Vincent set-up a cot next to the table and chairs under the awning, laid the gun on the table within arms reach, but put his earplugs in his pocket. Any silence from the animal choir would be a sure giveaway that something was amiss.

Vincent kept dosing off finding it hard to keep his eyes open, but about midnight he suddenly sat-up. He thought he had been dreaming, but then he heard it again, a rustling in the bushes at the foot of the hill. A flock of birds rushed out of the trees and the frogs stopped croaking. Vincent stood up and grabbed his gun, aiming it at the bushes below. With the light of a full moon, he noticed movement in the tall grass. Then he saw it . . . crouching low and moving slowly toward his position was a full-grown female lion. He aimed the gun at the predator and was about to shoot when two lion cubs came running out of the bushes, slipping and sliding on the rain soaked field toward their mother. She turned and growled at them. Vincent's finger slipped and the gun went off with a jolt; the glowing muzzle flash temporally blinded him. He heard a loud cracking sound, blinked several times to refocus his eyes, then raised the gun again, aiming toward his predator. But he saw nothing; it had disappeared. Keeping the rifle tightly against his shoulder ready to shoot, Vincent turned in all directions waiting for the lion to pounce. His heart was pounding and beads of sweat dripped from his forehead. Then he heard a ruckus at the edge of the trees and turned with his gun at the ready. He breathed a sigh of relief to see the lioness running in the opposite direction with her cubs in tow. Relaxing his grip on the gun, Vincent laid it on the table and rubbed his aching shoulder. He had heard the bullet hit something; he wondered what he had shot.

With dawn finally breaking, Vincent made a fresh pot of coffee, and then saw the victim of his bullet. A large splintered branch dangled from a Sycamore Fig tree; its marble-size fruit scattered beneath it.

Claude woke to the amusing, croaking and frolicking of frogs as they shot out of the grass sending sprays of water with each leap. She reached for her camera, laughing at the playfulness of these small creatures.

"I'm afraid the last laugh will be on us," said Vincent.

"Whatever do you mean?" she asked.

"Look around you. That ceaseless deluge during the night has turned the surrounding grasslands into a swamp."

"Oh dear, I see what you mean. It will definitely be slow going. Let us pray that the undercarriage of the truck will be at a height greater than the water," she replied.

"How did you sleep? he asked.

"That must have been some storm last night," said Claude. A loud clap of thunder and a flash of lightning woke me, and then I went right back to sleep." She sat down at the table then noticed the damaged tree. "Did the lightning hit that tree?" she asked while they ate breakfast.

Vincent then told her of his encounter with the lions and shooting the tree. "I would have shot her had I not seen the cubs."

"And had you, I would not have spoken to you for the rest of the trip," she said.

"Maybe not, but you would have been alive. Interesting thing about that tree," he continued. "It's a fig tree known in the Bible as the *Tree of Life* because so many animals live off its fruit, but in this incident it saved the life of the lioness and her cubs from a bullet."

"That's quite a coincidence," she said.

"Coincidence . . . I think not," he replied.

After breakfast, they quickly packed up the truck, double-checking that the supplies were tightly secured, and then slowly made their way down the hill. As Claude cautiously maneuvered the truck over the highest ground she could find and still stay close to the river, Vincent kept a watchful eye out for a suitable bridge crossing.

Traveling to remote mission posts brought about its own set of precarious circumstances. The bridges were often rotten from neglect. The continual pounding of the water against the pilings frequently jeopardized the integrity of the structure, not to mention the devouring effects of the tropical insects.

"I see a bridge up ahead. The swollen river has risen to about ten feet under the bridge. At least it's still standing and it looks wide enough for our load," he said. "Let's just take it ever so slowly."

Claude approached the bridge with trepidation. "It looks a bit rickety, but I know we must give it a try . . . we have been traveling for miles looking for a bridge." She negotiated the first half of the bridge as it creaked and groaned under the weight of the vehicle. Suddenly the whole truck lunged forward when a rotten wooden plank gave way. The bridge began to sway . . . the other rotten planks began to crack under the weight.

"Lord save us!" yelled Vincent. The truck plunged straight down. The impact of the splash spewed water through the windows of the truck with such force it drenched its occupants when they came to an abrupt stop.

"Are you all right?" he asked.

"Yes, I believe so, and you?"

"A bit humiliated and wet, but I'll live. It appears that we have landed on a sand berm in the middle of the river."

"So God has answered your prayer after all," said Claude. "Oh, look, the Lord has sent some angels! The natives on the river bank are waving at us and several are swimming out with ropes!"

Vincent smiled, "Praise the Lord. He does work in mysterious ways."

The natives worked several hours digging the truck out of the wet sand. They were finally able to secure the ropes to the front bumper of the truck and pull it to safety. The natives were excited to hear from where these strangers came and proud to show off their many handmade crosses. With the vehicle in need of drying out along with its occupants, Claude and Vincent were happy to accommodate their rescuers with the tales of their journey and to have a safe place in their huts for a good night's sleep.

Starting off the next day in fine spirits and with a collection of hand-carved wooden-crosses, *The Blue Cruise* continued its journey south toward the Mission Kabinda. Although the engine had dried out, its performance was most troubling. It coughed and backfired its way through the tall grasses of the Bush, sputtering, stopping and restarting about every two miles. Claude pressed on until white billowing smoke crept from under the hood.

"I guess this is as fine a place as any to set up camp," she said, trying her best to add a bit of levity to an otherwise trying situation.

Vincent dug the firepit, lit the wood and placed the grill over the top. He stood to stretch and watched the sky slowly turn into a brilliant reddish-yellow glow. "Have you ever seen such a glorious sunset?" he asked.

"It's a renewal of the soul and a reminder of just how small we are in the overall scheme of things," she said.

"Small among the multitudes, but very precious and significant in His sight," replied Vincent. They set-up their tents and lit the kerosene lanterns. While Vincent prepared the evening meal, Claude inspected the truck for any damage.

"It appears," she sighed, "that the radiator grate is totally clogged with the seeds from the tall grass." Then with the patience of an angel and armed with only a hairpin, she meticulously plucked out each seed from the grate, allowing the radiator to breathe freely again.

After their evening meal, Claude was so exhausted that even the frog chorus did not disrupt her sleep.

With an early morning start on the 11th of June they arrived at the Kabinda Mission just as the bells began to toll, announcing the start of the worship service. Natives of all ages filled the church in quiet, respectful devotion, but after the sermon the church became a community center with boisterous, happy laughter as the congregation became involved in numerous activities geared toward involving the local families.

The next day Lady Kinnoull and Father de Moor were given a tour of the schools run by the Brothers of Charity. Vincent turned to the Father Superior.

"I must commend you on a job well done. Your schools should serve as a model to other missions. The professional schools here are excellent and will go hand in hand with the increase in the enrollment of children in the parochial schools."

"We do try hard to involve the natives in positive ways; in being a partner in their children's education and spiritual growth," replied the Father Superior.

"And there is one area of most significance to me of which I am so pleased to see," said Claude. "And that is the influx of natives to high-level offices."

"This mission will one day be theirs to run. It is crucial that they understand the importance of the task at hand," replied the Father Superior.

They were able to spend a few more days at the Kabinda Mission, and then *The Blue Cruise* continued on its missionary journey toward Elisabethville, 670 miles away.

"Oh . . . look a that." Claude pulled to the side of the road. "I've got to get a picture." She grabbed her camera and jumped out of the truck. Across the road stood twelve to fifteen giraffes among a grouping of Acacia trees. Claude focused her camera on their long black tongues, which they slid along the branches, removing the top leaves and filling their mouths. She wished she could have recorded the sounds of the giraffes munching on the leaves.

"Those trees must be at least fifteen to twenty feet tall," said Vincent when Claude returned to the truck. I was looking at them through the binoculars . . . amazing when you see these animals up close."

"Did you see the length of their tongues?" she asked. "They looked about two feet long."

"I read somewhere that their tongues are black to protect them from the sun and that the thorns of the Acacia cannot penetrate through its thick skin," said Vincent. "It's surprising to see that there are still leaves on the trees, for each giraffe needs to consume up to seventy-five pounds a day of the moist Acacia leaves just to get enough water to survive. Otherwise they risk being attacked when they drop down to drink from rivers."

"I think I was able to get some great shots of them," said Claude. She started the engine and they were back on the road.

After two more days of camping and visiting isolated missions, their food supply was running low. While picking up fresh produce in a village market they walked next to a flatbed truck piled high with giant gorilla skins and elephant tusks still dripping of blood. The vile stench of the slaughter caused Claude to gag. She felt her stomach churn and ran to the side of the road where she lost her breakfast. Vincent came to her aid with a wet cloth and a cup of water.

"There ought to be a law against that type of torture to animals, have they no compassion? Who are these people?" she cried.

"You must keep your voice down," Vincent said in a whisper. He held the cool cloth on the back of her neck, helping her back to *The Blue Cruise*. "They are known as poachers and there are laws against them, but in isolated areas the villagers fear that the poachers would retaliate against them if reported."

Claude climbed back into their vehicle and pulled the map from the glove compartment. "Well, I'm going to mark on the map the location of this village . . . I'll show it to the proper authorities and let them deal with it. I just can't stand by and do nothing!"

Map of Africa showing the route traveled to visit over 112 missions. The solid black line is first leg of trip from Marseille to Cape Town. The journey home is shown in the broken line from Cape Town to Paris. (From *La Croisiere Bleue et les Missions D'Afrique* book)

Chapter 17

Watch Out For Crocodiles!

On the 14th of June, *The Blue Cruise* arrived at a river that presented quite a dilemma. They discovered that there was no permanent bridge on which to cross the river, only a floating pontoon bridge that hardly appeared safe for people, let alone a vehicle. The native operating the apparatus assured them it was very strong; passengers would be at the front and the vehicle would be strapped to the back section of the floating bridge. With a little apprehension and a lot of prayer, Vincent helped the native operator secure the truck and equipment to the back section of the pontoon bridge. Claude decided she would supervise this process from the safety of the driver's seat in the vehicle.

Vincent watched the operator pull on the rope attached to a pulley on the dock at the other side of the river. Everything seemed to be going fine as the floating bridge started to glide across the water. When they reached the middle of the river they felt a jolt.

"We must have hit something in the river," yelled the operator. "We're snagged on something."

Vincent looked over the sides of the bridge for any debris that they may have snagged. "I don't see anything that we could be caught on," he yelled.

The operator ran back to the truck and quickly untied the ropes that were securing it to the railings.

"What are you doing?" asked Vincent.

"If that vehicle goes, I don't want it to take us down with it." He ran back to try the rope pulley again.

"Get out of the truck!" yelled Vincent. But just as he yelled, the pontoon bridge broke apart . . . the section with the truck went adrift, with Claude in the driver's seat. The release of the back section propelled the front part of the bridge closer to the other dock. The operator frantically tugged on the rope pulley.

"CROCODILES! CROCODILES!" he yelled.

"What?" Vincent yelled. He looked in the direction of the truck. It began taking on water. The truck started to slide, throwing it off balance. Claude quickly assessed the situation.

"Lord give me speed and strength," she prayed. Closing her eyes, she plunged into the shadowy murkiness of the water below. The strong current pulled her down and away from the equipment as the platform drifted down the river with the truck precariously hanging over the side and taking on water.

Claude opened her eyes and swam toward the light above. Breaking through to the surface she heard frantic yelling to SWIM FASTER! SWIM FASTER! She knew her life depended on it.

On shore two men jumped into a rowboat trying to reach her, but she had summoned up an inexplicable strength and with great strokes she collapsed safely at the water's edge into Vincent's arms. He carried her safely to the dock. A native woman came running with a blanket and wrapped it around her.

Claude looked up at Vincent. "Once again our guardian angels have protected us," she said.

"And for that we are truly thankful," he replied. "Unfortunately, we forgot to pray for the truck." He looked down the river, but was amazed to see that the truck had not been swept away after all; it had become lodged on an embankment that jutted out into the river.

With the help of a group of natives, it did not take them long to remove the vehicle from the water; but it took three days to restore the drowned engine. After completely disassembling the motor, it became obvious the immersion in the water seriously affected some of the parts, causing considerable damage.

Once all the components were wiped dry, Claude carefully put everything back in place on the engine and climbed into the driver's seat. Vincent along with a couple of natives forcefully pushed the truck through the tall grass for several miles until finally arriving at a train station. They were able to obtain passage for themselves and their vehicle. They rolled it up a ramp and onto an empty flatcar. After securing the truck, they boarded the passenger car of the train for a much-welcomed ride bound for Elisabethville.

Elisabethville was one of the centers nearest to the frontier in the southern part of the Belgium Congo bordering Rhodesia. With *The Blue Cruise* still under repair, Claude and Vincent were shown the Salesian Fathers' Mission, located fifteen miles north of Elisabethville in Upper Lunpuia.

"I can see that the significance of this relatively young mission is in its remarkable professional schools," said Vincent, himself a professor. He was once again impressed by the education provided to the natives by master teachers. But the hour was getting late so they returned to Elisabethville for one last night with their missionary hosts.

In the morning, they found the engine of their truck had fully recovered from its untimely dive. They quickly replenished supplies and then veered eastward to Fort Chiniama in Rhodesia, arriving in the afternoon on the 28th of June.

A Floating Pontoon Bridge carrying *The Blue Cruise* across a crocodile invested river (Photo provided from *La Croisiere Bleue et les Missions D'Afrique* book)

Chapter 18

Rhodesia and The Legend of Bishop Smith

So far in their travels Claude had observed that the natives had a genuine love and respect for the missionaries, but in Rhodesia the atmosphere changed; the love and respect had turned to worshiping the missionary, who was now considered the master and father. This idolization of the missionary by the natives had a most profound effect on the conversion of souls to the Catholic religion. Bishop Larue and his thirty-five priests administered this successful parish of Bangueolo. Together they evangelized almost two thousand villages. The zeal of the missionaries realized the fruit of sixty-seven thousand Catholics and forty-six thousand new catechisms.

After the evening meal, Claude asked, "Bishop Larue, what is your secret for the conversion of so many natives to the faith?"

"Providence definitely had a hand in this success," he laughed. "Many years ago a Bishop Smith came to this region of fierce and formidable warriors and was visiting the chief of the tribe. Well, things did not go very well and their visit ends with a threat from the native king of the region. He recommends that the bishop leave immediately, otherwise, he would be killed without mercy. But the bishop surprised the king by saying, 'It's a shame, I would just treat and cure your illness.' Then without further ado, Bishop Smith departed."

"So he wasn't killed?" asked Claude.

"No, the bishop's reply had perplexed the king. He also realized that the bishop had left behind a bolt of colorful fabric. The king immediately sent a native to tell the bishop what he had left behind. But the bishop said it was a gift for the king to keep, which left a good impression with the king."

"Then the bishop was left alone to carry out his missionary work?" asked Vincent.

"Yes, but a few months later, the king fell ill and his sorcerers, soothsayers, even his doctors could not find the cause of his discomfort. This made the king very upset and he finally sent emissaries to the bishop. Although it was never stated what the king's illness was, it was obvious to Bishop Smith, who must have treated a similar illness before and was able to relieve his discomfort. With his illness gone, the king recognized and trusted the bishop as a great healer. Thus Bishop Smith was allowed to set up clinics in Rhodesia with the first missionaries."

"But that still does not explain why the bishops are still treated like kings in this area," said Claude.

"You are quite right," replied Bishop Larue. "One day the king requested the presence of Bishop Smith and told him that he was near death. He told the bishop that he has many wives and children, but when he dies his brother would be the heir and, as king, would have all the deceased king's family killed. Knowing that the bishop was a compassionate and godly man, the king asked the bishop to take his place when he died so his family would be spared. Although a strange proposal, Bishop Smith saw the good that would become of it and agreed. As king of the natives in Bangueolo, he became master of a very large family that he had to protect. So the first order of the new monarch was to stop the killing of women and children of deceased kings. And his next concern was to forbid polygamy in Christian marriages, finding husbands for each individual wife. The festivities were grand, and with so many lives saved, the natives called the place Chilouboula, *place of issue*. Since then, bishops and missionaries are revered by the whole population."

"What an amazing story," said Vincent. "To think that this one act of kindness done years ago, of the bishop becoming king, spared the lives of so many.

"The Lord does work in mysterious ways," said Claude. "And it also appears that the lack of missionaries and money is the only reason, one might say, why this country is not entirely Catholic."

They decide to visit the various posts in the Bangueolo area to discover their teaching methods and see firsthand the results of their evangelizing. Claude was interested in studying each of the missions and how their various methods worked in the different areas, and how the results compared.

After much inquiry, both Claude and Vincent came to the same conclusion that Bishop Larue already had. It is the parents that need to be converted first, making up the backbone of their apostolic activity, requiring years of study until they have acquired a perfect knowledge of the Catholic religion. From there the missionaries assimilate the natives' customs and religious spirit together, forming a cohesive conversion that becomes the building block for a strong family unit.

On July 29th, *The Blue Cruise* team left the Chilubula Mission, home to Bishop Larue and his small kingdom for God, and headed further southeast toward the shimmering waters of Lake Bangueolo also known as Bangweula.

There were many rivers throughout Rhodesia, and finding a suitable bridge that would hold the weight of their vehicle was becoming a dangerous undertaking. They finally spotted a bridge with the proper width and decided to take a chance. Slowly they ventured across but once more the bridge collapsed under the weight, sending the truck and its occupants into the river below. Although they landed in a shallow part of the river, it still took several distressful hours to remove their truck from the riverbed. The heat of the day dried them quickly, and with cooler nights, a restful sleep made them forget the fatigue of the day.

Bishop Larue's influence was seen over a wide area. *The Blue Cruise* arrived at the Lake Bangueolo Mission post where they were greeted by the joyful laughter and smiles of a group of native children running around the vehicle.

"What a blissful sight," said Claude. "Their round little bellies and ebony faces smiling with the joy of the Lord shinning through will one day make a beautiful portrait." She stepped out of the truck with her camera in tow and immediately started taking pictures of the frolicking children.

"You must be exhausted from your travels," said the head bishop to the new arrivals. "We are about to partake of our afternoon meal. Please join us for we are most anxious to hear about your journey."

During the meal, Claude and Vincent learned about the work that the nuns at the post were doing at the nearby leper colony.

"Are you not a little apprehensive about your own health while at the leper colony?" asked Claude of one of the nuns.

"My dear Countess, the good Lord has placed us here for a reason. These suffering people are God's children, too, and need our love. Our lives are in His hands," replied the sister. "What most people don't realize," she continued, "is that leprosy can be stopped from progressing if treated with the proper medication at an early stage."

"And I am one of those people who did not know that," said Claude. "I would like to join you tomorrow when you visit the leper colony, to see first hand the work you do there."

"We would be most honored to have you join us," she said.

The rest of the afternoon and evening brought much needed laughter as Vincent and Claude recounted the many times that *The Blue Cruise* ended up in the river.

The next morning, the head bishop accompanied Father de Moor and Lady Kinnoull in their truck following the sisters' vehicle to the leper colony.

When they arrived, Vincent looked around quite surprised. "I expected to see the area fenced off," he said.

"Most people do," replied the bishop. "We felt that these people were stigmatized enough by the physical impairment of this horrific disease. Shunned by family and friends and separated from society by fences and gates made them prisoners in their own land. We tore down the fences to let them know that God has not forsaken them and that they can still play a vital role in their society."

"But what can they do with the deformities that they have?" Claude asked.

"Their deformities should be treated as any other handicap," said the Bishop. "When first confronted with this disease, it can feel like a death sentence. But a great deal has been done in the medical field to help alleviate much of the problem, as you will see by observing the sisters in their daily work."

The colony stretched out before them, looking like any other village. Thatched roof huts were scattered throughout the acres. There was a clinic, a grocery and merchandize store, a school with children running around on a playground, and of course a chapel with a steeple and cross.

"The children . . . I didn't expect to see children here," said Claude.

"I'm afraid leprosy knows no age limit," said the bishop. "Fortunately doctors have discovered that this disease spreads through nasal mucosa rather than skin to skin contact. Some have a natural immunity to it, but unfortunately others are not so lucky."

"As you can see," continued the bishop, "the men who have deformed or amputated legs can still use their arms and those with damaged arms have strong backs and legs. Together they have learned to work as a team to keep their colony in good working order. They have built a water trough using hollow bamboo branches that carries the river water up to the colony using a diesel fueled pumping system that we were able to supply from generous donations. They have also learned to make traps from bamboo to capture small wild animals to feed the colony."

"I see several large huts. What are they used for?" asked Vincent.

"They are classrooms," replied the bishop. "In the first building, the missionary brothers hold classes to teach the men how to use bamboo in the construction of furniture and the second building is were the missionary sisters hold sewing classes for the women, providing them with brightly colored fabrics. Those that cannot sew help prepare meals and keep the colony clean. The third building across from the playground is where the missionary sisters teach the children of various ages."

"We are here to help in any way we can," said Claude.

"We can certainly use your help. The afternoon clinic is about to open. We provide changing of bandages and the distribution of medication to help relieve pain. The sisters will show you what to do."

After awhile, Claude became numb to the sight of missing or deformed limbs, as she helped apply medicine and changed bandages. But the most heartbreaking were those who shied away under hooded cloaks . . . in shame of their disfigured faces.

Chapel was held in the evening to introduce the two outsiders. Claude talked about their journey and their many mishaps, which brought much needed laughter. She explained that one of their tasks was to convince Europeans of the urgent need for their financial support to the Catholic missions in Africa. With their support, more clinics could be built to provide medical supplies and schools.

After the service, a man in a hooded cloak motioned for Countess Kinnoull to come to him. He pointed to her camera slung over her shoulder.

"Yes, I take pictures of the Catholic missions to show donors of the wonderful progress that has been achieved by their support."

"My picture, would it help bring more donor support?"

"Perhaps," she said.

He pulled the hood from his face revealing boil size blisters across one side. "Madame, your eyes show me much kindness . . . I hope my picture will help." He flashed a large smile showing several missing teeth. Claude fiddled with the focus on her camera, blinking to ward off the tears filling her eyes.

Countess Kinnoull on the right helping to apply medicine and bandages at a
Leper Colony (Photo from *La Croisiere Bleue et les Missions D'Afrique* book)

While driving back to the main mission, Claude commented to
Vincent, "In all the places we have visited on our journey so far, I find
myself most deeply moved by this leper colony. Watching these angels
of charity and participating in the things they do, has convinced me that
these sisters are a bit of everything that is goodness and virtue in the
heart of a missionary. I am amazed at the strength of mind of these
sisters who have looked upon such wounds to heal."

"Indeed," said Vincent. "We leave with fond memories of God's
amazing work being done here. But now we must return to the sweet
calm of the shimmering waters of Lake Bangueolo for our last night,
with only the rustling of unseen insects with their treacherous bites!"

"Sounds like we will need to unpack the earplugs and misquote netting," said Claude.

The next day they headed southeast toward Broken-Hill, seeking out the more isolated Catholic missions where their help would be most needed.

"There is one place where we must visit," said Vincent. He directed Claude to drive only a short distance out of their way where they could stop for lunch.

"What in the world is that thundering sound?" she asked. Then she saw the cause of the noise, and stopped the vehicle by the side of the road. A waterfall with a width of three hundred feet stood before them. Its thunderous explosion of water cascaded over a three hundred foot drop.

"This is Victoria Falls," said Vincent. "Isn't it amazing?"

"I have never seen such an enormous and powerful waterfall," said Claude. "Why, the sound reverberates right through the truck." The place was swarming with tourists. She grabbed her camera. "I must take a few pictures," she shouted over the deafening noise.

"Take your time, I'll pick up some lunch at that food stand over there," he shouted back.

After lunch, they left the awe inspiring Victoria Falls and headed south in the direction of Cape Town, the seat of the vicariate of the Western District.

"I must say that I seem to be at odds with myself," said Claude.

"Whatever do you mean?" he asked.

"Well, I come from the bustling city of Paris . . . but I now find that after living the life we have for several months, among those less fortunate and in the most remote areas, that I'm completely unprepared mentally for throngs of tourists."

"Yes, living the life of a missionary can change your whole perspective on what is or is not important in life. What you once held so dear may now have absolutely no relevance in your life what so ever," remarked Vincent.

When they arrived in Cape Town they found a very modern city with streets aligned at right angles and where thousands of cars entered the city from every direction. Life was hectic here as it was in most civilized countries.

The parish centers were accustomed to routine habits and schedules, which they stuck to religiously. Claude waited patiently, anxious to report on their mission research in central Africa, where the Bushmen had their freedom and openness of space. Their report dealt with the difficulty of traveling in such remote areas and the request for much needed vehicle tires for the missionaries, along with the need for more medical supplies and educational materials. The time allowed for Lady Kinnoull and Father de Moor to give their presentation was not nearly enough to cover the entire pressing needs of the various missions they had encountered during this first half of their trip.

After reporting on the impressive statistics of the missions, *The Blue Cruise* headed up the coast to Durban, glad to be away from the bustling city of Cape Town and anxious to continue their assistance at the missions in remote areas.

Chapter 19

The Journey Home

The occupants of *The Blue Cruise* started their journey home on August 29, 1929, hoping to be back in Paris by Christmas. After a treacherous drive from Cape Town along a curving and cliffhanging road, Claude stopped the truck at an outcropping overlooking the Indian Ocean.

While eating lunch, the sound of the ocean crashing on the rocks below was interrupted by a noisy braying sound. They looked around for a heard of donkeys.

"It's coming from down there," said Vincent pointing to the beach below.

"I don't believe it," said Claude. Grabbing her camera, she stood near the edge of the cliff hoping to get a good shot. She focused the lens on an animal family standing no taller than two feet, wiggling their short flat tails and braying at each other as they took turns flapping their flipper-like wings before sliding off the rocks into the ocean below. Two minutes later they waddled back onto shore with fish in their bills.

Claude snapped many shots of the funny creatures. "It's amazing," she said. "I never knew that Africa had penguins . . . did you?"

"It never crossed my mind," said Vincent. "That water must be awfully cold. I always think of snow when I see penguins."

"This is definitely something to write home about." Claude picked up her journal, adding a few notations and a quick sketch of the black and white sunbathers.

After a few hundred more miles, the weary travelers arrived at the port city of Durban. They spent the night at a small mission outside the city, where the missionaries told them of four new clinics that had been operating for only a few months. After reviewing their map of Africa, it was decided that they would add these new clinics to their list to see if they needed any supplies. Their marked route took them inland, arriving in Basutoland the next day.

This area was the most mountainous with some peaks towering 10,000 feet. From a distance, the dark mountain range seemed impenetrable. As *The Blue Cruise* got closer they saw narrow gravel roads spreading out around the dangerously steep face of the mountains.

"Maybe, we should not have added these four clinics to our itinerary," said Vincent looking out his window and down the side of a cliff. I don't think the truck is going to make it on such a steep grade."

"Nonsense," she replied. "We can't desert the clinics, they may be in need of fresh supplies. I'll take it easy," she patted the dashboard. "*The Blue Cruise* hasn't failed us yet."

She cautiously maneuvered the battered truck along the mountain road, only occasionally grinding the gears, finally coming to a stop at the pinnacle. Stretched out before them were luxuriant green valleys surrounded by snowcapped mountains. Slivers of streams and rivers crisscrossed the landscape. They stopped only long enough to take pictures, then slowly headed down to the valley floor. They were able to locate all the clinics and the missionaries were most grateful for much needed medical supplies before the winter snows made the mountain range impassable.

"I keep forgetting that it's winter here. The cooler temperatures are so refreshing compared to the steamy Congo," said Claude. "While you do the inventory on the remaining supplies, I'm going to wash up in that small river over there." She grabbed a towel and a bar of soap.

"Watch out for snakes . . . want my knife?" asked Vincent.

"I think it's too cold for any snakes, today. Like I said before, if I need you, I'll scream." Claude longed to put her tired feet into the river. She removed her muddy hiking boots and pulled off the heavy socks releasing a rush of heat. She rolled up her pant legs then walked to the edge of the river stepping into the cold water. The soft sand on the river floor oozed over her toes like a massage. Bending down to splash water on her face, she felt a strong suction tugging at her feet. Trying to lift one foot out, she began to sway, almost loosing her balance. She was stuck! Any movement caused her to sink even deeper into the gooey mud . . . she was now up to her knees!

"Vincent!" she screamed. "Help! I'm stuck!

When he heard the screams, Vincent automatically grabbed his gun and ran to the river. She tried to turn toward him, but sank to her waist.

"Don't move!" he yelled. "You're in quicksand! I need the rope from the truck. Whatever you do DON'T MOVE!" He ran back to the truck and grabbed a coil of rope.

When they heard the yelling, the missionaries from the clinic came running out pulling a donkey with them.

"We thought you had left," said one of the priests. "We should have told you about the quicksand. The donkey will pull her out once you get the rope around her."

Claude heard a commotion, but didn't dare try to move. She felt the suction of the quicksand tugging at her legs and stomach . . . it was hard to breath.

"Claude, listen to me!" shouted Vincent. "I'm going to throw this lasso over your head, but don't move until I tell you to. And DO NOT put your hands in the sand!"

Vincent swung the lasso over his head sending it flying toward Claude. It missed her by a foot, splattering mud on her face. He quickly pulled the rope back and swung it over his head several times working up momentum then flung it out with more force, the rope found its mark finally surrounding Claude, but she didn't move.

"I'm going to slowly pull the lasso tighter," yelled Vincent. When it gets close enough to reach, I want you to put your hands above your head."

Claude felt her heart thumping in her chest and sweat dripping down her face; the circle of rope was drawing closer and closer. Instincts told her to reach out and grab it, but her arms shot up into the air. Vincent yanked sharply on the rope, cinching it tightly around Claude's waist. The other priests quickly tied the rope to the donkey and they slowly began to drag her from the suction hold of the quicksand.

Once safe on the grass, a nun came running up with a blanket. Vincent wrapped it around Claude . . . swooped her up and carried her into the clinic where the nuns took over. Hot wet towels were brought in to remove any remains of the quicksand, then a tub with oil of lavender water enveloped Claude in a soothing warmth, relaxing her aching muscles. One of the nuns retrieved a set of clean clothes from the truck while another removed all the mud from Claude's boots.

An hour later, Claude walked out with a smile on her face and thanked all who had come to her aid. The missionaries insisted that they at least spend the night and had two rooms prepared for them.

The next morning they joined their hosts for a breakfast of bacon, eggs and pancakes before starting out on the next leg of their journey.

The plan was to continue north traveling over six hundred miles back to the Chilubula Mission. Along the way, they would visit several new missions that the Catholic headquarters in Cape Town informed them were in need of replacement supplies. Occasionally their road trip was hastened by a train ride. Finally on September 15th they arrived at Lake Bangueolo, glad to be back at the Chilubula Mission and home of Bishop Larue as promised.

"My friends, it is so good to see you again," said the Bishop as the travelers stepped out of the truck. "How was your trip to Cape Town?"

"It was quite busy and congested," said Claude. "But one thing that we did discover was that there are less conversions in the busy cities compared to the rural and secluded areas."

"Yes, that is true," replied Bishop Larue. "Often the poor, not having the comfort of material things, seem to grasp the depth of spiritual awareness and are led to the Lord much quicker than those with wealth."

"I must say that I prefer the uncomplicated lives of these devoted Bush people," replied Claude. "I know for myself that even though I come from wealth, I had to slip almost to the end of my rope . . . before the Lord caught me."

"Ah, but the seed was planted in you at a very young age. It just wasn't ready to bloom until now," said Vincent.

Another bishop came up to see what all the excitement was about. "Countess Kinnoull and Father de Moor, I'd like to introduce you to Bishop Jan van Sambeek, one of our most dedicated missionaries," said Bishop Larue. "He is about to take a well-earned thirty day retreat after twelve years of hard work."

"It's a pleasure to meet such a devoted servant of the Lord," said Father de Moor, shaking the priest's hand. Sambeek was a middle-aged man of medium height and slim build. He wore thick, round horn-rimmed glasses and sported a brown handlebar mustache and an untidy beard showing a few flecks of grey.

"We often recognize the heroism of the soldiers during war," said the Countess, "but look around you, let's not forget the unsung heroism it takes for these missionaries to venture out into the unknown wildlife of rural tribal regions of the Bush. Here are the heroes, the missionaries who lay down their lives every day to save just one soul."

"They are not forgotten," replied Father de Moor. "For there is no gift greater than the reward that God will bestow upon them . . . for a job well done."

Their plan to continue to visit other missions was temporarily put on hold when two of the mission's priests became ill and needed to return to Europe. Father Sambeek was also in need of a ride, so *The Blue Cruise* travelers availed themselves to assist the priests to Tanzania where they would be able to board a train. There was now plenty of space in their truck, since most of the medical supplies had been delivered to the various missions. Vincent prayed that the two hundred and fifty miles to their next stop would be without any mishaps.

As they were leaving the wetlands of Bangweulu, hundreds of animals were seen knee-deep in water.

"What kind of animals are those with the long spiral horns?" Claude asked Father Sambeek.

"Those are known as Lechwe, similar to antelope, but only found in the wetlands of South Central Africa. The females are a light golden brown with white bellies, the males are darker in color and have the spiral horns."

A blue grey bird with a seven-foot wingspan swooped past their truck in full dive for a meal in the marsh.

"Now that was an adult Shoebill, recognized by its blue color and shoe shaped bill covered with speckles," said Father Sambeek as *The Blue Cruise* continued on a rather bumpy dirt road heading toward Lake Tanganyika.

Once they reached the lake, Claude was able to book passage on the *Kogoma* stern-wheeler for herself, Father de Moor, their new mission friends and their one-ton truck. After the missionaries were settled and comfortable, Claude met up with Vincent on the outside deck.

"I was just talking with the captain," said Vincent. "Apparently Lake Tanganyika is the world's longest freshwater lake. It extends four hundred miles in a general north-south direction and averages thirty-one miles in width."

"It feels so isolated out here in the middle of nowhere, but I feel very privileged to be able to provide assistance to the missionaries," she replied.

They passed a secluded cove with sandy beaches and palm trees. Large patches of floating water hyacinth plants with their shiny, dark green leaves and bright white flowers moved gently with the breeze across the blue waters of Lake Tanganyika.

The Blue Cruise disembarked at Kigoma in Tanzania, while their ailing missionary friends continued north by train on their return to Europe. Father Sambeek had enjoyed the company of the occupants of *The Blue Cruise* so much that he asked if he could accompany them on their journey back to Algiers. Claude and Vincent agreed that the strength of another man might come in handy, knowing that the rainy season was fast approaching.

Around September 23rd, *The Blue Cruise* traveled toward Burundi and Rwanda. They stopped at several missions along the way, studying reports and discovering that in these regions there had been a flood of new converts despite the very strict catechism instructions and examinations. Claude asked why?

"With the upper class and the leaders in the region embracing the Catholic faith, the natives have followed," said one of the missionaries in the area. "However, this creates another problem. There are too few of us missionaries to meet all the spiritual needs of the population."

"It appears," said Claude, "that once again the Lord has arranged for me to be in this exact place at this very precise time."

"The Lord is never wrong," replied Vincent.

"What do you mean?" asked the missionary.

"I am most honored," said Claude "to be in the position to offer a substantial donation to establish a new post. I pray that this will somehow help alleviate the burdens by providing more missionaries and cut down on the travel time between missions."

"Bless you, sister, but it is we who are honored," said the missionary. The word spread quickly and soon the brothers and sisters of the mission surrounded the Countess, wanting to know more about this monumental gift. The Bishop arrived with a procession of native children running around him curious to see this petite lady who drove such a big truck.

"Countess Kinnoull, we are most humbled by your overwhelming generosity," began the Bishop. "We have been praying for an angel's help with this most significant, but enormous, responsibility of bringing souls to the Church; yet the harvest is great and we are in need of many more missionaries to support their spiritual needs. You are an answer to prayers. The sisters have assured me," continued the Bishop, "that the only name for this new mission post should be . . . *Our Lady of the Angels*. For that is precisely who you are and will always be to us."

With many blessings and prayers, *The Blue Cruise* set off on a one hundred mile trip from Gitega, Burundi, to Kabgayi, Rwanda, but the road that they thought would be only a short stretch turned out to be plagued with many unforeseen obstacles. Claude skillfully maneuvered their truck around potholes, over washed-out roads and across small rivers where there were no bridges. Father Sambeek, eager to help, offered his assistance several times in pushing the vehicle out of a sticky situation. The mud-clogged vehicle coughed and sputtered so many times that they were forced to sleep under the stars while the truck rested. Despite their vehicle problems, there was much laughter when they stopped to camp. Claude was delighted to hear of Father Sambeek's mission work while they enjoyed the savory cooking of Father de Moor. However, not all their camping experiences were so pleasant. With daytime temperatures in the 90's there were frequent tropical rains, and the drop in temperature to the low 60's at night brought uncontrollable shivers, not to mention annoying swarms of locusts.

On October 7th, billows of smoke pouring out from under the hood of the truck, announced their arrival at the Nyundo Mission. It took fifteen days to receive the needed parts to repair the damage to the engine.

Anxious to be on the road again, they pressed on toward Nangara, visiting three new missions along the way and spending two days at Roungou, a mission they had enjoyed on the first leg of their journey.

While in Nangara on October 28th, *The Blue Cruise* team received an urgent call from the *Fathers of the Sacred Heart* for more medical and food supplies; several of the missions had been isolated by flooded roads and downed bridges. They wrote down the coordinates of landing strips that had not been damaged by the rains. If they could get someone to fly in the provisions, then the natives would use canoes to transport the supplies to the isolated missions. *The Blue Cruise* immediately headed south by way of the Avakoubi Mission arriving in Stanleyville, also known as Kisangani, on October 31st.

It was in Stanleyville where they were forced to take a few days rest while a torrential rainstorm blanketed the area. Fortunately there were rooms available at a local hotel.

On the morning of November 4th Claude laid out a map on a table in the restaurant and circled the missions in need of supplies, marking the coordinates for the closest landing strips. A waiter came by to refill their coffee cups.

"Sir," said Claude. "We need to find an airfield where I can fly supplies into the missions that have been inundated by this deluge of storms. Is there one in or near Stanleyville?"

"Yes, Miss. The Simi-Simi Airfield is a few miles on the western outskirts of the city of Stanleyville," he replied.

After breakfast Claude and Vincent headed to the small airfield, leaving Father Sambeek behind to find new supplies that they would need upon their return.

The truck jostled along a rutted dirt road heading toward the airport sign in the distance. After passing through the entrance gate Claude pulled to the side of the road and stopped the truck.

"Isn't it a beauty?" she asked.

Parked next to the dirt road stood a doubled winged De Havilland D.H. 50. Droplets of water from last night's rain clung to its wings and glistened in the morning light.

"It is a most impressive aircraft," remarked Vincent.

"Well, it's even more impressive to fly," she said.

"What do you mean? You're not thinking of flying this, are you?" he asked.

"Now, don't tell me you're worried. I've spent many glorious hours in the cockpit of a beauty just like her."

"Is there nothing you can't do?" laughed Vincent.

Arrangements were made to rent the plane for a few days. After packing the plane with medical supplies, they plotted their route to Banalya, almost directly north of Stanleyville.

Although she had been trained on the 2-seater De Havilland DH37, Lady Kinnoull was quite familiar with the 4-seater De Havilland DH50, which she had flown from London to Paris with Harley on several occasions.

The ground crew handed Claude a clipboard with a preflight checklist and assured her that the plane had a full tank of gas and plenty of oil, but she insisted on checking it herself. She walked around the plane giving it a final visual check, then looked into the cockpit, which had been modified to leave more space in the back of the fuselage for the transport of supplies. Satisfied with the condition of the plane, Claude and Vincent climbed aboard, put on leather helmets and adjusted their goggles.

She checked the ailerons and the magnetos, giving thumbs up to the man standing by the propeller who had removed the wheel chocks. He gave a strong downward pull on the prop and the engine fired up.

"Here we go," said Claude feeling a rush of adrenaline as she increased the rpms to 1500.

Vincent said a quick prayer while they taxied toward the runway. Claude looked for any air traffic, checked the windsock to determine the direction of the air current, and then accessed the runway heading into the wind. When they reached a speed of 42 mph the aircraft was airborne. She pulled back on the stick and they began to gain altitude.

"It seems very odd having a Countess fly me over Africa," yelled Vincent. "Whatever possessed you to take up flying?"

"For the thrill of it. And to see the frightened look on people's faces when they see that I'm the pilot . . . sort of like the look on your face right now." Claude laughed.

"I'm not frightened," he said.

"Well, haven't you ever wanted to do something, just for the thrill of it? Or out of character?" she asked.

"Yes, I know just how you feel. When I became a spy during World War I, it was exciting, something a priest wouldn't normally do. But I also did it for my country."

"Exactly, totally out of character; a countess flying and racing cars and an honest priest being a secretive spy. You feel indestructible. That's the thrill."

Below they could see the overwhelming damage done by the prevailing storms. Roads were impassable and the overflowing rivers swallowed bridges. Dead animals floated in the fields. An occasional truck could be seen embedded in mud.

Lady Kinnoull's joy of flying had turned into a mission of mercy. They were able to fly in to missions built on high ground with landing strips. It took several days to transport not only medical supplies, but also food and drinking water. As they flew back to Stanleyville they watched dozens of natives load their canoes and head out on the treacherous journey to the isolated missions.

After returning the plane they picked up Father Sambeek and continued their journey. From Stanleyville they drove north to Bondo where its Bishop insisted that they visit Bangui, a two hundred mile detour.

When *The Blue Cruise* arrived on November 12th, they found the Bangui Mission in the midst of a huge enthusiastic celebration of the faithful. After the celebration, Father Sambeek stayed behind to help his fellow priests. Claude and Vincent got in their truck and headed across the mission field toward some terraced houses where the missionaries had prepared lodging for them.

"Listen," said Vincent.

"I don't hear anything,"

"That's just it," he replied. "There is an ominous eerie stillness that I don't like."

She stopped the truck and turned off the engine. "You're right, there are no birds, no crickets, no animal sounds at all. What's going on?"

A clash of thunder broke the silence as swirls of dust and leaves swept across the road in front of them.

"It must be a storm approaching," said Vincent.

Claude reached down to restart the engine but it was too late. The truck was slammed with such forceful winds that it lifted them up and threw the one-ton vehicle on its side. They looked back in horror as the storm descended on the Bangui Mission, sending roofs flying in every direction. Cyclone force winds whipped through the area with such speed that within one minute the whole mission was destroyed: the church, the school, and the terraced houses built by the monks were gone.

Father Sambeek rushed to their aid, helping Father de Moor and Lady Kinnoull climb out of the truck. They both staggered around dazed and confused from the sudden and unexpected ruin of the mission. Everyone was in tears, running around making sure there were no serious injuries. They walked through the rubble assessing the damage. All the roofs were completely torn off, walls were caved in and crushed furniture was strewn about. They walked around the crumbled wall of the church. The roof had collapsed onto the altar.

"Look!" yelled Claude, pointing next to the altar.

The one remaining item that was untouched by the cyclone was a statue of the Virgin Mary standing stately among the fallen ruins.

The head Bishop of the mission called all his people to gather around the statue.

"We must pray a prayer of Thanksgiving . . . to the Lord and to the Virgin Mary for the protection of the saints through this horrific storm. Not one serious injury among us. Buildings can always be replaced, but a life is precious in the eyes of the Lord. And now, Divine Intervention has protected our lives. We are truly blessed."

Claude looked around at the tear stained faces of the missionaries and the new converts. She turned to Vincent.

"I now know what I must do," she said.

Claude walked over to the Bishop and asked if she could say something.

"May I have your attention," said the Bishop. "Countess Kinnoull would like to say a few words." Everyone turned toward the Countess.

"In my journey throughout Africa . . . I have grown to have a deep appreciation and respect for the hard work and devotion of missionaries, whose whole lives are devoted to the spreading of the Gospel among people in far off countries. You do this with no thought of your own comforts or needs, other than to glorify the Lord and seek new converts to the faith. I have also seen how the Lord has worked in my life, by putting little detours here and there along this journey. He seems to know better than I where I should be and when. And so it is now that I find myself on a two hundred mile detour, to be here with you at this very moment in time. I was honored to participate in your wonderful celebration earlier today, only to be heartbroken along with you when before our very eyes your beautiful mission was destroyed. But these ruins were just buildings. The Lord does not live in these buildings. He lives within our hearts. And when you evangelize this joy and love of the Lord to others you are planting seeds in their hearts. You may never see the fruits of you labor, but the Lord will see the harvest of many new converts because of your hard work. The Lord is all knowing. And I believe that is why He has placed me here with you today. I have the honor to be in a position to offer the much needed financial support to pay for the full cost of rebuilding your mission."

A gasp of surprise could be heard from the crowd. Then in the half-ruined church without a roof, the parishioners joined hands surrounding the statue of the Virgin Mary and broke out singing a joyful hymn of gratitude.

The men at the mission helped to right *The Blue Cruise*. Claude and Vincent checked their supplies for any damage, and then organized the interior of the truck preparing for their next stops in Chad and Niger.

"It fills my heart with joy to see smiles of optimism back on the faces of these brave men and women," said Claude.

"Father de Moor, Father de Moor," yelled a young missionary running toward the truck. "We have just received word that all of Chad and Niger is flooded and impossible to pass!"

"I see," said Vincent. "Looks like Providence is in control again."

Staying on, they used the next few weeks to aid their friends in clearing the mission of all debris, and preparing the grounds for new construction.

There were immense lowlands in this region and all the bridges had been destroyed. Claude managed to requisition several boats and with the help from some of the missionaries they were able to build a pier and a new bridge. She admired the tenacity of the missionaries and tried to model her work after them, but found this virtue did not work without a lot of patience. It was another eight days of practicing patience before the waters finally subsided enough to show solid ground.

Taking a chance on the break in the weather, *The Blue Cruise* set off in a northwesterly direction toward Garoua. What would normally take over fourteen hours to drive turned into a number of starts and stops due to the impoverished road conditions from the recent flooding. They had been warned about the late November Harmattan winds blowing down from the Sahara Desert, but decided to continue on their journey anyway.

"I don't know how they can possibly call these roads," said Claude as they jostled from one side of the road to the other, swerving to avoid giant potholes and crumbling roadway.

Seven hours later the hot Harmattan winds blew in as predicted, raising temperatures to 95 degrees Fahrenheit and covering their vehicle and the road ahead with heavy sand, severely limiting visibility.

After hitting a rather large pothole, that sent the occupants of the truck hitting their heads in unison, Father Sambeek hollered, "Stop the truck and let me out!"

"Are you out of your mind?" asked Claude.

"Just give me a pole and a flashlight and I'll forge a trail for us. This truck is not going to take much more banging around and neither are our heads."

"I agree with that," said Vincent. "I believe we have just what you need on the side of the truck right behind you. There are a couple of wood poles from our tents, and I have a flashlight under the seat up here."

"Also grab that piece of canvas by the tent pole. Put it over your pith helmet and tie it down with a piece of rope. It will protect you from the blowing sand," said Claude.

As Father Sambeek cleared a path around numerous potholes, Claude drove the coughing and sputtering truck in the direction of the flashlight. After about an hour, the winds subsided, a clear road opened up ahead of them and they were able to make up some time. They arrived in Garoua on December 5th.

Before thinking of herself, Claude immediately started to make the necessary repairs to the truck. She also sent a telegraph back home requesting vehicle parts and tires to be sent immediately by air transport to Gao in Mali. It would, however, be a while before they could visit the Gao Mission; the entire engine and radiator had to be cleaned of sand before they could continue their journey.

The many delays of flooding, cyclones and engine problems had set *The Blue Cruise* months behind their original schedule to be back in Paris by Christmas. So with their truck now free from sand and engine problems, they set off for Kano, Nigeria. What should have been only a distance of twelve and a half hours turned into a two-day drive over worse roads than they had ever encountered before. The tires were being held together only by continual prayers, for they were averaging four to five punctures a day. This kept the good Father Sambeek busy mending tires, a job he assigned himself.

They finally arrived in Kano on December 16th and were greeted by a very friendly reception from the Fathers of African Missions of Lyons. After repairs, *The Blue Cruise* was on the road again.

From Nigeria they made a brief stop in the northern tip of Benin. Claude parked the truck and got out to stretch her legs. She noticed a group of women in the colorful dress of native Africans sitting at a stall with baskets of handmade dolls. She asked if she could take their picture. The women flashed bright white smiles and then posed in a more serious manner, each looking contemplative at the dolls they held in their hands. Claude snapped a few photographs, bought several of their homemade dolls, then rejoined the men waiting by the truck.

"Well, I see you have purchased yourself some Voodoo dolls," said Vincent. "Do they come with pins?"

"On my word," she gasped. "I had no idea!"

"You both have it wrong," said Father Sambeek, chuckling to himself. "Voodoo is completely normal in Benin and other regions of Africa. It is recognized as an official religion. It has none of the negative connotations it has in Europe or America. In fact, it is more than a belief system; it is a way of life, including culture, philosophy, language, art, dance, music and medicine."

"Now I'm intrigued," said Claude. "Please tell us more."

"The Voodoo spiritual world consists of Mahou, the supreme being, and about 100 divinities, or Voodoos, that represent different areas in a person's life. Voodoo priests ask these divinities to intervene on behalf of ordinary people. They have nothing to do with sorcery or black magic. These people do not stick pins into dolls to cause misfortune. It's similar to our Catholic faith with its many saints."

"Surely you can't compare our God to theirs?" she asked.

"No, but you must understand that these people are not aware of any other god. Yet once introduced to our Lord, they see the similarities and convert to the Catholic religion quite easily. They use different Voodoo dolls for the different areas in their life. Similar to the rosary beads that we use when we pray."

"I must say, Father Sambeek, that it is we who are fortunate to have your company during this portion of our journey," said Vincent. "Not only are you an excellent tire mender, but you have enlightened us with your historical knowledge of this area."

"Ah, but it is I who is blessed to be included on this most marvelous journey."

Without further delay, *The Blue Cruise* continued on course to the mission Niamey, Niger, arriving on Christmas Eve.

"I know that we did not expect to be celebrating Christmas so far from our country during this festival so dear to the Christian heart," said Vincent. "But Providence has surely placed us here for a reason."

"Indeed," said Claude. "We are here to witness the mystery of our faith being celebrated in the most diverse regions. A sincere devotion to Jesus is occurring on this very day in the heat of Africa as well as under the gray skies and freezing temperatures of our own country. Just listen to the natives sing with such conviction and devotion for the celebration of the Divine Christ Child's birth."

"Just as precious memories have been seared into our hearts of Christmas celebrations from the past . . . the Holy Spirit has forever sealed within our hearts a love and devotion for the Lord. Let us on this Christmas morning unwrap the gift the Lord as so graciously bestowed upon us, the gift of eternal salvation, and share it with others," said Vincent. The three of them took Holy Communion and then sang the French Christmas carol, *Le Divin Enfant* (*The Divine Child*) before joining the rest of the mission for a celebration breakfast.

The travelers were anxious to get started, not knowing how long their truck would continue to function. The next day they arrived in Gao, Mali to a warm reception from the town's people. Gao is located on the River Niger about two hundred miles east-southeast of Timbuktu on the left bank. Upon receiving the request for new tires, the French government had sent orders to the directors of the regions to offer any necessary assistance to *The Blue Cruise*.

"It is wonderful to receive such an enthusiastic welcome, but my main concern are the tires," said Claude. "Just look at the wheel rims. We've been riding on the inside track of the wheels and now the tire tread is totally gone. Where is our shipment?"

"You're right. The supplies you ordered should have arrived before us," said Vincent. "I'll do some asking around. In the meantime why don't you and Father Sambeek get us settled at the mission. It looks like we might be here for awhile."

About an hour later, Vincent returned with some bad news. "It appears that the plane transporting our precious tires was in an accident and we are looking at another week before the shipment arrives."

"That should give me plenty of time to repair the wheel rims and check for any other damage before we cross the Sahara Desert," said Claude.

It would take eight more days for the tires to arrive before *The Blue Cruise* could set out on their perilous journey across the Sahara Desert to Algiers.

Chapter 20

Crossing The Sahara Desert

After sending out the requested tires, the French government telegraphed the Sahara officials, asking them to monitor and protect *The Blue Cruise* along its route. They agreed to provide a native guide, named Mohamed, who could lead them across the desert to the supply posts along the way. This knowledge put the occupants of *The Blue Cruise* at ease as they ventured into Algeria.

While waiting for their guide, the director in the area gave them a hand radio for any emergency that might occur during their crossing.

Much to the surprise of Claude, when Mohamed finally arrived he had brought his own transportation, a Dromedary Camel.

"I thought you would be riding in our vehicle," she said to him.

"No, no," said Mohamed. "My camel is more reliable."

Years of life under the scorching Sahara sun had etched deep lines in the man's brown, leathery face. His head was wrapped in a turban of white cloth, his body clothed in a black Arab robe. He led his camel to a watering trough. They all watched in amazement as the camel consumed more than thirty gallons of water in a matter of minutes.

"My camel is now prepared to travel for several days with no food or water," said the guide. "Let's go!" The camel kneeled down and Mohamed climbed upon its back. He adjusted his robe revealing a dagger and gun holstered at his waist, then he and his camel trotted off in the direction of Reggane, Algeria.

Claude turned to the other occupants of *The Blue Cruise* and smiled. "Why, this is just like being in the movies," she said, turning the key in the ignition. The truck started up with no problems, much to their relief.

"Follow that camel!" said Vincent. "Countess, if you are ever in need of a job, I can highly recommend you as a first-rate auto mechanic." They enjoyed a good laugh as they started on their last stretch to Algiers and home.

Despite the levity, they were all quite aware of the difficulty of crossing the Sahara with its many hazards.

Claude kept the truck at a steady speed so the tires would not sink into the sand that covered what little of the road she could see. "I am in awe," she said. "Just look at these magnificent golden sand dunes spread out before us. Only God could paint with such an incredible color palette to create this remarkable landscape."

"And let's not forget the animals He created that live in this landscape," said Father Sambeek.

"I know that camels live here, but what other animals could possibly survive the hot days and cold nights?" asked Claude.

"Although the temperature may only register eighty-degrees Fahrenheit, it can feel much hotter because of the lack of cloud cover and the reflections off the golden sands," said Father Sambeek. "Jackals and several types of hyenas roam the Sahara. Rodents, snakes and scorpions thrive in this desert environment. There is also a very small fox that makes its home in tunnels in the sand dunes during the day and comes out at night to prey on the rodents."

"Are any of the snakes poisonous?" Vincent asked.

"I don't believe the snakes are, but the yellow Deathstalker scorpion with its five-striped smooth-tail has a very dangerous venom containing large amounts of toxins."

Up ahead, the camel had lowered itself on the road and the guide slid off. Claude slowed the car to a stop. Relaxing the tension that had built up in her hands and shoulders, she got out of the car and the others followed.

"What are you doing?" she asked.

"Looking for a marker with a five painted on it," replied Mohamed. "But the sand has covered everything. It is called Poste Maurice Cortier, also known as Biden 5." The guide looked around. "Over there," he pointed. They followed him.

Half buried in sand was an old grey metal gas can with a large red 5 painted on it.

"What is the marker for?" she asked.

"It will let you know that there is a source of supply nearby. Could be water or gasoline," he replied.

"What are those mounds of dirt?" asked Vincent, pointing a short distance off the road.

"It looks like wells," said Mohamed. "Let's go look. Bring some containers."

The men carried a few empty water barrels and Claude grabbed her camera. Not wanting the truck to get stuck in the sand they left it parked on the road. The guide rode the camel and the others trekked behind. The eerie silence was only interrupted by the grinding of the sand beneath their feet and the occasional disapproving grunt from the camel.

"This is incredible," said Claude when they reached the mounds of dirt. She adjusted the lens on her camera. "I've never seen anything quite like this."

Before them stood a serpentine trail of hundreds of mounds of dirt resembling a colony of mole holes, but each one large enough to hold a person.

"Why would they dig so many wells?" she asked, while continuing to photograph the strange looking moonscape in the middle of the desert.

"I think I can answer that one," replied Vincent. "In the Middle East they call this a qanat, a gently sloping underground channel constructed to lead water from a high water table to farmland or a village below. In this case, the first shaft is called the Mother Well because they struck water at the beginning of the water table. Every few feet another access shaft is dug for construction or maintenance and to let air into the qanat channel. It also allows access for nomads traveling across the desert. They can drop a bucket down the shaft to retrieve water. Even though the water table keeps getting deeper and deeper, the qanat's water-carrying channel keeps the water supply within reach with a bucket as it gently slopes toward a village. This is often the only way for people to live in these desert villages."

Again the camel knelt down in the sand and the guide slid off its back. He fetched a bucket and long rope that had been tied to the side of the camel. Slowly he lowered the bucket down into the Mother Well, trying not to disturb the mounds of dirt. The men opened their water barrels and filled them from the bucket. They each got a chance to experience retrieving water from the well.

Mohamed dipped a wooden ladle into the bucket. "Drink?" he asked offering the ladle to Lady Kinnoull. She took a long drink then hesitated.

"Why, I'm pleasantly surprised," she said. "It's quite cold and refreshing, with just a bit of a salty taste."

The guide smiled, tied the bucket to the side of the camel and they returned to the truck.

Although it was only about four hundred miles to their next stop in Reggane, they still had to travel through the Tanezrouft Region. This is known as the *Land of Terror* because of its having the harshest environment on the Sahara . . . a place where water, landmarks and vegetation are practically non-existent.

Claude had been exhausted from keeping a steady foot on the accelerator while driving through the sand, which covered every inch of the road. The reddish and golden sands were mesmerizing, lulling the occupants of *The Blue Cruise* into a false security. Suddenly sharp rocks jutted out from under the sand like a tiger pouncing on its prey.

Claude's quick reaction time while racing cars in England sprung into action. She could no longer follow the camel's path, but swerved around tire-piercing rocks with endurance and determination. The scorching heat of the desert brought beads of sweat to her forehead and her tight grip on the steering wheel only exacerbated the nagging tension across her shoulders.

The sand blowing across the jagged rocks turned into the finest and most irritating dust imaginable, permeating any open crevice.

It was a welcomed sight when the piercing rocks finally disappeared and the landscape turned back into red and golden rolling sand dunes. Lady Kinnoull stopped the vehicle and they all got out to stretch their legs.

The still cold water from the well was a welcome respite, and with dusk fast approaching they decided to set up camp. While Claude and Father Sambeek assembled the tents, Vincent started preparing the evening food. Their guide joined them for the meal and warned them about how quickly the desert night could turn dangerous. The drastic temperature changes from the steaming heat during the day to the freezing cold of the night has caught many a foreigner off guard.

"Keep an eye on the horizon," Mohamed warned. "The greatest danger is an unexpected sandstorm. Or worst, desert raiders." The other men offered to share their tent with the guide, but he preferred using his camel as his pillow.

When night fell upon them, the stars in the sky lit up the heavens.

"When I look at the magnificence and splendor of God's creation above us I am in awe, and I have a hard time trying to understand why some people can deny His existence," said Claude.

"Without city lights to dull the image, one is humbled at the wonderment of God's power," replied Father Sambeek. "And to think that all of the stars you see could fit on a pin head compared to God's glory."

"And an AMEN to that," said Vincent.

He and Father Sambeek agreed to take turns at watch, allowing their driver, Lady Kinnoull, to get a full night's sleep.

Vincent took the first watch. The night temperature in the desert had dropped dramatically to thirty-eight degrees Fahrenheit. He put on a heavy jacket and pulled the hood up over his ears. He picked up the binoculars from the folding table and scanned the horizon for any trouble. In the last two hours, there had been nothing but silence.

He looked at his watch. It was almost midnight; he had one more hour to go, then Sambeek would take over. Vincent prepared a fresh pot of coffee; Sambeek would need it. He poured himself a cup, sat back in a canvas chair and put his feet up on a crate. The hot cup warmed his numb fingers. Taking in a deep breath of the aroma of freshly perked French Roast coffee, Vincent closed his eyes, savoring the first sip.

Suddenly a loud scream resonated across the desert. Vincent dropped the cup, spilling hot coffee all over his jacket and reached for his double barrel elephant gun. The screaming didn't stop and barking and snarling noises joined the choir.

Claude and Father Sambeek came running out of their tents.

"What on earth is that noise?" she asked.

"Not sure," said Vincent. "But it appears that the desert takes on a whole new personality in the night."

The guide still lying on his blanket against his camel, smiled, then joined the hyenas in a hearty laugh. "Welcome to the desert night life," he said. "They won't bother us, but I see that Father de Moor has things well in hand if they do." He noticed the gun in Father de Moor's hand.

"How long do they keep this up?" asked Claude.

"This is their play time," replied Mohamed. "They'll be running around for hours." He turned over and pulled his blanket up over his head.

Vincent opened his gun case, retrieving three sets of earplugs and passed them to the others. "Sambeek, you're up in an hour," he said while pouring himself another cup of coffee.

The next morning they got an early start, arriving in Reggane on January 9th. Then pushed on to the small oasis town of Timimoun where they again replenished their supplies. By now they felt that any serious danger was in the past and decided to release their guide.

They spent the next four days at the White Fathers missions between Timimoun and Golea El. It was near here in El Menia, Algeria, where they visited the Tomb of Charles de Foucauld.

Ever since reading about the French priest at St. Augustine Church in Paris, Claude had felt a kinship to this man who had led a similar life as hers. She now knelt down at the foot of his tomb and wept. When she stood, she ran her hand across the top of the tomb, outlining the words etched on the top; *Cry the Gospel With Your Life,* a phrase that Charles was known to proclaim.

"Yes, my brother, I will cry the Gospel with my life," said Claude. "And I pray I will one day meet you in Heaven." She bent down and kissed the top of the tomb.

Then Vincent and Father Sambeek joined her and they prayed, asking the pious hermit of the Sahara to raise the hearts of the apostles who realize the dream of his life.

The trio finally reaches Ghardsia on January 14th. The badly worn tires were a concern, but soon they faced another more challenging problem when the second rear spring on the vehicle broke. With no garage in sight, Claude decided to replace the spring herself.

When they first started to prepare for this journey, the Countess had insisted on bringing along as many spare parts as possible, a reflection on her racing days.

Father Sambeek jacked up the truck and removed the wheel. Claude got to work. The men were amazed by the swiftness with which she performed the task of replacing the spring.

"Again you surprise me," said Vincent. "Your capabilities seem to have no boundaries."

"I can do all things through the Lord who strengths me," she replied with a smile.

The one hundred and twenty-six miles from Ghardaia to Laghouat revealed hills of half stone and half sand. An occasional strong wind obstructed their view of the road causing them to stop several times. They prayed that their vehicle would survive the last few miles to Laghouat.

The swaying palm trees and orchards of Laghouat were a welcomed sight for the weary travelers and they stopped to stretch their legs. They decided with only two hundred miles to Algiers that they would press on toward their goal. The fear of more vehicle problems reined in Claude's desire to race full speed ahead to Algiers.

Finally, on January 16th, *The Blue Cruise* arrived at the Algiers Port with prayers of praise for the Divine Protection of *The Blue Cruise* and tears of joy from the pure exhaustion of its massive undertaking. They were greeted at the docks with much fanfare. The French government had been kept appraised of their whereabouts by hand radio and now a band began to play as officials escorted the occupants of *The Blue Cruise* over to a makeshift platform. Father de Moor and Father Sambeek stepped back and let Countess Kinnoull speak for all of them.

"*Deo Gratias*! Thanks be to God!" said Lady Kinnoull looking out over the crowd. "Thanks to Divine Protection, we have finally arrived at the port to take us home. We have traveled over twenty-two thousand miles in the space of nine months. We have traversed the great African continent from north to south and south to north, visiting and assisting in a record 126 mission posts. Six new mission posts were founded and four vicariates have received significant aid. It has been an extensive, grueling and at times perilous journey. But the magnificence of God's glory has overshadowed any difficulties and brought many joys in seeing the harvest of thousands of new converts.

"The needs are urgent, for there are too few workers to help with the immense rise in those longing to know God in this vast continent. We will never forget the courage and sacrifice of the devoted missionaries that serve in these remote areas. We are forever connected with the precious assurance of the belief of *Only One Flock, One Shepherd!*

"So it is with great humility that *The Blue Cruise* declines all invitations, both official and public, that could give *The Blue Cruise* honor and glory that only belongs to God. Let each of us all do something according to his or her means: for the missions, for church services, and even on our own doorsteps where communistic beliefs are beginning to seep into our neighborhoods."

A loud applause rose from the crowd. Father de Moor and Father Sambeek joined Countess Kinnoull. They waved to the crowd and then returned to their truck, where they said goodbye to their traveling companion Father Sambeek. They exchanged addresses, promising to keep in touch.

"May I take some photos of the two of you with *The Blue Cruise* truck?" asked a reporter.

"Of course," replied the Countess. "Any publicity to draw attention for the reason we took this journey is most appreciated."

"By the way," said the reporter. "I don't know if you are aware of this, but you have just broken the world record in miles for trans-crossing the African Continent in a Citroen truck."

"Well, if it wasn't for the hand of Providence, we would never have completed this journey. So again, to God be the glory."

Vincent and Claude watched as their faithful *Blue Cruise* truck was hoisted into the cargo bay of the *Lamoriciere*, a three hundred and seventy foot long passenger ship that serviced the Marseille-North Africa route and would be taking them to France.

"I can't believe that we are finally homeward bound," said Claude as they ascended the gangplank.

The Blue Cruise at the end of its journey through Africa
(Photo from *La Croisiere Bleue et les Missions D'Afrique* book)

Chapter 21

The Yoke of Christ

Jack and Florence Newbury had been busy preparing for Lady Kinnoull's return to Paris. Florence had made a turkey dinner with all the trimmings, and Jack had washed and gassed the car along with taking the poodle, Ali Baba, in for a grooming. All was ready when *The Blue Cruise* pulled up in front of the apartment.

"Oh, Miss Enid, what a pleasure to see you after such a long time," said Florence. Her husband tried to control the dog, but it pushed its way through to its master, jumping up and licking her face.

Lady Kinnoull wrapped her arms around Ali Baba. "Boy, did I miss you," she said, giving the poodle a big kiss on its head. "Next time I travel you are coming with me."

"It's so good to have you home safely," said Jack.

"It's wonderful to be home. Father de Moor will be joining us for dinner and we'll tell you all about our journey."

The two men unloaded the truck, stacking boxes of camping equipment and cartons of films and photographs in the sitting room, then washed up for dinner.

It took a few days for Claude to acclimate back into the Parisian lifestyle she had left almost a year ago. The parties and material things that meant so much to her artistic friends in Paris, now seemed quite insignificant compared to the work of her new missionary friends spreading the Word of God to some of the poorest people in the world.

She missed the participation in the works of each mission they visited on their African journey. Her life had made sense then; she experienced a calling that had touched her soul. She looked at her reflection in the mirror on her dressing table and knew what she wanted to do.

Vincent was busy in his office at St. Augustine Church preparing his lesson plans for the next group of new converts when Claude walked in.

"Well, what a pleasant surprise. Have you adjusted to Paris life again?" he asked.

"Not exactly," she replied. "That's why I'm here. I've come to a decision about my life that I need to discus with you."

"This sounds quite serious," said Vincent. He put down his lesson plan and turned his full attention to his friend.

"Well, ever since we've returned from Africa, I've been having conflicting feelings. I find I miss our missionary friends, but more than that, I miss being involved in their work. Yet I missed Paris, too. However, I do believe that the Lord is showing me that perhaps I should become a nun."

"A nun! My, this is serious," said Vincent.

"Well, I can't think of anything more rewarding than to live a life devoted to carrying out God's work. I get excited just thinking of the possibilities." She sat down at a desk across from Vincent.

"You must do what you think your heart is telling you," he said. "But there are different orders of nuns that you should be aware of before you make your decision. Let me call in Sister Margaret, she can explain all the differences to you."

After careful consideration, Claude decided to become a member of the Third Order of Our Lady of Mount Carmel (Discalced). As a Third Order Nun, she was allowed to keep her personal possessions. With her influence and money in tact, she felt better able to serve the Church.

When a newspaper article on the desperate struggle of poor single women with children caught her eye, Claude decided to establish a hospice for the terminally ill women that the hospitals would no longer accept. At her own expense, she set up this hospice on the Rue de la Bien Faisance at Paris-Suresues in 1933, calling it *Consolation.* An appropriate name, for she was offering these suffering souls comfort and the reassurance that somebody cared. These women stricken by cancer finally had a loving, caring place in which to complete their final journey and were allowed to have their children stay with them.

Three times a week, Claude donned her nun's habit, carefully placing the brown cloth scapular over her head and adjusting the two-sided apron-like part of the habit. She considered it the yoke of Christ and wore it with devoted reverence. Claude picked up a clipboard and her Bible. Now she was ready to make her rounds as the directing nurse. Her top priority was making sure that the women received everything they needed to make them comfortable during their stay.

She had learned many things from the nuns at the missions in Africa, especially while assisting them with aid to the lepers. Looking up into the eyes of those unfortunate souls and seeing pools of tears when she sat next to them, holding their hands and washing their wounds, had shown Claude that a little bit of human dignity goes a long way.

Now she would sit and pray with these terminally ill women, holding their hands and reassuring them that their children would be taken care of, and that through the blood of Jesus they too could find peace. Before dying, these women and young mothers out of wedlock had found an angel in Sister Claude Kinnoull, entrusting their children to her to be raised.

Claude remembered how at peace she felt a few months prior in Kongolo where she was entrusted with the care of sick native babies. Now she felt a duty to find loving homes for all these soon to be orphaned children.

Sister Kinnoull was true to her word, finding homes for all but four older children who remained in her care; two girls and two boys whom she later sent to the best boarding schools to be educated at her own expense, and to whom she later gave dowries.

Chapter 22

Artistic Expression

Claude had placed several items on the back burner while focusing on setting up the hospice. Now that it was properly staffed, she decided to take the time to delve into the many boxes that had taken over her sitting room. She began opening the containers, then realized that there were hundreds of photographs and films. The thought of having to sort through the whole pile by herself was overwhelming, so she decided to elicit help.

A few hours later, Vincent arrived with a projector. Florence had prepared some refreshments for the showing of the films. She and Jack were excited to finally see the footage of the journey. Together Claude and Vincent sorted through the boxes of memories.

"Well, I must say," said Jack after an entire day of viewing their incredible African pilgrimage, "you have enough fine footage there for several full length movies. I'm sure that there would be a lot of people interested in your journey."

"Now that we have seen the quality of the films and photographs, I agree with you," said Vincent. "We need to have them professionally produced. I'll do some calling around."

About a week later Claude and Vincent found themselves in the international office for *Missionary Propaganda Through Films,* headquartered in Paris. They sat in the waiting room with anticipation, holding the boxes of neatly catalogued film footage. These cartons didn't just hold films; they held their dreams of reaching many unsaved souls for the Catholic faith.

The receptionist stood up from her desk, "Monsieur Bonaire, Head of Film Production will see you now."

Saying quick prayers to themselves, they followed her down a long hallway to a large mahogany paneled conference room.

The receptionist knocked on the open door. "Monsieur Bonaire, I'd like to introduce you to Countess Claude Kinnoull and Monsignor Vincent de Moor."

"Please come in and have a seat. I've followed the newspaper's account of your mission trip to Africa and felt from the beginning that it had the makings of a movie."

"Well, here are all the films," said Father de Moor. He set the boxes on the conference table.

"We've gone through all of them and have marked each film container in chronological order," added Countess Kinnoull.

"My word," said Bonaire. "It looks like with the proper editing and dialogue we could have several full length feature films here. I can't guarantee that will be the case. After all, my production committee will have to view all the films and make their recommendations."

"Our goal in doing these films," said the Countess, "is to draw interest to those who don't always attend church; for them to become aware of the heroic and self-sacrifice of Catholic missionaries. By doing so we are hoping to open their eyes to our faith, and at the least, draw financial support for these warriors of the Lord."

"The task you seek is not an easy one. You must understand that almost the entire film industry is in non-Christian hands. Unless the film is sufficiently interesting, and, for that matter, technically correct, it could very well be rejected."

"We not only put the matter into your hands, but it's been in God's hands from the beginning," said Countess Kinnoull. "I'm sure the two of you can work something out. Good day, until we hear from you."

That year, the *Film Bureau* along with their secular contacts, *Productions Cinematographique,* went on to produce several important movies from those very films – *Unvarnished Africa, Croisiere Bleue,* and *The Sahara.* These were followed by three more films in 1934 – *Mysterious Africa, Pagan's Progress,* and *The Secret Front (*a spy film that was reproduced in the English version under the title *Spied For England*).

Years later, when interviewed by reporters, Countess Kinnoull revealed taking part in a film, playing a secret agent. Although most unusual for a nun, it was completely understandable considering her growing desire for artistic expression.

Ever since she had returned from Africa, the many faces of both the missionaries and the newly converted natives had haunted Claude. Their facial expressions showing their joy of knowing the Lord was something she wanted to capture forever . . . not just in her mind, but also on canvas.

Claude found an old sketchpad she had left behind her bedroom door. She grabbed a handful of drawing pencils and headed to the dinning room table. Florence brought in a breakfast tray.

"Oh, Miss Enid, I'm so glad to see you sketching again. Should I have Jack retrieve your easel and paints from storage?"

"Yes, and have him set it up in the sitting room now that all the boxes are gone," she replied. "Also tell him to have the car ready in about an hour. I'm going to pick up some fresh paints and visit with a few friends this afternoon."

"Very well, Jack will be most delighted."

Claude had missed the weekly café meetings with its eclectic mix of artists and writers. She was especially looking forward to political discussions with her good friend Viscount Leon de Poncins, a fellow aristocratic Catholic author who had recently published a number of books on the secret powers behind revolution.

She felt comfortable and at home walking around the trendy, bohemian Montparnasse district. Her friends didn't judge her; they were all struggling to find their voice in art or writing, or both. It was a welcomed sight to see the faded green and cream awning of the Café Le Select on the corner at 99 Boulevard du Montparnasse. Claude walked past the outdoor seating and entered into a world unchanged by the modernization of many other cafés. Polished, mirrored walls reflected the light from colorful art deco lamps hanging above dark varnished tables with matching bentwood chairs. She passed the over-crowded bar and headed to the back of the room where several red leather banquettes lined the walls.

"There she is," shouted Leon. He waved. "Over here, Claude. We've saved a spot for you."

"We were discussing Agatha Christie's new novel *Murder On The Orient Express*. Have you had a chance to read it yet?" asked one of her friends.

"I'm afraid not," replied Claude. "But I do enjoy her work."

"Then we will change the subject so not to spoil the read for you," said Leon. "We've all been following the exciting account of your mission trip," he continued, "and I bet you have come up with some wonderful ideas for your art work."

"Actually I'm having my easel set-up today and came down to buy some new paints. This time I'm going to try my hand at portraits."

"Fate is with you today," said Leon. "A friend of mine, Ignacio Zuloaga, is having an artist reception this evening and I'd like you to join me. I do believe that he would be able to help you in your portrait painting endeavors."

"Oh, you must meet him," said another friend. "He is recognized abroad and in Spain as the foremost portrait painter of the day."

"How exciting," said Claude. "I'd be happy to join you."

"I'll pick you up at 7 p.m.," said Leon.

"So tell me, I've been away almost a year, what is the political climate like now?" she asked.

"Those Red Leftists are seeping into our educational system," said a woman in the group. "They don't come right out and say they are communists, they go about it in a sneaky way. They infiltrate by putting teachers in at every level of education."

"Well, what can be done about this?" asked Claude.

"Revolution," replied Leon. "Eventually the people will get fed up with the propaganda and will rebel. I spell it all out in my book."

"I know from my experience in Africa that one person can make a difference," said Claude. "We should all do our part, whether financial, journalistic or artistic to fight this communist infiltration."

"Ah, spoken like a woman with the character of a crusader," said Leon. They all laughed and agreed to meet again the following week.

Leon arrived precisely at 7 p.m. to escort Claude to the Paris Salon showing of Ignacio Zuloaga's most recent paintings. When they arrived the salon was bustling with a Who's Who of the art world. Ignacio stood in the shadows sipping a glass of champagne while watching the reactions of his fellow artists.

Leon and Claude made their way through the crowd.

"Leon my friend, I'm so glad you could make it. And who have we here?" asked Ignacio.

"May I present Countess Claude Kinnoull. She just mentioned today that she wants to try a more realistic approach to her artistic endeavors, more toward portrait painting. Of course I insisted that she meet you, the world's best portrait painter."

"So, my dear, how long have you been painting?"

"I've spent a few years doing free flowing impressionistic work. But ever since my journey to Africa . . . I've been haunted by the faces of the people I met. I want to capture that image. I want to paint their eyes . . . so one can see deep into their souls."

Ignacio had been introduced to quite a few people calling themselves by royal titles to impress him, but he saw something entirely different in this countess. He saw in her a sincere desire to develop a technique of portrait painting that causes a person to want to linger on the painted image. It was a technique he had spent years learning.

"I'm always eager to encourage young artists," said Ignacio. "I have a studio here in Paris, but I'm only here for a few months out of the year. We could start tomorrow, meeting twice a week for three months, if you are serious about lessons. We can talk about the price after my showing."

"Price is no consideration," said Claude. "And I prefer to pay in advance so the money issue does not interfere with the creative process."

"Very well, we can start tomorrow at two o'clock at my studio in the Montparnasse District." He handed her a card with his studio address.

"Until tomorrow," she said, as a group of admiring fans swarmed around Ignacio.

Thus began a long lasting friendship of mutual respect between student and teacher. Claude's art improved dramatically over the years. She had numerous showings at various galleries throughout Paris. Although Ignacio was in Paris for only a few months out of the year, he always looked forward to working with Countess Kinnoull. He told her that she should come to Spain where he could continue with her lessons. She assured him that one-day she would, but for now her many commitments, especially at the hospice, did not allow for much traveling.

Chapter 23

The Countess Sub Rosa

Claude had always looked forward to the once a week café visits with her artist and writer friends. However, as of late, their light-hearted banter had turned toward much more serious issues. The unstable political situation in neighboring countries upset Claude. She decided to consult with Father de Moor regarding those concerns.

"You might think me a bit unstable when you hear my proposal," said Claude as she sat down in Father de Moor's office.

"Nothing you do would surprise me," he replied.

"There is something that has been floating around my brain for awhile. Since you were a spy during the last war, I thought you might be able to help me."

"Now I am intrigued!"

"Do you think I have what it takes to be a good spy?"

"What on earth are you talking about, Claude? Now, you want to switch from being a nun to . . . a spy?"

"Well, not exactly. I'd still be a nun. Like you remaining a priest, while a spy."

"Oh dear, have I become such a bad influence on you?"

"Don't be silly. You've been a great role model. You've taught me to standup to injustices and to help those unfairly treated. The world news is troubling and I'm noticing how the Communist Party influence is invading our daily lives . . . I want to do something about it."

"Well, in that case, to answer your question, yes, I think you have all the makings of a great spy. Your title of countess allows you into places that the average person cannot access. Your petite size throws off any suspicion. Your knowledge of automobiles and planes is a great asset. You are a determined and professional individual who has lived in both high society and low missionary conditions. Being a nun is a good cover for your protection. But you lack one thing that is crucial; you have no training in weapons."

"But you could teach me that, couldn't you?" she asked.

"You would definitely need training on how to handle a small handgun. And yes, I could teach you a few tricks of the trade. But I can't emphasize enough that this is a dangerous business. The people you would be spying on would not think twice about taking your life. The question you have to ask yourself is would you be able to take another person's life to protect yours?"

"That is a hard one," replied Claude. "I pray that God will not put me into a situation where I would have to use a lethal weapon. However, if I was in eminent danger of being killed and there was no way out, than I would not hesitate to use a gun."

"Then the best concealed weapon for you would be the .32 Colt automatic. It's small, at 7 inches long, and only weighs 24 oz. It holds 8 rounds and is extremely accurate," said Vincent. "I'll check with the *Deuxième Bureau* and see if they can use you. If they agree, we'll start your training next week."

"Jack and Florence will certainly be surprised if I become a spy."

"Well, they must never know. Nobody must know!" said Vincent. "Your viability as a spy is dependent on secrecy. Your life depends on it! Now you go home and seriously think this over. I'll let you know what the Bureau says."

A week later, Claude felt the cold steel of a 1903 .32 caliber Colt handgun in the palm of her hand.

"Its quite lightweight," she remarked in surprise.

"Yes, it is a perfect pocket gun," said Vincent. "But safety first. Always make sure to clear the gun before you work on it. Remove the clip and check the chamber. There is a manual safety lever and a grip safety that won't allow the gun to go off if it is dropped by accident. There are two very small sights you can use for aiming, however, if you hold both arms straight out and shoot, you should hit your target with no problem, considering the extreme accuracy of this weapon."

Claude followed his every instruction and was surprised when she loaded the gun and shot her first round. "Why, there is hardly any recoil at all."

"That is why many women prefer this gun. But above all, you must remember that this is a deadly weapon and if you pull it out to use it; you are aiming to kill whatever or whomever is threatening you."

"I understand," said Claude. She reloaded the gun. Her training in self-defense continued for several weeks until any reactions to threatening circumstances became automatic to her. Her final test involved several Bureau spies. She was given a sealed envelope to be delivered to a specific location by a precise time, while touching base at several shops throughout Paris without being detected along the way.

Claude was up for the challenge. She left her apartment at noon as instructed and observed several suspicious looking people on both sides of the street. She walked quickly in and out of alleyways and stores and thought she had given the other spies the slip. However, she caught the reflection in a store's window of a man across the street, awkwardly trying to hide his face with a newspaper. Having been trained to suspect everyone, she slipped into a dress shop and went quickly into the dressing room. From the over-sized handbag she was carrying, Claude retrieved a short blond wig, a wool sweater, a long skirt and a pair of walking shoes. She changed clothes and then rolled up the dress she had been wearing, tied it around her stomach and pulled the sweater over it. When she stepped out of the dressing room, Lady Kinnoull could not be found; she was replaced with a blond, pregnant woman who was having a dizzy spell.

"Oh, my dear, you look rather pale. Please have a seat on this stool," said the salesgirl. "Would you like me to call you a taxi?"

"That would be most kind of you. I'm afraid I've over exerted myself today."

A rumbling of thunder could be heard in the distance and the rain began to fall. When the taxi arrived, the salesgirl told the pregnant woman to lean on her. She opened the door and held an umbrella over their heads and escorted the woman to the taxi.

"Where to, lady?" asked the driver.

"Turn right at the end of the street, then go for a block and turn left." At the end of the block she told him to turn left again. "Now you can let me out at that very large cathedral."

"Lady, we've just gone around the block."

"Indeed, and hasn't it been fun?" She paid the driver, then stepped out of the taxi and ran into the church. She hurried down the outer aisle to the main offices.

"Excuse me, Sir, aren't you Father de Moor?"

The priest turned around. "How may I help you?"

She reached into her over-sized handbag and pulled out a large, sealed envelope. "I believe this is for you."

Father de Moor's mouth dropped open, then he laughed. "I knew we could count on you. I'm most pleased with your progress."

Chapter 24

The Spanish Civil War

After World War I a peace reigned over Europe. However, this was a different Europe with changing borders and the emerging of new nations. Germany and Austria were especially affected, for they had to not only relinquish a lot of territory to the victors of the last war, but were expected to pay restitution to other countries for damages that had occurred. This was not an easy task considering that most of the countries involved in World War I were now in debt. The winning countries began borrowing money from the United States with no means of repayment. The situation grew worse when inflation in many countries made it impossible for people to save any money.

In 1929 when the stock market crashed in the United States it brought about the Great Depression. The effects were not constrained within those borders, but spread throughout Europe, leaving little chance for the damaged continent to recover. The poverty level rose dramatically, with millions of people out of work. This was now the perfect breeding ground for two movements to assert their powers:

(1) Communism – Known as the Left, was a political Karl Marx theory, advocating class war leading to a society in which all property is publically owned. Each person works and is paid according to their abilities and needs.

(2) Fascism – Known as the Right, wanted a strong national government. Fascists sought to unify their nation through a totalitarian

state that promoted the mass mobilization of the national community. They were hostile to liberal democracy, socialism and communism. They have a devotion to a strong leader and an emphasis on ultra nationalism and militarism.

In 1931 the spread of the Great Depression brought dire consequences to Spain, forcing out Prime Minister Primo de Rivera. The next five years brought battles between Socialist, Marxist and Stalinist groups.

The Vatican viewed Communism and National Socialism as great threats to the Catholic Church. Those threats came to the surface on May 17, 1933, when the Spanish government enacted the *Association Law,* requiring all heads of religious orders to be of Spanish decent. Members of religious orders were forbidden to work in any industry or trade. There was uproar when church schools were eliminated and religious orders were not even allowed to teach secular education. When the Pope strongly protested against this, the government confiscated all church property, yet allowed the clergy to remain in Spain and maintain the property. For the next three years, without schools to provide an income, the priests and nuns lived off the fruits and vegetables that the church land produced and the meager donations of faithful parishioners, themselves almost destitute.

The Communist Party's insidious spread of influence and control seeped into every nook and cranny of peoples' lives. The Party believed in a clean sweep of everything, aiming to start from nothing. Spanish youth groups merged with the communist youth groups and were told that they must spread their new beliefs through dominance by using the torch, oil, and dynamite to clean wounds that plagued Spain. These wounds were allegedly the rich and the priests. Landlords fled for their lives when communist militants confiscated their mansions and land for equal use by all people. The preamble of the Madrid Socialist program was a complete endorsement of communist-style, ultimate revolution, the destruction of the existing society down to its roots.

Revolutionary mobs burned five churches, a convent, a seminary, and a Catholic school in the southern port city of Cadiz. When General Franco arrived two days later, he exploded in anger at the military governor of the city:

"Is it possible that the troops of a barracks saw a sacrilegious crime being committed and that you stood by with your arms folded?"

The governor informed Franco that the government in Madrid had forbidden him to intervene in such matters.

"Such orders," snapped Franco, "since they are unworthy, should never be obeyed by an officer of our army."

The revolutionaries were having their way, burning churches all over Spain. The Center of Catholic Studies was destroyed and almost four hundred holy images removed.

Finally, in February 1936, the Popular Front Government was elected, much to the consternation of the Republican left-wing militants. These militants were so enraged that they plotted a rampage of anarchy and atrocities. They were determined to rid Spain of all connection to the Catholic religion. Destroying the churches and their religious relics was not enough; they now aimed to ridicule the bishops, priests and nuns hoping to run them out of Spain for good. But the faithful remained steadfast in their beliefs. They prayed with passionate intensity and sang praises to the Lord with unwavering devotion. But this just intensified the anger that the communist militants felt toward these seemingly unbreakable souls.

When Italian troops invaded Addis Ababa, Ethiopia, on May 9, 1936, with a triumphal win, it emboldened Mussolini. Two months later he traveled over three thousand miles to intervene in the affairs of Spain. But by now, General Francesco Franco serving in Spanish Morocco had heard of the slaughter of the priests, nuns and bishops by the Republic of Spain. Franco, being a devote Catholic, decided to save his beloved Spain from this barbarism. He contacted Mussolini, who provided the aircrafts needed to transport Franco's Nationalist Army back to Spain.

During the Spanish Civil War both sides (the Nationalists and the Republicans) were guilty of atrocities. But Republicans perpetrated the worst brutalities against Catholic clergy with eleven bishops, over sixteen thousand priests and almost three hundred nuns savagely slaughtered. It was these atrocities that championed Countess Kinnoull's commitment to Franco's cause.

Franco's mental development as a child grew into a dual personality later in life. This mental confusion formulated from his being subjected for many years to his father's absolute power and indifference, clashing with his mother's quiet, soft-spoken upbringing of their children in the Catholic religion. These fluctuations in Franco's mood swings became most evident when on September 28, 1936, a formal decree announced that Franco would assume all the powers of the new state. A commander in the African army who at one time had Franco under his command stated, "You don't know what you've just done . . . you don't know him like I do. If you give him Spain, he is going to believe that it is his. He won't let anyone replace him, either during the war or after until he is dead."

With the condemnation and slaughter of Catholics by the Republic, the Nationalists turned the war into a Christian crusade. Pope Pius XII compared the Christian heroism of the Nationalists with the barbarous atheism of the Republic, bestowing on Franco the higher power he needed to convince the international community to support the Nationalist cause.

Always a strong Catholic, Franco's thoughts turned more to religion than ever. His practice of almost daily devotions contributed to what eventually became a sense of mission. Franco was now perceived not only as the defender of Spain, but of the Catholic faith. With such recognition a grand and lavish ceremony was planned for October 1, 1936, to welcome the new Chief of State at his headquarters established in the Episcopal Palace in Salamanca. Franco's picture began to appear on cinema screens and on the walls of offices and schools, giving him the title of Caudillo (compared to the title Fuhrer).

On March 23, 1937, Franco summoned General Emilio Mola to discuss the assault on the Republican controlled city of Bilbao in Northern Spain. It was agreed that an attack would proceed with no regard for the local population, which consisted of many Basque Catholics. This brought about a distressing situation for Franco. He needed to distance himself from what he knew would be a tragedy for some innocent lives, but an unavoidable condition of civil war. He traveled to Pedraza Castle in the province of Segovia, about one hour drive from Madrid, where he was the guest of Claude's art teacher and friend, Ignacio Zuloaga.

Father de Moor received disturbing accounts of the atrocities committed against fellow priests, nuns and bishops at the hands of the Republic of Spain, which he sadly conveyed to Countess Kinnoull one Sunday after church.

Vincent handed Claude the newspaper. "You would think there would be more coverage on the horror being committed against the Spanish Catholics . . . instead only articles of praise for the heroism of Spain's Republic forces and their desperate need for supplies."

Claude skimmed through the articles and glanced at the propaganda pictures . . . then she saw it. "This can't be!" she yelled. "Look at this picture." She held up the newspaper for Vincent.

He looked at the picture and read the caption. *A gathering of friends assisted George Harley Hay, the 14th Earl of Kinnoull, in loading emergency food and medical supplies onto his large yacht, headed for the beleaguered Republican Forces in Spain.*

"Is this the man you were married to?" he asked.

"The one and only . . . I hope he rots in hell for what he's doing. To think he was a secret communist all these years. No wonder we never saw eye to eye on things." Her face flushed with anger.

"Now, Claude . . . we best be leaving the decision on who goes to hell or not up to the Almighty."

"Well . . . maybe the Nationalist Army will blow his yacht to smithereens before it can get into port." Shocked by the cruelty shown to the Catholic religion and its people, she looked at Vincent with tear-filled eyes.

"Maybe what is really needed is a counterbalance to all this propaganda," he said.

"You are absolutely right. This is something I can do," she said. "In France, our old Christian world sleeps unaware of the danger, as the sleepwalker who skirts the abyss of night without even thinking of the danger. They must wake up, look beyond the Pyrenees Mountains where Communism lives, and believe that the danger is real. They must wake up and fight against it."

The time had come for Countess Kinnoull to leave for Spain.

Knowing she could not mention the real reason for her visit to Spain, Claude informed Florence and Jack that she would be leaving her Paris apartment and her cherished poodle in their capable hands while she continued to pursue her desire to study portrait painting under the tutelage of Ignacio Zuloaga at his studio in Spain.

"How long may we expect you to be away?" asked Jack.

"I'm afraid it will depend on how attuned I am at producing a more realistic approach to my paintings."

"Well, rest assured your apartment and the dog will be well taken care of, and waiting for your return," said Florence.

Ignacio was thrilled that the Countess had finally taken up his offer for lessons at his home. He insisted that she stay at his estate so they could discuss art into the evenings. When she arrived in the middle of March, 1937, she was shocked to see that his home was actually the Pedraza Castle, which he had bought in 1925 and totally remodeled.

"Countess Kinnoull, I'm so pleased that you have finally accepted my invitation for art lessons in my beloved country of Spain. I'll have your luggage taken to your room, but first I would like you to meet my daughter, Lucia." A slender young woman with cropped, dark brown, wavy hair, about the same age as the Countess, descended the stone stairs to greet their guest.

"I'm excited to finally get to meet you, Countess Kinnoull. My father has told me so much about your artistic abilities. He sees a promising future in art for you. And I am honored to have been selected as your escort and guide to see our beautiful city of Pedraza."

"Oh, but it is I who is most honored to be under the tutelage of Spain's most admired artist, and to finally meet his family."

"I'm afraid my wife and son are traveling throughout Europe and are not expected back for another month," said Ignacio. "But knowing how well you young people enjoy the nightlife, Lucia is looking forward to showing you some of Spain's incredible clubs. Although I enjoy being a recluse in my castle in the evening, you might enjoy the Spanish nightlife, which gets started around ten. Now, Lucia show the Countess to her room and we will meet later in my studio."

Claude was pleased with her room and grateful that the fireplace had been lit; she had become chilled by the cool damp weather. It was a comfortable room filled with massive dark mahogany furnishings trimmed with decorative wrought iron. Two large windows framed in stone offered a picturesque view over the countryside that stretched for miles. She noticed that the maid had carefully emptied her suitcases, placing the contents neatly in the corner armoire. Before leaving on this trip, Vincent had given her several dark leather suitcases with false bottoms to store eavesdropping equipment, cameras and her gun. But at the last minute she decided to use her stylish tapestry luggage, which she felt was much more appropriate for a countess to own, thus hoping not to draw suspicion to herself from inquisitive servants. One could not be too cautious during these trying times in Spain. However, as a photojournalist, she carried a large camera case that did have a false bottom, which contained her gun, ammunition and false identification in case of an emergency. Claude quickly freshened up and rang for the maid.

There was a light knock on the bedroom door. The Countess took one last look in the mirror then opened the door.

"You rang for me, Madame?" A stout, gray haired, middle-aged woman stood before her. She wore a mid-calf, black dress covered with a heavily starched white apron, looking as if she could handle anything that might occur in the castle.

"Yes, I am to meet Mr. Zuloaga in his studio and need some directions."

"I will be pleased to show you, Madame. Just follow me. My name is Inez and if you need anything during your stay with us I will be happy to be of service."

"Thank you, Inez, for the warm welcome. How long have you worked for the family?"

"Oh, since the children were first born. You see, I started as their nanny and now look at me; thirty years later I'm running the whole castle. Well, here we are at the door to the master's Tower Studio. Enjoy your afternoon."

Claude opened the door and stepped through into a brightly lit circular room with Spanish tiled floors and tall ceilings. Paintings in all sizes covered the walls.

"I see you have found my hideaway," remarked Ignacio upon seeing the Countess.

"Thanks to my amiable guide, Inez."

"Our dear Inez. I believe this castle would be in ruins without her capable managerial competence. But now we must start your lessons. I have placed an art easel next to mine so we can capture the natural light from the windows. The warm glow of the afternoon sun puts me in a most contemplative mood."

Claude perused the collection of various themed portraits hanging on the walls. "I see that you have developed a realistic style of Spanish tradition with your impressive bullfighters and flamenco dancers."

"Fortunately I have family and friends who are willing models. Perhaps I will have the opportunity to capture you in a beautiful Flamenco attire before you return to Paris?"

"I would of course be most honored to have my portrait painted by the great Zuloaga."

"You flatter me, my dear. Now let's see if I can teach you the technique of capturing a person's soul through the pools of their eyes." And so their afternoon art lessons began.

Claude was an astute student and quickly embraced Ignacio's intermingling of earth tones, using slight degrees of difference in the intensity with muted tones of maroon, black and grey pigments.

"Do not be afraid of bold, heavy strokes in portrait painting," he said. "Dainty, timid brush strokes give you away as a woman. And few women find it easy to break into a predominately male venue. Using your chosen name of Claude will cause your work to be admired for its artistic value."

"I see where your dark, broad brush strokes draw attention to the light facial tones, and to the facial expression of your subject," she said.

"Precisely. And for your next lesson we will work on the subtle, mystical sadness of the Spanish soul as seen through their eyes. But for now I will retire for an hour and meet you in the library for cocktails and discussions of the world political scene."

Although time had slipped by quickly, Claude welcomed the respite and the hot pot of tea and biscuits waiting upon her return to her room. By the time 6 p.m. approached, she had changed into a black evening gown and had found her way to the library. One of the servants was tending to the logs in the massive stone fireplace while another had brought in a tray of cocktails, followed by Lucia wearing an aquamarine sequined evening gown and her father wearing a less formal black dinner jacket.

"Has father told you of our plans for this evening?" asked Lucia. She helped herself to a cocktail from the tray the servant was holding.

"I'm afraid we have been so busy in the studio that we haven't had time to discuss it," said Ignacio, handing a cocktail to Claude. "Both you ladies look lovely tonight."

"Well, we are having a simple dinner here with father at about eight, then you and I will explore our beautiful little village of Pedraza de la Sierra. There are several magnificent restaurants that provide entertainment starting around ten."

"Sounds delightful," said the Countess.

"Pedraza is one of Spain's most charming walled villages, dating back to medieval times when people needed protection from invasions. Although we have only five hundred residents, we allowed hundreds of people seeking shelter during the Civil War uprising to remain and feel safe within our walls," remarked Ignacio.

"As a photojournalist, I heard the most horrendous reports of atrocities against the Catholic Church and the murderous slaughter of innocent priests and nuns."

"Yes, it was all true," he said. "We remained safe in our walled-in village in the middle of nowhere. But those seeking sanctuary with us were in a state of shock, barely able to describe the horrific conditions and the monstrous animals into which our fellow Spanish citizens had become."

"What happened when Generalissimo Franco was appointed the new Chief of State?" she asked.

"All I can say is thanks to God and to Franco for being our liberator from this totally chaotic, destructive behavior. There are still areas in the northern Basque region that are fighting against Franco. Even though I'm from Eibar, which was leveled by Franco's liberation, I know he is a Catholic and will eventually bring peace to all of Spain. We will work with all our strength to rebuild a New Spain. To

Spanishize our country and get rid of all outside influences. That is my dream in art. I will dedicate the years that are left to me to that end."

Claude now knew that she had a true political ally in her friend, someone she could depend on if the situation presented itself.

A servant came into the library and rang a bell, "Dinner is served, Sir." Ignacio held an arm out for each of the ladies and escorted them to the dinning room.

By 10 p.m., Ignacio excused himself for the evening and Lucia and Countess Kinnoull were whisked away in a chauffeur driven automobile to visit the clubs in the village.

The ladies were dropped off at the only entrance to the town, which opened into a labyrinth of narrow cobblestone streets.

"I've never seen such an unusual city," remarked Claude

"Notice the homes of the aristocracy embellished with their personal coats-of-arms," said Lucia. "Citizens of Madrid often come here seeking the calming tranquility of the surrounding Guadarrama Mountains, but can still enjoy a varied night life with our numerous restaurants."

They turned the corner walking into a wide-open area.

"Here in the center of the village is Plaza Mayor, with its rustic colonnades and balconies often serving as a bullfighting arena. You must see at least one bullfight before you leave Spain."

"I have such a love for animals that I'm not sure I could endure the killing of the bulls," replied Claude. "Besides there doesn't seem to be any other way to escape but by the front gate and I think the bulls know that."

"Bull fights are such a part of our culture," said Lucia, "that we don't give it a second thought. Why would you want to escape? You're perfectly safe here. We have no crimes precisely because there is only one way out. Ah, here we are at our first venue. Entertainment by the Spanish gypsies can be mesmerizing," she warned.

They entered the Café Cantante and were seated near the left side of the stage. The lights dimmed and a single spotlight showcased a striking silhouette of a flamenco dancer against the drawn curtain. As the guitar music began to play the curtain slowly opened to reveal a slender, dark haired woman in crimson. She was dressed in a high collared but low backed traditional flamenco dress with a cascading ruffle from her knee to her ankle. The dancer slowly raised her arms above the white roses clipped to the sides of a tightly coiled braid at the back of her head, gracefully moving her hands to the rhythmic beat of the music. The guitarist methodically increased the beat as his tenor voice recounted the courageous struggle of the Spanish gypsies' life. The dancer began a complex rhythmic pattern of toe-heel clicking steps swirling from side to side across the stage, keeping beat with the guitar while her upper body moved with grace . . . allowing her hands to tell the story. A thunderous applause with a standing ovation followed the performance.

"Did I not tell you that you would be mesmerized by the gypsies?" asked Lucia.

"The whole audience was mesmerized," said Claude. "The dancer, the song, the guitar . . . threaded together they formed the perfect tripartite art form. It was amazing to watch."

They had a few more drinks then moved on to several other restaurants whose entertainment could not compare to the flamenco dancing. The last place had a much more sedate atmosphere with only a single piano bar, but with a most intriguing clientele.

The ladies were seated and ordered coffees. The piano player surprisingly was playing Cole Porter music and several couples were dancing. Several tables to their right sat two German officers and another man in a suit with his back to them. When the waiter brought their coffees he also delivered a message.

"Compliments of the gentlemen in the uniforms at the table near the back." Both ladies turned toward the men and raised their coffee mugs to thank them.

"I hope they don't ask us to dance," said Lucia. "I don't want them to know who I am."

"We don't want any trouble, Lucia. If they ask, it's better to dance with them and not lie about who we are. They are Germans and will find out who we are, if curious."

The ladies sipped their coffees and when the song ended, the two officers approached the table. Claude immediately recognized the slate-grey trousers with their wide outer stripe of scarlet worn with knee-high, glossy-black jackboots, as the uniform of a general.

"We couldn't help but notice that you two lovely ladies are alone," said the older of the two officers. "I am General Field Marshall Hugo Sperrle and this is General Wilhelm Ritter von Thoma. We were wondering if we could have the pleasure of this next dance."

"It is the least we can do since you have paid for our coffees," replied Claude.

"But you have us at a disadvantage," said Sperrle. "You know our names, but with whom do we have the pleasure of dancing?"

"I am Countess Claude Kinnoull and this is my friend Lucia Zuloaga." The Countess stood and Hugo Sperrle bowed, clicked his heels and offered his arm. He was a bear of a man with a close-shaven head and eyes as cold as steel. Claude was glad she had worn high-heels.

"Zuloaga, a name I'm quite familiar with," said von Thoma. "But it is Ignacio Zuloaga whose art I've admired for years. Any relationship?"

"That would be my father," replied Lucia.

"Then I am honored to be dancing with the beautiful daughter of a world renowned artist."

Lucia lucked out, thought Claude. General von Thoma was definitely the better looking of the two. He was tall and muscular. There was a kindness in his eyes, a cultured man with an appreciation of the arts. The music began to play as the couples approached the dance floor.

"Tell me, General Sperrle, what has brought you to this quiet walled village of Pedraza out in the middle of nowhere?" asked the Countess.

"Sometimes even active military men long for a bit of respite from the constant ravages of war. But you are not from Spain, either. Do I detect an English accent, maybe a slight hint of French?"

"You are very astute, General Sperrle. I was born in London but now make Paris my home."

"And what brings you to Pedraza?" he asked.

"I'm a guest of Ignacio Zuloaga, studying portrait painting."

"Perhaps another time, another place, you could paint my portrait?"

"Perhaps," she replied.

As the general swirled her around the dance floor Claude felt his hand on the small of her back, pulling her closer. She could tell that this was a man used to getting what he wanted. The smell of alcohol reeked at every word he spoke. Finally the music began to slow. As he twirled her one last time she caught a glimpse of the man who had been seated with the generals. She recognized Ramón Serrano Suñer, the brother-in-law of Generalissimo Franco.

When the piano player took a short break the men escorted the ladies back to their table.

"May we join you?" asked General von Thoma.

"I'm afraid we must be leaving," said Countess Kinnoull, "I have a busy day tomorrow.

"Please allow us to escort you ladies safely home," replied General Sperrle.

"Thank you, but that won't be necessary," said Lucia. "Our chauffeur is waiting."

"Then thank you for a most enjoyable evening, ladies," said von Thoma.

"Perhaps we will see you again," said Countess Kinnoull.

"Perhaps," replied General Sperrle. Adjusting his monocle, a stern but curious look clouded his face as he watched the ladies leave.

Chapter 25

An Unexpected Guest

It did not take long for the village to learn that a Countess was a guest of Ignacio Zuloaga. Soon invitations arrived requesting her appearance as guest of honor at several of the more influential residents' estates. This was most welcomed by Claude, since her title allowed her access to people in aristocratic positions in society. She would also be able to maneuver among high government officials attending such parties without attracting suspicion. This access put her in a position to keep the Paris and British Bureaus abreast of any communist activity that might come up in overheard conversations; they were also especially interested in Franco's movements.

It was customary in Spain that a gentleman did not call on a lady until at least noon because of the into-the-early-morning hours of parties and entertainment. Though Claude would have preferred to sleep in, she set her alarm for eight o'clock. She did not want to be disturbed while coding a message to Vincent regarding any suspicious activities during the week. She was anxious to report of the sighting of Ramón Serrano Suñer dining with the two generals, and was curious why they were meeting in such an isolated village.

Claude finished her message and inserted it into a crocheted bookmark. She quickly dressed and grabbed both her camera and Bible, placing the bookmark in the middle of the book. She quietly went downstairs to the kitchen where she found Inez busy baking muffins.

"My, you are up early, Lady Kinnoull. May I offer you something to eat?"

"Thank you, but I'll wait and eat when the others are up. Last night in the village I saw a church bell tower and thought I might attend an early service, if there is one, and take a few pictures."

"That would be the Church of San Juan and there are several services throughout the day. I'll call the chauffeur."

"That would be most kind," she said. "I'll wait outside."

The chauffer dropped the Countess off at the gate to the village and said he would wait for her. She covered her head with a lace scarf and entered the Church of San Juan just as the service was about to begin. Only a handful of parishioners were in attendance. Dipping her fingers in the Holy Water, she knelt and made the sign of the cross. She sat near the back of the church on the right side closest to the confessionals. Claude bowed her head and prayed that she was doing the right thing.

Those in attendance stood as two priests entered followed by a dozen choirboys chanting a familiar Latin hymn. As they sat back down, a few latecomers filed in to the pew across the aisle. Claude turned to greet a woman sitting next to her. Out of the corner of her eye she caught sight of the tall, polished black boots of a German officer's uniform. Her breath caught in her throat as her Bible slid to the floor. Reaching down to pick it up, Claude got a better look at the officer and gasped. Pulling the lace scarf further down on her forehead, she hoped to better disguise her face. What was he doing here, she wondered.

After the final benediction and the parishioners stood to leave, Claude quickly made her way to the end of the pew, hoping not to be noticed by the officer. She entered confessional box #2 as instructed, closed the door, and promptly latched it shut. She kneeled on a cushioned bench facing a paneled window. A priest on the other side slid the panel open, revealing an iron grate between them.

"Forgive me Father, for I have sinned," she said with her head bowed waiting for the password.

"My child, we have been waiting for you. What news do you have?"

Breathing a sigh of relief, she slowly pulled the bookmark from her Bible and slipped it through the grate. The priest removed the coded message and returned the bookmark to the Countess.

"Bless you, my child. Say three Hail Maries and be on your way."

She left the confessional a bit sadden not to receive some communication from Vincent. Even though he had said that her assignment would be to send information only, rather than receive any. Claude knew he was only thinking of her safety, but she was still hoping. She nervously looked around, expecting the officer to be lingering behind waiting for her. But he was nowhere in sight. Perhaps he didn't see her after all.

Stepping outside, she removed the lens cap from her camera remembering to take a few pictures of the church. Suddenly a heavy hand touched her shoulder and wouldn't let go. She felt her heart skip a beat.

"I see that even a countess has secrets to confess." A deep voice whispered into her ear. A cold chill swept over her. Claude quickly turned, coming face to face with the German officer that had been in the church.

"General von Thoma! What a pleasant surprise. I would never had pictured you as a Catholic," she said.

"I never said I was," he replied.

"Then what are you doing here?" She asked while putting the lens cap back on her camera.

"Actually I was hoping to see Lucia again before we head out. I saw you enter the church and was waiting for her to join you."

"She'll be sorry to have missed you. I believe she will be out of town for a few days."

"Then perhaps I can drive you back to the castle?"

"Oh, that won't be necessary. The chauffeur is waiting for me."

"Have a good day, Countess Kinnoull." They both nodded. She headed back to the front gate, daring not to turn around. Her heart was still pounding after she was safely inside the car. As they drove off, Claude took a quick look back. General von Thoma was talking to another officer. She felt her throat tighten and put her hand on her neck. No! He was talking to General Sperrle.

Later in the afternoon Claude continued her art lessons with Ignacio.

"I understand that you and my daughter had an interesting evening the other night."

"Yes, it was my first encounter with flamenco dancing and it was marvelous."

"Did you not have another encounter later that night?"

"Are you referring to the two gentlemen who bought us coffee?"

"I'm referring to the two German Officers that you danced with. Claude, I know we both fervently back Generalissimo Franco and that Hitler's military has come to his aide . . . but I do not trust Hitler. Nor, his generals, and neither should you."

"In these unsettling times it is hard to trust anybody. I can assure you that I will be cautious around strangers."

"Speaking of strangers, we will have some unexpected guests with us tonight for dinner," said Ignacio as he added a speck of highlight to the deep-set eyes of the matador in his painting. "Notice how the slight highlight draws you into his soul."

"Who are your special guests tonight?" Claude added some bolder strokes to her painting, which seemed to please her mentor.

"Let's not spoil the surprise." Ignacio smiled, adding a tinge of red on the bull's eye to finish off his painting.

Not knowing who to expect at dinner, Claude chose a classic, but alluring calf length evening dress. While its black silk was demure enough to convey dignity, her bare arms shone through the lace bolero jacket that topped it. Primarily covered, yet partially bare, she felt ready for anything. Setting off the simple elegance by adding a single strand of pearls with matching earrings, and she was ready to meet Ignacio's surprise guests. Having been a guest herself for several weeks, Claude had finally mastered the many different corridors and stairs and swiftly found her way to the library for cocktails.

Upon entering the room she noticed two men with their backs to her, deep in conversation while warming their hands near the fireplace. One stood tall and slender while the other was short and stout, appearing rather insignificant next to the tall one until he turned around. His large and commanding dark brown eyes captivated Lady Kinnoull and brought a smile to her face.

"Gentlemen, I'd like to present to you Countess Claude Kinnoull," said Ignacio. "Lady Kinnoull, it is my profound honor and privilege to introduce to you Generalissimo Franco and his brother-in-law, Ramón Serrano Suñer." Both men smiled.

Standing before her was a man with a lion's heart and a steel-hard backbone. "This is a most pleasant surprise," said Countess Kinnoull. "It is an honor to finally meet the man who is saving the Spanish Catholics from elimination and fighting the poisonous infiltration of communism."

"The pleasure is mine," replied Franco as he kissed Countess Kinnoull's hand.

"But Ramón Suñer, you look familiar," she said. A servant interrupted with a tray of cocktails for the guests.

Ramón's smile turned into a puckered pout. He jerked his head back and reached for a cocktail, spilling some of his drink onto the tray.

"Now, I remember where I saw you . . . it was late one evening in one of the restaurants in the village. You were with General Hugo

Sperrle and General Wilhelm Ritter von Thoma, if I'm not mistaken," said the Countess.

"No . . . no, I do believe you are mistaken, Lady Kinnoull, for I have just arrived this evening to meet with Franco."

Ignacio raised his glass. "A toast to Generalissimo Franco, Godspeed in rebuilding a New Spain – free, great and unified!"

They held their glasses up. "To Generalissimo Franco!"

"Now you must all follow me to my studio, and bring your drinks with you," said Ignacio. "I'm celebrating having finally finished a painting that pays tribute to the Nationalist defenders. I would be most honored to unveil it in your presence tonight."

As they made their way to the tower, Claude asked Ignacio, "Is not your daughter joining us this evening?"

"I'm afraid Lucia had a previous engagement and sends her regrets."

When they entered the studio, Ignacio directed their attention to a large painting in the far corner that was draped with a paint stained covering.

"It is with the highest respect to those who have given the ultimate sacrifice for our great country of Spain that I unveil for you tonight the *Siege of the Alcázar*." He pulled back the cloth to reveal the scene when the Nationalist defenders refused to surrender; despite the building they occupied being engulfed in flames. When they stepped closer to admire the detail of the struggle and the powerful brush strokes typical of a Zuloaga painting, Claude couldn't help but notice an unspoken pain was alive and shimmering in the dark pools of Franco's eyes.

"Bravo, Ignacio, bravo," said Franco. "If only we all had the visual perception of an artist, then this civil war would have long been over."

"Just look around you," said Ramón. "What wonderful portraits you have painted, Ignacio. You should paint one of Franco."

"Indeed," said Franco. "Ignacio, I will commission you to paint a formal portraiture of me as soon as this civil war is over."

"I'd be most honored," replied Ignacio.

They continued their discussion on art during dinner, where Franco learned of Countess Kinnoull's passion for portrait painting.

"This is quite a remarkable lady," said Ignacio. "Lady Kinnoull, you should tell Franco of your exciting but dangerous adventure to Africa. Would you believe this petite woman managed to drive a truck back and forth across the continent of Africa, delivering medical aid to Catholic missions?"

"Your looks are quite deceiving," said Franco. "You have the character of a crusader. Perhaps you could be of use to me."

"I was going to ask you about that. Being a photojournalist for the British *Catholic Herald* and the *La Croix of Paris* newspapers, I've noticed the awful propaganda that spews forth from the Republic side. The truth of the horrific situation with the Spanish Catholics seems to get no coverage. Perhaps I can help give a more positive view of the Nationalist side that might turn the British and French toward your cause."

"Excellent idea," said Franco. "I'll recruit you into my Intelligence Service which will give you the opportunity to ride along in my army as a photojournalist, capturing my liberation of Spain. What do you say?"

"I would jump at the chance," replied Lady Kinnoull raising her glass to his.

"I'm afraid I must be going, duty calls," said Suñer. "Thank you Mr. Zuloaga for your wonderful hospitality, and it's been a pleasure meeting you, Countess Kinnoull. Franco, I'll keep you posted on the activities we discussed earlier. Good evening." The rest of the party retired to the library for after dinner drinks.

Countess Kinnoull excused herself for a moment and returned to her room. She was excited and wanted to assure Franco of her loyalty. She took a check from her purse then returned to the library.

She liked Franco and saw in him a kindness that others did not see. And now she would have a chance to alert the British and French Secret Service of Franco's every movement.

Franco saw in her an opportunity to advance his cause to an international audience, but what he didn't expect was for Countess Kinnoull to hand him a check for £10,000 to support his anti-communist crusade.

"Generalissimo Franco, I know if given the opportunity I can convince British and French Catholics to champion your cause. I offer this check to show my loyalty to you and the Christian Crusade."

"I know that an angel is in my presence and I'm most humbled by your generosity," replied Franco. "But now I must speak frankly with you so there is no misunderstanding. If you agree to ride with my army as we liberate my beloved Spain, there will be shocking things you will see that both sides have been guilty of. You mentioned meeting General Sperrle, head of the German Luftwaffe, and General von Thoma, head of the ground force, Condor Legion. We need their support to win, however they disobeyed my explicit orders to bomb only strategic and specific areas of known Republic holdings in Guernica. Instead they used that town for their own military practice, demolishing everything and everyone in sight. Now it is up to me to liberate what is left of their blundering stupidity."

"I will focus my articles from a liberator's point of view and will show a side of this war that is not being told," replied Lady Kinnoull.

"For that I'll be most grateful. But there is one other thing that causes me pause," said Franco. "You mentioned seeing Ramón with these generals."

"I may have been mistaken, but it certainly looked like him from what I saw."

"My brother-in-law objects to the increasing role of the Catholic Church in our politics and he accuses me of riding on a cult of personality. He is increasingly becoming a thorn in the side of our party by criticizing too many of its policies."

"I'm sorry to hear that," said Lady Kinnoull, "I'll certainly keep it in mind. When do we leave?"

"We'll be leaving tomorrow morning after breakfast. I'll have my assistant type up a form indicating that you are my official war correspondent. And another thing, Countess Kinnoull, for your own safety we will refer to you as Claude, my photojournalist."

Ignacio refilled his guests' drinks. "The hour is late my friends. Before we retire let's raise our glasses for a toast to a successful mission. May we all meet soon in more peaceful times when Spain is whole once again."

Chapter 26

War Correspondent in Franco's Army

Excited and nervous, Claude stared at the piles of clothes strewn across the bed. She had brought only two pairs of dress trousers, which were totally inappropriate for riding around in a jeep with dirty, sweaty men. She was about to ring for Inez when there was a knock at the door.

"Come in," she said. Inez entered with a large duffle bag.

"I was just about to ring for you. I suppose you have heard that I'm off to war tomorrow. And look, I've only brought a couple of pairs of good trousers."

"Oh, my dear, I have heard all about it. Generalissimo Franco's assistant has packed this duffle bag with two khaki uniforms and a helmet that he insists you wear at all times. I've also found an old pair of winter boots and several wool socks that use to be Lucia's. Now you try on the uniforms and if they need any hemming, I'll do it for you tonight."

"You are an angel, Inez." Claude smiled.

"I'm no angel, but it's an angel you'll need for being crazy enough to ride in Franco's army. You do know that there are those who want to see him dead?"

"This is a Christian Crusade, Inez. Franco has God's army on his side and the Lord is using me to tell the world about it."

Inez fought back tears and gave the Countess a hug. "I hope you know what you are doing. I'll pray for you and light a candle at mass tomorrow. Ring if you require any help, I need to plan a hearty breakfast for all of you."

Claude tried on the uniforms and decided a belt to hold up the pants and rolling up their legs would work fine. The boots from Lucia fit perfectly with the addition of a pair of heavy socks. She hung the rest of her clothes back in the armoire. Her camera case fit snugly in the corner of the duffle bag, and in its false bottom she hid her passport, money and gun. Several notebooks and pens were added on top of the false bottom along with her camera and film. Then Claude relaxed in a hot bath and shampooed her hair, not knowing the next time she would enjoy this luxury. That night she wrote a letter to Father de Moor explaining her change of plans.

The next morning after a lavish breakfast several jeeps arrived for Franco and his entourage. Claude handed the letter addressed to the Saint Augustine Church in Paris to Inez, instructing her to give it to one of the priests when she attended mass in hopes they could forward it to Paris. She thanked Ignacio for his generous hospitality and promised to return soon to retrieve her belongings.

The motorcade proceeded north toward the town of Guernica. The German Luftwaffe had exceeded their orders to bomb strategic Republic sites. Instead General Field Marshall Hugo Sperrle, the first commander of the Condor Legion, used this opportunity to demonstrate to Hitler the Luftwaffe's air superiority by dropping a deluge of bombs in the town of Durango on the road between Bilbao and the front. The retreating Basque forces entered the town of Guernica. This is where the Luftwaffe displayed its most powerful demonstrations of flagrant disregard for Franco's orders to only bomb strategic Republic sites. Instead, the Luftwaffe decimated the town of Guernica where the fleeing Basque had gone to seek refuge. Franco was outraged and sought Claude's assistance in providing positive propaganda to the international news services. With her war correspondent credentials, Claude was able to send updates to the British *Catholic Herald* and *La Croix of Paris* newspapers, whenever she could wire out her stories.

Claude saw firsthand the tragedy of Spain. She lived day by day on the front where she was shocked at seeing the results of the killings of the civilian population. Etched forever in her mind were the scorched, mutilated bodies of sacrificed Catholics, their grotesque corpses dangling from meat hooks on display in the windows of butcher shops. The same was discovered in Toledo, Barcelona, and Gerona; witnesses described even worse daily mutilations done to nuns and priests. Praying for people to wake up to the horrendous atrocities being committed against the Spanish Catholics, Claude wrote: *"How can one believe an ideal like communism that gives life to such monsters? The time has come to act."*

She would later learn that almost no one outside the Catholic Church knew about the thousands of priests, nuns and Catholic parishioners martyred during the Spanish Civil War.

Franco's army headed toward Navarre. As the trucks approached the town, people gathered on both sides of the road to welcome Franco's army with flags waving and chants of "Long live Christ the King, Long live Catholic Spain." The people of the Navarre region had banded together; men, women and children of all ages joined to fight for God and Country alongside Franco. He and Claude walked with the people to the top of a mountain that displayed a large cross; all the while singing hymns. They knelt at the cross and prayed for a united Spain. Franco was so choked with deep emotion he could not speak, but his actions spoke for him. With tear filled eyes, Franco planted a large Spanish flag next to the cross and the fervent chants continued.

With most of Spain now on Franco's side, his army sought to liberate Madrid. The troops had grown to include the volunteer army of men from Navarre. Claude was brought to tears on many occasions, but to hear these men devoutly pray and recite the rosary every night in the trenches touched her heart. She wrote how these men at night would sing religious and patriotic songs with such fervor that their voices rose into the air and flew towards the enemy trenches. Far from lessening the men, it made them stronger and more courageous. They were full of faith and patriotism, which is why they stood well above their enemies. They threw themselves into the fight without thinking of the number of opposing forces, nor of the difficult terrain. Their courage was excessive, reckless and daring. Claude held many a young, fatally wounded soldier in her arms as they made the sign of the cross, then looked toward the sky and in a murmur exhaled their last breath and last earthly love, "Long live Christ the King, Long live Spain."

Franco's army was given a boost of patriotism with the steadfastness of the Navarre people. Together they were fighting a Holy War. Although the Communist Revolutionaries had a strangle hold on Madrid for two and a half years, the Catholic Nationalists persevered to the end, and in the end won.

On March 31, 1939, Franco announced the end of the war to a thunderous applause. A victory parade comprised of thousands of veterans marched through the streets of Madrid.

Generalissimo Franco declared: "Our State must be a Catholic State, socially and culturally, because the real Spain was and is Catholic."

Spain's new government gave full freedom to the Church with the recognition of all human rights, and mandated religious instruction at all levels of formal education.

On May 20th, Franco attended a Te Deum Service of Thanks, in the Church of Santa Barbara in Madrid, offering this prayer: *"Lord, benevolently accept the effort of this people, which was always Thine, which with me and in Thy name, has vanquished with heroism the enemy of truth in this century."* Then Franco laid his sword before the high altar, with the solemn promise to God and Man never to draw it again save in defense of his country against invasion. Ever since that day Spain has known peace, and the full freedom of her people to practice their Catholic faith.

Claude sent off her last articles on the Spanish Civil War and then thanked Franco for allowing her to ride along with his army.

"But it is I who should be thanking you, Lady Kinnoull. Your positive and perceptive articles have turned the international community in my favor and I am in your debt. If ever I can be of service to you, please don't hesitate to call." Franco kissed her hand, then instructed his assistant to drive Countess Kinnoull back to Pedraza. For her work in his Secret Service, Franco awarded Countess Claude Kinnoull the premier *Order of Isabel the Catholic* medal.

After a few days of rest and sitting for her portrait to be painted by Ignacio, she packed her bags and was on the next flight to Paris.

Painting of Countess Kinnoull by Ignacio
(Photo graciously provided by the Anita Roy Family)

Chapter 27

Return to Paris

Claude was glad to be back in Paris, but her time at home would be short lived. She tried to purge from her mind the gruesome savageries inflicted upon Catholics she had witnessed as a war correspondent. She strived to fill her days with lighthearted pleasures; walking her poodle, meeting with her artistic friends, and improving on the painting techniques she had learned while in Spain.

Although Claude had supported Franco during the Spanish Civil War, she never trusted Germany. When Hitler made a pact with Stalin on August 23, 1939, she decided to get involved by working with the Allies against the German-Communist alliance. When Hitler invaded Poland on September 1st, Britain and France were duty-bound by an agreement they had made with Poland to come to their aid if they were ever invaded. So a declaration of war against Germany was declared on September 3rd.

With her experience playing a spy in a movie and her collaboration during the Spanish Civil War, Claude now found herself wanting to get involved again. She sought guidance from her spiritual mentor and friend, Monsignor Vincent de Moor.

An awareness of the presence of the Lord wrapped her in a comforting serenity when she entered the sanctuary of Saint Augustine Cathedral. She found Father de Moor in his office.

"I was wondering if I might have a word with you, if you are not too busy?"

"I am never too busy for you. Please have a seat and I'll fix us some tea," he replied.

"I was just getting settled back into a normal routine," she said. "But now I find myself about to be immersed in another war."

"Immersed, in what way?"

"After having seen firsthand the destruction of Spain in its horrendous civil war, I just can't bear to see my beloved Paris occupied by a Nazi regime, or communists. I must be involved. I cannot just sit by and do nothing. I need your advice."

"Oh, Claude, it is not my advice you must seek, but God's guidance."

"But Vincent, I have been praying continuingly since war was declared against Germany for God's guidance in how I may be of service. I feel the Lord has led me to you for assistance in this matter."

"I see," he said. "I do believe that your experience in Spain could be of considerable use to the French and British."

"You mean by identifying communists?"

"Yes, the British and French Secret Services could use you, not only for uncovering the communists agents in France, but also Nazi agents working as spies ahead of any invasion. While riding along with Franco's army you were privileged to observe German officers, in contact with Franco and Hitler. These men could very well now be spies sent ahead to rid France of anyone aiding the Allies. Your recognition of any German officers whether in uniform or in civilian disguises in France would be a tremendous help to the Allied Forces. However, I worry for your safety. While in Spain Franco and his army could protect you. But now you are on your own and those men you might identify, well, they just might recognize you first."

"Surely there will be other agents that I work with?"

"You'll meet a few contacts, but most of the time you are bound to be on your own. I'll introduce you to my friend in the French

Resistance; perhaps your experience in Spain could be of some help to them."

The French Resistance was aware of Claude's involvement in Franco's army through her many newspaper articles and welcomed her assistance. They were convinced that her ability to recognize certain German spies could indeed benefit them.

Claude so desperately wanted to make a difference, and set about her task with a passion. While dining and dancing at the finest restaurants and clubs in Paris, and attending theaters and art galleries, Countess Kinnoull became an expert in the identification of German officers.

Because of her title the Club owners would always offer her the best seating, which was usually next to one occupied by the most boisterous Germans. They did love their alcohol and loved to brag. Claude never let on to anyone that she fully understood the German language. She would only speak in French or English, and played ignorant to anything that was spoken in German . . . all the while taking copious notes in a small notebook that fit snugly in her evening bag.

One night after dancing with Maurice Utrillo, an artist friend, she was walking back to her table when a very drunk German stood up from his table just as she was passing. His hand snagged the delicate chain handle of her evening purse sending her comb, lipstick and small notebook flying. The clumsy drunk picked up the notebook and flipped through the pages.

"*Excusé moi!*" he said in slurred French. He handed the notebook to the Countess whose heart was pounding so loud she thought everyone could hear it. Maurice retrieved the other contents. "I buy you both drinks," said the German.

"No thank you," said Maurice. "We have another engagement."

Claude was glad that before her trip to Spain she had developed her own form of shorthand . . . not even Father de Moor could decipher it.

"Well, that does it," said Jack. He threw the newspaper down on the table, then took another sip of coffee and a bite of croissant.

"What's the matter?" asked Florence.

"With the invasion of Poland, it has forced the hand of France to declare war on Germany."

"Well, surely our soldiers will go to Poland to fight the Germans. We're safe here, aren't we? Poland is on the other side of Germany, quite a distance from us." She sat down at the table and picked up the newspaper.

"My dear, if you read the whole article it says that the Germans have already taken Poland and now their tanks have crossed into Belgium. It says they have spies everywhere."

"What are we to do, Jack?"

There was a loud pounding on the front door. They both stared at each other.

"You stay here. I'll get the door," he said.

Two men dressed in black trench coats and fedoras stood before him.

"What can I do for you gentlemen?" asked Jack.

"We are looking for Countess Kinnoull," said the taller man.

"I'm sorry, but she is visiting friends for a few days. Would you like to leave a message for her?"

"It's a shame that we missed her. We had the pleasure of meeting Countess Kinnoull while in Spain. She mentioned that she was from Paris, so we thought we would look her up."

"She told us that she had a wonderful time in Spain," said Jack. "She'll be disappointed to have missed you. Would you like to leave your names and phone number where she can reach you?"

"No. When exactly do you expect her back?"

"In about five days, I believe. May I at least have your names?"

"Just tell her it was the gentlemen she and a friend danced with, while in Pedraza." The two men turned in unison and left.

Military officers, thought Jack as he closed the door.

"What was that all about?" asked Florence. "I heard you say Miss Enid would be gone for a few days, visiting friends. She never mentioned anything of the sort to me."

"Just protecting our girl," said Jack. "We don't know what happened in Spain. I'm sure she will have an explanation when I pick her up from the art gallery tonight."

"Why, Jack, you lied to those men."

"One can never be too sure, when it comes to spies," he said.

"You're just being silly. Who on earth would want to spy on Miss Enid?" She went back into the kitchen to wash the dishes.

Claude had just finished saying her good-byes when she saw Jack pull up in front of the art gallery. He opened the car door for her.

"How was the show?" he asked.

"It was wonderful. I must say that it's been fun getting back among my artist friends and viewing their newest creations. And how was your evening?"

"It was most unusual, Miss Enid."

"Well, tell me all about it. What happened?"

"We had a visit by two men who said they danced with you and a friend while in Spain. Funny thing . . . the one who spoke was not a Spaniard. He had a German accent and refused to leave a name or contact information. Is there something I should know?"

"All I can tell you right now is that I do know who these men are and I don't want to run into them again. What did you tell them?"

"I had just read about German spies infiltrating France when there was a knock on the door. Even though these men were dressed in civilian clothes, they didn't look to me like they were here for a social call. I told them you were away for about five days visiting friends."

"Good. That will give me some time."

"Time for what?"

"Jack, I can't go into specifics with you, now . . . but I do think that you and Florence should go on a vacation to England."

"Good heavens, Miss Enid, what have you gotten yourself into?"

"Listen to me, Jack. It is important that I know if anyone is watching the apartment. I'll crouch down in the seat as you drive by the front. Check to see if anyone is lurking across the street or sitting in any parked cars. Then we'll go in the alley entrance."

Jack drove slowly down the street trying to imagine where he would hide if a spy. "It doesn't look like anyone is on the street or standing around in any alcove. There are several cars parked on the street, but I don't see any occupants." He drove two blocks further then turned back, going down the alleyway behind her apartment.

Florence had just cleaned off the kitchen counters when she heard a noise at the back door. The knob slowly moved and the door began to open. Florence grabbed a butcher knife . . . her hand shaking and heart pounding.

"Good heavens!" she exclaimed when Lady Kinnoull and Jack hurried into the kitchen. "You were about to give me a heart attack. Things have been a bit nerve racking this evening with all this talk about spies. Did Jack tell you?"

"Sorry," said Lady Kinnoull. "We didn't mean to startle you. And yes, he informed me of what happened."

"I told him how silly he was to think that spies would be looking for you. Well, I've had enough for one evening. I'm off to bed. Coming Jack?"

"I'm going to have a little night cap, then I'll be there." He poured Miss Enid and himself a drink.

"Jack, I know I owe you an explanation. But I promised Father de Moor that I wouldn't say a word to anyone about what I was up to. However, I now realize that my good intentions of not informing you and Florence may have put your lives in danger."

"Father de Moor is involved?" Jack couldn't believe what he was hearing.

"Let me talk to Father de Moor first, then I'll give you a full explanation. In the mean time, I suggest that you talk with Florence about taking a vacation to England."

"I'll wait for your explanation, first," said Jack. "Good-night Miss Enid."

That night, Claude tossed and turned with visions of that evening in Spain . . . General Hugo Sperrle swirled her onto the dance floor and into his arms . . . his heavy, uneven breathing on her cheek as he held her close. Too close, she recalled. Just thinking of it sent chills up her spine. And now, he was in Paris. Looking for her.

She sat up with a jolt. Someone had snitched. But who had betrayed her? She thought of all the people she had met while in Spain and those in Franco's army. Only one name kept coming back to her . . . Ramón Suñer, Franco's brother-in-law. He had denied that he had been with General Sperrle and General von Thoma when she mentioned seeing him at the restaurant that night in Spain. It had to have been him, she thought.

It was just starting to get light. She decided to slip out before anyone else got up. Claude pulled her bag of disguises out of the closet. She combed her reddish-brown hair back into a bun, covering it with a short grey wig and leaving a few straggling hairs falling over her eyes. A faded navy-blue skirt touched the tops of a pair of well-worn black walking shoes. A tan, flowered, loose-knit sweater hung past her waist. Claude dipped her finger into a circular canister of brown shoe polish, dabbing a few age spots onto her hands and adding a dusting of white powder to her face, she was pleased with the results.

She dragged a chair over to the bay window and stood upon it. From that height she was able to look through an opening in the drapes without any movement. It appeared it was too early for any activity on the street. She put on a tan raincoat and covered the wig with a brown and yellow flowered scarf, tying it tightly under her chin. She finished the look with round wired-spectacles, sitting low on the bridge of her nose.

Claude quickly wrote a note for Florence and Jack, saying she went for an early walk and to meet friends for coffee. She grabbed a large tote bag, crammed with a change of clothes, and quietly left the apartment. She looked up and down the street, but saw no activity. Claude walked slowly with a limp, trying to stay in character. At the far end of the block she noticed, out of the corner of her eye, a man coming out from the side of another apartment building and heading her way. Her heart began to pound but she kept her slow walk, even when the man called out to her several times.

"Madame!" he yelled and touched her shoulder.

Claude jumped and turned around.

"Sorry. Didn't mean to scare you," he said.

"Bad hearing," she said in a loud voice and pointed to her ears.

"That building you came out of, is that where Countess Kinnoull lives?" he shouted.

"Yes. Lovely lady," she replied in a loud voice.

"Is she there now?" he shouted.

"No . . . no, I think she's visiting friends. As I recall . . . she mentioned something about Switzerland. Yes, that's it. She's visiting friends in Switzerland."

"Do you know when she will be back?"

"Oh, that's not my business. These young people come and go as they please. Must go now, first one to the market gets the pick of the crops." She turned and limped away.

A few blocks further, Claude limped into the Saint Augustine Cathedral. A nun rushed over to her.

"May I help you?" she asked.

"I realize it is quite early, but Is Father de Moor here?"

"He is always one of the first to come in," she replied. "I'll take you to his office."

Father de Moor was talking with another man when the nun interrupted them.

"Excuse me, Father de Moor. This woman has asked to see you. I'm sorry, but I forgot to get her name."

He turned and looked at the elderly woman standing in the doorway. "No need for introductions. We are longtime friends. Thank you, sister. That will be all." He closed his office door.

Father de Moor turned to the man he had been talking to. "Pierre, I'd like to introduce you to Countess Claude Kinnoull."

"No, this cannot be the Countess Kinnoull that others have described to me."

"She's the one and only," replied Father de Moor. "And dressed as she is, she must be in some danger. Lady Kinnoull, Pierre is with the French Resistance."

"What gave me away?" Claude asked.

"Your ring that your mother gave you. I would not have recognized you, otherwise."

"I must be more careful." She twisted the ring off her finger and put it in her pocket.

"Pierre has informed me that we are both in danger."

"Let me explain," said Pierre. "Countess Kinnoull, you have been able to alert the French and British to so many Nazi agents that Hitler has placed a price on your head.

But you are not the only one. During World War I Father de Moor was once ordered poisoned by Franz von Papen, Vice-Chancellor under Adolf Hitler. He managed to escape that threat, but we have learned that he is being hunted again and also needs to elude capture."

"I had two German officers that I met in Spain come looking for me yesterday," she said. "And then today, I was stopped and asked questions about Countess Kinnoull. It was a good thing I decided to dress in disguise. But now, what are we to do?"

"If France falls into Hitler's hands and his army proceeds toward Paris, it will be essential that both of you not fall into the hands of the

Gestapo. In order to protect you both and safeguard other Allied agents, arrangements have been made for you and Father de Moor to fly to England," explained Pierre.

"But I can't leave Ali Baba behind," she said.

"Who is Ali Baba?" Pierre asked.

"It's her poodle," replied Father de Moor.

"Well, take the dog on the plane with you," said Pierre.

"You don't understand," she said. "There's a six-month quarantine on animals flying into England. That's like locking your child up for six months, I won't hear of it."

"I won't go without you," said Father de Moor.

"Are you telling me that you would put other agents in danger because of a dog?" Pierre asked.

"I suppose not. But I have an idea that might help us," said Claude. "I'll let you know tomorrow if it works."

With Hitler's push to reach Paris, time was of the essence to move. Countess Kinnoull sent an urgent phone call to Generalissimo Franco, asking for his help. Franco's reply was that he could be of no assistance while they were in France. But remembering Countess Kinnoull's generosity in her support of his cause, he would make arrangements for safe passage for the Countess, her dog and Monsignor Vincent de Moor on the last ship departing on October 4, 1940, from Lisbon to New York . . . if they could find a way to cross into Spain.

Excited about the news, Claude limped out of her apartment in her old lady disguise, anxious to inform Vincent of Franco's help. She was surprised to see Pierre in Father de Moor's office.

"Is something wrong?" she asked.

"Yes, Pierre has informed me that the Germans are advancing quicker than expected. They've crossed into France. Should be in Paris by late tomorrow."

"We still have a way out, Franco has agreed to help us," said Claude. "We just have to make it to Lisbon by October 4th."

"That might be harder than you think with gas rationing," replied Pierre. "You may have to walk some of the way. The Resistance can help out with short distances and I've mapped out several safe houses from Paris to Bordeaux along country back roads. It's best to travel at night and the dog must be muzzled while on the road."

Claude and Vincent, both realized that receiving assistance from priests and nuns along the way was no option considering the price put on Father de Moor's head. The Germans would surely have surveillances specifically aimed at Catholic churches. No they would definitely have to rely on others.

"I suggest you both continue to wear disguises until safely onboard the ship," said Pierre. "And Countess Kinnoull, you must not go back to your apartment."

"But I must inform Jack and Florence. I need to pack and get Ali Baba," Claude protested.

"Write down what you will need taken care of and I'll get word to them. You'll see them later," said Pierre.

Claude wrote instructions to Jack and Florence and promised to explain everything that night. Pierre left to hand deliver the letter.

In the meantime, she and Vincent had to come up with a few disguises and Claude knew exactly where to look. The basement of the church had a room for sorting dropped-off donations. She and Vincent rummaged through the bags of clothing looking for some country peasant outfits, but turned out looking more like gypsies.

Vincent donned a wide pair of brown trousers tucked into black calf-high leather boots. He added a velvety, brown vest over a tan shirt with long billowy sleeves. He turned around.

"What do you think?" he asked.

Claude burst into laughter. "No respectable gypsy would be caught without his fedora. I think I saw the perfect one over on the hat table."

Vincent tried on two hats and decided on the black one. "Is this better?" he asked.

"Perfect," she said. "I see no signs of a priest, but to be on the safe side, maybe you should add a hoop earring."

"Now, that's where I draw the line. And what about you, have you found anything useful?"

"I've decided to stay as an old woman for the time being. But once in the country, I'll slip into my gypsy disguise. It would be difficult walking with a limp all the way to Spain."

They bundled the clothes into shopping bags and waited for their transportation.

At 5:45 PM, an elderly woman limped her way down the block to La Pâtisserie des Rêves (Pastry Shop of Dreams) at 93 Rue du Bac. As she opened the shop's door a gold bell jingled, announcing her presence. "Bonjour," she said with a smile on her face.

"Bonjour Madame. You are just in time, we'll be closing in a few minutes," said the store clerk.

Five minutes later, an *Acme Plumbing* van parked in front of the Pâtisserie. A tall man in white overalls got out and grabbed a toolbox. A black beret shadowed his face. When he entered the shop, the clerk pulled the shades on the windows and changed the open sign to closed.

"We've been expecting you," said the clerk. "Please follow me." He led the man into the back kitchen.

"Well, it looks like you weren't followed," he said, sitting down at the table.

"Vincent, you look just like one of the locals," said Claude.

There were three loud knocks at the back door.

"That should be Pierre with our other guests," said the clerk. He looked through the peephole to confirm, then let them in. Jack, Florence, the dog and Pierre quickly entered.

Florence struggled to keep Ali Baba calm. She looked at the people sitting at the table.

"Where's Miss Enid? We're supposed to meet Miss Enid." She dropped the dog's leash and he ran over to the old lady sitting at the table.

"I'm right here, Florence." Ali Baba jumped up and licked the old lady's face.

"Oh my goodness! It is you! I would never had recognized you if it wasn't for Ali Baba." Florence and Jack sat down with the others.

Claude quickly explained her involvement as a spy while in Spain and as a photojournalist in Franco's Army.

"Good heavens! You could have been killed," said Florence. She shook her head in disbelieve.

"And who is this other gentleman?" asked Jack.

The plumber removed his beret and smiled.

"Father de Moor!" Jack couldn't believe it. "Well, I can say one thing for sure. I know that if Miss Enid is traveling with you, I won't worry about her."

Claude reached out and touched Jack and Florence's hands. "I don't know when we will meet again, but be assured that once I'm settled in America I'll be sending for you both." She took an envelope from her pocket. "Now here is the name and phone number of my solicitor in London. I'll be in contact with him and he'll know how to reach me." Claude handed the information to Jack along with two plane tickets to England.

"I've packed everything you requested," said Florence. "Even a bag of dog food and some extra bones." Tears began to roll down her cheeks. She pulled a crumbled hankie from her pocket and dabbed at her eyes.

Claude got up and limped to her aid. Florence looked at the old woman and smiled. "That will be me in a few years." Everyone laughed easing the tension in the room.

"It's good that we depart on a happy note," said Claude. She gave her friends a hug, then put the muzzle on Ali Baba. It was time to go.

Pierre thanked the clerk for his help. Cautiously he opened the back door and checked the alley, then ushered the others into the truck. Vincent and Jack sat in the back with Ali Baba while the ladies rode up front with Pierre.

Their first stop was the airport to drop off Jack and Florence. Pierre stopped the truck about a block away . . . Gestapo spies might be at the airport. As they drove off, Claude watched her lifelong friends mingle in with the other passengers entering the terminal. She felt relief . . . now they would be safe.

The idea of driving straight through on their own was preferred, but with the strict restrictions on gas, it was out of the question. Their modes of transportation varied from cars and trucks to horse drawn wagons. Traveling was slow due to the magnitude of people running for their lives. Vehicles out of fuel, stranded on the sides of the roads, were pushed into the fields to make room for the mass exodus of refugees flowing toward the west and to Spain; hoping to obtain passage to a new and better place.

The farmers along the way offered food and clothing to any in exile, and since the French love their animals; Claude's poodle was treated with equal kindness.

Claude and Vincent stayed out of sight during the days, resting in the farm homes of gracious patriotic French citizens.

The haggard old lady with a limp that had started out on this journey had disappeared; instead an energetic young gypsy woman, dressed in a white puffy sleeved blouse with a patchwork full-skirt of various shades of blue, bounded out of the barn. She wore hiking boots, and a long red scarf worn low on her forehead, which tied in the back, covered most of her hair. Glimmering gold hoops dangled from her earlobes. Claude threw a black crochet shawl across her shoulders.

"Well, what do you think?" she asked.

Vincent laughed. "We look like a couple of misfits thrown off the Gypsy bandwagon."

A farmer came from behind the barn driving a horse drawn cart filled with hay and a standard size poodle. Vincent helped Claude up. She patted Ali Baba on the head and gave him a bone. He happily settled down to chew on his new treasure, before the muzzle was put back on. Vincent tossed their two suitcases onto the hay, and then climbed aboard.

"I can only take you about ten miles," said the farmer. "It'll be dusk soon and my eyesight at night isn't what it use to be."

"We appreciate any help in reaching the border," replied Claude.

The cart pushed on a bit further than ten miles, but when the sun began to set, the farmer pulled his cart to a stop.

"This is as far as I can go," he said. "My wife put together some sandwiches, fruit, freshly baked cookies and a couple of jars of lemonade for you." He handed them a canvas bag with a tie string top. "Godspeed to you both."

Having slept most of the day, they made good time traveling from dusk to dawn. They stopped at several safe houses along the way. The Resistance provided transportation whenever possible. But once they reached Bordeaux they had to walk the last three hours to the border.

Indian summer in late September had been a blessing, bringing unusually warm temperatures, but now a crisp breeze chilled the air. Autumn burst forth with splashes of red tingeing the trees across the majestic Pyrenees Mountains.

Countess Kinnoull and Father de Moor were fortunate, they had their visas and passports along with Franco's assistance once they reached the border; but thousands would wait for days, begging Spain to allow them free passage to Portugal and on to the main port in Lisbon and the dream of a better life.

Chapter 28

Journey to America

A black Fiat Cabriolet pulled up to the shipping dock in Lisbon, and parked near the gangplank of the Greek Liner, the *Nea Hellas*. The driver got out and unloaded a pair of suitcases and a rather large, standard size poodle sporting a muzzle. He managed to weave in and out of the people starting to embark and handed the dog to a steward. It began to drizzle as he made his way back to the car.

His two passengers had their heads bowed in prayer, but immediately looked up when the car door opened. A rumbling of thunder and a crack of lightning lit up the sky, bringing forth a steady downpour. The patter of rain against the canvas roof of the car beat out an unnerving rhythm. The only thing Countess Kinnoull heard in the beat was, *'Got To Get Out, Got To Get Out, Got To Get Out!'*

Vincent gave a tip to the driver and Claude handed him an envelope addressed to Franco, expressing her profound appreciation for obtaining their passage. They waited until the last person in line was on board. They looked around to see if anyone stepped out from the shadows that might be a Nazi spy, then ran up the gangplank, grateful to have umbrellas covering their faces.

The *Nea Hellas* was the largest Greek flagged ocean liner at the time. It was almost six hundred feet long and seventy feet wide. Its six steam turbines were capable of sixteen knots and at that rate it was expected to take nine days to reach America.

Those fortunate enough to have arranged passage filled the decks and lined up against the railings, waving a farewell to their war torn countries in optimistic hope of a life in a new land. This ship was the bridge to their future.

Claude got her dog settled down and the steward was kind enough to provide a bowl of water and some meat scraps from the kitchen. She took a thirty-minute nap, and then met Vincent in the first class smoking room.

A haze of smoke hung in the air. The room was large but cozy, with mahogany paneled walls. Intricate designs were etched into the frosted glass doors and four layers of ornate white crown molding framed the ceiling. Three foot carved plaster friezes of flowered garlands graced two sides of a gold-framed mirror, which hung squarely over a welcoming fireplace. The room was filling up with an array of high society from many different countries; all trying to escape the ravages of war, all with their own tragic stories to tell.

A steward walked through the room ringing the dinner bell. Claude and Vincent made their way to the dining saloon. The ship was at full capacity so no single seating was allowed. They were shown to a table with a most diverse group of fellow travelers.

A British lady in her sixties sat across from them. Claude recognized her right away.

"Viola Harvey, it is so good to see a familiar face! The last time I saw you was about two years ago at the gallery in Paris, when you had that wonderful show of your sculptures," said the Countess. "May I introduce you to Monsignor Vincent de Moor." He started to stand.

"Please don't get up," said Viola. "I remember the wonderful accounts in the news of your travels through Africa with Countess Kinnoull and the aid you brought to all those missions. I'm honored to be sharing a table with you."

"Let me introduce myself," said a white haired gentleman sitting next to Viola. "I'm Count Maurice Maeterlinck."

"It is nice to meet another Belgian," said Father de Moor. "If I recall correctly, did you not receive the Nobel Prize in Literature?" he asked.

"Yes, it was in 1911. That award was the culmination of my life's work," replied the Count with a smile.

A waiter interrupted offering a choice of a white Chardonnay or a red Merlot.

"I'll take the Merlot and just keep it flowing," said the middle-aged woman sitting next to Maeterlinck. "What a wonderful table with such interesting people. I'm Alma and this is my husband, Franz Werfel. He is also a poet and writer."

"How interesting," said the Count. And what do you do, my dear, while Franz is writing?"

Alma played with the collar on her black satin dress. The anguished exodus from France and the grueling journey across the Pyrenees Mountains on foot had etched the fear of survival on her face. But you could tell that at one time she had been a true beauty, with her tall slim stature and dark brown hair piled high on her head.

"I've always been musically inclined, since I was a teenager," she replied with a sadness pooling in her deep-set hazel eyes. "I've been able to expand on my music interest by composing songs for both voice and piano."

"I think that's marvelous," said Countess Kinnoull. "I would enjoy, and I'm sure the others would also, if while on our voyage you might consider entertaining us in the Music Room."

"Perhaps in a few days when I'm more rested," said Alma.

"I feel so blessed to be here," said Viola. "Yet I feel guilty for my happiness while I know that others left behind are still suffering."

"Remember that happiness is as contagious as gloom," replied Count Maeterlinck. "It should be the first duty of those who are happy to let others know of their gladness. And let me say by raising my glass that I am indeed happy to be here with all of you, sailing to freedom in America."

"Hear, hear!" They all said in unison raising their glasses to a new life.

The waiters began to serve the dinner.

It had been awhile since those escaping the terrors of war had seen such an abundance of food. The first course, a Greek rice soup was followed by a baked Fish Normandy.

"Monsignor de Moor, I'm so glad that you are at our table," said Alma. "Something strange happened to Franz and me while we were in Lourdes waiting for our papers to be approved for travel. I ran across the most interesting little booklet on Saint Bernadette."

"One of my favorite saints," remarked Father de Moor. "Did you by chance get to visit her grotto at Massabielle?"

"Oh yes, we visited it several times and it made a deep impression on us. The sermon and the music so moved me that I had to cry and hide my face. It tore at my heartstrings. On our last day in Lourdes, Franz disappeared for awhile, but I must let him finish the story . . ."

"I was so moved by the life of Saint Bernadette," said Franz, "that I felt drawn to visit her grotto one last time. It's hard to explain the incredible power of the Holy Spirit that overwhelmed me. It was like a dream, I was in a trance, looking down from above my body. Then I heard myself vow to the statue of Saint Bernadette, that when we get to America safely, I'll write a book in her honor. Every night since, I have dreamed of her life."

"You've had an incredible awakening," said Father de Moor.

"I wish you Godspeed in your endeavor," said Countess Kinnoull, "for she is a special saint to me, also, and I'm blessed to have a first relic of Saint Bernadette. It's a tiny piece of her bone incased in a small, crystal covered container."

The servers interrupted with a choice of entrees of roast turkey or cold roast lamb, served with a baked potato or French fried potatoes and a side of sautéd Spanish celery. A salad of boiled red beets ended the main meal. Turkish coffee was served with a chocolate pie dessert surrounded with slices of apples, watermelon and oranges.

After dinner, those interested were entertained in the Music Room with Rossini's *Barber of Seville.*

Before retiring to their cabins, Vincent accompanied Claude with a stroll along the deck to the delight of a grateful Ali Baba. It was pitch black, a starless night. Not even the moon could be seen through the shroud of dense fog dripping with dampness.

Claude stood still and cocked her head slightly to one side. "Did you hear that?"

"Hear what?" he asked.

"Listen!" she whispered.

Several voices could be heard coming toward them. Their conversation was unclear, but their thick German accent was undeniable. Claude felt her throat constrict and her heart pounding erratically. Surely they hadn't been followed onto the ship. A sense of dizziness overwhelmed her. She reached for the railing to keep her balance.

"Are you all right?" asked Vincent. A middle-aged couple strolling arm-in-arm, nodded as they passed by.

"This seems like a dream," said Claude. "I'm afraid I'll go to sleep and wake up in the nightmare of running from the Gestapo, always looking behind to see if I'm being followed. Why, just hearing that couple's German accent, made me physically ill."

"You are not alone in your fears," said Vincent. "If you like, the steward can bring meals to your cabin. But just remember . . . this ship is filled with those whose lives have been shattered. There are bound to be some German Jews trying to escape. Their only hope is a safe journey to a new life in a country known for its freedoms and liberties. God willing, our nightmares will end and be replaced with the promise of new beginnings."

"You're right. Everyone on board is escaping from the tyrannies of war. I will not let the enemy win by allowing fear to run my life," said Claude.

The next few days brought rough seas, with swells crashing on the deck that kept most passengers hunkered down in their cabins. The *Nea Hellas* was on a constant ebb and flow as the sea surged. Finally, after seven days there was a break in the weather and the sun burst forth from a bank of clouds. Everyone gathered outside grateful for the fresh air and calm seas once again. The wet decking glistened under the sun and the stewards were busy wiping down the wooden deckchairs.

Claude walked Ali Baba around the ship several times. On returning to her cabin, a steward had left a bowl of meat scrapes for the dog. She turned a light on for Ali Baba and made her way to the First Class Writing Room.

The room had several writing desks and sofas, but Claude was the only occupant. The beautiful weather had kept others out on the decks. She sat at a desk by one of the windows and using the ship's stationary, wrote a letter to Jack and Florence. She hoped they had made it safely to England and told them of their escape through Spain.

That evening during dinner an announcement was made that the war was spreading toward Greece and that in all probability their ship, the *Nea Hellas*, was making her last crossing until after the war.

After dinner Vincent and Claude enjoyed a starlit, clear sky, while taking their nightly promenade with Ali Baba.

"Isn't it strange," she remarked, "how this great ship is making its last transatlantic voyage and so are its passengers, with no hope of a return until after the war, and maybe not even then."

"Ah, but I'm sure you will again one day walk along the River Seine and visit the Saint Augustine Cathedral which has helped to change your life in such measureable ways," said Vincent.

"I look forward to that day." Claude smiled looking out across the vast ocean.

The next morning the weather was once again mild, with the promise of a sunny day. Everyone was out on the decks, chattering with their fellow passengers.

"You can just feel the excitement in the air," said Claude as she and Vincent stepped to the railing. The *Nea Hellas* had left the vast Atlantic Ocean and was passing through the Narrows connecting the Lower Bay and the Upper Bay in New York Harbor.

"Look, there she is," shouted a youngster. "The Grand Lady, I can see her on the horizon!" Everyone rushed to the railing to catch their first glimpse of the Statue of Liberty.

The ship's Captain made an announcement on the loud speakers: "It has been my privilege to deliver you from the land of tyranny to the land of freedom. As the Grand Lady would say, *'Give me your tired, your poor, your huddled masses yearning to breath free.'*" Cheers resounded and many wept with joy. The stewards passed out brochures with information on the Statue of Liberty.

"This brochure says that Lady Liberty's feet are in fact standing among a broken shackle and chains," said Vincent, "and her right foot is raised as if moving forward, away from oppression and slavery."

"I remember seeing the small version of the Statue of Liberty near the Eiffel Tower in Paris," said Claude, "but I never noticed her feet. If we get a chance, we must take the ferry over to Bedloe's Island and get a better look."

The Captain made another announcement on the loud speakers: "We will be lowering the anchor in the harbor while health officers board the ship to look for any signs of diseases. Once the ship inspection is complete, doctors will check the health of all first and second-class passengers. These passengers will then be able to disembark once we dock in New York City. All third-class passengers passing the health check will have to wait for ferryboats to transfer them to Ellis Island where immigration processing will proceed. We will be calling names in alphabetical order. In the meantime, all dining-rooms are open for full service."

While enjoying their last meal on board the ship, Claude and Vincent discussed their plans for when they disembark in New York.

"I've heard so much about New York City and would enjoy seeing a play or musical production while we are here," she said. "Oh, and since we're so close to Canada, I've always wanted to visit Quebec. I've heard that it is a city that does everything French. And what would you like to do?"

"I would like to visit Los Angeles, California," replied Vincent. "I heard that one of my students is now a teacher at the Catholic Diocese in Los Angeles. And I, also, would like to visit Quebec. In my study of miracles, I read about the Basilica of Sainte-Anne-de-Beaupré a major Roman Catholic place of pilgrimage. A place where miracles have been seen."

"Tell me more," said Claude. The waiter brought a fresh pot of tea.

"Sainte Anne is known as the patron saint of sailors," said Vincent.

"That's quite right, sir," the waiter interrupted. "I once served on a ship in that area. The tale goes . . . that some sailors who became shipwrecked off Ile-Oeuf on their way to Quebec City built their first church. One of the builders, who walked with a cane, was able to walk independently once the church was completed. Ever since, any visitor to the church with a walking impediment who prays, it is said, has left their canes, crutches and walking aides behind as a testament to their healing."

"That's wonderful, a definite point of interest to us," said Claude.

"Enjoy your visit," said the waiter as he cleared their table.

"We shall be like nomads," said Claude, "living for awhile in New York City, then in Canada, and eventually driving across the United States to California."

"Sounds good to me," said Vincent.

The *Nea Hellas* finally passed the health inspection and was permitted to pull up anchor and dock at the port in New York City. Father de Moor and Countess Kinnoull along with her poodle disembarked and got into a taxi.

"Where to, folks?" asked the cab driver.

"Well, we're not really sure," replied Claude. "Can you suggest a nice hotel near the tourist attractions?"

"No problem." The taxi driver smiled. After weaving in and out of side streets for about twenty minutes the driver announced: "Here we are folks. The Wyndham New Yorker Hotel located in Manhattan's Garment Center, central to Pennsylvania Station, Madison Square Garden, Times Square and the famous Empire State Building." A porter from the hotel came over to assist. Vincent paid the driver and they followed the porter to the registration desk.

"Do you have reservations with us?" asked the desk clerk.

"I'm afraid not," replied Claude. The clerk looked at her then at Vincent with his priest collar, holding the dog's leash.

"We are quite busy with several ships arriving, but I'll see what we have. Will you be needing one room for the two of you?"

"No," replied Vincent. "We'll need two single rooms and the lady has a dog."

"We do have several single rooms on the third floor and there will be an extra charge for the dog. Please sign the register book." They both signed the book and were given keys to their rooms.

The clerk rang a bell and a bellboy, dressed in a stylish uniform of navy blue trousers with a gold stripe, a bright red jacket adorned with rows of gold buttons and sporting a red pillbox hat held on by a dark blue chin strap, arrived to push the cart with their luggage. "This is Johnny the Bellboy," said the clerk. "If you have any questions, he's your man." Johnny stood only forty-seven inches tall, but the smile on his face told them he took pride in his job. They followed Johnny to the elevator and up to their rooms. He informed them that the Benny Goodman Big Band was playing in one of the ballrooms that night and if they were hungry the hotel had five restaurants. He was given a generous tip and promised to be back with some meat scraps for the dog. They were both tired from their long journey, but agreed to meet in the lobby in two hours to check out the restaurants and entertainment.

Chapter 29

They Were Like Nomads

They spent the next three days playing tourist. Johnny the Bell Boy suggested that they take the time to see New York's World's Fair before it closed on October 27th.

They had already visited the Empire State Building and took the ferry out to Bedloe's Island where they climbed to the top of the Statue of Liberty's crown, taking in the view of New York and the harbor. They also remembered to take a picture of Lady Liberty's feet among the broken chains.

On their third day in New York City, they took a morning taxi to Flushing Meadows-Corona Park where 1,216 acres of the New York World's Fair spread out before them. They were handed a brochure that explained how the theme for the fair started out as *Dawn of a New Day,* showing visitors a look at the world of tomorrow, but in 1940 the theme was changed to *For Peace and Freedom* as the war in Europe escalated.

"Let's start at the Theme Center," said Claude, looking at the map of the fair. Vincent agreed.

They approached two stark, white, monumental buildings, the seven hundred foot tall Trylon building and the Perisphere. They stepped onto a moving stairway that led them inside the Perisphere then onto a moving walkway high above the floor level. They looked down upon a model of the city of tomorrow and then exited by a curved walkway named the Helicline.

"Look at all these vibrant colors on the avenues emanating from the Theme Center, like colorful spokes on a wheel," said Claude.

"It appears that each of the avenues leads to a different zone," remarked Vincent. "I have a feeling that you might enjoy the Transportation Zone." They followed the blue avenue just south of the Theme Center.

"What an incredible display of lighting," she said. "The further we walk from the Center, the lights shine a darker shade of that color hue."

A large General Motors sign graced the entrance to the first building in the Transportation Zone. When they entered the massive 36,000 square foot building, the visitors were buckled into moving chairs that transported them over a huge diorama of a futuristic section of the United States. Before them was an amazing array of miniature highways, towns, 500,000 individually designed homes, 50,000 miniature vehicles, waterways, and a million miniature trees of various species.

"I have the strangest feeling that either we are shrinking or the diorama is gradually becoming larger," said Vincent.

Claude laughed, "I do believe you are right. As we move through the exhibit, the cars and other elements of the exhibit are beginning to appear life-size."

When the ride ended, they found themselves in an area that was an actual city intersection with multistory buildings. Numerous stores lined the streets where visitors could discover the latest and futuristic General Motors and Frigidaire products. They decided to enter the Ford Pavilion, following the crowds to the entry platform of the Road of Tomorrow. A brightly colored Ford car pulled up, Vincent got into the back seat and Claude sat in the front. The driver took them along the dream highway of the future for a half a mile, then up the spiral ramp and around and through the building itself, all the while explaining the impressive features of the car. When the ride was over the driver handed her a business card and brochure detailing the exclusive discount available to visitors of the World's Fair if they were interested in purchasing a new car.

Claude looked at the name on the business card, *Mr. Joseph Porter, Manager.* "How soon can one take delivery of this car, Mr. Porter?"

"This particular model is available now. I'd be happy to show you the various colors that are ready today, if you would like to see our showroom here at the fair."

"I am in need of a reliable vehicle for a long trip," she said. "And I have particularly enjoyed the suspension of this model."

"You have excellent taste, Madame. Excuse me, but I don't believe I caught your names?"

"I'm Countess Claude Kinnoull and this is my friend Monsignor Vincent de Moor." They followed him to the showroom to see the variety of colors available. It didn't take Claude long to make up her mind.

"All the colors are beautiful," she said, "but I find myself drawn to the more sedate, black, 4-door sedan with the white sidewalls."

"A good choice for a long trip, and plenty of storage in the trunk," said Joseph. "Would you like the radio intact or removed?"

"Why on earth would you remove the radio?" asked Vincent.

"It seems that there has been an increase of accidents. Apparently there are some people whose attention has been distracted from their driving while listening to the radio. It has become our policy to ask the client's preference in that regard," replied Joseph.

"I'll definitely need a radio," said Claude.

"We just have a few papers to fill out, and of course your means of payment or credit, and the car will be yours." Joseph smiled handing her a packet of papers to sign.

"I prefer paying cash, which you will receive when you deliver the car early tomorrow morning to the Wyndham New Yorker Hotel," replied Claude. "You do know where that is, don't you?"

"Absolutely. I'll personally deliver the car of your choice to your hotel tomorrow." It has been a pleasure doing business with you, Countess Kinnoull. Until tomorrow."

They continued their visit of the Transportation Zone by climbing to the rooftop of the Ford Pavilion where racecar drivers performed non-stop along a figure eight track. Much to Claude's amusement, the B.F. Goodrich Building provided exciting, close-up viewing of stunt drivers performing daredevil shows.

"Reminds me of some of the stunt driving you performed while in Africa," remarked Vincent." Claude rolled her eyes and smiled.

On the way to the exit, they were treated to the exciting introduction of RCA's first black and white 5-inch tube television sets. As a special surprise, they, along with the other visitors leaving the park, could see themselves on television. They also watched the Franklin D. Roosevelt's speech and the opening ceremony of the World's Fair.

When they returned to their hotel they stopped in to hear the Tommy Dorsey Band and finished with a dinner at one of the restaurants in the hotel.

"I know that the tourist attractions were exciting, the food tonight was fabulous and the entertainment was delightful . . . but I sense something is bothering you," said Vincent.

"I feel so guilty enjoying myself in such a lavish way," she said. "There was so much hope for the future shown at the World's Fair, but then I remembered what we have been through and what are friends in Europe are going through now. I feel the sidewalks closing in on me, such masses of humanity, no matter where I turn in this city. The freedom is wonderful, but I need to breath the freedom. Instead I'm feeling stifled."

"I believe the Lord is telling you that it is time to move on. What you need is a good long drive to release some of that frustration. Or perhaps you are a bit homesick for Paris."

"You might be right on both counts."

"Then we will be off tomorrow for Canada," said Vincent. "Once the car is delivered, we'll pack up and be on our way."

Joseph Porter pulled up in front of the Wyndham New Yorker hotel at 7 a.m. in the new sedan. He asked the desk clerk to alert Countess Kinnoull of his arrival.

Claude had retrieved her money from the hotel's safe and packed her luggage the night before. She rang for Johnny the Bellboy, who arrived promptly with a cart. He followed the Countess and her dog to the elevator where Father de Moor was waiting to ride down with them. Both tipped Johnny, thanking him for his superior service.

In the lobby, Countess Kinnoull handed an envelope with the cash payment for the car to Mr. Porter, along with a substantial tip for having gone out of his way to deliver the car as requested. He handed her the keys and explained that the car needed to be driven slow for the first one hundred miles to break in the engine, then the oil needed to be changed.

The morning's temperature was a brisk thirty degrees, but the clerk at the checkout desk said the weather report predicted temperatures to start rising with a week or two of Indian summer weather. For now, Claude was glad she had a warm heavy coat and gloves. Ali Baba quickly settled down for a nap with his blanket on the backseat as they left New York City heading toward the Canadian border. Joseph Porter had provided them with a map, which showed Quebec was about nine hours away.

"I'll let you drive to Albany, then I'll have the oil changed and take over the driving," said Claude.

"Well, that's a relief," he replied. "With you behind the wheel, we should arrive in Quebec well before teatime." They decided that stopping every two to three hours would work best, so they could all stretch their legs.

Once Claude took over the driving, she increased the speed as Vincent occasionally dozed off. The country roads seemed to go on for miles and the traffic was almost nonexistent. They followed US 9 north toward Canada and the Rouses Point Border crossing. The closer they got to the border an impressive color palette took over as the bright green tree foliage sprang forth with bursts of brilliant flaming red, orange and yellow hues.

At their last break before the border they consumed all the fruit they had purchased along the way and let Ali Baba fetch a few sticks to stretch his legs. When they finally reached the border crossing they had all their papers in order, including the dog's and were quickly allowed to pass into Canada. By the time they reached the village of Sainte-Anne-de-Beaupré, Claude had managed to cut about an hour off the drive, arriving just in time for afternoon tea.

The charming village nestled along the Saint Lawrence River transported her back to her beloved France, with its horse drawn carriages, sidewalk cafés and quaint winding avenues. Even the street signs were reminiscence of those in Paris.

Continuing down the main street, the magnificent white Basilica of Sainte-Anne-de-Beaupré came into view. Its intricate spiral towers stood stately as bookends to the arched entrance. The Romanesque Revival style of the church was built in the form of a cross. The building stood over a hundred yards high and extended the same distance in length with the width varying from sixty to seventy yards. Claude pulled the car into the parking lot. She found a shady spot and rolled the windows halfway down to give the dog some air while they toured the basilica.

"Why don't you go ahead and I'll catch up with you inside," said Vincent. "I'll check in the office to see if there might be accommodations available for a few days."

"Be sure to tell them I have a dog," she replied as he headed off.

Countess Kinnoull draped a lace scarf over her head before entering the Basilica of Saint Anne, honoring the mother of Mary. Stepping across the threshold, a calming peace reigned over her, a quietness blocking out all other noise. She dipped her fingers into the stoup holding the Holy water; the extra droplets fell from her fingers, splashing back into the vessel, each plop awakening an emotion of memories. She knelt and made the sign of the cross, then prayed:

"By this Holy water and by Your Precious Blood, wash away all my sins O Lord."

The built-up tension she had been carrying for so long, gave way to a flood of tears. She finally felt safe from the Gestapo's grasp.

She felt a connection to this place, or was it to the women? Claude wondered. She stood in front of the consecrated chapel where the relic of Saint Anne, given by Pope John XXIII to the shrine, was on display. Claude admired the awe-inspiring stained glass window of the chapel, showing Saint Anne's role as protector of those who are small and humble and those who suffer. She lit a candle, then knelt and prayed.

Vincent finally caught up with Claude. "We've been invited to stay a few days with the nuns and priests of the basilica and you'll be happy to know that they are all quite fond of dogs."

"I'm so pleased to hear that, for I've been reading in this pamphlet that there are two hundred and forty stained glass windows in the basilica; far too many to see in one day."

"Well, we better get started," replied Vincent.

The next few days were a refreshing blessing for the Countess. The nuns and priests proved to be a very intellectual group, expounding on the history of the basilica that a small pamphlet could not possibly incorporate.

But time was of the essence, for winter weather was fast approaching and they had a long drive ahead. They set about packing up the sedan and then with many prayers and blessings from the Basilica of Saint Anne, they retraced their route to New York and continued on to Illinois.

Chapter 30

Route 66

"According to this map," said Vincent, "Chicago is where we pick up highway Route 66 that would take us all the way to California . . . about a 2,278 mile trip."

"A mere pittance compared to our African journey of 22,000 miles on roads that were at times nonexistent!" replied Claude. "And it doesn't look like we'll have any problems with lodging. Several motels are marked along the route."

Four hours after leaving Chicago, they reached the town of Edwardsville where they stopped at a market to purchase items for a picnic lunch. Vincent spread a blanket on the grassy knoll overlooking the Mississippi River while Claude prepared sandwiches and fruit for their lunch. Ali Baba ran free along the river's edge, stretching his legs and rolling on the grass.

"It's just the way Mark Twain described it in his books," said Vincent as they watched a riverboat with its enormous paddle wheel navigate upstream. With lunch over, Claude called her dog back to the car and they headed to the toll bridge that would take them into Missouri. After paying their 35 cent per person toll, they received a pamphlet describing the Old Chain of Rocks Bridge as one of the longest continuous steel truss bridges in the country, measuring more then five thousand feet long with its most distinctive feature being a twenty-two degree bend in the middle. This allowed boats passing underneath to align with the strong current of the Mississippi River.

"Certainly not like the bridges we crossed in Africa," said Claude.

"Especially the ones our truck fell through," laughed Vincent.

Route 66 offered a vast, picturesque overview of the uniqueness of America. It meandered over the countryside, rising and falling as it curved its way across the Ozark Mountains of Missouri; skirting along the vast plains of wheat rippling in the winds of Kansas; hugging the landscape of rolling hills to the Great Oklahoma Plains; and maneuvering around the whirling tumbleweeds on the sweeping flatlands of the Texas Panhandle. Texas was where Route 66 reached its midpoint.

With only a few cars in sight, Claude increased the pressure of her foot on the gas pedal, experiencing the independence of the road and its sense of freedom. It was the same thrill she had encountered on the racetrack. Nearing the New Mexico border she slowed the car and pulled into the last gas station in Texas. She gave the car a thorough check-up, replacing all the belts, changing the oil, checking the tire pressure and adding more water to the radiator. Vincent took Ali Baba for a walk and then replenished their picnic basket, not knowing how far it would be to the next store.

The Badlands of New Mexico proved to be a fascinating region of desert landscape broken up by sporadic mountains, with sandstone bluffs where one could see openings to natural caves and unusual rock formations. When they reached Arizona, Route 66 snaked across a moonscape of desolate mountains where periodic patches of Prickly Pear Cactus seemed to appear out of nowhere.

Claude, being an artist and photographer, decided to take a side trip to the Painted Desert and the Petrified Forest National Monument, where they enjoyed a picnic lunch and marveled at the multi-hued landscape from light shades of purple to bright coral colors mixed in with patches of green and brown grasses. She took several pictures of the area, forever capturing the colorful landscape for future paintings, before heading back to Route 66.

A rumbling of thunder could be heard and flashes of lightning struck in the distance. Black ominous clouds began to fill the sky, blown in by an increasing wind. They decided it would be better to stay in the next town to ride out the storm headed their way. So far they had been blessed with very mild weather throughout their drive across America. There were several bouts of rain and wind, but nothing that caused them pause. Ali Baba on the other hand was now pacing back and forth on the backseat, sensing the thunder growing closer. Claude was relieved to see a motel vacancy sign and pulled off the road toward the Wigwam Motel office in Holbrook. Vincent secured two rooms for the night, each room being in the shape of a teepee.

"Looks like we are in for a taste of the Wild West," said Vincent, handing Claude the key to her room. "You're in Teepee 4 . . . I'm in Teepee 3."

"Let's hope there are no wild Indians tonight," she laughed, taking the key.

While Claude settled Ali Baba down for the night, Vincent walked over to an adjacent café and ordered dinner to be taken back to their rooms before the slight drizzle that had just begun turned into a downpour.

The next morning, after a restless night of torrential rains, thunder and lightning, Claude woke to the heartening sight of the sun. This time she was happy to relinquish the driving to Vincent as they headed out on the last leg of their trip to California.

"I see on the map that Kingman is only 252 miles from Holbrook. Let's take a break there and have a late lunch, then I'll take the wheel," said Claude.

"The dog might have to relieve itself, a bit sooner than that," remarked Vincent. "Flagstaff is almost halfway . . . we should stop there and stretch our legs. In the meantime, why don't you catch up on some much needed sleep? Your car is in good hands. I'm not the least bit inclined to speed."

"That sounds good to me," she replied, reclining her seat and closing her eyes.

Vincent watched in the rearview mirror the desert environment slowly fade into the distance as the elevation gradually rose. The largest Ponderosa Pine forest in North America soon replaced the fields of Prickly Pear Cacti.

Driving through the heart of the Coconino National Forest, the temperature began to drop and he turned on the car heater. Snow-capped mountains could be seen in the distance. Finally at the 7,000-foot elevation, they had reached Flagstaff. Claude woke when the car stopped and rubbed her hands together. "My, its awfully warm in here," she remarked.

Vincent turned off the heater and then grabbed their jackets from the backseat. "Here, you'll want to put this on before we get out. The high elevation has dropped the temperature by twenty-eight degrees." They got out to stretch their legs and took the dog for a walk through the forest.

"I've been thinking about our trip across these United States," said Claude. "I can't help but marvel at how the diversity of the landscape from state to state, like the diversity of its people, appears to have woven together a most colorful tapestry of American History."

"Keep in mind," replied Vincent, "America is a very young nation compared to Europe; its comprised of immigrants from all over the world, some of the best and brightest people have made their home here. But with the war breaking out in Europe, more will surely be flocking to this country for its liberty and freedom."

"Just imagine the growth this country will be facing with the influx of all those people. Why, right now, this route 66 that we're driving on, is the only totally paved highway across America," said Claude. "But in a few years I bet this country will be covered with paved roads going in all directions."

When they returned to their vehicle, Vincent retrieved the dog's bowl and filled it from the water hose at the gas station. While Claude checked the tires and refueled the car, Vincent bought a couple of apples from the adjacent fruit stand and again they were on their way, hoping to make Kingman by two o'clock.

With Providence providing clear weather and Claude in the driver's seat, they arrived in Kingman just before two. They pulled into the Chevrolet-Buick gas station next to the Gaddis Café, taking care of the needs of the car and the dog before entering the restaurant.

"You folks just sit anywhere you like and I'll be with you in a minute," said a stocky built woman with striking red hair piled atop her head.

They chose a booth close to a window where they could keep an eye on their vehicle and Ali Baba. The car's windows were rolled down half way and the shade from the building protected the poodle.

The waitress brought over the menus, "Where're you folks from?" she asked, setting down two glasses of ice water on the plastic, flowered tablecloth.

"We're from Paris, France," replied Claude.

"My, you're a long way from home. Welcome to Kingman," said the waitress. "I'll give you a few minutes to look over the menu. Oh, and be sure to save room for dessert. We have fresh apple pie, hot out of the oven." She went back into the kitchen and returned five minutes later.

"What'll it be folks?" She removed a pencil from behind her ear and a receipt book from her apron pocket.

"I'll have the hot baked ham sandwich with French fried potatoes and coleslaw, with a pot of tea," said Claude.

"And I'll also have a sandwich, but make mine the hot roast beef sandwich, with coffee," he said. "And we will both try your apple pie with ice cream."

"Good choices," said the waitress.

After they had finished dessert, the waitress brought them their check. "Where you folks headed?" she asked.

"We're headed to California, taking Route 66 all the way to the end in Santa Monica," replied Vincent.

"Beware," said the waitress. "You folks are headed for the *Bloody 66.*"

"What do you mean?" asked Claude.

"It's the notorious Sitgreaves Pass through the Black Mountains. So steep some travelers have requested us locals drive their cars or tow them over the pass. It's a dangerous, twisting road, and if that's where you're headed, you don't want to try it at night," said the waitress. "You best be leaving right now if you want to get through it before dusk."

"Thank you for the warning," said Vincent. They paid their bill and headed for the car.

"Sounds like we're in for an interesting ride," said Claude.

"If you're still tired I'll be glad to take the wheel for awhile," replied Vincent.

"Are you kidding? Who's the racecar driver here? This sounds like my kind of course."

"That's what I was afraid of," he said, getting into the passenger side of the car.

They left the security of Kingman, heading into the unknown desolate landscape of the Black Mountains. They drove for what seemed like miles on a back road through the isolated flatlands, snaking their way along the base of the Black Mountains until they reached a rickety old hand-painted wooden sign stating: ED'S CAMP – KEEP OUT–NO TRESPASSING!

"Well, I must say, I don't think we would want our car to break down in this area," said Vincent. Suddenly Route 66 made a sharp turn and began to ascend the Black Mountains. The sporadic patches of grasses and cacti now turned into dark black soil with sharp jagged rocks.

"That was some incline in elevation," remarked Claude when they reached the pinnacle of the mountain. "I recall a racetrack in England that had an extremely steep incline, but nothing like this."

The route began its abrupt downward descent fraught with dangerous hairpin turns. The road began to twist and turn, hugging the hillside with no guardrails for protection.

"I can see why you would not want to try this drive at night," said Claude. "I really have to struggle to keep the car from veering into the other lane and pray that any vehicle coming toward us won't encroach upon our lane."

"That would be double prayers we're putting in, and let's not forget that there are NO GUARDRAILS!" Vincent looked nervously down the mountainside into the abyss thousands of feet below.

Claude slowed the vehicle the best she could, careful to pump the brakes on the way down. Her shoulders and arms ached from the tense maneuvering of the steering wheel, and mental exhaustion had set in from the strict concentration required to drive the treacherous mountain pass. By the time they had reached the base of the Black Mountain, she was more than glad to let Vincent take over driving the rest of the way into Needles, California.

They arrived just as the sun was setting. Vincent pulled the car into the parking lot of the grand El Garcés Hotel next to the railroad depot.

"So far, I'm quite impressed with California," said Claude. "Imagine going from Wigwams in Arizona to this most elegant Neoclassical, Beaux-Arts style hotel."

"Only the best for the Countess who saved my life," replied Vincent.

"I did not save your life."

"The pure fact that I am here and not down the side of the Black Mountain is more than proof for me that you did indeed save my life."

"And Providence did not have something to do with it?"

"I should say it did. It secured a desire in you to want to learn to race cars and look where it has landed you. That knowledge you acquired as a racecar driver has allowed you to skillfully maneuver this treacherous route through the Black Mountains and land us safely here."

"Then we do indeed have a lot for which to be grateful."

While Claude walked Ali Baba, Vincent arranged for two rooms for the night. She agreed to meet him in the lobby in three hours and they would go to dinner.

Vincent was glad he had made reservations at the Harvey House Restaurant in the hotel. He could see that it was very popular since the tables were filling up fast.

Claude met up with Vincent at the lobby entrance to the restaurant. She wore a simple black sheath with long sleeves and a square neckline graced with a single strand of pearls.

"Don't you look lovely tonight, and punctual as usual." He offered his arm and escorted her into the restaurant. The Maître d' immediately showed them their table by a window overlooking the garden. A cascading fountain was the focal point and the needle shaped mountains, silhouetted against the sky in the background, appeared as if stately sentries protecting the city. Claude noticed the table was set with exquisite Irish linens and the finest china and silver.

"I was reading about Fred Harvey in some of the literature explaining the history of the Harvey Hotels and his celebrated Harvey Girls," said Vincent to the waitress about to hand out their menus. "And I can tell by your impeccable uniform that you indeed must be one of them."

"Yes, Sir. We Harvey Girls feel fortunate to be working for a man with such honesty and integrity. His strict standards for high quality food and first class service have successfully brought a new, higher standard of both civility and dining to a region often regarded as the Wild West."

The waitress handed them the menus and while she explained the evening specials, Claude observed the young girl's professional uniform. The crisp, starched uniform consisted of a black skirt hanging no more than eight inches off the floor, with opaque black stockings and black shoes. Her long-sleeved black blouse was overlaid with a white apron, covering the entire uniform except for the sleeves. Her hair was neat and pulled back with a white ribbon. They made their dinner choices and the waitress scurried away to place their order.

"I couldn't help but notice that none of the Harvey Girls wear any makeup and their uniforms are almost like those of a nun," said Claude. A busboy brought them water and an Indian basket full of hot rolls and butter.

"Perhaps it is for the same reason that nuns dress the way they do, as do I with my black slacks, jacket and white collar," replied Vincent. "They are obviously trying not to draw attention to themselves. Their whole purpose is to serve the public."

"Like parallel worlds," said Claude as she reached for a hot roll from the basket.

"You might say that. But now, let's thank the Lord for the food we are about to partake," he said. They bowed their heads and he said a quick prayer for their food and for continued blessings on their journey ahead. When they looked up their dinners had arrived. The size of the portions caught them by surprise.

"We at the Fred Harvey Restaurants like to provide a good value for our traveling public," said the waitress noticing their surprised look. "If you need a container to take some of the food back to your rooms, please don't hesitate to ask."

The freshness of the food was a delight to their palates. "I wish I had the room to savor the rest of this delicious meal," said Vincent, "but alas I'm afraid Ali Baba, will be treated to a gourmet meal tonight."

"Between your steak and my chicken, he certainly will not be wanting," replied Claude.

"According to the map, it looks like we only have a four and a half hour trip to the end of the line," said Vincent.

"Yes, I'm looking forward to seeing the Pacific Ocean. I think it best to leave early in the morning, due to the heat of the Mojave Desert.

And if I could trouble you to walk my dog, I'll go get gas and make sure we have plenty of water."

"My pleasure," said Vincent. "I'll also check us out at the front desk. One less thing to do in the morning."

Claude pulled her car into the Texaco station near the hotel. "What will it be, Miss?" asked the gas station attendant.

"Just need the tank topped off, check the tire pressure and make sure there is enough water in the radiator."

"Where are you headed, Miss?"

"Hope to see the Pacific Ocean some time tomorrow."

"There's a caravan of cars leaving in about thirty minutes if you want to join them. I wouldn't recommend that you drive across the Mojave by yourself, especially at night. Always best to travel in a caravan. The Mojave can be quite the endurance obstacle for any vehicle."

"Thank you for your concern, but I'm not traveling alone and we will be leaving early in the morning."

"If you're aiming for a daytime crossing, then I might suggest you purchase one of these canvas water bags to hang in front of the radiator. The evaporation of the water in the bag helps to cool the radiator and in an emergency you could drink the water." The attendant held up a large 11 by 17 inch rectangular flax and canvas bag, imprinted with the image of an Indian chief with a red and white-feathered headdress on one side. The other side had a red outline of the State of California. The price of $1.70 was inked at the top near the metal clasp that held the coiled rope handle, and a metal screw top covered the opening for filling and drinking.

"Not a bad idea," said Claude. "Add one of those to my bill, please."

"If you've got the time, may I suggest stopping at Roy's Café in Amboy. Great food, best hamburgers around," said the attendant. "And the Amboy Crater is something to see."

"Sounds interesting. Thank you for the suggestion."

The sun was just beginning to rise when they set off for Barstow. Coyotes howled their good-byes and red-tailed hawks soared overhead. The Mojave Desert stretched out before them in ever changing elevations.

"I find it quite interesting how God has created such unique cacti. Just look at the Mojave Yuccas projecting their needle pointed leaves, like daggers protruding from the rocky slopes. Even the groves of towering Joshua Trees possess some type of needle like spikes to protect them from intruders or parasites," said Vincent.

"As a teacher, you see it from a scientific point of view. As an artist I marvel at the uniqueness of God's color palette," she remarked. "His wide brush strokes of various shades of tans, browns, reds and greens of the desert landscape, against the backdrop of a clear blue sky, fills me with wonderment of His Majesty."

"Yet there are those who would question His existence," said Vincent.

"And that is why you have been blessed with the gift of teaching. You have a unique way of presenting the Lord's story, which I know has brought about the salvation of many a lost soul."

"Even if only one soul is saved, it has been worth it," said Vincent.

"Then it's been worth it," said Claude, "for you've helped save my faith."

"No, you were always in God's grace, but had just taken a side path. It was your choice whether or not to reverse that path. I for one am very pleased that you made such a wise and right decision."

"Look up ahead," said Claude. A flock of birds were swarming over a dead animal on the road. As the car approached, the featherless-headed birds flew off the carcass, yet continued to circle their prey from above.

"Those are vultures," said Vincent, "and from the size of the carcass, it looks like a dead coyote."

Claude swerved into the other lane, missing the bloody animal. The vultures swooped down, wasting no time resuming their meal. She continued to make good time, having not passed a single car since they left the town of Needles. They arrived at the halfway point to Barstow and decided to stop at Roy's Café, recommended by the Texaco Gas Station attendant the night before.

After lunch they headed south of the town to see the Amboy Crater created by the only volcano on Route 66. Signs along the route had piqued their curiosity with *TAKE ROUTE 66 AND CLIMB A VOLCANO!*

"Well, here it is," stated Vincent as they stood atop the extinct cinder cone crater formed by black lava rock rising above a twenty-seven square mile lava field. Claude took several pictures, but they decided not to climb down into the crater and continued on.

Once they reached Barstow, Claude filled up the car and checked the tires and belts. They agreed that there would be no more stops until they reached the ocean.

Two hours later they parked the car near the entrance to the Santa Monica Pier. A large neon sign declared *The Santa Monica Pier, Yacht Harbor, Sport Fishing, Boating and Cafés.* They walked to the end of the pier and watched a group of teenagers body surfing.

"End of the line for Route 66," said Vincent.

"And what an ending," replied Claude.

Screams of fear and delight could be heard as children of all ages climbed the one hundred and twenty foot high *Shoot the Shoots* ride and boarded the flat bottom boats for a thrilling thirty degree water chute drop into an enormous deep pool. As they walked back along the pier with the dog, they enjoyed watching the other rides. The *Aerial Swing*, *Speedboats* and the *Flying Planes* were all big hits with nobody seeming to mind the long lines.

"Before it gets much later, I think we should drive back to Los Angeles to meet with your former student at St. Vincent Church," said Claude.

"I believe it's not that far from here," replied Vincent when they reached the car. He pulled out a scrap of paper from the pocket of his jacket. "According to this note, St. Vincent is located at the corner of Adams and Figueroa." He picked up the map of Los Angeles and showed Claude the quickest route from Santa Monica.

They arrived at the parking lot of St. Vincent Catholic Church in Los Angeles about 4 p.m. The stately cathedral had an ornate, decorative entrance with detailed carvings in white limestone. The five-story bell tower resounded precisely on the hour, announcing the end of the afternoon service and sending pigeons flying from the belfry in all directions.

Claude looked up at brightly colored tiles covering a forty-five foot diameter dome, glistening from the hot afternoon sun. "The whole church with its white limestone is almost blinding from the sun. I hope they don't mind my bringing Ali Baba along . . . much too warm to leave him in the car."

When they entered the church office a receptionist looked up from her typing. "Good afternoon, how may I help you?"

"I was wondering if Father Sebastian Ambrozini might be available. I'm an old friend from Paris," said Father de Moor.

"You are in luck, he just finished Mass and should be here any minute. Please have a seat. May I offer you some coffee, tea or water?" asked the receptionist.

"A cup of tea would be delightful," said Lady Kinnoull. "And could I trouble you for some water for my dog? I have his bowl here."

"Of course, no problem. I love dogs." She took the bowl and went into a backroom to fix the tea.

The door to the office opened and in walked a priest. "I don't believe my eyes, could this really be Father de Moor all the way from Paris, France?" The men shook hands and then embraced.

"My, you are a sight for sore eyes," said Vincent. "I'd like to introduce you to Countess Claude Kinnoull and her trusty poodle, Ali Baba."

"It's a pleasure meeting you, Countess Kinnoull. Why don't we all go to my office? It's just down the hall."

"Why don't you two gentlemen catch up on old times? Your receptionist is making me some tea and getting the dog some water, and then I'd love to spend some quiet time touring this magnificent church," said Lady Kinnoull.

"Well, when you finish the tour, please join us in my office," said Father Ambrozini. "Vincent and I have a lot of catching up to do."

The receptionist returned with a pot of tea, some cookies and a bowl of fresh water. "Eileen, you take good care of Countess Kinnoull. She would like to tour the church after she has her tea. This is my teacher and mentor, Father de Moor. He and I will be in my office reminiscing about the good old days."

"It's a pleasure to meet both of you. I have some brochures about our church that might interest you, Countess Kinnoull. You can leave your dog with me while you visit our church, if you like."

"That's most kind of you." Claude gave the water to her dog along with a handful of dog biscuits, picked up a *Sunset* magazine from a side table and settled back to enjoy her tea. The magazine focused on the Western States and one article in particular piqued Claude's interest.

"Eileen, I've just read the most fascinating article about a little village called Carmel-by-the-Sea, one hundred and twenty miles south of San Francisco. Have you ever been there?"

"I myself have never been there, but some of my friends rave about it. They say the town is filled with the most interesting characters. I believe they called them free spirited bohemians, writers and artists who believe in avant-garde, innovative ways of doing things. Is that where you're headed?"

"I'm giving it some thought," replied Claude, "and if I may take you up on your offer to leave my dog with you, I would like to tour your church."

"Of course . . . here is a brochure describing the various statues and sculptures."

Claude took the brochure and headed out on her self-guided tour. Afterwards she found Vincent and his friend laughing about fond memories of their time in Brussels and Paris.

"Did you enjoy your tour?" asked Father Ambrozini.

"Very much. The high relief sculptured panel of John the Baptist and Jesus with the delicate undercut areas of their hands and feet was amazing. But I was most intrigued by the very modest statue of St. Vincent de Paul. He was a saint that I was not familiar with. To learn that he is known as the *Great Apostle of Charity,* and then to look at his portrait next to his statue, you can see the gentleness captured in his eyes."

"Yes, Saint Vincent de Paul was known for his compassion, humility and generosity toward the poor. That is what we teach in our school. From the very youngest to those accepted for the priesthood, we teach the honor and privilege of serving the poor."

"I have some good news," said Vincent. "A vacancy for a teaching position here has just become available and Sebastian has offered me the job."

"Congratulations! What a wonderful beginning to a new life in this country. It appears that Providence is indeed at work again for you and me. I've read about a colony of artist and writers that live in a village called Carmel, just south of San Francisco. Their bohemian lifestyle intrigues me and I think it might be a place where I could settle in quite nicely," replied Claude.

"That is a cause for joy. We'll celebrate with a special dinner tonight. I've also arranged accommodations for the two of you," said Father Ambrozini. "Countess Kinnoull I hope you don't mind staying with one of the nuns. She loves dogs. And Vincent will bunk with me until his studio apartment is ready."

They were all up early the next morning to say farewell to Countess Kinnoull and to pray for her safe journey. "Father de Moor, I'll be sure to write and inform you of my new address once I'm settled, and I'll expect a visit from you in the near future."

"It may be sooner than you think since this teaching position is only temporary." He waved as she drove out of the parking lot.

Once out of Los Angeles and well on her way up the coast on Highway 1, Claude enjoyed the time to savor the solitude and reflect on the many choices she had made in her life that led to her coming to the United States.

When she arrived in Santa Barbara it was still very early and the Santa Barbara Mission was not open to the public. She let the dog run around while she took pictures of the grounds, located on a knoll between the Pacific Ocean and the Santa Ynez Mountains. A sign posted in front of the mission explained that of the twenty-one California missions, only the chapel at the Santa Barbara Mission has two identical bell towers, and that the Chumash Indians built its extensive water treatment system with aqueducts and reservoirs.

A thick fog crept in from the sea, dripping its ocean mist over the landscape. Claude whistled for Ali Baba. He jumped onto the passenger seat, sticking its head out the window of the car. Claude retraced the route back to Highway 1, heading north.

On the map it looked like the road followed the coastline, but in reality it took sudden detours inland with switchbacks up and over hillsides. Claude was up for the challenge, her racing car mode automatically clicking in. Fellow drivers out to enjoy a leisurely ride along the Coast Highway were bewildered to have a car seemingly showing up out of nowhere and then suddenly pass them. The only thing occasionally slowing her down was her desire to capture on film the thunderous explosion of frothing waves smashing against the rugged cliffs of the serpentine coastline. A few miles further, the road again took a slight turn inland where the bright afternoon sunlight filtered through the heavily wooded area of the Santa Lucia Mountain Range. When the road curved back toward the ocean there were several turnouts where one could stop and appreciate the spectacular ocean views.

Claude pulled into one of the wide turnouts at the junction of Partington Ridge and Highway 1. She let the dog out to stretch its legs then tied the leash to the guardrail. In the distance a thick bank of fog hovered over the ocean. She was adjusting her camera lens, focusing on the scene before her, when a massive, dark-colored Humpback Whale breached the surface of the water, shooting an exhalation spray ten feet high, through its blowhole. She snapped a photo just as the enormous mammal arched its back, then dived into the depths of the ocean below, hurling its black and white fluked tail fin against the surface of the sea, sending a spray almost as long as its fifty foot length.

Glad to have had her camera at the ready, Claude took several more shots. She then got the dog back into the car and they continued north on Highway 1. Forty-five minutes later she turned left onto Rio Road, passing by the Carmel Mission. When the road branched, she kept to the right, merging onto Junipero Street, which took her into the village of Carmel-by-the-Sea.

PART 3

Countess

Chapter 31

Carmel-by-the-Sea

Countess Kinnoull pulled up to the Hotel La Ribera at the corner of Lincoln and 7th Street. Its white Spanish Mediterranean façade was reminiscent of the European style that she had seen while in Spain. A doorman came down the red brick steps to help with her luggage. At the registration desk, Ali Baba sat obediently next to her.

"How may we help you, Madame?" asked the clerk.

"I read an article while in Los Angeles that praised your hotel as one of the show places of the Monterey Peninsula, and decided that this would be the first place I'd visit. I'm new to the area and not sure how long it will take before I'm able to find a place of my own, and of course I have my dog to consider. You do allow dogs, don't you?"

"Yes, we allow dogs. But with an extra charge, of course. We have available a room with a fireplace, sitting area and access to a patio."

"That sounds lovely," she said while signing the registration book.

The clerk looked down at the signature. "Countess Kinnoull, it is a pleasure having you and your pet join us. And if you need anything just call the front desk." The clerk rang a bell and a bellboy retrieved the key and showed her to her room.

It didn't take long for Countess Kinnoull to assimilate into the free spirited, bohemian lifestyle of the artists and writers in the village of Carmel. Her first order of business was to visit the mission she had passed on the way into town. As soon as she started attending the church, she was introduced to many residents who shared her European background and cultural interests. Word soon spread that she was looking for a home to rent until she could find the right place to buy. When the Fletcher Dutton house in the Carmel Highlands became available, Lady Kinnoull decided to rent it because of its light and airy artist studio that opened onto a garden patio.

Once settled into her rental house she immediately set up a workspace and began painting. She decided to start with the American landscape with its ever-changing tapestry of colors and textures that she had just experienced. Claude hoped that the cruel and vicious images of the brutalities of war, that had etched such an indelible impression on her mind, might finally have a chance to fade. She began to paint, but struggled to erase those nightmares. After many starts and stops, it finally became clear to her that the bombing of Paris was now something she wanted to tell the world about, in a way they would never forget. What better way than through her art? She was fortunate that this artist studio had tall ceilings, a perfect place to accommodate her massive easel. Her first painting with its larger-than-life characters told the story of the bombing of Paris, which she had witnessed while escaping from the city.

Those fortunate enough to be invited into her studio were stunned that this petite young woman could be the artist behind the canvases of such grand proportions more commonly associated with male artists. Deep, haunting hues lured one into the complex emotions shown on her subjects' faces and into the depth of their story.

Word soon spread that a countess had moved into the area. Lady Kinnoull began receiving numerous invitations to dinner parties where she was to be guest of honor. Upon hearing that she had studied portrait painting under Zuloaga, the local gentry requested appointments with the Countess to have their portraits painted.

One could see the profound Spanish influence evident not only in the strength of her color palette on landscapes, but also in the inclusion of peasant blouses and casually draped shawls in several portraits. Lady Kinnoull had a conviction that strength and integrity should be paramount in her life, and it is noticeable in her paintings. Her artwork was as uncompromising as her belief in the Catholic Church.

It wasn't until Countess Kinnoull met Una and Robinson Jeffers that her painting commissions thrived. The Jeffers' cultivated social circle of friends included those who were either very successful in their fields or extremely wealthy; many who wanted their portraits painted. Through this friendship, Lady Kinnoull was allowed to capture Robinson Jeffers at the waters' edge on a remote boulder, depicting his loneliness. She was also able to capture a serious pose of the distinguished English journalist, author and broadcaster Dr. Richard Roberts.

Lady Kinnoull had an uncanny sense of the mood of each of her clients, whether the dramatics of a war scene or the casualness of a young girl, the seriousness of a journalist or the loneliness of a poet. Countess Kinnoull went on to paint the portraits of at least sixteen prominent Carmel residents.

Countess Kinnoull in her Carmel Highlands Studio painting
The Bombing of Paris as she remembered it (San Francisco News 8/19/1941)

Susan Porter painting
(Provided by the Harrison Memorial Local History Library)

Countess Kinnoull with oil painting of Vera Lehmann
(Provided by the Harrison Memorial Local History Library)

Painting of Chief Red Eagle, by Countess Claude Kinnoull,
(Provided by the Harrison Memorial Local History Library)

Painting of Poet, Robinson Jeffers, by Claude Kinnoull,
(Graciously provided by The Tor House archives)

A self-portrait of Countess Kinnoull (graciously provided by the Hess Family)

Mosaic created by Countess Claude Kinnoull
(From a Monterey Herald newspaper clipping)

Adoration of the Virgin painting by Claude Kinnoull
Hanging in the Saint Angeles Church in Pacific Grove, California

Countess Kinnoull in her artist studio
(Photo from the Monterey Herald newspaper)

Chapter 32

Carmel During World War II

On December 6th, 1941, twelve submarines of the Imperial Japanese Navy were lurking in the Hawaiian waters near Pearl Harbor. They were poised to attack any U.S. Pacific Fleet ships that might try to escape after their planned air attack. However, the surprise attack proved so successful that not a single American ship was spotted at sea for several days.

On December 7th, the Japanese bombed Pearl Harbor; which lead to the idyllic village of Carmel being drawn into the war. Countess Kinnoull's greatest fear that the war she had fled from would one day catch up to her was becoming a reality.

Although it was this bombing that drew the United States into World War II, the Axis countries (Germany, Japan and Italy) would soon be pitted against the Allies (the United States, Great Britain and the Soviet Union).

With the imminent fear of a west coast invasion, a draft was proclaimed and four hundred and eighteen Carmelites enlisted. Local residents took up vigils, scanning the horizon for enemy planes. The Monterey Presidio's Army Commandant ordered a practice emergency evacuation of the entire village of Carmel. For the first few weeks of the war, mandatory blackouts had residents installing blackout shades and painting (or taping out) the headlights of vehicles. The whole peninsula was cloaked in an ominous darkness while soldiers patrolled the beaches. Firemen were instructed on how to deal with explosions from bombs, should the village be attacked.

The proximity of Carmel to the U.S. Naval Postgraduate and Army Language Schools in Monterey had placed the sleepy artist village in a precarious position. The coast guard ordered the Monterey harbor closed, freezing all ships in port. Any private planes at the Monterey Airport were grounded until further notice. Commercial Airlines were still operating, but no Japanese were allowed to fly and all baggage was inspected. Warning systems of four blasts on fire whistles meant the extinguishing of all lights in the entire area; the all clear consisted of two blasts. Severe penalties would be incurred for failure to observe the order, since one single violation might mean the loss of thousands of lives. Realizing the acute danger to vital Monterey Bay, civilian and service officials acted in quick succession to put the area on a war footing.

On December 10th, the *Monterey Peninsula Herald* stated that credible sightings had placed enemy aircraft not only off San Francisco, but also along the Monterey and Los Angeles coasts. They were pleased to report that the total blackout alarms in those areas proved most successful, for no bombs were dropped.

While the military and citizens of the small seaside towns looked to the skies for enemy planes, a more menacing plot was set in motion.

Nine of the twelve Japanese submarines that had been positioned near Pearl Harbor were now headed to their prearranged targets. They were strategically located along the Pacific coastline based on prewar intelligence, giving them the best opportunity to attack the shipping lanes used by American merchantmen. Four subs were sent to the most important locations: Los Angeles Harbor, San Francisco Bay, the mouth of the Columbia River and off the Strait of Juan de Fuca near the Port of Seattle. The remaining five subs were sent to locations that the Japanese considered less crucial, but would still see the most action: Cape Blanco, Oregon, and the rest were in California: Cape Mendocino, Monterey Bay, Estero Bay, and San Diego.

On Saturday, December 20th, pleasant weather and mild temperatures brought scores of golfers to their favorite seaside courses. Blackout air raids had become less frequent and the residents of Carmel were trying to get their lives back to normal.

Countess Kinnoull was walking Ali Baba along the cliffs overlooking Carmel Beach. She watched the playfulness of two seagulls and a double crested cormorant bobbing on the waves, searching for their next meal. A sudden surge of large swells sent the birds flying towards the cliffs. But something else caught Lady Kinnoull's eye. She reached into her purse and retrieved a small set of binoculars; one of the things she had learned as a spy was to always carry a pair. She adjusted the focus on a patch of black, billowing smoke about three miles off shore. As the object came into view, the name *Agwiworld* was clearly visible. The massive oil tanker appeared to be making zigzagging maneuvers to outrun something. Lady Kinnoull positioned her focus on the ship's wake. About five hundred yards behind the tanker was a Japanese submarine. The gunners were trying to aim the deck guns while large swells thrashed them out of shooting range. The sub circled and dodged, attempting to get broadside of the oil tanker, but never succeeded. As the American ship zigzagged closer to land, the sub fired a last round from its gun deck then submerged. A bright glimmer in the sky appeared. Two Navy bombers dropped depth charges where the sub had just submerged. It was never seen again.

Although the war never touched the mainland, the citizens of Carmel did whatever they could to help. There were periodic Scrap Drives; gas, sugar, butter and leather shoes were rationed as well. Some even took in servicemen and their wives, so they could be together one last time before going overseas.

Countess Kinnoull had thought she would be out of harm's way in America, but now the war appeared to be getting closer; she needed a safer place to live. She had witnessed first hand what the Nazis did to spies and knew that Hitler had placed a price on her head and those of other French Resistance operatives.

She let her friends in Carmel know of her search for a more secluded place. Several people suggested the old Watson estate that was built back in 1925 for West Point graduate and World War I pilot Col. Henry L. Watson and his family.

After viewing the sprawling estate tucked away among a forest of oak and pine trees, Countess Kinnoull decided to first rent, then eventually buy the property. The 6,800 square foot hacienda had a reddish, clay barrel tile roof and was situated on sloping acreage with its own stream. Its seclusion near a dense forest seemed isolated enough, yet was still within easy walking distance to the village. She felt the size of the estate would be a perfect place to harbor any of her French Resistance friends fleeing the war (although that need never was substantiated).

The high ceilings in the main living room allowed plenty of space for her massive canvases to be displayed properly; however the natural lighting she needed for painting was insufficient. She decided that the shack behind the house could be rebuilt as a studio, but for that she would need the help of a local handyman.

During this period of time in Carmel one of the most expeditious ways of getting your requests known was by the local bulletin board, located between the post office and the Rollo H. Payne's Village Restaurant on Dolores Street.

The Countess put pen to paper, requesting a hardy handyman for help on her estate. She put on her walking shoes, leashed her poodle and the two headed into town to pick up her mail and post the notice.

The bulletin board consisted of panels of wood from part of an old fence. Numerous notes of various sizes and colors had been nailed or taped to the wood along with lost gloves, a shoe missing its laces, and a scarf here and there.

After Lady Kinnoull taped her notice to a board she turned to see an elderly man dressed in rustic cowboy attire complete with blue jeans, a leather fringed jacket and a ten gallon hat, whispering to her poodle. Ali Baba, appeared to be mesmerized.

"Looks like you have a way with animals."

"Yes, ma'am. Ever since a little boy, animals and I get along." He stood and removed his hat. Dark deep-set eyes framed by sun-worn leathery skin revealed the ravages of harsher times. "You need help?" He pointed to the note she had just taped to the board.

"Well, yes."

"I'm your man. I help you."

"But you don't even know what I need help with."

"No problem. Stars tell me last night opportunity comes my way."

"And you believe in the stars?"

"Nature and I on same spiritual plane."

"I need someone to help me rebuild a studio. Do you think you can do that?"

"Lucky you, I build many things and live by lumber yard."

"What is your name?"

"Red Eagle, at your service."

"Well, Red Eagle, I'm Countess Kinnoull. If I agree to have you help me with my studio will you listen to my spiritual journey?"

"Deal," said Red Eagle. He tore the notice off the bulletin board. "I start today?"

"No, you can start tomorrow morning." She drew him a map to her residence on the back of the notice, and thus began the start of a lifelong friendship.

Chapter 33

Red Eagle

R ed Eagle warmed his hands around a mug of strong black coffee. He watched the sun burn away the early morning fog that drifted through the tall pine trees near his weathered cottage. He had been fortunate to find this place at the edge of the lumberyard. Some would describe it as a small shanty, but to Red Eagle it was his home. It also came with a dilapidated barn, which he was able to restore, adding stalls for his two horses. Always up at the crack of dawn feeding them, Red Eagle enjoyed watching the tiny village by the sea slowly awake to another day.

When he reached the barn, he placed the coffee mug on a tree stump and pulled two carrots out of his pocket. An eagle circled overhead then disappeared. A good sign thought Red Eagle as he entered the barn.

"How are my beauties today?" He broke the carrots in half and fed them to his beloved Bay horses, Mink and Buzzard. He stroked their reddish-brown coats and black manes. "Well, Mink, it looks like you are going to meet a countess today."

He saddled his horse, attached a bag of tools and nails and set off on this new adventure.

They trotted down Torres Street past Tenth Avenue to an old wooden gate at the entrance to the Kinnoull estate. From horseback, Red Eagle unlatched the gate and proceeded up the dirt road toward the hacienda at the top of the sloping hill.

The forest was overgrown, its natural state creating an isolation Red Eagle admired. Communing with nature is good for the soul, he thought.

Countess Kinnoull waved for them to come up to the front porch. "What a beautiful horse," she said. "You can hitch him here at the tree next to the porch."

Red Eagle liked this lady who was short like him. She was dressed in overalls and a plaid shirt with her hair pulled back with a scarf. She stood erect and determined, a woman not afraid to get her nails dirty. A most admirable quality in a woman, he thought. He tied Mink's lead to the tree and followed the Countess around to the back of the house to a small shack.

Countess Kinnoull noticed Red Eagle's calloused hands and was pleased that she had found such a hard worker. She had immediately felt a bond with him on the day before, when Ali Baba had been so entranced with this stranger.

"May I ask, what is the history behind your name?

"Red Eagle means keen sight and soaring flight. I was born in 1870 into the Choctaw Tribe of Fort Worth, Texas. It is old tribal custom that the first thing my father saw when he left the tepee, after holding me for the first time, was a red eagle. So that is what he named me."

"Your father was very wise to name you Red Eagle, for you do have keen sight into the ways of animals."

"I never knew my father," replied Red Eagle. "I was only a year old when he mysteriously disappeared. It was my Uncle Red Wolf that helped to raise me. He was a great medicine man and taught me the Indian arts of medicine and the traditions of the woods and trails. How about you? How do you come by the name Countess?"

Lady Kinnoull smiled, "Well, I was living in England at the time. I was young and foolish and in love with a racecar driver, who just happened to be an earl. We hastily got married, but it did not last. Now, looking back, I can see how the Lord had a different plan for my life all along."

"I, too, have been to England. When I was ten years old my mother died and Mr. Cody, the great Buffalo Bill, was in town and came by to watch the building of the Santa Fe Railroad. I liked his horse and was talking to it, he wondered who I was. My uncle was once a performer in the Buffalo Bill Wild West Shows and introduced us. When Mr. Cody heard that I was an orphan, he adopted me with my uncle's permission."

"So, Buffalo Bill Cody became your father?"

"Yes, and what a great man he was. He taught me how to break horses and how to do tricks with a lariat. By the time I was thirteen, I could stick on the back of anything with four legs. I became part of the Pony Express in his Wild West Show. The next thing I know, the whole show is on a boat to England where we performed for Queen Victoria in London."

"How long were you with the show?"

"I would alternate between the shows and the life of a cowboy on the Texas open range. When I was sixteen, my Uncle Red Wolf became very ill and called me to his bedside. He told me in words I'll never forget; 'a man can face death bravely if he leaves no black cloud in his life.' Then he died. His words haunted me, but it wasn't long after that when I met a beautiful Indian girl named Bright Light from the Cherokee Tribe. We soon married and the next three years were the happiest of my life."

"What happened after three years?"

"We lived on a farm near Houston, raising corn and potatoes. I was the medicine man for all the animals in the region. Then my wife became pregnant. But when the baby was born there were complications and both she and the baby died. I was a medicine man, but could not save them. After that I went back to the life of a cowboy and a Wild West performer."

"How tragic. My heart goes out to you." She placed a hand on his shoulder. "We have a lot in common. I, too, lost a child when he was only a few months old. It turned my life upside down . . . but the good

Lord rescued me from a downward spiral. He gave purpose back to my life."

"Who is this Lord you talk about? Sounds like Big Spirit in the sky."

Lady Kinnoull was excited to have such an inquisitive, captive audience as Red Eagle. While they cleared out the shack, they talked about each other's spiritual journeys and the Countess marveled at the vast knowledge that Red Eagle had acquired in the course of his seventy-one years.

During the next few weeks they worked hand in hand to change the dark and dingy shack into a proper artist studio, engulfed in natural light with a high ceiling. But that was not the only thing changing. As the days turned into weeks, the strangers were becoming friends.

The God that Countess Kinnoull talked about reminded Red Eagle of the Indians' Great Spirit in the sky, and the Saints he compared to the relatives that had gone before him and now watched over him. By the time the artist studio was ready for occupancy, Red Eagle's heart had embraced the Catholic faith.

Sunday mornings became special to Red Eagle. He would dust off his cowboy boots and stand proud in his only suit, waiting for Countess Kinnoull to pick him up for the short drive to the Carmel Mission. With his conversion to Catholicism, Lady Kinnoull became his godmother and continued with his instructions in his new faith.

"It has happened," said Red Eagle one day after church. "It is as you said. God has shown me the way I must go."

"What do you mean?" she asked.

"I know what I'm meant to do. Since I can no longer perform in the Wild West Show, it is up to me to show others the Indian ways. To talk about the Wild West before there are none of us left."

"A most admirable cause," she replied. "It's a wonderful feeling when you know that you are doing the Lord's will."

From that day forth, Red Eagle became Carmel's famous purebred Choctaw Indian Chief. He was proud to be an honorary member of Carmel's Boy Scout Troop 86, instructing not only them, but Girl Scouts and anybody else who wanted to learn woodcrafts and Indian folklore. He also enjoyed performing rope tricks for the troops at the USO Club.

Chief Red Eagle in his full Indian Chief attire.
(Photo provided by Harrison Memorial Local History Library)

Red Eagle in his only Sunday suit.
(Photo provided by the Harrison Memorial Local History Library)

Red Eagle at his farewell performance
(Photo provided by the Harrison Memorial Local History Library)

Chapter 34

Village Life

Settling into village life, Countess Claude Kinnoull decided to take a more involved interest as a resident, striving to keep the charming aspects of her adopted European-style village-by-the-sea intact. She became quite vocal whenever new developments, in the guise of progress, threatened to change the village. She preferred to address each council member and the mayor individually when it came to voicing her concerns rather than attend the council meetings.

Village development was not the only concern of the residents. There had also been a big protest when restaurants were no longer providing freshly caught fish that residents had become so accustomed to. They later discovered that the local Japanese fishermen who supplied the restaurants were told to stay away from the beaches, and had their fishing boats impounded. Shortly after that, all Japanese were rounded up and sent to relocation camps for the duration of the war.

However, the Japanese were not the only people sent to relocation camps. Those who came from countries such as Germany and Italy, or aligned with the Axis countries, also came under severe scrutiny for fear that there may be spies among them.

Countess Kinnoull empathized with their persecution, but fully understood the ramifications that even one spy could generate. She herself knew that her own actions as a spy had more than once foiled the enemy. She justified any decisions she made during the war with the knowledge that even one miscalculation on her part could have meant her death or the death of those with whom she worked with in the French Resistance.

When the threat of invasion was no longer an issue for the Monterey Peninsula, Carmel returned to its idyllic way of life. Countess Kinnoull wrote to Father de Moor in Los Angeles, apprising him of her new address and that if any of their fellow resistance fighters were in need of escape, they would be welcomed at her new home.

Now that her studio was finished, the Countess continued during the day with portrait paintings of local residents, but her evenings were lonely. She decided to finally put pen to paper and begin the novel she had been thinking of writing; an outline of a story began to materialize. She was determined to incorporate a little of herself in each of her characters. Having traveled extensively throughout her life, she appropriately named her book *Come Home, Traveller.*

One evening while writing, her concentration was disrupted by a scratching noise outside. Peeking through the curtains of her office she was amused to see several raccoons ambling across the deck, occasionally stopping to pick at a few acorns that had dropped from the large oak tree near the railing. Ever since her return from Africa where she saw the mutilation of animals by poachers, Countess Kinnoull had felt compassion for animals. She now decided to do something for her newfound friends.

The next morning she retrieved some wood pieces leftover from the remodel of her artist studio and constructed a ramp long enough to stretch from her office window to the deck below. When twilight turned to darkness, she opened the window and placed a tin pan with dinner scraps and dog food on the windowsill. She then poured herself a cocktail, sat back with her feet up on the desk and waited for the show to begin. Soon there was a rustling in the bushes. Four masked bandits scampered across the deck, then cautiously maneuvered up the ramp to reap their reward. Animals of habit, the raccoons quickly became accustomed to this nightly ritual; every night around 8 p.m., the

Countess looked forward to her rendezvous with her new evening companions.

After several weeks of writing, Lady Kinnoull was pleased with the direction her novel was going, but decided that she could benefit from the organizational skills of a good secretary. Inquires at the mission for someone with secretarial skills brought forth several names. After interviewing the ladies, she chose a petite, middle-aged woman with a French background.

Lauretta Barrabe was excited to be working for a countess. She, like Lady Kinnoull, was a devote Catholic and made time every day to pray at the Carmel Mission. Although she enjoyed speaking French with her new employer, she also knew her place and respected the Countess's privacy.

Her first order of business was to sort through and organize the extensive amount of notes from Lady Kinnoull's travels to Africa and Spain. Lauretta became a loyal and trusted employee for the rest of Countess Kinnoull's life.

Chapter 35

An Old Friend

One day a letter arrived that pleased Countess Kinnoull. Her good friend and godfather would be arriving in a few days.

Monsignor Vincent de Moor was most alarmed when he received word that the German Gestapo had been inquiring of his whereabouts at several Cathedrals in France and Belgium. Not wanting to put others in harms way, he took a sabbatical from his teaching position in Los Angeles, for the duration of World War II. He decided to take Countess Kinnoull up on her offer of a safe haven at her home in Carmel.

Lauretta was pleased with what she observed of the gentleman who had just knocked on the front door. He wasn't at all what she expected Monsignor de Moor to look like. He was a man of tall stature with a receding hairline of stark white hair, quite the fatherly type and with a most congenial countenance.

"Lady Kinnoull is finishing a portrait and will be in very shortly," said Lauretta. "I'll show you to your room."

Father de Moor followed her upstairs to a large size room with a sitting area and view over the garden below. It had been a tiring journey from Los Angeles and he was glad to have the time to freshen up.

The Countess had just come in from her studio when Father de Moor entered the front room.

"Vincent, my dear friend, just your presence gives me such joy."
She gave him a welcoming hug. "I trust you had an enjoyable drive
along the coast?"

"Beautiful scenery, but a very tiring winding road," he replied. "I
miss our stimulating conversations to while away the hours."

"I can't tell you how many times I have clung to those memories of
your wise counsel like a life preserver in a stormy sea."

"That counsel comes from someone much wiser than I. For what
I've learned from the Lord, I'll gladly pass on to anyone who will
listen." His smile was that of a proud father. He looked around the room
with its cathedral ceilings. The walls were adorned with several large-
scale canvases.

"I see you have put to good use your painting lessons from Zuloaga.
I'm most impressed. I can understand why local residents would be
honored to have their portraits painted by not only a countess, but a very
accomplished artist at that."

"Such kind words from my dearest friend mean a lot to me. Yes, if
it weren't for Ignacio I would still be painting impressionistic, pretty
little flowers. He taught me to paint with bold strokes and to be
uncompromising in the size of my canvases."

"I can't help but notice this massive fireplace mosaic. Was this done
by you?"

"Ah, you surprise me." She smiled. "Vincent, do you not recognize
some of the pebbles?"

"You mean to tell me that the rocks you collected in Africa are part
of this mosaic?"

"I remember you thought I was being foolhardy when I collected
rocks wherever we stopped."

Vincent laughed. "I don't recall ever seeing a mosaic quite this size,
especially in a home. Most impressive."

"I decided to stop with this mosaic when it grew to eight feet by
eight feet. I created it with pebbles not only from Africa, but from

wherever I traveled . . . even as far away as Japan and Mexico. Notice the shells, forged iron, brass and obsidians that were added for more dimension." She ran her hand over the mosaic.

"It was actually the obsidians with their dark, glass-like volcanic formations picking up light reflections that drew my eye to the artwork."

"I call this *The Tree of Life*. Every time I look at it, something new catches my eye. I chose the title from the *Tree of Life* fig tree that you shot in Africa . . . remember?"

"How could I forget? But I also noticed the beautiful mosaic pathway leading to your front door. Is that your work, too?"

"Yes. I had so many pebbles and other mosaic pieces leftover that I expanded the art to the pathway."

"Your talents never cease to amaze me. But I see there is another well-known painting hanging by your fireplace. Is that an original Maurice Utrillo?"

"Isn't it lovely? I met Maurice when I first moved to Paris and we became good friends."

"I've always enjoyed the clean, simple lines of his cityscapes," said Vincent.

"When he gave a gallery exhibit of his Post-Impressionism style showing the streets of Paris, there was one that always drew me in," she said. "Maurice noticed me lingering by this street scene of the Church of St. Severin. He came up behind me and said, '*When a painting captures your heart, then it must be yours. My gift to a dear friend.*' He then took it off the wall and handed it to me."

"Excuse me, Lady Kinnoull," Lauretta interrupted. "I'll be leaving for the evening and will see you in the morning. It was a pleasure meeting you, Father de Moor." She placed a tray with two glasses and a bottle of Sherry on the coffee table.

"The pleasure was all mine," he replied, shaking Lauretta's hand. After she left they both settled down on the sofas across from one another.

"I've met so many interesting people since I moved here," Claude continued while pouring their after dinner drinks. "The intellectuals make for stimulating conversations and the artistic bohemians without inhibitions in their art, writings, and way of dress captivate me with their *joie de vivre* philosophy."

"Sounds like you have found a bit of paradise right here on earth. The estate is beautiful; you're living in the tranquility of a forest, and just a close walk into town. You well deserve this serenity that has finally found you."

"There are still times when I wake from a nightmare of being captured by the Gestapo, but only those who have walked in our shoes can possibly understand what we've been through."

"It will fade with time, my friend, and I think you have found an enchanting place in which to finally plant your roots."

Chapter 36

A Dinner Guest

Lauretta arrived for work at 9 a.m. ready to transcribe the latest chapter of *Come Home, Traveller.* A tantalizing aroma of bacon, sautéed beef sirloin tips with herbs and spices and the light browning of carrots and onions wafting through the house drew her to the kitchen.

"Good morning, sir. For a moment I thought Lady Kinnoull had hired a chef."

"In a way you might say that is what I am," replied Father de Moor, stirring several pots on the stove. "Has the Countess recounted to you our adventures in Africa?"

"Yes, indeed. What an exciting and fulfilling experience that must have been."

"I was the one doing all the cooking during that trip. It is a favorite pastime of mine. During my time in Paris, I was fortunate to acquire the secrets of mastering the art of French cooking from a chef who attended our church."

"Well, if it tastes as good as it smells, I'd say Lady Kinnoull is the fortunate one."

"I'll make sure to put aside some for you to take home."

"Oh, it was never my intention to impose on you. I just came in to make a pot of tea."

"It's no imposition. I've made more than enough for several meals. I insist you have some, and you'll find the tea kettle is still hot."

"Well, I certainly wouldn't want to insult a guest." Lauretta smiled. She filled a small teapot and then returned to her office.

Claude enjoyed rising early, experiencing the wonderment of the garden unfurling its creative majesty. The kaleidoscope of colors was breathtaking. She clipped a variety of blooms for that evening's dining table.

"Good morning," said Claude, placing the basket of flowers on the kitchen counter.

"And what a good morning," said Vincent. "Your timing is perfect. The pot of tea is ready and orange currant scones are fresh out of the oven, and dinner is simmering." He filled a vase with water. "Let's put these flowers to rest in the water so we can have breakfast while it's still hot."

"I must say . . . I certainly have missed your cooking." They sat down to enjoy the meal together.

"There is a gentleman that I would like you to meet, so I have invited him for cocktails and a late dinner tonight. But I do not expect you to cook the meal; I thought perhaps a nice restaurant in town."

"Nonsense, you must indulge me. You know my passion for cooking. This is not work, but a pleasure for me. Besides, it is the least I can do when you have so graciously allowed me to stay here. Now, tell me of this gentleman you have invited."

"His name is Noel Sullivan . . . I met him at the Carmel Mission. He serves as the church organist and is well known as a concert singer. Noel has given the most wonderful solo performances at the mission. He studied voice and music in Europe and lived for awhile in Paris."

"Then he should be a good judge of my French cooking. I'll look forward to meeting this friend of yours."

While Claude worked on her novel and Lauretta typed the chapters, Vincent walked Ali Baba into town. He went in search of a good Burgundy wine to accompany the evening's meal and purchased two fresh loaves of French bread and some chocolate éclairs. When he returned, Lauretta was about to leave for the day.

"But wait, you can't leave without your dinner," said Father de Moor. He quickly dished up a portion of the *Boeuf Bourguignon* that had been simmering all day along with some boiled potatoes, buttered peas and several slices of bread. *"Bon appetite!"*

"Thank you so much, I'm looking forward to this meal. The aroma throughout the day has made me quite hungry. Have a good evening, Father de Moor."

Noel Sullivan arrived precisely at 7 p.m. for cocktails and was delighted to learn that Father Vincent de Moor was the chef for the evening. After introductions they all agreed to dispense with formalities and just use their first names.

"It has been awhile since I've prepared my favorite *Boeuf Bourguignon* recipe. I do hope you both will be gentle with your food critique." Vincent poured their cocktails.

"This will be delightful. I haven't had good French food since I left Paris."

"I've been telling Vincent how fortunate we are at the Carmel Mission to have such an accomplished musician and concert vocalist." Claude motioned them to sit by the fireplace.

"Well, this may surprise you, Vincent, but I attended the Jesuit colleges of St. Ignatius and Santa Clara. Unfortunately, I discovered that my interests leaned more toward the musical than the academic."

"The Lord blesses us all with our own special gifts. You are fortunate to have found yours at a young age and have brought many years of joy to others because of it."

"I suppose that is one way of looking at it. We all have different callings or gifts, as you so aptly put it. Sometimes it just takes a bit longer than others to find that path."

There was a rustling noise outside along the balcony.

"What on earth is that noise?" asked Vincent.

Claude smiled. "It is my nightly visitors. Follow me . . . you must be very quiet." They entered her office, dimly lit by a Tiffany desk lamp. The two men stood in the shadows while she opened the window. "Good evening, my little friends. So sorry I'm late with your meal, but I have company this evening." She placed a bowl of dog food outside on the windowsill, and then sat down at the desk. The three watched as a parade of five furry masked bandits scampered up the ramp, devoured the dog food, and then ran off into the night. She closed the window and turned to her guests.

"Those raccoons put on quite a show," said Vincent.

"I knew you were fond of domestic animals, but did not know it extended to wild animals," said Noel.

"I'd take care of any animal if I see that there is a need," she said as they walked back into the living room.

"I was just thinking that with your love of animals, you would make a great asset to the Society for the Prevention of Cruelty to Animals," said Noel. "You must give it some thought. In fact I'll mention your name to the board at our next meeting. It's been said that the only way to make a difference around the Peninsula these days is if you are an influential member of a board."

"I'll think about it," replied Claude.

"You both must come visit my Hollow Hills Farm in Carmel Valley," he said. "I, too, have a love of animals. Wait until you see my menagerie of dogs, sheep and goats."

"I'd enjoy seeing your farm," said Vincent. "Have you lived there long?"

"I made it my permanent home in 1939."

"Didn't you once live in San Francisco?" asked Claude.

"That's correct. When my father became ill, I returned from Paris to help take care of him. And, Claude, this should interest you as a writer; we lived in a house my mother had purchased from Mrs. Robert Louis Stevenson. She wanted a home for the Carmelite nuns who had come to

San Francisco. One of those nuns was my sister Ada, now known in religious life as Mother Agnes of Jesus."

"I wasn't aware that one of your sisters was a nun," said Claude.

"Yes. In fact she now resides at the Carmelite Monastery. Why don't you both join me when I visit her next week? It's a lovely drive. The Monastery with its sweeping ocean views holds a special place in my heart, but not just because of my sister. When my father died, he had willed a large sum of money to Ada and she in turn offered the money to build the Carmelite Monastery. So appreciative were the nuns that they allowed our father, Francis J. Sullivan, to be buried in a tomb under the altar and statue of St. Joseph, which can be seen from the nun's oratory."

"We would be delighted to meet your sister," said Claude. "I've seen the magnificent chapel on the hill while driving to and from the Big Sur area, but have never stopped for a service there."

"Let's continue this conversation in the dinning room," said Vincent. "Dinner is ready to be served."

Chapter 37

The Carmelite Monastery

The early morning fog had finally dissipated. Looking out from the passenger side of Noel's car as they drove south on Pacific Highway 1, Countess Kinnoull felt the warmth of the sun on her face and became mesmerized by its glistening reflections off the foaming surf.

"Looks like a beautiful day for a walk along the beach," said Vincent.

"I'm not sure how long you plan on visiting Carmel," replied Noel, "but if you get the chance you must visit Point Lobos. It's just up the road a bit on the right. There is a cove with emerald green water where it is believed that Robert Louis Stevenson was inspired to write *Treasure Island*. It's a great place to hike or have a picnic."

"I'd enjoy a good hike," said Vincent.

There was a dip in the road, and then on the left they could see a grey metal cross appear to grow from the hillside. As they got closer, they saw that it stood stately atop the red tiled roof protecting a white bell tower.

"There she is," said Noel turning the car left onto a narrow road. High on the hill before them stood the Carmelite Monastery.

They parked at the top of the hill. Stepping out of the car, Claude felt a quiet tranquility. She stood captivated by the majestic landscape of the thickly forested Point Lobos Reserve on the left and the undulating waves of the ocean below.

"What a magnificent view," said Vincent.

"Yes, our family was most pleased by this location chosen for the monastery." They followed Noel up the long flight of stairs to the chapel. "Notice the two shields above the arch. The left one is our Sullivan Family coat of arms and the other is the seal of California. Our family owed our good fortunate to the many opportunities we found in California. If you let your eyes wonder to the arch above the circular window, that is the shield of the Order of Our Lady of Mount Carmel. Directly above that at the top of the building is the sculpture of Calvary with Jesus on the cross emanating against the sky."

They entered the chapel and followed the center aisle to the main altar. To the left side of the altar were the statue of St. Joseph and the tomb of Francis J. Sullivan.

Noel knelt at the tomb and bowed his head. Lady Kinnoull read the Latin inscription on the tomb, *"The just will be held in eternal memory. Here rests in the peace of Christ, Francis J. Sullivan (1851-1930) who has founded this church and monastery."*

The appointed time to visit his sister Mother Agnes was fast approaching, so they made their way along the side aisle. Claude stopped to admire the woodcarvings along the wall. They were the fourteen Stations of the Cross depicting the birth, life, death and resurrection of Jesus. Her thoughts wandered back to an earlier time when she had strolled the path where Jesus had walked in Jerusalem.

They descended the steps from the chapel and took the path to a side building, which housed the nuns. Noel rang the doorbell. A voice on a speaker asked their business and then told them that Mother Agnes would be in the first Speaking Room. A buzzer sounded and the three entered into a lobby where a sign indicated that the Speaking Rooms were to the left.

The Speaking Room surprised Lady Kinnoull with its rather large size, since the only furnishings comprised of an oriental rug covering the dark hard wood floors and three overstuffed wingback chairs. The chairs were facing an opening in the wall that was closed off by shutters. When they sat down, the shutters were pulled back to reveal Mother Agnes. Diamond shaped iron grillwork kept the nun cloistered from them, but there was enough room between the bars enabling them to shake hands when introduced.

"It is such a pleasure to finally meet you, Mother Agnes," said Countess Kinnoull. "Your brother has told us so much about you."

"The pleasure is all mine," she replied. Mother Agnes was draped head to toe in a dark brown robe and headdress. "You and Monsignor de Moor are well known to us at the Carmelite Monastery. We followed your exciting and dangerous mission trip through Africa written up in the *Catholic Herald*."

"Did you know that Countess Kinnoull insisted on driving the truck during the whole trip and that afterwards she became a Third Order Nun?" asked Father de Moor.

"No, I wasn't aware of that," she replied with a smile.

"Oh, yes. She was a feisty young convert, never afraid to try new things." They talked about several of the more amusing events that happened on their trip, enjoying a good laugh. Then things turned a bit more serious as Noel and his sister reminisced about their family. The time had passed quickly, when Mother Agnes stood.

"What a most delightful afternoon. It has been a pleasure meeting you, but now I must go."

Father de Moor and Countess Kinnoull said their goodbyes, and then Noel held his sister's hands in his. They gazed into each other's eyes; both shared a beaming smile in silent visions of their childhood days. He bent down and kissed her hands.

Watching her brother leave the room left an ache in her heart, but Mother Agnes refused to surrender to the tears welling in her eyes and slowly closed the shutters.

The Carmelite Monastery in Carmel, California

Chapter 38

Life After The War

World War II was winding down with the surrender of the Germans on May 8, 1945, but it took almost an additional four months for Japan's formal final surrender.

Carmel's residents were looking forward to the return of their hometown soldiers. The whole town was arranging plans for patriotic celebrations, grateful that the war had finally ended. It was over for most of the residents, especially for the families of the returning soldiers, but not for the families of the twenty men who gave the ultimate sacrifice.

The citizens of Carmel gathered together to discuss the importance of establishing a permanent memorial to the fallen soldiers. Countess Kinnoull had seen first-hand the heroic deaths of soldiers, while as a war correspondent in Franco's army. She agreed with several residents that a serene and meditative place was needed to honor such a memorial.

After much contemplation it was decided that Devendorf Park at the entrance to the village would be the recipient of this honor. A plaque listing the names of all twenty fallen soldiers would be embedded in a large granite boulder positioned near a park bench. A flagpole was erected next to the memorial. The American flag, the banner under which they fought so heroically, would forever honor the memory of these brave hometown soldiers.

The Countess longed to return to her beloved Paris and to check on the condition of her apartment, but she was aware that massive devastation had occurred throughout Europe. Also, the Atlantic Ocean was still a minefield of unexploded bombs, restricting all transatlantic crossings. She chose instead to occupy her time by finishing her novel and continue painting.

Encouraged by her friends, Countess Kinnoull applied for and was accepted to the Carmel Art Association. As her knowledge of art expanded, her paintings began to take on a more spiritual awakening.

One afternoon there was a tapping on her studio door. "Sorry to disturb you," said Vincent, poking his head into her artist's domain. "I was wondering if I might get a glimpse of what keeps you so late in your studio."

"Come in." Claude turned from her canvas. "I've been working on a difficult composition. This is a small version of what will be a more involved, larger work of the Crucifixion."

"Very nice. I wish I had artistic ability," said Vincent. "Stick figures are about my speed and even that is debatable." He looked at the other paintings in her studio. One in particular caught his eye. "Oh my, I think you have outdone yourself on this painting. I can feel the powerful emotions emanating from their faces." He stepped closer to study the painting. Her meticulous attention to detail moved him. "The Lord has truly blessed you with a special gift," he said.

"I call that one the *Adoration of the Virgin*. It's not quite finished."

Lady Kinnoull spent her days painting and her evenings after dinner writing. She felt fortunate having Vincent as an extended houseguest. But he was more than that. He had grown from her spiritual mentor to a trusted friend and confidant. She considered him family and enjoyed their late afternoons with cocktails, intellectual conversations regarding world affairs, much laughter over their many journeys together and challenging games of chess.

One evening after feeding the raccoons she sat down at her desk and reread the last page she had written in her novel. She smiled. Only two little words are missing, she thought. She hit the return bar on her typewriter twice and added THE END.

A few days later, Lauretta knocked on the office door.

"Come in," said the Countess, who had been clearing papers off her desk.

"It's like giving birth," said Lauretta. "Here's your baby." She handed a 9x12 inch box to Lady Kinnoull. "There are two manuscripts, one is the original and the other is the carbon copy. I've made all the changes you indicated."

The Countess opened the box and looked at the contents. The top paper read: *Come Home, Traveller* a novel by Claude Kinnoull. She grinned, "This has been a long time coming." She put the carbon copy in her desk. "Let's kick this baby out and see if it can fend for itself." They both laughed, then Lauretta tied the box with twine and double knotted it.

"Well, it's all set for its trip," said Lauretta. "I'll take it to the post office today."

By the end of the year, a special delivery box from Doubleday & Company arrived for Claude Kinnoull. It was the advance copies of her newly printed book. Early copies had already been sent to national and local newspapers in time for the January 1947 book review columns.

"Why, this calls for a celebration," said Vincent. "How about I cook up some hors-d'oeuvres and you invite a few friends over to ring in the New Year?"

"I'm quite excited and would like to thank the people who have been most helpful with their editing expertise. Yes, I think a party is in order. But because of the late notice, I'll only invite a few friends."

Always one to enjoy culinary creations, Vincent was pleased that only six people were invited for the celebration. As he brought in platter after platter of delectable delights, one in particular caught everyone's eye. Using crackers as book covers and thinly sliced cheese as pages, he had handwritten with a paste of black olives the title *Come Home, Traveller* on each cracker. A few minutes before midnight he passed a tray of glasses filled with chilled Champagne, offering one to each guest.

"If I may have your attention, please. We are celebrating not only the beginning of a new year, but . . . let's all raise our glasses to our host Countess Kinnoull. It gives me great pleasure to announce the launch of her much awaited book, *Come Home, Traveller.*"

"Hear, hear!" Their voices rang in unisons. "Speech! Speech!

"First off," said Lady Kinnoull, "I have a signed copy of my book for each of you. And second, I'm so blessed to have such good friends who freely offered me advice and encouragement while I labored over the whole process of my first novel. Now, as much as I abhor reviews of any sort, I know I can count on all of you not to hold back on any scholarly assessment that your intellectual prowess demands. I wish you all a blessed new year ahead." The clock chimed twelve times. They all raised their glasses.

"Happy New Year!" They shouted in unison.

Once the book reached the bookstores, reviews began to appear in local and national publications. Having always been leery of art reviews, Lady Kinnoull was pleasantly surprised by the overwhelmingly positive reviews from top literary critics.

"In many years of work in a city far from California, this reviewer cannot remember meeting so impressive, so remarkable a first novel. Though Lady Kinnoull has chosen a subject of all but insuperable difficulty and unbearable sadness, she treats it with a sureness, an economy of effort, an apparent ease which seem the result not only of talent amounting to genius, but of long practice in a most exacting art; and the result is a little masterpiece." . . . H. IDE

"The first thing to be said of Claude Kinnoull's haunting and memorable book is that it is one of the richest, most carefully observed and finely reasoned novels I have read for years . . . it has self-control; in style and presentation. They who read **Come Home, Traveller** *as a novel of pity, of man's search for truth and constancy will find it, on that level a gripping and unusual story; but to read it only on that level will be to miss its most rewarding quality. There is art, great art, though never the greatest, where the work means exactly what it says, neither more nor less. But especially in literature, there is art in which the real quality is implicit, a thing of overtones . . . An art where the words are overcharged, carry more than their plain meaning, sometimes more than the author is aware of."* . . . *R. ELLIS ROBERTS*

The many positive reviews and feedback from friends overshadowed the one or two unfavorable reviews.

Well known in the local art circles, Countess Claude Kinnoull was guest of honor in a whirlwind of literary activities to launch her new book. The Village Book Shop in Carmel held an author signing and discussion around its fireplace. Later the same day, the Countess was at the Poor Scholar Bookshop in Monterey for another book signing. Mr. and Mrs. Ellis Roberts hosted a sherry and "Oxford Cup" party where those who had read the book had five minutes each to discuss their favorite parts of the novel.

The Carmel Book Sellers had a most impressive program on a Sunday afternoon of January 26th for their *"Author's Afternoon"* discussion. Tea was served at four o'clock with a most unique table decoration of Roman candles, which were lit to celebrate the publication of the novel. One of Countess Kinnoull's paintings, *The Girl in a Green Shawl* was on display in the main salon, where she happily autographed copies of *Come Home Traveller.*

Chapter 39

Bon Voyage

"I'm going to miss you," said Lauretta, "but I know that this is something you must do. After two years of enduring peace in the world, it surely must be safe to travel to Paris."

"In the next couple of weeks I'll put together a list of things that I would like you to do for me while I'm gone. In the meantime, I'm planning a cocktail party on the first Saturday in May, to say *au revoir* to my friends before I depart for Europe. Here are the invitations and the guest list. I'll need you to address them for me."

"I'll see to that right away." Lauretta took the invitations and guest list and headed back to her office. Glancing over the names, she was most pleased to see that Red Eagle had been invited.

To ease Ali Baba's anxiety of not being able to travel with her, Claude brought home a playmate for him. A dark-haired pedigreed standard size poodle named Sylvie.

On Saturday, May 1, 1947, a light ocean breeze swept through the trees bringing a balmy seventy-degree temperature to the village. What a perfect afternoon for a cocktail party, thought Lady Kinnoull. She was delighted that of the thirty-nine invitations sent, there were no regrets.

As the guests began to arrive, the Countess reflected on the many intellectual people that she had grown to know in the short seven years since her move to this artist enclave by the sea. She now considered all of them her dear friends.

Father de Moor was amazed at the variety of influential people in her circle of friends. While pouring cocktails he met fellow clergy, a few doctors and lawyers, artists, several playwrights and authors including the famous poet Robinson Jeffers and his wife Una, along with the renowned and talented Indian Chief, Red Eagle.

"May I have your attention," said Lady Kinnoull standing by the entrance to the dinning room. "I want to thank you all for coming. I knew I could count on all my dear friends to be here. Since word has come that the minesweepers have finally cleared the Atlantic Ocean, passenger ships are now able to commence their transatlantic voyages. That means that in about two weeks, I'll be sailing to France then on to England. I wanted to say good-bye to all my friends for I'll be away for at least four months."

"Well, this calls for a toast," said Noel Sullivan. "Let's all raise our glasses to Countess Kinnoull for a safe journey abroad and for a successful launch of *Come Home, Traveller.*"

The party continued on for several hours until Claude bid *au revoir* to the last of her guests.

"I must say that I enjoyed meeting your most eclectic circle of friends," said Vincent as he cleared away the last of the cocktail glasses. "They are quite diverse and opinionated."

"That's the way I like them," said Claude with a smile.

"I still wish you would reconsider and allow me to travel with you across the United States."

"You of all people should know that I'm quite capable of taking care of myself. Besides, I need you to stay here and care for the house and the dogs."

"They will be the best fed dogs around and I'll even remember to feed your little night burglars."

"I knew I could count on you, my friend. Now, there is another matter that I would like you to consider."

"It's always a mystery with you," he said as they sat down for a game of chess.

"I know you are quite accomplished at building things, so I was wondering if you might be interested in building a small guest house. I have more acreage than I know what to do with. Is that something that might interest you?"

"Well, I would have to check with the City Planning Commission regarding building permits. But yes, this is something I could do for you. I'll get some paper and you can show me the type of home you were thinking of."

"No, this isn't for me," said Lady Kinnoull. "It is my gift to you. We can walk the grounds tomorrow and pick out the perfect spot. I'll leave the funds for the building supplies and permits, but you'll have to build it."

"Sounds like I have overstayed my visit."

"Oh, I did not mean for it to sound like that. Your friendship means a great deal to me. Why, I look forward to our long conversations and your challenging games of chess. You see, when I return from Europe I will be bringing back with me the couple that worked for my mother until she died, and then worked for me in Paris. You remember them."

"Oh, yes. Florence and Jack. I remember how excited they were on our return from Africa."

"Since they will be living in my house I thought you might enjoy more privacy, but still be close by on the property. I do hope you'll agree."

"But of course. I've been thinking of retiring from teaching and this would be an ideal location. I'm sure I can get Red Eagle to give me a hand. He did a fine job on your artist studio."

"Then it's settled. Tomorrow we'll find the perfect location and talk with the City Planning Department."

Time passed quickly and the day for Countess Kinnoull's departure had arrived. Vincent placed two suitcases and a picnic basket in the trunk of her car.

"I've packed you several sandwiches, fruit, cookies and water along with a thermos of hot tea. That should give you a good start. The maps are in the glove compartment with Route 66 clearly marked."

"I knew I could depend on you to think of everything. I figure that the roughest part of the trip will be crossing the dry barren desert. But if I start across before dawn I should be fine. Did you pack my toolbox?"

"It's in the trunk along with a flashlight and some flares. The spare tire is in good condition, and I've added several mechanical belts and that water bag you picked up in Needles, just to be on the safe side. I know how you consider the roadway your own personal race track."

"Hopefully I won't collect any speeding tickets along the way. Now, where are my children?" She turned and called the dogs. They bounded from the backyard, stumbling over one another vying for her attention. She kissed each dog on the head. "You kids mind Vincent. I'll expect a good report when I get back." She threw a ball and the dogs took off. Father de Moor said a quick prayer asking for guidance and a safe journey for her.

"I'll send you a letter now and then," said Claude. "And I wish you success on your building project." She waved as she drove down the driveway. Once outside the gate, there was a grinding of gears and billowing of smoke from the tires spinning on the dirt road as she sped up Torres Street on the first leg of her journey.

With building permits in his pocket, Vincent had enlisted the help of Red Eagle in clearing the land and laying the foundation for a one bedroom, one bath cottage across from the Kinnoull estate. They had accomplished a lot in one week and were proud of the progress.

"Countess Kinnoull will be surprised when she returns from Europe and finds a completed guest house," said Vincent. "I hope she had a safe trip to the east coast."

"You need not worry about her. She is one hardworking lady. Very determined," said Red Eagle. "She would have made a good squaw." They both laughed, and then packed up their tools for the day.

Red Eagle mounted his horse. "See you in church tomorrow, my friend."

"Come by the house after the service and I'll fix lunch," said Vincent. "There's a new recipe I want to try, if you feel like being a guinea pig."

"I never turn down food." Red Eagle smiled, then galloped up the hill.

After fixing the dogs' evening meal, Father de Moor strolled into town to pick up a few items from Decker's Market on Ocean Avenue and then picked up the mail at the post office. He was pleased to see among the bills and advertisements that there was a letter addressed to him postmarked from Canada. Anxious to hear what Countess Kinnoull had to say, he walked over to Devendorf Park and found a bench warmed by the late afternoon sun. Placing the groceries next to him on the bench, he tore the end off the envelope and opened the letter.

Dear Vincent,

I hope all is well on the home front and the kids are minding you. The trip across the vast continent of the United States was mostly uneventful. Except of course for the downpour and tremendous thunder and lightning storms that illuminated the dessert landscape before entering Arizona. The trip seemed to pass quickly, perhaps because I was familiar with the road conditions of Route 66 or that of my speed. I'm happy to report that I have not collected any tickets along the way. The Highway Patrol has such nice gentlemen.

I have met some wonderful people along the way. Many Europeans are heading east hoping to sail to Europe to check on relatives and

property. It was good that I booked passage when I did because I fear
that all passenger ships will be filled to capacity. I write in haste for I'm
about to board the ship. I'll write again once I'm settled in Paris.
Best Regards
Claude

Vincent folded the letter placing it back in the envelope and smiled. No need to worry about her, he thought. She appears to be doing quite well on her own. Picking up the bags of groceries, he headed home.

The gate at the beginning of the Kinnoull property in 1940
(Photo graciously provided by Jean Neito)

The road leading to the Kinnoull Estate on Torres Street in 1940
(Photo graciously provided by Jean Neito)

Chapter 40

News From Europe

The days passed quickly while Vincent and Red Eagle continued their work on the small cottage. Two weeks later another letter arrived this time it was postmarked from Paris.

Dear Vincent,

It is with a sadden heart that I view my return to France through eyes of sorrow. The destruction is so overwhelming. Diseases are running rampant mainly caused by malnutrition. Milk is nowhere to be found because all cattle were either killed or stolen by German soldiers. Adults fare the worst going without in order to provide for their children.

Towns in the countryside and on the outskirts of Paris were hit the worst. Bombed-out buildings cover the landscape. Factories and lumberyards are now piles of rubble. Men and women scour the towns looking for labor in exchange for food. There is plenty of work to be done, but with gasoline rationing there are no trucks to haul away debris. Things look very bleak, indeed.

Arriving in Paris, I'm shocked by the contrast. Paris has been mostly spared the destruction of allied bombings. Our beautiful cathedrals and museums still exist, but thieves have taken our country's most treasured art pieces. We can only pray that those who have stolen these irreplaceable treasures also appreciate art and are protecting these valuable pieces.

My apartment almost fell into the hands of a wandering pack of hoodlums, but my neighbors managed to chase them off and took turns keeping vigilance over the building. There will be food and gas rationing for a long time to come. When I talk with the French people they are all worried what the future will bring. Most spend their time with physical worries – getting enough to eat and wondering how they will keep warm this winter. Others worry about the political situation. Many of the people in France whose political sympathies were with the Communist Party have become anti-communist.

I feel that communism has lost out, particularly in the towns. But the strength of their Communist Party lies in the weakness of other parties, and in the fact that the communists are so well disciplined and organized.

The one thing I'm afraid of is that America will go to sleep and not keep up with her researches, her military power and her awareness of the imminent danger. If she goes to sleep, the world is going to be dominated by communism.

I pray that it will be brought home to all Americans in some way so they could realize how Europeans are actually suffering from lack of food, that they would want to do everything they could on the simple grounds of one human being helping another.

I'll be travelling to England next week and hope to have better news. I trust all is going well on the home front.

Best Regards,
Claude

Father de Moor decided that what the Countess needed was a cheerful letter from home.

Dear Claude,

The ravages of war can be devastating, but at least the bombings have ceased and the reparation can begin no matter how slow, it's a new beginning.

Glad to hear you will be going to England soon. I expect your book to be a big hit over there.

Here on the home front, progress on the cottage is being made albeit quite slowly with all the building inspections that are needed. Red Eagle has been an enormous help bringing in all the cement blocks for the foundation. The land has been cleared and the foundation finally poured. The framing should be going up next week.

The kids are doing fine, but wonder where you are. They take turns walking into town with me for the mail and groceries. They look forward to Saturdays when they romp on the beach, and then come home for a bath.

Looking forward to hearing about your trip to England.

Best Regards,
Vincent

When Countess Kinnoull arrived in England she found that London had received the brunt of the bombings and the countryside had been left relatively safe, just the opposite of what she had witnessed in France.

The roads and buildings were in shambles, making driving a car around London impossible. Lady Kinnoull hailed an approaching Hansom cab. The driver pulled back on the reins of the one-horse driven cab and stopped in front of her.

"Yes, Miss, how can I be of service?" asked the driver stepping down from the spring seat. He offered his hand to assist her into the cab.

"I didn't realize that horse drawn carriages still existed."

"Not for long, I'm afraid. This will be the last year that a horse cab license will be issued in London. If you ask me it is a mistake. Why if it weren't for my Bessie a lot of high society folks would be hoofing around London on their own feet, with this gas rationing and all. Now where do you desire to go, Miss?"

"I'm looking for 6 Raymond Building in London. I do hope it is still standing," said Lady Kinnoull.

"That one I know. Faired much better than others, though the road is a battleground to maneuver. Hold on tight, Miss. It's bound to be a bit bumpy."

Countess Kinnoull smiled. Surely not as bumpy as some of the roads in Africa, she thought.

After being jostled to and fro while the driver skillfully guided Bessie around bomb craters and building debris, they finally came to a sudden stop in front of the Raymond Building. The driver jumped down and offered his hand helping Lady Kinnoull out of the cab.

Once inside the lobby, the Countess perused the roster of occupants by the mailboxes. She ran her finger down the long list, stopping at a familiar name noting the office number.

She entered the elevator and pushed the button of the floor she needed. Nervous, she kept licking her lips. Had her plan worked? The elevator stopped and the door opened. Taking a deep breath she tried to relax and stepped out into the hall.

Countess Kinnoull recalled the time when she was so desperate to break away from the Earl. How hurt she felt when her well-meaning friends told her not to divorce. And their shocking advice that she could now save face by paying off the Earl's debts with her inheritance after her mother died. But it was Ernest, the energetic young solicitor, not her friends, who stood by and helped her through a most public and humiliating divorce.

Entering the room, she saw no secretary, but an inner office door was open and the minute the man behind the desk saw her he jumped to his feet.

"Countess Kinnoull, what a pleasure to see you again after all these years. The minute I received your letter I started working on your plan."

She stood silent, shocked how the ravages of war were etched across his face. Fatigue had settled in deep furrows on his brow and his once lively eyes were now pools of sadness.

"Ernest, I've been so concerned for all my friends in England and France. The minute I heard that the minesweepers had given the all clear for travel across the Atlantic, I booked passage. I'm pleased that my letter arrived safely."

"I'm afraid that the postal service has been quite sporadic since the war. I only received your letter last week."

"I know that I have given you such short notice, but I could think of no one better than you to tend to all the details. Have you found the couple?"

"Actually, they found me. About a week before your letter arrived, the Newburys came to my office seeking any information regarding you. They said that you had recommended my office if they ever needed help."

"So you know how to contact them?"

"Yes. They have been living in the northern countryside. When the bombings started over London it was ever so frightening . . . not only for the adults, but especially for the children. The London Blitz was a new form of warfare that was terrifying. For fifty-seven consecutive nights the relentless bombings were taking their toll not only by destroying or damaging more than one million London houses and killing more than forty thousand civilians . . . but by traumatizing the children to the point of hysteria. Something needed to be done, so the government stepped up by offering to evacuate the children by trains to homes in the countryside. It was called *Operation Pied Piper*."

"I recall reading about it in the paper. Are you saying the Newburys were involved with that?"

"Let's just say that they were able to help the teachers who traveled on the trains. There were millions of children torn from their parents heading into an unfamiliar situation for their own protection . . . not knowing when they would ever see their parents again. Older couples traveling to the countryside pitched in to help the best they could."

"I am so relieved that Jack and Florence have survived these years of torment. Did you tell them of my desire to have them return to the United States with me?"

"They were overjoyed to hear of your plan to give them the opportunity to work for you again and to move overseas . . . away from the rubble of war-torn countries."

"It will, however, take a few months to secure their proper papers. Most government building were damaged and the makeshift offices have been inundated with passport requests."

"Ernest, I'm so glad you are working on their behalf. I'll pay them a visit and see a few other friends while I'm in England for two weeks. Once back in France, I'll wait for their arrival and then I'll book our passage to New York."

"I wish I was going with you. From what you've told me of Carmel, it sounds like a perfect place to recuperate from the ravishes of war."

"I hope some day you will come for a visit. I really mean that. I can't thank you enough for all the help you have given me over the years . . . it has really meant a lot to me."

"That's most kind of you, my friend." He walked her to the elevator. "Have a safe trip home."

"Until we meet again," said the Countess. She smiled and pushed the down button to the lobby.

The two weeks Countess Kinnoull spent in England was a time of joy seeing old friends, but heartbreaking sadness also overwhelmed her, which she described in a letter home.

Dear Vincent,

England is no longer the England where I grew up. A strange and unfamiliar country has emerged from the ravages of war. Two years have passed since the country fought this heroic war, but the people are still living in squalor. Public buildings go neglected with broken windows and deep shrapnel scars. Once the pride of neighborhoods, sidewalks go un-swept and overgrown gardens are besieged with crumbled newspapers and strangling weeds.

The fighting spirit that had kept the English people going during the war is now gone. The people stand in long lines, the spirit drained from their faces. There is a lack of basic necessities: food, decent housing, money, and job prospects. Everything is rationed including food, gasoline, coal and clothing.

The people are growing weary, but they persevere for in all this sadness there appeared one bright light. I was told that during the massive bombings of London, a bellowing ring of fire surrounded the historic Saint Paul's Cathedral. The people watched in horror as the flames crept closer and closer. The massive dome, crowned with a gold cross, stood defiant against the crackling fingers of the scorching flames as if emitting a protective shield that quenched the fire into glowing embers. Not one spark touched the Cathedral. The people believe that this was a sign that God had not forgotten them.

I was able to meet with my solicitor while in England and he has submitted all the paperwork needed to obtain passports and visas for Jack and Florence Newbury. It will however take a few months, but they will be joining me in Paris and I'll be booking passage for the three of us at the end of September.

I hope all is going well with the cottage and that the kids are behaving.

Best Regards,
Claude

Glad to be back in Paris, Claude strolled along the Boulevard du Montparnasse, stopping at the corner in front of Café le Select. A lot had happened since her carefree days among her eclectic artistic friends. She entered the café with the trepidation that her friends had all moved on, until she heard her named called out.

"Claude? I don't believe my eyes. Come join us." A man at a far corner table stood and waved at her.

"My dear Leon, I was hoping you would be here." The two embraced. She sat down next to her good friend. "Do the others still come?" she asked.

"I'm afraid we have all been scattered in different directions since the war. Occasionally one or two will pop in for a chat, and then they will be off for several months. But I'm forgetting my manners. Claude I'd like to introduce you to a fellow journalist, Drew Pearson from America."

"It's a pleasure to meet you," said Drew. He stood and shook Claude's hand.

"I'm quite a fan of yours," said Claude. "I enjoy reading your column *Washington Merry-Go-Round.* "

"Now, the last I heard, you were headed to Spain when the Germans invaded France," said Leon.

A waiter came to their table. Claude ordered a pot of tea. "Yes, that was a sad time for me. I was able to obtain passage on the last ship to the United States. I've been living in the small artist village of Carmel-by-the-Sea in California."

"Drew and I were just discussing the deplorable conditions that the people of Europe are living under."

"I was shocked," said Claude. "Two years after the war, people are still living in poverty. Everything is rationed. I've heard that all of Europe is that way. People are finally realizing that communism is not the way to go and are turning from it."

"But if something is not done soon, the communists will gain their following by supplying food to all the desperate and hungry

Europeans," said Drew. "Why just the other day, I was at the train depot doing an interview when a few carloads of grain were delivered, and the communists were being praised and thanked with much fanfare. I was affronted that the people had forgotten so quickly why the war had been fought. I personally believe that the United States could surpass the communists in sending food to the desperate, hungry Europeans."

"I agree with you," said Claude. "If only it could be brought home to all Americans in some way so they could realize how Europeans are actually suffering from lack of food. They would surely want to do everything they could on the simple grounds of one human being helping another. America needs to wake up."

"And we as journalists can make a difference," said Leon. "We can inundate the newspapers throughout the United States with articles and opinion pieces urging the good people of America for help."

"Then we must act in earnest when we return to America," said Drew.

Several months later, Lady Kinnoull met with Jack and Florence Newbury in Cherbourg, France. They were listed on the first class manifest of the *S.S. Mauretania* sailing from Cherbourg on September 24, 1947, to arrive at the port of New York on September 30th.

There was, however, another traveling companion with the Countess who was not listed on the manifest. Little Valentine de But, a three-month old French poodle with a royal pedigree, had captured Lady Kinnoull's heart while in Paris and now brought much joy to all those onboard the *S.S. Mauretania*. On their last night at sea, Lady Kinnoull sent a telegram to Father de Moor with the approximate arrival day and time to expect them in Carmel.

Chapter 41

Homecoming and The Friendship Train

Lauretta placed a vase with freshly cut flowers on the dining room table. A light breeze from an open window carried the sweet scent of roses wafting across the room. She wanted everything perfect when Lady Kinnoull and her guests arrived.

Father de Moor had gotten up early and put a roast in the oven, then bathed the dogs in anticipation of her late afternoon arrival. He checked on the roast, basting it with its savory juices, and then set the oven timer for another hour. He was looking over his dinner list, making sure nothing had been forgotten, when the roar of a car shifting gears could be heard as it climbed the short hill to the house.

"Sounds like they have arrived," Father de Moor announced.

Lauretta closed the door to her office and rushed to the front entry. She no sooner opened the door than two very jubilant poodles bounded their way out, jumping up on their master and licking her face the minute she stepped out of the car.

"I've missed you, too, my darlings." She kissed each dog on the head. "Now, I've got a surprise for you." She reached into the backseat of the car and brought out a wiggling black curly haired puppy. As she held it in her arms, each poodle sniffed the dog. Satisfied that her poodles would accept the new puppy, she placed Valentine on the ground and the three ran off into the back yard.

When the Newburys got out of the car, Father de Moor introduced them to Lauretta.

"You must be exhausted from your travels," she said. "Let me show you to your room." Jack picked up their suitcases and they followed Lauretta upstairs.

"I see you have been very busy," said Claude to Vincent.

"Yes, the cottage is finally finished. I put the last baseboard in today. Would you like to see it?"

"Of course. Let's see it now, while Jack and Florence get settled."

The cottage nestled among the trees pleased Countess Kinnoull.

"I like the design. Although small with only one bedroom and bath, it appears larger with the step down into the bedroom and kitchen. You will get a lot of use out of the brick fireplace in the living room when the fog rolls in from the ocean."

"I have all the necessary comforts," he replied.

They stepped outside. A bistro table with two chairs and a few potted geraniums added charm to a wall-enclosed patio off the living room.

"You did a wonderful job for the first phase."

"What do you mean, first phase?"

"You're going to need a carport to protect your vehicle from the pine trees oozing sap. And of course, leave it to a man to forget the all important laundry room."

Vincent laughed. "Why, I thought I'd just hand wash a few items when needed and hang them on a line out back."

"Of course you did." Claude smiled. "You can draw up the second phase plans and submit it to the planning department next week." They walked back to the main house to join the others for cocktails.

"Vincent, did I mention to you that I had tea with a Mr. Drew Pearson while in Paris?"

"No, I don't believe so. But I do know of him from his columns in the paper. He seems a most passionate man about any subject he writes about."

"Indeed," said Claude. "We were discussing how important it is for Americans to realize that Europeans are still starving. Their crop fields were destroyed during the war and their animals slaughtered, or stolen."

"How awful," said Vincent. He passed around a tray with cocktails.

"You would think that the countries would start getting back to normal by now," said Jack. "Unfortunately with rationing still going on it's nearly impossible."

"My heart goes out to the innocent children," said Florence. "They were sent on trains out into the countryside to live with strangers; then when they return to the city, they find it in ruins. Their homes were destroyed and there is a food shortage."

"Yes. Help is still desperately needed. Mr. Pearson and I decided to write articles explaining the situation in the hope of raising donations. I've almost finished my article and will have Lauretta type it up tomorrow and send it off to the *Monterey Herald*. The Americans need to know that the war against communism is an ongoing battle and we must not let our guard down."

"You've always been one to rally the troops when it comes to community involvement," said Vincent.

After dinner, they all retired early. Jack and Florence were excited to finally be in America and back with Countess Kinnoull, who promised them a tour of the property the next day.

Before Countess Kinnoull's article appeared in print, Drew Pearson, on October 11, 1947, had saturated the media and radio broadcasts with his vision of a *Friendship Train* delivering boxcars of food to Europe.

Fearful that Europeans, in desperate need, would turn to the communists for help, Drew played on the Americans' patriotic and moral duty. He asked Americans to donate food from their homes, restaurants, gardens, and fields. His call for help was such an astounding success that it turned into a competition as to which state would send the largest amount of provisions.

Inside each crate of food there was a tag with the first and last name and address of the donor. On the outside of the packages were the words: *"All races and creeds make up the vast melting pot of America, and in a democratic and Christian spirit of good will toward men, we, the American people, have worked together to bring this food to your doorsteps, hoping that it will tide you over until your own fields are again rich and abundant with crops."* The message was also written in Italian and French and printed beside the American flag.

On November 7th, only five weeks after Drew Pearson made his impassioned call for help from the American people, *The Friendship Train* turned into three trains with a total of 270 boxcars. By December 18th, the much-needed supplies arrived by ship at Le Havre, France. The food was distributed throughout France and Italy by both French and American organizations.

Several days later, Father de Moor read an article in the newspaper about the success of *The Friendship Train* and rushed up to the main house. He found Lady Kinnoull in her artist studio.

"I thought you might like to read this article," he said, handing her the newspaper.

As she read the article by Drew Pearson a smile brightened her face. "This is marvelous," she said looking up at Vincent. "It says here that no money was ever spent on the boxes of food, the train or the transporting of the goods by rail and trucks; the loading and the use of the ships were all free. The Americans can look at themselves with great pride for doing such an outstanding job."

"The most amazing thing," said Vincent, "is that this whole humanitarian project did not involve the government at all, but was run entirely by the American people with their love and moral belief of helping fellow human beings in need."

"It goes to show you," said Claude, "how one person can make a huge difference when he puts all his passion behind a good-hearted idea."

"I like to think that Providence also had a hand in it. You can keep the article if you wish." He looked up at the easel. "Looks like you're taking a break from portrait painting."

"Yes, I'm trying out a new project, *The Mysteries of the Rosary*. I'm giving it a more modern style."

"I see that the size of the canvas is considerably smaller."

"That's because when I finish there will be fifteen pieces illustrating the life of Jesus and when displayed, they should be grouped together."

"Then I shall take my leave so you may proceed with this most admirable endeavor."

"Thank you for showing me the article, it has brightened my day. Are we still on for a game of chess later?"

"I wouldn't miss it," said Vincent. Three frisky dogs darted past him as he headed back to his cottage.

The Cottage Vincent de Moor built on the Kinnoull Estate

As the years wore on, Countess Kinnoull filled her days with charities, animals, art, writing, and community involvement. Her pedigreed poodles were a much-loved attraction at the local dog shows.

Countess Kinnoull presenting one of her beloved pedigreed poodles at the local dog show. (Reproduced by permission of the Monterey County Herald newspaper)

Although her days were filled with various activities, the Countess hungered for something more. Just being involved in the community was not quite enough for her. She was used to being assertive and in control. Words from her friend Noel Sullivan kept haunting her. *It wasn't enough to be on committees where all the busy work is done, one had to aim for a position on the board of those committees where the real decisions were made, and where one could truly make a difference. But if one wanted to be a mover and shaker on the Monterey Peninsula, the most prestigious board position was that of the Society for the Prevention of Cruelty to Animals.*

Chapter 42

The SPCA

Countess Kinnoull parked her car near the corner of David Avenue and Lottie Street in the coastal town of Pacific Grove, only five miles northwest of Carmel. She wanted to see for herself the quality of the organization that Noel had suggested she become involved with.

A small cottage was the only house on the block. An etched wooden sign with the initials SPCA confirmed she was at the right place. She introduced herself to the manager, who gladly gave her a tour of the premises, hoping this may be a prospective donor.

"As you can see, we are not nearly large enough to accommodate all the poor, pathetic creatures brought here for our help. It breaks my heart at times, it really does. We try our best to take care of God's creatures, but as you can see, so much more needs to be done."

Countess Kinnoull was not impressed by what she saw. The stench of urine and fecal matter reeked from the earth floors of the two fenced runs, one for dogs and the other for cats. She covered her mouth and nose with a handkerchief and followed her guide.

"Sorry for the smell, but the volunteer who helps clean up after the animals is running late today."

Dozens of wooden kennels were lined up across the yard. Dogs started barking at the presence of people. Anxious faces with sad eyes looked hopefully at them through the slats in the kennels.

"I'm shocked," said Lady Kinnoull. The words stuck in her throat as she fought back tears. "How can this crude shelter offer any warmth or comfort to these animals, not to mention the control of the spreading of diseases?"

"We do the best we can with the money that is donated. I assure you that a veterinarian sees each animal when they come in, and they are given a nutritious meal once a day along with snacks. Our volunteers bring in old blankets and towels whenever they can and try to take them out for walks twice a day."

"I'm sure you are all doing the best you can." Lady Kinnoull took one last look around.

"If only we had more donations and more people willing to adopt an animal," said the manager.

"Perhaps I can be of some help in that area. Thank you for the tour and you'll be hearing from me."

On the drive home, Countess Kinnoull smiled to herself; at last she had found a cause she could feel passionate about. She immediately contacted Noel Sullivan with her wishes to become a member of the SPCA.

Knowing what her influential circles around the Monterey Peninsula could mean for the organization, Noel suggested at the next SPCA board meeting that she be welcomed not just as a new member, but as a member of the board. It was agreed that a woman of her international stature could be beneficial to the organization.

In 1949 Countess Claude Kinnoull was elected as the newest member of the SPCA Board of Directors and became one of its most avid supporters, working tenaciously for the protection of animals.

When local veterinarians were unavailable, Red Eagle's knowledge as a medicine man sometimes carried over into the animal world. Lady Kinnoull, along with many other residents, often brought their sick dogs, cats and horses to him. They believed in his powerful connection with animals and his ability to cure their pets. The community of Carmel-by-the-Sea had such deep respect and admiration for Red Eagle

that when he became ill, the police would check in on him every hour to
see if he needed anything.

One day, Father de Moor, sat down with his morning coffee and
local paper. On the front page was a headline that made his heart sink.
He quickly ran up to the main house with paper in hand. He found Lady
Kinnoull in her studio.

"Claude, I'm afraid I have some very sad news." He handed her the
newspaper. The front-page headline was something she knew was
coming, but wasn't prepared for.

"Red Eagle, Carmel's Own Icon of the Wild West, Dies"

"My dear, dear friend," said Claude. She felt her throat tighten as
she choked back tears. "Did I ever tell you that I was his godmother?"

"He told me while we were building the house," said Vincent. "He
said that his spiritual journey had collided with yours."

Claude smiled. "I can just picture him soaring to loftier heights with
the wings of an Eagle." She brushed aside tears with the back of her
hand. "His was a life well lived."

Vincent put his arm around Claude's shoulder. "Let's go back in the
house and I'll read the rest of the article to you. But first I'll put on a pot
of tea."

The article went on to say that Chief Red Eagle had died after a
lengthy illness on January 10th. There was to be a Requiem Mass held
at the Carmel Mission and he was to be buried in Monterey's Catholic
Cemetery. He was a simple man and when he knew he was dying, he
wrote down that only a plain concrete marker bearing his name should
identify his grave.

After Red Eagle's death, Claude's days turned into shadows.
Florence and Jack tried their best to encourage her, but to no avail. In
desperation, Jack let Ali Baba and the other two dogs loose in her room.

The dogs seemed to do the trick. After they licked away the tears and sadness, Claude could not help but laugh. She decided that work at the SPCA would be the best way to honor Red Eagle's memory; after all, they had shared a deep love for animals.

Although the SPCA is a world-renowned organization, each chapter is a separate entity governed by its own policies and board of directors. Being an author, Countess Kinnoull volunteered to undertake the editorial tasks of the organization. She oversaw their newsletters and magazines, as well as the brochures used in fundraising drives. Her efforts and way with words began to pay off. New donations and memberships started pouring in.

Work on remodeling the David Avenue shelter commenced, but every attempt was hindered by complicated zoning restrictions. Although the day-to-day operations at the kennel began to improve, with more and more animal loving volunteers spending extended time with their wards, the need for expansion became increasingly apparent. However, when the neighbors started to complain about barking dogs it became obvious that increasing the David Avenue facility was out of the question.

That afternoon Countess Kinnoull drove over to the Catholic cemetery and parked her car by Red Eagle's grave. While she tugged at the blades of grass that had encroached upon the cement marker, she recounted to Red Eagle the struggles the SPCA was having in securing permits to improve the David Avenue shelter. She then placed a bouquet of his favorite wild flowers from her garden on his patch of ground. She looked around at the nearby headstones and was saddened that Red Eagle had requested such a plain marker. She knew that years from now the etchings in the stone would naturally fade with time, and the knowledge of Chief Red Eagle's connection to Carmel would also grow dim. She said a prayer for his soul, and then headed back to town.

Chief Red Eagle's Grave Marker

Countess Kinnoull stopped at the Carmel Craft Studio to talk with its manager, Fred Klepich, about her visit to the cemetery. Both being members of the Carmel Art Association, they decided something more accessible than a grave marker was needed to honor Chief Red Eagle. It needed to be something that people would see every day. The matter was brought up to the City Council. After much deliberation, it was decided that a wooden plaque with a carved head of an Indian in feathered headdress should mark the alleyway where Red Eagle traveled every day to and from his cottage in the back of the Murphy Lumber Yard. Countess Kinnoull and Fred Klepich said they would cover the cost of the sign.

On the day the plaque arrived, friends and council members were present when Countess Kinnoull had the distinct privilege of nailing up the sign while Fred Klepich held the ladder for her. She had this to say about her dear friend:

"Red Eagle could read only very little and could write no more than his name. He had no formal schooling, yet he was wise in many ways, civilized in his simplicity and he possessed education of the heart. For those of us who were honored with Red Eagle's friendship it will be a lasting satisfaction to see his name, inscribed on this attractive sign, enter the list of Carmel's outstanding citizens and become an honored part of our city's legend."

Eight years after Red Eagle's death, he finally acquired the formal recognition to be indelibly placed into the historical records as one of the enduring characters whose life has made Carmel such a unique village.

On this special day, Countess Claude Kinnoull, the benefactress and godmother of Red Eagle, transformed a dusty alleyway between San Carlos and Mission streets just south of Ocean Avenue, into the Red Eagle Trail. He will now be forever immortalized into the history books of the little village of Carmel-by-the-Sea.

Marker for the Chief Red Eagle Trail as seen today

Countess Kinnoull hanging plaque for Chief Red Eagle Trail
(Reproduced by permission of the Monterey Herald newspaper)

Chapter 43

A Most Generous Gift

Since the arrival of Jack and Florence Newbury, Countess Kinnoull knew that the day-to-day running of the household and her dogs was in good hands, which allowed her to once again immerse herself in her art.

The deadline to finish the painting of the *Adoration of the Virgin* for an Easter Exhibition at the Carmel Art Association Gallery was fast approaching. The spiritual realm of this painting kept her focus on heavenly things, helping her to escape the often distressing and heart-rending world news of nations rebuilding in the aftermath of war. She finally finished the painting in 1949. After an encouraging show at the gallery, Lady Kinnoull presented the *Adoration of the Virgin* as a gift to be put on permanent display at St. Angela's Catholic Church in Pacific Grove.

"Jack and I thoroughly enjoyed finally seeing your art displayed in a gallery," said Florence, who had just entered the studio with a pot of tea and some freshly baked scones. "We were so pleased hearing all the wonderful comments that the people were saying about your art. You're finally getting the recognition you rightfully deserve."

"Please stay and have tea with me and tell me how you and Jack have been. I get so busy with my art and the SPCA that I don't often have the time to sit and chat."

"Well, Jack and I certainly enjoy our work, except for the occasional aches and pains as one ages."

"Do you miss Europe, being such a long way from home?"

"I can tell you what I don't miss is the constant noise from all the rebuilding after the war. We're so grateful that you wanted us to join you here in Carmel."

"We've known each other a long time. To me you are my family. It's a comfort having you both here with me again."

"And you are like a daughter to us," said Florence as she poured their tea.

"What do you hear from that young niece of yours in England? She is always so prompt with a thank you card whenever I send a care package."

"I just received a letter yesterday from Jean and she says that there's less rationing now that the fields are producing again. And is excited to report that she and her fiancé Harry will soon wed. The sad part is they must postpone their honeymoon for a while since a lot of money was needed for her fiancé's medical bills from injury sustained during the war."

"How is he doing?"

"He's much better, and beginning to eat solid foods. The doctors believe he will have a full recovery, but it will just take time."

"Well, I think there is something I can do about this. I have an idea for a wedding present I think might please them. I'll be sure to write her."

Near the end of April in 1950, the Countess wrote to Jean who was living in England.

My Dear Jean,

We have all been thinking of you so much and are delighted at the news this evening that Harry is beginning to take food again and you should see more rapid improvement from now on. It will be a real answer to prayers – yours and ours.

Now, I am going to make you a suggestion, which I want you to consider carefully. Your Harry will certainly need a long period of rest, and probably a change of air, so what I am suggesting is that you should, as soon as he is well enough, get married and come out here for your honeymoon. I would pay all your travelling expenses and of course any other expenses that you might incur while here and would rent a nice little house for a month for you to be on your own – as one should be on a honeymoon! It would be my wedding present to you so I hope you will accept, and then enjoy it . . .

Countess Kinnoull continued to list five reasons that Jean and Harry should accept her wedding gift and suggested that any time before or after August would be best because she had previous business arrangements for that month. She then signed her letter *Miss Enid,* for that is what Jean had always called her.

Jean and Harry were overwhelmed by Miss Enid's generous offer. They set sail in the early fall from England on one of the larger Cunard Ocean Liners to New York, and then on to Carmel.

The young married couple were wined and dined by Miss Enid every evening at a new restaurant. Florence and Jack were brought to tears of joy by the outpouring of love and generosity she showered upon their niece and her husband.

One day the Countess decided Jean and Harry needed to see the beauty of Yosemite National Park, so they all piled into her car and drove about five hours to the park.

They spent the weekend photographing the splendor of the park's breathtaking landscape and enjoyed hand feeding the deer that freely roamed the forest.

When the month came to an end, the Newburys were sad to see their niece and her husband head back to England. However, in 1967 they did return to live permanently in Carmel with their two daughters, Sally and Ruth. That was also the year that Jack and Florence decided to buy a home of their own. They found a house close to the Kinnoull estate on Viscano Street.

Countess Kinnoull on the right feeding a deer in Yosemite National Park with Jean (Photo graciously provided by Jean Nieto)

Countess Kinnoull taking photo in Yosemite National Park.
(Photo graciously provided by Jean Nieto)

Chapter 44

The Mysteries of the Rosary

During the summer of 1955, Countess Kinnoull took time for a one-man show displaying her portrait paintings, drawings and mosaics at the Hidden Village Gallery of Monterey.

"What a lovely evening," said Claude after returning from the art show. "I was most pleased with the turnout."

"The diversity and boldness of your paintings brought in so many admirers," said Vincent. "There was one person in particular who was asking me all kinds of questions about you."

"No better person to ask than you," she replied. "Perhaps the person was interested in purchasing one of the paintings?"

"Actually, he is a Jesuit from the Santa Clara University, just south of San Francisco. Apparently the university has opened its own art gallery and museum. They have exhibitions several times during the year. He had heard about you and came down to view your paintings."

"How did he hear about me?"

"From our mutual friend, Noel Sullivan. Apparently he supports that Jesuit University and recommended that the gentleman take a look at your art."

"And was the gentleman interested?" asked Lady Kinnoull as she set up the chess set for their usual evening game.

"He was especially taken by the *Adoration of The Virgin* on loan from St. Angela's Church. But when I told him about the series of paintings you were working on for *The Mysteries of the Rosary,* he gave me his card and asked me to have you get in touch."

"He couldn't have come and talked with me himself?"

"Seeing you with a group of admirers, he did not want to interrupt a possible sale for you." Father de Moor handed her the man's business card.

"I'll give him a call tomorrow. Now let's get on with our game."

The next day she called the number on the card and spoke with the manager of the de Saisset Art Gallery at the Santa Clara University.

"Well, it looks like I'm going to be in another art exhibit next year," said Claude to Vincent when he appeared in the doorway to her studio.

"Glad to hear it. You should be out showing your art. When is the show?"

"The grand opening will be held in 1956 on Friday October 26 at 2 p.m., there is to be a tea, concert and art show. I do hope you will be able to attend."

"I wouldn't miss it and I'll be sure to tell our friend Noel Sullivan of the date. He will be most pleased."

Since moving to California, Countess Kinnoull's style of painting had been strong, but simple dramatic portraits. Her compositions of figures showed an emphasis on character with a well studied, limited color range. But when she began the *Mysteries of the Rosary* her style changed to a more modern accentuation, with bold bright colors producing effects resembling stained glass.

The rest of the year passed quickly. The Countess continued the finishing touches on the *Mysteries of the Rosary* in preparation for the October show. Invitations had been sent out more than a month before and there was an excitement in the air in anticipation of opening night.

Claude had been painting all morning and decided to take a break. After fixing herself a cup of tea, she picked up the unread morning paper and sat down at the dinning room table. She always turned to the society pages first to see which of her friends had made it into the news.

She took a sip of tea and glanced at the headlines. She felt her throat begin to close up. She started coughing . . . her hand began to tremble; tea splashed down on the newspaper and rolled onto her lap. Grabbing a napkin, she dabbed at the newspaper trying to preserve the article. The smudged black headline again jumped out at her.

Noel Sullivan Dies of a Massive Heart Attack!

Lady Kinnoull's eyes filled with tears as she tried to finish reading the article that recounted the long list of accomplishments of a most esteemed member of the Carmel society.

She couldn't believe that her dear friend Noel Sullivan, the one person who believed in her talents enough to get her paintings publically displayed in an exclusive show, at the now prestigious de Saisset Art Gallery, was gone! His dying on September 15th, just a few weeks shy of the art exhibit broke her heart, making her more determined than ever to put on a good show in his remembrance.

Friday, October 26 arrived with much anticipation. Countess Kinnoull woke early to a familiar aroma wafting through the house.

"Good morning, Jack. If I didn't know better, I'd say you were preparing the evening meal. It smells wonderful."

"Yes, we do have some lucky dogs here. I thought I'd have their meat and vegetables cooked before we head out to the gallery. I have tea steeping, let me get you a cup."

"That would be lovely." She looked out the kitchen window, glad to see the sun was already up.

"Wonderful day for an art show, Miss Enid." He handed her a teacup.

"Thank you, Jack. I think I might drive up a little early and check on the display. It's important the paintings be hung in the correct order. Perhaps Father de Moor could ride with you and Florence?"

"It would be our pleasure. Don't you worry about a thing. We'll see you before the program begins."

On the drive up north, Countess Kinnoull released any nervousness by engaging in her favorite pastime, the thrill of acceleration. While fast speed seemed to calm her, she knew it often terrified her friends. With an eye on the rearview mirror she sped along, trying to stay one step ahead of the highway patrol and any more tickets to add to her collection.

Finally arriving at the university, Countess Kinnoull turned into the almost empty parking lot and found a large oak tree to give her car shade from the warm and balmy 70-degree temperature. She was glad to have arrived early. She ascended the wide expanse of stairs leading to the lobby of the Spanish style de Saisset Museum and Gallery and was pleasantly surprised at its size. The two-storied façade of windows allowed a warm glow of sunlight to flood the room. She crossed the lobby to an auditorium and looked in.

"Countess Kinnoull, I recognize you from your picture. I'm so honored to meet our featured artist. I'm Mrs. Richard and I'll be in charge of the afternoon tea. I bet you're interested in seeing how your paintings are displayed."

"Yes, that is why I came early." She followed the woman across the auditorium. Several large round tables with white linens were interspersed throughout the room. Low circular glass vases filled with yellow roses, white carnations and baby's breath decorated each table. The main long tea table was covered with a gold lace tablecloth and anchored at each end was an elaborate silver tea service. Silver trays of varying heights displayed a variety of finger sandwiches and petit-four cakes. Tall, delicate china vases filled with long stem yellow roses ran the length of the table.

"Oh, Mrs. Richard, you have out done yourself! What beautiful decorations. You put on such a lovely tea. I can't express my gratitude enough."

"I was hoping you would be pleased. Now, if you go through those double doors on your left, they lead into the gallery. If you need anything be sure and let me know."

The moment she entered the gallery, she knew her art was in good hands. The curator had hung the paintings precisely as she had instructed. Although the gallery was filled with a variety of her art in oil, gold leaf and enamel, it was *The Mysteries of the Rosary* that took center stage. Stretched out across an entire wall was the life of Christ. She took her time reviewing each painting.

"The angels will be singing in heaven today." A deep voice from behind startled her.

The Countess turned around. Father de Moor stood with a big smile.

"I hope the angels like modern art," she said, smiling back.

"Didn't you know that any time a saint expresses a love for their savior, angels break out in a chorus? Speaking of music, the concert is about to start. Shall we join Jack and Florence?"

The auditorium was beginning to fill as people streamed in from the lobby.

"A most impressive room," said Vincent as they sat down at their reserved table.

The orchestra began to tune their instruments, preparing for the concert of religious music selected to set the mood for the unveiling of *The Mysteries of the Rosary.*

Countess Kinnoull later gifted the entire set of fifteen paintings to the Sisters of the Carmelite Monastery.

The Mysteries of the Rosary

Joyous Mysteries

Renunciation

The Visitation

The Birth of Jesus

Presentation in the Temple as a Baby

Finding Jesus in the Temple Preaching

The Sorrowful Mysteries

The Trial

The Scourging

Crown of Thorns

Carrying the Cross

The Crucifixion

The Glorious Mysteries

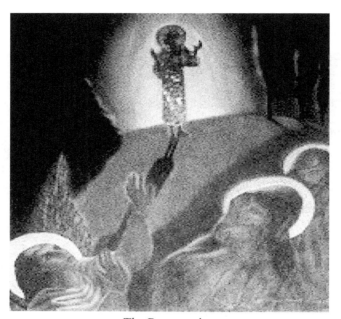

The Resurrection

The Ascension

The Holy Spirit

The Assumption of Blessed Mary Into Heaven

The Coronation

The Photos of the Mysteries of The Rosary were graciously provided by
the Sisters of the Carmelite Monestary

Chapter 45

Changing Times

The 1950s were contentious times in the village of Carmel. A group of thirty-three merchants formed a local Carmel Business Association, causing the residents to flock to the City Council meetings in outrage.

The Business Association tried to reassure the townspeople that they had no designs on their traditional way of life, but the residents would have no part of it, for they knew the association would try to lure new tourist businesses to their village.

One of the most vocal residents for keeping Carmel from commercialism was Countess Claude Kinnoull. She seldom attended the City Council meetings, but instead felt more comfortable going directly to the mayor or individual council members to voice her displeasure. This time her friends convinced her that as many residents as possible were needed for a good showing.

The City Hall, once the All Saints Episcopal Church, stood proudly on a hill with its brown wooden façade, bell steeple and large double doors giving the appearance that calming serenity awaits; not the often controversial disputes that the Council meetings were known for.

Countess Kinnoull made her way through the crowded vestibule, glad to see many familiar faces. She took a seat close to the public podium.

Mayor Horace D. Lyon called the meeting to order. "I can see by the wonderful attendance tonight that you all have a lot on your mind, but first there are a few items we have to clear from our docket

"First, the City Council has unanimously agreed to lift rent control since this wartime ruling has been determined no longer applicable or necessary.

"Seond, for those who have had concerns about the construction work that has been going on for over a year at the Carmel Mission, I'm happy to announce their new convent has been blessed and dedicated.

"Third, since we are on the subject of religion, the Planning Commission has finally granted a permit to the Presbyterian Church to construct a chapel at the junction of Junipero and Ocean Avenue.

"Fourth, we have had numerous complaints about male nakedness around town, so the City Council has put forth an ordinance that states that men must wear shirts while on the streets."

After the laughter subsided it was the public's turn to speak. Lady Kinnoull went to the podium.

"Mayor Lyon, Council Members and fellow residents, my name is Countess Claude Kinnoull and I've been a resident here since 1940. I, like many others, moved to this tranquil village-by-the sea to get away from the hectic city life. I draw your attention to the plaque that hangs directly behind you. It so eloquently states:

"The city of Carmel-by-the-Sea is hereby determined to be primarily, a residential city wherein business and commerce have in the past, are now, and are proposed to be in the future, subordinated to its residential character . . .

"The founding fathers of our charming little village were so concerned that those in charge should fight to keep Carmel-by-the-Sea from becoming a commercialized tourist destination that they engraved that mission statement onto a plaque, so that future Mayors and City Council members would be forever reminded of their duty to the residents above those of business before they made any decisions regarding development."

"Yes, Countess Kinnoull, we are well aware of the plaque on the wall and try to do the best to improve our city," said one of the Council members.

"But that's the point," continued the Countess. "What businesses consider as growth and improvement may very well lead to the destruction of the ambiance and charm that we residents have grown to love about our village. I, along with many of the people here tonight, are concerned that most shops that cater to residents are being quickly replaced by the more lucrative tourist gift shops which have now grown to twenty-three. And we oppose the Jade Tree Motel, planned for Junipero Street, because of its massiveness and towering height. After all, we already have forty-six motels and hotels, how many more do we need? Then to top it off, I read in the *Pine Cone* newspaper that there are plans to build a three-story Carmel Plaza on Ocean Avenue, which will cover an entire block. What are you thinking? I implore you all to reread the mission statement on that plaque each and every time you walk into these chambers before you make a decision, and to remember that we, the residents, voted for you."

Loud applause resounded through the audience. It was going to be a long evening.

The battle between the residents and the Business Association has never ceased, which is a good thing. The ambiance of this European style village-by-the-sea remains intact, although the shops have adapted through the years to reflect the ever-changing demographics of the throngs of tourists that delight in the uniqueness of this special place. However, the town's shops were just an indication of other changes about to happen.

Thunder rumbled in the distance and the wind picked up as Vincent and Claude quickened their pace across the cobbledstone courtyard of the Carmel Mission. Father de Moor looked up at the threatening dark clouds that appeared to have settled above the chapel.

"Looks like the angels are quarreling today," he said as they entered the narthex.

"And on a Sunday, no less," said Claude. She secured her lace head covering, dipped her fingers in the Holy Water, knelt and made the sign of the cross.

An usher handed them both a program, then they made their way down the aisle to the front row pew. Waiting for the service to begin, Claude glanced at the program. She nudged Vincent.

"I wonder what this is all about?" She pointed to the last item on the program. It read: *Please remain seated for an important announcement.*

"Probably a collection for something, or someone," he replied.

The choir began to sing while a few stranglers found their seats. Claude missed the clear operatic voice of her dear friend Noel Sullivan. Not a whisper could be heard when his singing brought the whole congregation into the reflective reverence and adoration appropriately needed to worship the glory of God. But now, distracting murmurs could be heard while the choir sang.

When the priests came forward to celebrate the Traditional Latin Tridentine Mass, dressed in their finest vestments, the congregation became silent. Ornate gold framed religious artwork and massive golden candlesticks adorned the altar. With their backs toward the congregation, the priests knelt on the steps leading to the altar. They raised their hands in adoration. Lady Kinnoull felt a chill. She could feel the presence of the Lord as the priests chanted Latin prayers of exaltation to Christ and raised the chalice in His honor.

When the service ended the congregation remained seated, wondering what the special announcement might be. One of the priests went to the podium facing the audience.

"I want to thank all of you for remaining and I'll only take a moment of your time. On this Sunday, January 25, 1959, Pope John XXIII has given notice of his intentions to convene the Second Vatican Council. As many of you know, the First Vatican Council was cut short when war broke out. Although the role of the Papacy and the congruent relationship of faith and reason were completed, the pastoral issues concerning the direction of the Church were not addressed. The Pope wants to adress relations between the Roman Catholic Church and the modern world. He plans to convene the Second Vatican Council in Rome calling for a worldwide gathering of 2500 Catholic cardinals, archbishops and bishops. We will keep you updated as soon as we hear anything. *Benedicam tibi et vade in pace.*"

Countess Kinnoull looked at Father de Moor. "I don't understand. What does this mean?"

"It means that the Catholic Church will be changing to suit the modern world. Just exactly what that means we won't know until the Council actually meets. It might mean changing the language of the Mass to be understood by more people."

"But I like the church the way it is. It's the beauty of the Latin Mass that first drew me to convert to Catholicism. But once I learned more about my new religion, I began to realize the reverence to the Lord that each traditon meant. When the priests turn their backs on the congregation and face the cross, they were worshipping the Lord. They do not try to appease the congregation as you see in other religions. It's the reverence implied by the traditions that mean so much. You don't think they will take it away, do you?"

"I doubt they would take away something so meaningful to so many. But the question still remains, is the Latin Mass relevant in today's modern society?"

"Yes, it is relevant," said Claude as they walked through the parking lot toward her car. "You can travel anywhere in this so-called modern world and walk into any Catholic Church and understand the service because they are all spoken in Latin. Maybe I should start a petition going."

"Not so fast," replied Vincent. "This will be a long process. Just getting 2500 cardinals, archbishops and bishops together in Rome is a monumental task in and of itself. Most of these men have their schedules booked for the entire year. You are probably looking at more than two years before any major decisions will be coming forth from Rome. Can you imagine trying to get all those men to agree on adopting new church policy?"

"You're right, but we cannot sit by and have our traditions trashed so the church will fit in with modern society. We can start writing letters now. Do you know any cardinals or archbishops?"

"Actually you may already know an archbishop who I think would be very receptive to a letter from you regarding this issue."

"When did I meet this archbishop?" she asked when they reached her car.

"Do you mind if I drive?" asked Vincent. "There is something I'd like to show you in Carmel Valley."

"Go ahead." Claude tossed him the keys and got into the passenger side of the car. "Now, about that archbishop?"

"Well, during our adventures in Africa we may have met a Father Marcel Lefebvre. Early on in his work for the White Fathers in Africa, Marcel showed a remarkable aptitude in teaching other priests dogmatic theology and Sacred Scripture. It has been said that he was very popular with his students not only for his pleasant and smiling demeanor, but that he always stood firm in his principles. His keen interest in math equipped him for the challenging position of keeping the seminary's finances in order. Another area in which he excelled was his mechanical knowledge in maintaining all the missions' vehicles in good working condition. This particular gift landed him the appointed job as the mission driver, which took him to the numerous missions throughout the vast area of Gabon in the Congo."

"You're quite right. Surely we must have run into him, but after almost a year of meeting with so many priests in our travels it would be hard to remember all their names. And now that he's an archbishop, you feel that he is the one I should write to regarding my concerns?"

"Yes, I think he would be a good start."

"Well then, if you can work on getting his address, I'll start writing the letter. It will be interesting to see where Archbishop Lefebvre stands on this new modernism of the Church."

They drove along the serpentine Carmel Valley Road where the sun always seems in abundance. Massive oak trees dotted the landscape. Vincent turned onto a narrow side road, then pulled into a clearing and parked the car.

"Well, here it is." He got out of the car and Claude followed.

"But there is nothing here but a vacant lot."

"It won't be vacant for long, once I build the stone house."

"I don't understand. Are you not happy in the cottage on my property?"

"Now don't be upset with me. I've always had a dream that when I retired I would have my own little piece of land."

"How could I ever be upset with you? I'm happy for you. Now show me how the house will be laid out."

He broke a twig off an oak tree and drew the design for his house in the dirt.

"Your cottage has been wonderful and you gave me the opportunity to hone my building skills. But I'm afraid the damp ocean climate is causing my bones to ache in my old age. I've been searching for a warmer climate and when this piece of property came on the market, I jumped at the chance. Since I will only be a few miles away, I hope we can continue our evening chess games?"

"But of course," replied Claude. "And can I still expect your fabulous French cooking wafting through my kitchen every now and then?"

"I wouldn't have it any other way," he said.

Father de Moor was finally at peace. His dream of owning land and building his very own cottage by the sweat of his brow, was becoming a reality. For the next two years, his humble abode was a meeting place for several young priests. They spent many an afternoon in deep, philosophical discussions regarding the different interpretations of the Bible. However, he never missed a visit to Countess Kinnoull's home, for their appointed evening chess game and dessert.

It was a brisk November evening in 1961. Florence had just put away the dinner dishes, when the timer on the oven went off. She reached down with a couple of pot holders and smiled when she opened the oven door. Countess Kinnoull was drawn into the kitchen by the spicey aroma.

"Whatever you're cooking for dessert smells heavenly."

"It's one of Father de Moor's favorites, an apple pie," she replied.

Jack came in from feeding the dogs. "Can't wait to taste that pie." He looked at the clock on the kitchen wall. "Father de Moor seems to be running a bit late tonight."

"Yes. It's not like him to be late for anything," said Lady Kinnoull. "I hope his car didn't break down."

"I'll put the kettle on for some tea while we wait," said Florence.

"I tried to talk him into putting in a phone at his cottage, but he wouldn't hear of it. Now maybe he'll change his mind," said the Countess.

"If you like, I'll take a drive over there and pick him up," said Jack. "Maybe he fell asleep and forgot to set an alarm clock."

A vision of Vincent's strong arms carrying her mud soaked body from the quicksand gave her a chill. He needs me, she thought. "I'm going with you," said Lady Kinnoull.

"You two go ahead and I'll stay and keep an eye on things here," said Florence.

"Now, don't you eat any of that pie while we're gone," said Jack, trying to make light of the situation.

When they arrived at the cottage there were no lights on. Father de Moor's car was still parked in the driveway. They called out to him, but there was no answer. Jack pounded loudly on the front door.

"Father de Moor," he shouted. "It's Jack. Are you in there?" He tried the door knob, it was unlocked. They both entered into a darkened room. Jack felt along the wall for a light switch.

"Oh, dear Lord," said Lady Kinnoull, when the light illuminated the room. She rushed over to Father de Moor's body sprawled face up on the floor. "Vincent! Vincent! It's Claude. Can you hear me?" She held his cold hand, trying to find a pulse. "I can't find his pulse!" She looked up at Jack.

Jack put his hand on Vincent's neck, finding the carotid artery, hoping to feel a pulse, but there was none. "I'm afraid he's gone. I see no sign of a struggle and no blood stains. It looks like his heart just gave out." He gently reached over and closed the eyelids. "We'll need to call the police. The restaurant we passed on the way here, should have a phone."

"I won't leave him alone," said Claude, tears streaming down her face.

"I'll hurry," said Jack as he ran out the door.

Countess Kinnoull sat next to the body. "My dear, dear friend. Our lives were so intertwined. You were that father mentor that I so longed for, my godfather and teacher whose knowledge always amazed me. We certainly were a pair, weren't we? The two of us traisping across Africa. I, never afraid, knowing you were there with your hunting rifle and you, petrified with fear at my driving and flying. With us both relying on Divine Providence we made it through some harrowing experiences." She reached over and held his hand. "I know I should be happy for you, because you are in a better place with the Lord. But you leave an empty space in my heart, a space that will ache everytime I see a chess set and recall those long conversations we had, as we tried to solve all the world's problems; oh, how I'll miss those." She heard the approaching siren of an ambulance. "I'll miss you!" She bent over and gently kissed his forehead, placing his hand across his heart. "May you rest in peace, my dear dear friend."

Monsignor Vincent de Moor had died on November 18, 1961.

Harold Willis, Florence Newbury, Father de Moor, Jean (Willis) Neito, with Jack Newbury along with the Willis girls: Ruth and Sally standing in front of Father de Moor's stone house (Photo graciously provided by Jean Neito)

Saddened by the loss of her dear friend and godfather, Claude felt like the world was closing in on her. She longed for those friends who really understood her. But the irreversible hands of time were ticking faster . . . for those few remaining.

Florence brought up a breakfast tray to her room. "You really must eat something, Miss Enid. It's been a few days now. You can't keep on like this."

"I know you mean well, Florence. But I haven't been able to sleep and I just don't have an appetite."

"Well Miss Enid, I've been looking after you for many years. I promised your mother that I'd take care of you, and I'm not going to stop now. I'm going to draw you a warm bath while you eat some of that hot oatmeal. And if you give me any trouble, I might just have to call on Jack, and you know how ornery he can be." Florence propped Enid up with several pillows and stood staring until she ate a spoonful of oatmeal.

Countess Kinnoull smiled. She was lucky to still have such loving friends looking after her.

"By the way," Florence yelled from the bathroom. "Your editor keeps leaving messages for you to call. He's worried that you'll miss the Christmas deadline. Now, that's something that you should be putting your mind to."

"You are absolutely right, Florence. I have obligations and commitments to others that I need to honor. By the way, the oatmeal tastes delicious."

"Welcome back," said Florence with a smile of relief.

For the next few days, Countess Kinnoull immersed herself in finishing her short story, *The Unlikely One,* about a serviceman and his dog, which was published in time for Christmas.

Meanwhile, she continued with her writing campaign to anyone who would listen to her demands that the Latin Mass not be subjugated to any changes to placate modern society.

Once her book was published and the holidays were over, Providence stepped in again, at the March 1962 SPCA Board meeting. Two amazing women, both with a heart for animals, emerged to form a mighty force to be reckoned with.

British-born Countess Claude Kinnoull and Hawaiian-born Gwendolyn Rycroft May became the dynamic duo fighting against cruelty to all animals. They formed a friendship with a special bond that lasted a lifetime. When tipped off on abuses to animals, the two would head out in search of justice. Gwen with an official looking clipboard and Claude with a camera would approach the unsuspecting violator.

"Excuse me, sir," Gwen would say. "I'm from the SPCA and would like to ask you a few questions regarding your animals."

Then Claude would look around at the rolling hills and distract the man. "Sir, I've never seen such gorgeous countryside. I'm an artist and would love to paint this landscape. Would you mind if I take a few pictures for my work?"

"Nah, go ahead. It's even prettier when the wildflowers start to bloom," said the man.

As Claude aimed her camera at the surrounding landscape she ambled closer and closer to the dilapidated remains of a weather-beaten barn. Gwen skillfully maneuvered around so the man's back was to the barn. Claude zoomed in on the rib cages of the obviously malnourished workhorses in the corral. Adjusting the focus she took several close-up photos, then joined Gwen who was writing up a warning citation for the man to improve the conditions for his horses.

"Times are tough and I have no money for hay or oats. I can't afford a fine, lady. I'll get paid for my crops next week, then I can provide better for them."

"We can deliver a week's worth of hay and feed to tide you over," said Gwen, "but after that if you neglect them you most likely will lose them."

Driving back to the SPCA both ladies realized that their current facility was no longer adequate. They were going to need much more acreage that would allow for the care of larger animals and a wildlife refuge.

Many animal abuse cases were settled in court when the undisputed photographs of the malnourished horses, dogs and cats were brought forth by the dynamic duo trying to save them.

Animal supporters after hearing of the SPCA's land dilemma finally stepped up, providing money to purchase a nine-acre parcel between Monterey and Salinas.

A donation box for the SPCA
Countess Kinnoull brought it back from England

Countess Kinnoull with one of her poodles
(Photo graciously provided by The Anita Roy Family)

Countess Kinnoull with one of her poodles ready for a show
(Photo graciously provided by The Anita Roy Family)

Chapter 46

A Chance Meeting

It took until October 11, 1962, for the Second Vatican Council under the pontificate of Pope John XXIII to formally convene, and another three years for the Council to debate the renewal of Catholic doctrine in a modern timeline and perspective. On December 8, 1965, under Pope Paul VI, the Second Vatican Council convened for the last time.

When the results of the Council were made known to the church members, many applauded while others were in shock. The most obvious changes included the widespread use of native language in Holy Mass instead of the Latin language . . . and the subtle elimination of ornate clerical vestments, elaborate golden candle holders and intricately framed religious artwork. But it was when the priests performing the Holy Mass were instructed to face the congregation instead of facing east toward the Lord that Countess Kinnoull felt a profound sadness and outrage. Now it looked to her as if the priests were worshipping the congregation instead of the Lord. When contemporary Catholic music replaced the more traditional spiritual music, even with the accommodation for a set of drums and guitars, the Countess decided to leave the Carmel Mission and attend the more conservative service at the Carmelite Monastery.

Countess Kinnoull felt at home with the nuns at the Monastery and they enjoyed her company. She would often attend the chapel service accompanied with her two standard size poodles. The nuns didn't mind, so this went on for a while until others started bringing their dogs. Sadly, a woman attending services complained, which put an end to any dogs being allowed in the chapel. The nuns would take turns caring for the Countess's poodles while she attended mass. Sister Francisca said she enjoyed her talks with Lady Kinnoull, but sensed a sad soul. She often prayed for the Countess.

In 1966, the month of June brought only five days of summer weather before the fog crept in from the ocean, enveloping Carmel in a constant drizzling dampness that lingered under the canopy of towering pine trees.

Lady Kinnoull felt the chains of depression dragging her down and decided a vacation was in order. By the end of June she had packed her bags and was off to Paris, knowing that July and August were its warmest and sunniest months. She longed to stroll along the River Seine with its abundance of plein-air artists demonstrating their propensity for French Impressionism.

Although she was seeking warmer weather, Lady Kinnoull had forgotten how throngs of tourists also flocked to Paris for the summer. Unfortunately, all her friends had seemed to disappear on their month-long vacations just as quickly as the tourists had arrived. But she was not deterred. Dusting off her sketchpad she headed to the park a few blocks from her apartment.

The magnificent black and gold intricate grillwork on the massive double gate marked one of many entrances to the twenty acres of Parc Monceau. Although it was only a ten-minute walk to the bustling Champs-Elysées with its throngs of tourists, few ventured through these gates, much to the delight of the local residents. Beyond the gates one was transported into a different realm, transfixed into a dream-like state. Statues of writers and musicians were interspersed along dirt pathways shaded by stately trees of various hues of green, offering protection from the sun. Flowers bloomed profusely during the summer months, displaying a lavish array of colorful blossoms. Lady Kinnoull stood on a stone bridge looking down at a pond covered with floating lilies. She remembered that Monet had done a series of three paintings of this park in 1876 and then another two in 1878. Sitting down at a bench by the water she took out her sketchpad. A large Weeping Willow tree claimed an island for itself in the middle of the pond. She began to sketch.

Before she realized it, an hour had passed. While gathering up her sketches she noticed a folded newspaper at the far end of the bench. The word LEFEBVRE in a partial headline caught her eye. Could it possibly be . . . she wondered? She picked up the paper.

ARCHBISHOP LEFEBVRE VISITING THE LATIN QUARTER

The article went on to say that the Archbishop Marcel Lefebvre, who was elected by the Chapter of the Holy Ghost Fathers in July 1962 as their Superior General, was widely respected for his experience in the mission field. He was visiting 30 Rue Lhomond in the Latin Quarter to put in place major reforms of the seminaries run by the Holy Ghost Fathers.

He had caused quite a stir when he transferred several liberal professors to non-educational posts and ordered books by certain modern theologians to be removed from the seminary library.

The Archbishop had proposed the publication of a multilingual newsletter. It would provide information and examination of the Council's recommendations, which would help the bishops to make sound interpretation and take practical measures against progressivism. This he hoped would enable the bishops to take action on a worldwide scale to defend and promote the truth.

She put the newspaper in with her sketchpad. Providence has once again played its hand, thought Countess Kinnoull. She rushed home to make a historically significant phone call.

"Operator, I'd like to place a call to the Holy Ghost Fathers' Seminary at 30 Rue Lhomond in the Latin Quarter."

"I'll connect you now," said the operator.

Marcel Lefebvre had just placed his briefcase next to his luggage when the phone rang.

"Hello?"

"I'd like to speak to Archbishop Lefebvre."

"Speaking."

"Archbishop, I'm so glad I was able to reach you. My name is Countess Claude Kinnoull. Perhaps you remember me from my letters?"

"I do remember the name. It's a blessing to hear from a parishioner so passionate for traditional Latin services."

"It is imperative that I meet with you as soon as possible."

"I'm afraid that I'm leaving now for Orly Airport to fly back to Rome. But if this meeting is as urgent as it sounds, perhaps you can meet me there. I'll have an hour before my flight."

"Thank you for seeing me. I'll leave immediately."

Thirty minutes later an announcement crackled over the intercom at Orly Airport.

"Paging Archbishop Lefebvre, paging Archbishop Lefebvre. Please come to the Customer Service Counter. Your party is waiting."

Hearing his name announced over the loud speaker, the Archbishop made his way to the counter where he met Countess Kinnoull.

"Your Grace, I am honored that you would take the time to see me."

"My child, what is this urgency you speak of?"

"I have been most troubled since the Second Vatican Council convened. I fear for the Catholic Church and for the Traditional Latin Mass. Your articles regarding these concerns gives me much comfort in these trying times. I agree with you one hundred per cent, as do many of us, in the fight for the Traditional ways. And now I believe that Providence has placed me in a situation where I may be of assistance to you."

"I'm afraid I don't understand," said the Archbishop.

She reached into her purse and pulled out her checkbook. "I'm giving you a donation for your continued work in promoting the importance of the true Traditional Latin Mass and I will gladly give more." Along with a substantial check, she handed the Archbishop contact information for her English solicitor, who would expedite any further funds needed.

"Your generous and most unexpected gift will allow me to purchase the much needed office equipment to ensure a more professional newsletter. It will help keep up our fight for Tradition." He thanked and blessed the Countess, then hurried off to catch his flight to Rome.

The first edition of the newsletter appeared in August 1967 under the title *Fortes in Fide* (Strong in the Faith*)*.

Many influential liberal members of the Archbishop's large religious congregation began to criticize his motives, considering him out of step with the modern Church leaders and the Second Vatican Council recommendations.

In September 1968 a General Chapter of the Holy Ghost Fathers met in Rome. Their first order of business was to name several moderators to lead the Chapter's sessions instead of their Superior General, Archbishop Marcel Lefebvre.

Feeling that it had become impossible for him to remain Superior General of an institute that no longer wanted nor listened to him, Archbishop Lefebvre handed in his resignation as Superior General to His Holiness Pope Paul VI.

On October 28th, a new Superior General was elected who was willing to allow the demands for reform. When the Holy Ghost Fathers began to implement the changes called for, toward modernism . . . Archbishop Lefebvre left with a sad heart, but with a determination to train up priests in the traditional ways.

When Lady Kinnoull heard of his departure from the Holy Ghost Fathers, she also withdrew her longtime financial support of the White Fathers as they began implementing the modern changes in their missions in Africa. Instead, when Archbishop Lefebvre founded the St. Pius X Association in July 1969 for Priestly Training, Countess

Kinnoull paid the majority of the expenses for their quarters at the Don Bosco House in Fribourg, Switzerland. A short time later, she provided financial assistance to obtain the Seminary property Diocese of Fribourg in Écône, Switzerland.

Countess Kinnoull was adamant that the Traditional Latin Mass be allowed to continue because in her view it was the foundation of the Catholic faith. She stood by and supported Archbishop Lefebvre because he followed the laws of the Church in everything, except when it would adversely affect the defense of the Catholic faith.

Upon her return to her home in Carmel, Countess Kinnoull continued with financial support of the Society of St. Pius X and often corresponded with the Archbishop, who kept her informed of the growth of the Society. Whenever his schedule allowed a respite at the Society's retreat in Los Gatos, California, the Archbishop always welcomed a visit from the Society's benefactress.

Once back from Paris, Countess Kinnoull was eager to immerse herself in the everyday activities of the SPCA. By the late 1960s they were actively looking for a new property. After many disappointments and rejections, a large piece of land (along the Monterey-Salinas highway adjacent to the SPCA's current location) became available with a manageable price tag. Lady Kinnoull, now vice president of the SPCA, and Gwen May, executive director, explored the one hundred and fifty-eight acres along with William Kennedy, current president of the organization.

Countess Kinnoull, not wanting to annoy any neighbors with barking dogs, purchased the property with the help of another substantial donor, the Grover Hermann Family. They now had a total of one hundred and ninety-seven acres. The property was then donated to the SPCA in two parcels – one for immediate use and the other to be added later, if the SPCA continued to carry on its functions for all animals. The funds provided to purchase this property, which had been slated for a subdivision housing use, insured that it would now remain a wilderness in perpetuity. According to the deed, no portion of the land could be sold for any other use. They called the land *La Vega Verde* (The Green Fertile Valley).

"Well, now that the SPCA has a new location, we must act quickly to raise funds for the building of structures and fencing," said Gwen at a 1968 Board of Directors meeting.

"If we are to draw in the most influential donors," replied William Kennedy "then we need to present them with something that will tug at their hearts so they will open their deep pockets."

"I agree," said Countess Kinnoull. "I think the history of our SPCA, from its inception in 1905 to what it has now become, would show donors the importance of their contributions."

"That's a marvelous idea," said Gwen. "And I take it since you are the current in-house writer that you will take on this project?"

"I'd be honored," said Lady Kinnoull.

While the Countess worked on an in-depth history of the SPCA, two other members gave anonymously the sum of $100,000 dollars toward the construction of new buildings for *La Vega Verde*. The grand opening for the new facility was in 1967.

Lady Kinnoull spent many long hours scouring the minutes of past SPCA meetings from 1905 to the current date to formulate a cohesive historical account of the Monterey SPCA. Finally, in 1969 the task was accomplished and presented to the board.

"It is with great pride," said Countess Kinnoull, "that I present to you the much awaited culmination of the historical record of our beloved SPCA, *An Open Door: The Monterey County SPCA from 1905 to 1970.*"

A resounding applause and cheers filled the room as Lady Kinnoull passed around copies.

"As I say in the forward," the Countess continued, "*The aim of this work is to give a picture of a human endeavor kept going through two world wars and the Great Depression, through periods of apathy and times of prosperity by people who, succeeding one another over the years, shared a belief in the essential rightness and justice of what they were doing."*

The new, improved facility gave each dog its own indoor cage with an outdoor run; and with custom floor heating, all animals would now be comfortable even if temperatures outside dropped to freezing.

In April 1969 an obituary in the morning paper caught the eye of Jack Newbury.

"I say, Lady Kinnoull, this sounds like a person you would have enjoyed meeting. This George Whittell, Jr., was quite a character. It says here that he was a flamboyant millionaire who enjoyed piloting planes, fast cars and wild animals . . . now that's right up your alley. He at one time owned virtually the entire Lake Tahoe frontage on the Nevada side. And get a load of this; he actually had lions, elephants and a giraffe roaming his estate." He handed her the obituary page.

Lady Kinnoull read the article and smiled. "Jack, you didn't tell me the most significant part. Mr. Whittell prefaced his will with the following declaration: *'It is my desire the funds be used to relieve pain and suffering among animal, bird and fish life and to preserve, improve and perpetuate animal, bird and fish life . . . '* It goes on to say that after leaving $100,000 to the University of San Francisco, Mr. Whittell donated the bulk of his estate to the *Defenders of Wildlife,* the *Society for the Prevention of Cruelty to Animals,* and the *National Audubon Society.* But it doesn't mention if he wanted the national or local chapters to receive the proceeds."

"Does that mean the Monterey SPCA could receive funds?" asked Jack.

"It means that there will probably be a battle for the funds . . . I'm going to write out a grant request today. Bless you, Jack, for bringing this to my attention."

Countess Kinnoull submitted the history of the Monterey County SPCA from 1905 to 1970 along with a formal grant request to the

George Whittell Estate and prayed. The fact that so many local independent SPCA organizations were all vying for part of the funds could tie up grant requests in the courts for years.

While waiting for a reply on her request, Countess Kinnoull worked diligently to increase new membership for the SPCA. As head of the membership committee she helped to increase the membership by eighty per cent. At one of the many receptions given for new members, Lady Kinnoull met a woman who not only donated money to the cause, but also actually worked physically with the horses she so passionately fought to protect.

"Countess Claude Kinnoull," said one of the board members, "I'd like you to meet Sharon Andreason, a fellow horse enthusiast."

"It is a pleasure meeting a kindred spirit," said Lady Kinnoull, offering her hand.

"The pleasure is all mine, but did I hear correctly that you are a countess?"

"The title is helpful in raising funds, but you may call me Claude."

"Then Claude it shall be, and my wish is that we become good friends, for I'm new to the Monterey Peninsula."

"I'd like to hear how you became involved with horses and how the SPCA can be of help to you," said Claude. "I see two chairs by the window. Let's take our tea over there and you can tell me all about yourself."

The two ladies soon became good friends, having conversations about legal fights for horses during their many luncheons together. Claude told Sharon of her recent funding of an organization for horses and mules in Egypt and gave her contact information to organizations involved with horse abuse issues in the United States.

Sharon later supported these organizations for a while, but grew restless and found them not progressive enough. She decided to bring up these frustrations to Claude.

"You must never give up on your dream," said Claude. "Sometimes it only takes one person with a passion to get things moving in the right direction."

"What about the SPCA? Do you think they might be able to help more with abused horses?" asked Sharon.

"I'm afraid as I grow older I become more battle weary with the board trying to see eye to eye on projects. I fear that the land is not being used to its fullest for animals. While wildlife habitat is an important use of part of the land, there are other animals in need that should not be excluded. There is an area that would be perfect for the rescue and rehabilitation of horses and mules." Claude put her hand on Sharon's shoulder. "When I'm long gone, I hope you will rally for the cause."

"You can count on me, but let's hope you're still here to see your efforts fulfilled."

Sharon Andreason went on to put her energy and money into founding *Horse Power,* which got things moving in California and ultimately lead to national legislation.

In 1975 Gwen May and Countess Kinnoull resigned from the board of the SPCA. But the dynamic duo was not retiring from work. They founded the *Animal Welfare Information and Assistance* program, later known as AWAG (Animal Welfare Assistance group). This group provided financial and educational assistance to low-income individuals, families and seniors with pets.

Several years later, Countess Kinnoull's tenacious efforts in fundraising finally paid off when the Monterey SPCA received not one but two different grants from the George Whittell Foundation. The first funding helped to build an education center, which opened in 1979. The SPCA's humane educator, Judy McCormack, was able to teach and instill better humane attitudes toward animals in over 25,000 children a year.

The second, more substantial grant of $400,000 provided the means to build a much needed wildlife center on a hill overlooking the SPCA shelter. It opened in 1982 as the country's most elaborate facility of its kind, with custom-built cages and aviaries and its own veterinary hospital.

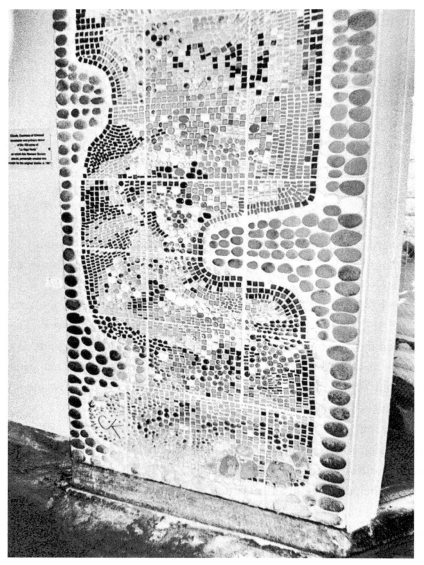

A mosaic at the Monterey SPCA made by Countess Claude Kinnoull

Chapter 47

The Changing of Staff

When Florence developed painful arthritis in her hands and Jack suffered from chronic back pain, they decided it was time to retire. With the Newbury's retirement, Lady Kinnoull began a search for a new cook and housekeeper. In 1975 Helen Dunn, a widow from Lake Forest, Illinois, became the chef and companion to Countess Kinnoull.

As the years wore on, Lady Kinnoull could no longer handle the everyday details of running her estate by herself. She sat down near the fireplace and looked up at the large colorful mosaic and reminisced about the years spent collecting the various pebbles and stones.

Helen brought in a tea tray with fresh scones and a pot of Earl Grey. "I thought this might cheer you up a bit, Miss."

"Thank you, Helen. Tea always seems to give me a much clearer mind. Would you be so kind as to ask Lauretta to please join me for tea?"

"Certainly, I'll bring another cup."

Lauretta sat across from Lady Kinnoull and Helen poured their tea.

"You seem troubled today," said Lauretta. "Can I help?"

"I am feeling a bit down. At seventy-five years old, I find I don't have the energy to get anything done. The poor dogs are beginning to suffer from my neglect. You wouldn't know by the way they look today, that they were once show dogs."

"I would offer to help you with them, but I'm afraid their size overpowers me. But I know someone who might be able to help. My sister Anita Roy is in need of a part-time job. She's a lot sturdier than I am and she loves animals. Right now she's staying with our mother and looking for a place to rent."

"Why don't you have her come this afternoon and I'll see how the dogs get along with her?"

That afternoon, when five foot tall Anita, dressed in black slacks and a long sleeved white blouse, approached the Kinnoull estate, two rambunctious, standard size poodles bolted from the front door heading straight for her. Having been warned by her sister of the dogs' playfulness, Anita stood firm and opened her arms wide.

"*Bonjour mes enfants.*"

When the dogs heard the same greeting that their master always spoke, they both jumped up on Anita and licked her face.

"Oh, you naughty boys. Leave the poor woman alone. Look what they've done to your blouse," said Lady Kinnoull.

"No harm done. What's a little dirt among friends? Countess Kinnoull, I'm Anita Roy. I believe my sister spoke to you about me?"

"Yes. She said you love animals, but did not mention that you also speak French."

"*Mais oui,*" replied Anita.

"I'm so pleased," said the Countess. "I miss the beautiful French language . . . talking to my dogs in French has not been enough. Now to be able to converse with another person in my favorite language will bring me such joy. Please come inside and I'll show you their routine."

That evening Anita had dinner with her sister.

"Well . . . I got the job," said Anita. "And I had the dogs eating out of my hands. Of course, it helped that I had treats for them."

"Now remember," said Lauretta, "I recommended you for this job. She is a countess after all, and deserves the respect of one."

"I did notice a faint air of nobility, but the moment I started speaking French all barriers came tumbling down. Why, you should have heard her laugh at one of my jokes."

"No! You didn't tell her one of your stupid jokes!" Lauretta's mouth dropped in a look of shock.

"She rather liked it . . . and came back with one of her own," said Anita. "I'm beginning to think that your countess might be a comedian in disguise."

"I won't have you talking about her like that," snapped Lauretta. "And when you are in her home you need to keep your place."

"Not to worry, sister . . . I'll wait until she warms up to me." Anita smiled.

While Lauretta was an excellent secretary, always dressed prim and proper with a most serious attitude, Anita was just the opposite. Her simpler, casual dress, bold opinions and feisty sense of humor endeared her to Countess Kinnoull. Knowing that Anita was looking for a place of her own, Lady Kinnoull offered her the house that Father de Moor had built on the property.

Each evening after her chores, Anita would visit Lady Kinnoull for a cocktail while they fed the numerous raccoons and conversed only in French, trying to out do one another with their jokes.

What started out as a part-time job taking care of the dogs turned into an enduring friendship. These two ladies from different social situations had a special bond. Anita reminded the Countess of herself when she was younger.

Countess Claude Kinnoull was a product of her time and class. She kept most people at a distance. She had a great sense of who she was, the wealth of her family, their nobility, and her title. Although she projected a formidable presence, like a miniature tiger, one sensed a certain loneliness. This became evident one Christmas.

Chapter 48

A Christmas to Remember

In the fall of 1979, at a private chapel in Monterey, California, a mutual friend introduced Nancy Welch to Countess Kinnoull. Ever since the Second Vatican Council convened, the believers in the Traditional Latin Mass kept this small chapel very much *sub rosa* (in secret). It's members often asked permission to bring new converts.

The woman standing before Nancy was barely 5'3" in heels, and was dressed in a suit of the latest haute couture style. A woman of substance, she thought.

Lady Kinnoull smiled at the woman about her same height that, like herself many years ago, was just now beginning her spiritual journey. "I understand that we are both converts to the Catholic religion and that you have also met with Archbishop Lefebvre."

"Yes, he did my confirmation last year."

"I know that the Archbishop spends some much needed rest in Campbell, California once a year. Perhaps you would like to join me for a visit the next time he is in the area?"

"That would be lovely," said Nancy. "I'll look forward to it."

They entered the chapel where Nancy was about to witness her first Latin High Mass. The sweet aroma of burning frankincense and myrrh permeated the chapel. When the singing of the Gregorian chant filled the room, a spiritual reverence transpired that Nancy had never felt before; an overwhelming sense of connection to the presence of the Lord. Tears streamed down her face when the service concluded.

"So what did you think of our Mass?" asked the Countess as they walked to their cars.

"It was magnificent. I can't believe what I have been missing. Why would this type of Holy Mass be replaced to satisfy the secular whims of society?"

"It is most disturbing, isn't it?" said Lady Kinnoull. "That is why we must be diligent and pursue the Holy fight to keep the Traditional Latin Mass as a sacred part of the Catholic Church."

"I wholeheartedly agree," replied Nancy, "for I am now totally converted to the Traditional Mass and will attend this private chapel from now on."

But to be a Traditionalist Catholic was to be on the fringe. They were often ostracized. The private chapel attendees were a disparate group, but passionate. At the time there was quite a controversy over the legality of holding a full Latin Mass. It soon became illegal to perform it. The Father who performed the Mass at the private chapel went to see the Pope about his predicament. He was finally given a rite of exception, which entitled him to say the Latin Mass until his death.

During the next six years, Countess Kinnoull called upon Nancy to drive up to Campbell whenever Archbishop Lefebvre was there on retreat. By this time the Countess was in her late seventies and tired easily, making the drive to Campbell impossible. Nancy felt honored to be of assistance, for by now she had learned that Lady Kinnoull was a great benefactress to the Society of Saint Pius X.

Their visits with the Archbishop were kept short because of his full schedule. Nancy recalled, "Being in his Excellency's presence was like being in a room filled with warmth and light. His eyes were intensely blue and he was delightful. When he smiled it was very warm and cordial, like an embrace, and you felt very blessed to be in his presence."

Although Nancy Welch and Countess Kinnoull had a few things in common, social status was not one of them. Nancy knew her place. After all, Lady Kinnoull was nobility, with rank, with money, with social status, and no one would just approach her; it just wouldn't be done. If she asked something of you, then you were more than happy to oblige. But you would never approach her.

One Christmas morning in 1983, with one act of kindness, that social barrier came tumbling down.

It was a mild 60 degrees with the sun beginning to appear through the clouds when the nine o'clock Christmas Mass at the private chapel concluded. As the congregation departed with wishes of a Merry Christmas, Nancy and Countess Kinnoull found themselves together on the steps outside.

"What a magnificent service," said Nancy.

"Yes, the Christmas Mass is one of my favorites," said the Countess. "I bet you have big plans for Christmas?"

"I do have an evening dinner engagement. What about you? Are you spending Christmas with friends and family?"

"No, not this year."

"You mean you're going to be alone on Christmas?" Nancy was shocked.

"It seems that all my friends are traveling."

"I have nothing to do until this evening. Would it be all right if I called on you for a visit this afternoon?" asked Nancy.

"Yes, I'd be very pleased to have you over for a visit. Let's say about two o'clock." Lady Kinnoull took out a notepad and drew a quick map to her house. "With no street addresses in Carmel, I find it is easier to draw a map rather than explain how to get to my house."

"Thank you, Lady Kinnoull. I'll look forward to our visit."

On the drive home, Nancy kept wondering if she had done the right thing by practically inviting herself to Countess Kinnoull's house. Wanting to take a gift, Nancy panicked when she realized that all the stores were closed for the holiday. What does one give a countess who has everything? She looked around her apartment, hoping to find something she could take as a gift. She dusted off an old bottle of Champagne she had been saving for New Year's Eve, tied a ribbon around an unopened box of chocolates that a neighbor had given her, then headed out the door, not wanting to be late.

With the very detailed map to follow, Nancy had no problem finding the Kinnoull estate, arriving right at the appointed time.

"Merry Christmas, Countess Kinnoull," said Nancy, handing the gifts to her hostess.

"How kind of you, please come in." She led Nancy into the living room. "I'll only be a minute. I've fixed a pot of tea. I'll get the tray and we'll head upstairs."

Nancy looked around at the many large portrait paintings, not realizing that the Countess had painted them. When Lady Kinnoull returned from the kitchen with the tea tray they went upstairs to a second floor study.

They enjoyed tea and scones and chatted for about an hour and a half. Their conversation was cordial, but very superficial. Countess Kinnoull had learned from her aristocratic background not to speak freely about herself, her background, her wealth or achievements, but had acquired the fine art of saying a great deal about very little.

When the visit came to an end, Lady Kinnoull walked Nancy downstairs.

"I've so enjoyed our visit. You have a beautiful home," said Nancy when they reached the foyer.

"Could you wait one moment, I have something for you," said the Countess. She went back upstairs and was gone for almost five minutes. When she returned she handed Nancy something in a white linen handkerchief.

Nancy gently opened the handkerchief. Inside was a small circular container with tiny brown flowers on the rim and a crystal clear cover. White velvet fabric lay underneath. And on it was a priceless gift, a chip of Saint Bernadette's bone.

Nancy gasped. "I came to the Catholic religion through a study of the Saints. I chose Saint Bernadette as my Patron Saint."

"Then you were meant to have this Relic and here is the paper of authenticity. Merry Christmas, Nancy."

Nancy was overwhelmed by her generosity, but felt sad that her own gift to the Countess of chocolates and Champagne was so insignificant.

But she need not have worried, for she had actually given Countess Kinnoull a much more precious gift. She had given of her time, the time to visit a lonely soul on Christmas Day.

A Relic of Saint Bernadette (Graciously provided by Nancy Welch)

Chapter 49

A Reflection

Countess Kinnoull filled her last few years with painting, writing and developing a philanthropist foundation for her many charitable causes. She was extremely generous when it came to a charity, organization, or cause that she held dear to her heart. The Countess was a champion to those unable to fend for themselves.

A cause she was most passionate about was education. On the campus of the Monterey Institute of International Studies, an affiliate of Middlebury College, sits a two-story house originally built in the 1930s. It's known as *The Kinnoull House* in honor of its benefactor, the Countess of Kinnoull. Her foundation, the *Sylvanus Charitable Trust,* funded the purchase and renovation of the structure for academic use. The Trust has also provided significant support for language curriculum over five decades.

So heartfelt was Lady Kinnoull for *The Society of Saint Pius X,* with its teaching priests of the importance of preserving the Traditional Latin Mass, that she added this mission statement to her *Sylvanus Charitable Trust: For the welfare of and prevention of cruelty to animals and advancement of traditional teachings and practices of the Roman Catholic Church as taught and accepted before the Second Vatican Council.*

In 1984, the Monterey County SPCA presented Claude with the first *Countess of Kinnoull Humanitarian Award* for her tremendous efforts in

founding of the Monterey County SPCA. Then in 1985, Countess
Kinnoull watched with pride as her longtime friend Gwendolyn May
received the same award. Gwen described Lady Kinnoull as *The Angel
in the Background.*

Although she tired easily from long road trips, Countess Kinnoull
still enjoyed the thrill of speed. She often raced around Carmel and the
Monterey Peninsula in her metallic gold Camaro, with its Cadillac
engine.

After numerous complaints of some maniac speeding through the
side streets of Carmel, the police set a speed trap to catch the culprit.
Just as the officer was parking his police car off a side road, a flash of
gold sped by him. He turned on his lights and pursued the offender, who
slowed the car to a stop. With ticket book in his left hand and his right
hand at the ready on his holster, the officer cautiously approached the
driver's side of the vehicle. The driver slowly lowered the window.

"I see you have a new car," said the officer.

"Yes, and she runs great," replied the driver. "Did I ever tell you I
was a racecar driver?"

"Yes, Countess Kinnoull . . . the operative word being *was*," he
replied. "The streets around here are not meant for racing. There are too
many animals and children running around."

"Oh, but I'd never hit an animal . . . or a child, for that matter. I'm
too good of a driver."

"Not good enough. You're breaking the law." The officer pulled out
his ticket book.

"Just tell me how much I owe you and we'll settle it right now." She
watched the officer fill out the ticket form.

"I'm afraid that's not how we do business. Please sign the bottom of
the form." He handed her the ticket book.

She quickly signed her signature. "There, now may I go?" she
asked.

The officer tore off her copy and handed it to her. "Here's your ticket and please note that this is more than a speeding ticket. You're to appear before the county court house within thirty days. I'm recommending that your license be revoked."

"Whatever for?"

"Countess Kinnoull, over the years we have issued you stacks of warnings and speeding tickets; so many that we could paper the entire police department with them."

"But I've always paid you promptly, haven't I? And in the forty years that I've lived here, I've never even hit a tree . . . now you can't deny that."

"That doesn't excuse you from breaking the law. Safety in our community comes first. Have a good day, Countess Kinnoull." The officer walked back to his vehicle. Lady Kinnoull slowly drove home.

A few weeks later, Anita was looking forward to her usual evening visit with Lady Kinnoull. She recited in her head the new jokes that she had practiced for several weeks. She thought for sure they would bring much laughter.

Claude sat in the driver's seat of her Camaro running her hands over the smooth burnished steering wheel, her eyes filling with tears. For several moments she stared into the rearview mirror to a flashback of more youthful days on the Brooklands' racetrack. Her hands tightening on the steering wheel, shifting gears as she accelerated up the steep incline. The roar of the engines and the smell of the oil and gas . . . it was all fading away, as was her life.

"They can't do this to me . . . they just can't do this," she yelled out loud. She stopped when she heard footsteps crunching on the gravel driveway. Quickly dabbing her eyes with the sleeve of her sweater, Claude opened the car door.

"My word, you scared me half to death," said Anita. "Am I too early?"

"You're right on time . . . I was just sitting there remembering my racing days. But now all that's over."

"Boy, I wish I could have seen you then." They walked toward the house. When they got into the foyer, Anita could see Countess Kinnoull's red swollen eyes.

"What's happened? she asked.

"They've gone and done it now."

"Done what? And who are they?"

"The police and the court have suspended my license for good. Apparently some neighbor complained . . . I'd sure like to know who it was. I might be fast, but I'm one of the safest drivers around. Now they have ruined my life!"

"I'll be happy to drive you anywhere you need to go," said Anita.

"You don't understand . . . my life is over! My car was my freedom. When I touch the steering wheel a surge of adrenalin pumps through my veins, it's what keeps me alive!"

"But they didn't take away your car, did they?" asked Anita.
Countess Kinnoull stopped and thought about it, then smiled. "You're right . . . they only took away my license." They both laughed.

"Now let me tell you some of my new jokes," said Anita as she closed the front door.

Chapter 50

The Harvest of My Dreams

In 1985, after a long illness, Countess Kinnoull had come to the realization that her days were numbered. She began to get her affairs in order.

Nancy Welch never forgot that day in May when she went to the private chapel and found out that Lady Kinnoull was quite ill. She knew that the Archbishop Lefebvre would be at the retreat in Campbell, so she made that fateful phone call praying that His Excellency would be able to visit his dying friend. Because of that call, Lady Kinnoull received the blessing from the Archbishop that her soul longed for. She found true serenity before her final journey. Two months later on Sunday, July 21, 1985, she left her earthly home for Glory.

A Rosary was recited for Countess Claude Marguerite Kinnoull on Wednesday July 24th, and her memorial service was held at two o'clock on the following day at the Carmelite Monastery south of Carmel.

Nancy Welch recalled arriving for the memorial and finding the chapel almost full. Although it was a closed casket, she learned that Countess Kinnoull wished to be laid to rest in her nun's habit, and as a last request, insisted on a High Requiem Mass, which was considered to be a Trinitarian right. Despite the fact that the Countess was a great benefactress to the Carmelite Monastery, Sister Francesca said that they so admired Lady Kinnoull that they would have performed the High Requiem Mass for nothing.

As the nuns sang the beautiful and haunting Latin chants, Nancy looked down upon the child-size coffin that protected the now petite and frail body of a once formidable and courageous woman of substance. The Countess never wavered in her religious allegiance to the Tridentine Mass, which during her travels she had been able to hear in every country she visited.

Countess Claude Kinnoull received many honors for her political, humanitarian and church activities during her life. She was presented with one of the highest honors in France, *Knight of the French Legion of Honor;* presented as a *Commander of the Royal Order of the Lion of the Congo* by Belgium's King Leopold; and Spain honored her as a *Knight of the Order of Isabelle the Catholic.* Pope Pius XI awarded her with the highest medals that can be awarded to the laity by a Pope, the *Cross Pro Ecclesia et Pontifice,* and as a *Dame of the Holy Sepulcher* whereby she upheld the works of the Latin Patriarchate of Jerusalem while preserving the spiritual duty of proclaiming the faith.

For over fifty years Countess Claude Kinnoull was a nun of the *Third Order of Discalced Carmelites.* She also held membership with the *Society of Western Artists, Monterey Peninsula Museum of Art, The Carmel Art Association,* and *The Tor House Foundation,* along with supporting many local and international charities.

Unfortunately, the Countess did not live long enough to see her and Sharon Andreason's dream come true. In 1992 the SPCA joined in partnership with *Horse Power (*now called *SPCA Horse Power),* an equine rescue and adoption organization that has been watching out for horses since 1992.

Always thinking of others, Lady Kinnoull left a few last words to her friends in the program she had prepared for her own memorial service:

For any who have held me in affection of friendship, I leave these thoughts:

Meditate sometimes, with devotion, upon the Beauty of God. Make of August 6, the Feast of the Transfiguration, the Feast of His Beauty – For it commemorates the day when, on the high mountain and before the gaze of His Apostles, He was transfigured, His Face shining like the sun – And they, "lifting their eyes, saw only JESUS, alone."

For the greater part of my life, One thought above all others has brought me peace in moments of dismay, serenity in grief – The thought that: Only One Thing Matters Absolutely. Suffering, good deeds, our efforts, our faults and all other things matter only in relation to it, in so far as they contribute or fail to contribute to that one thing – Whether in the close confines of time in which we live or in the timelessness to which we go; whether on this familiar speck of stardust which is Earth or in the furthest worlds and galaxies of God's Creation – worlds where beings beyond our ken and our imagining (our fellow creatures, no less) may have their dwelling – only this one thing matters: This one thing, which is – THE GLORY OF GOD – It is to this infinite Splendour that I offer the minuteness of my life, my death, my eternity

– Claude Marguerite de Kinnoull –

Archbishop Lefebvre recognizing the crucial role she played as benefactress to the Society of Saint Pius X, paid this tribute in an announcement circulated upon news of her death: *"She could consider the young priests of the Society as her children because without her help at the beginning it would not have been possible to fulfill our priestly work."*

Countess Claude Kinnoull made certain that upon her death the *Society of Saint Pius X* and the many and varied charitable causes that were dear to her were supported by her estate trust fund, which continues to this day to do her good work. She has come full circle. She dreamed of the day when the Traditional Latin Mass would again be allowed to flourish, and that animal welfare be brought to the attention of all mankind. A poem by her uncle *Noel H. Wills* in 1920 best sums up the realization of her dream: (Permission to use poem from Major Tom Wills, Miserden Park, Glos)

The Harvest of My Dreams

Still is there joy to win the golden yield,
Red glow of orchard, yellow gold of field
While Nature for my keeping
Gives a secret, as it seems,
I shall one day go a-reaping
The Harvest of My Dreams

When moves the slow scythe o'er my grassy grave
My heart shall garner all those friends I crave,
So, in my long last sleeping
Far beyond the bright sunbeams,
I shall than I know be reaping
The Harvest of My Dreams

Countess Claude Kinnoull's body was laid to rest at the San Carlos Cemetery in Monterey. She was so respected by the *Society of Saint Pius X* that every year a memorial service is held in her memory.

A young Enid Fellows

EPILOGUE

Dear Lady Kinnoull,

Providence stepped in one day and we were destined to meet. A paper from the deed to our new house floated to the floor and my eyes came to rest on a most curious thing: a seal from England stamped 'Kinnoull Estate.'

With my curiosity piqued, I began a journey of discovery that would last nine years. The road was fraught with obstacles, but I persevered. When roadblocks tested my endurance, Providence would nudge me in a new direction. Each new discovery brought me closer to unveiling the mystery of your life.

Your stage was the world and you played many roles. Though petite in stature, you grew into a formidable woman to deal with; you became a woman of substance. Through many trials and tribulations, which you endured admirably, you turned to the one solid rock that had always been there for you – God.

Your faith in Him became the cornerstone of a new life for you; no longer the young impressionable girl manipulated by others, but an accomplished and courageous woman who put on the armor of God and never flinched when called to fight for the less fortunate or show allegiance to a worthy cause, such as missionaries, education and animal welfare.

Your life is a life worth remembering, worth studying; a glowing example of how one person can make a difference.

As we end this journey together, I put the last drop of ink to paper from a pen you once owned, but now as a gift given to me I'll always cherish. From this day forth, when I walk down the street where I live and look up at the estate which will forever remind me of you, I will be smiling, knowing I am the richer for having known you.

May you rest in peace, my dear Countess Kinnoull
~Kathleen Ambro~

Countess Kinnoull in her later years
(Photo provided by Mike Brown)

The Tree of Life mosaic by Lady Kinnoull
(Graciously provided by the Hess Family)

Countess Kinnoull provided the funds for the Language Education Center at The Middlebury Institute for International Studies in Monterey, California

The painting of the Voodoo doll makers in Africa by Claude Kinnoull

The Countess and the Earl's Apartment at 47 Portman Square in London

The Kinnoull Estate in Carmel, California

Kathleen Ambro

The Dinning Room in the Kinnoull Estate in Carmel
(Graciously provided by the Hess Family)

The Living Room at the Kinnoull Estate in Carmel
Notice the *Tree of Life* Mosaic above the fireplace.
(Graciously provided by the Hess Family)

A young Enid Margaret Fellows

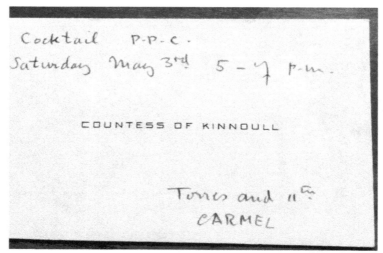

Countess Kinnoull's Calling Card
(Graciously provided by Kathleen Sonntag)

A Needlepoint Pillow Made by Countess Kinnoull
(Graciously provided by Anita Roy)

ACKNOWLEDGMENTS

When I set about to write of Countess Kinnoull's life it became a journey of many years and through those years I've been touched by the generosity and encouragement of so many people. I thank you all from the bottom of my heart and hope if I inadvertently left your name off the list, that you will forgive me.

Lee Andreason – a friend of Lady Kinnoull's who moved to Spain.

Fr. Jacques Emily - who always believed a book should be written about Lady Kinnoull. His kindness and prayers and knowledge of the workings of the Catholic Church have been immensely helpful.

Mark Gallegos – from St. Aloysius Retreat House for his quick responses to my many questions and for finding Father Francois Laisney for me.

Nancy Welch – for befriending Lady Kinnoull one lonely Christmas; and for making the most important phone call of her life to Archbishop Lefebvre. She will be greatly missed.

Mike Brown, former Carmel City Council member – he worked at the SPCA and often met with Lady Kinnoull to go over the books. His memories of Lady Kinnoull were delightful. He graciously provided a photo of Lady Kinnoull to be included in the book.

Elizabeth and Lou Ungaretti – grew up next door to Lady Kinnoull who always gave the Ungaretti children Godiva Chocolates for Halloween. They both had some great stories to tell. Lou will be greatly missed.

Nancy Larson – for pointing me in a new direction in my research.

Denise Sallee, Rose Franzen, Ashlee Wright and Jean Chapin – the Reference Librarians at Harrison Memorial Library's Local History Room.

Victor Henry, Dennis Copeland, Eboni Harris and Caroline May – the Reference Librarians at the Monterey Public Library.

Lisa A. Hoefler - the Director of Operations for the SPCA of Monterey County.

Ann Flower - coordinator of Public Services Library of the Monterey Institute of International Studies for sending me in the right direction for the Kinnoull House.

Erin Morita - Stewardship Officer of the Monterey Institute of International Studies.

Nathalie Mathurin, Assistant to Consul General de France in San Francisco – for the history on why Countess Kinnoull was given the honor of Knight of the Legion of Honor for her services to France during the war.

Vern Yadon, retired Director of the National History Museum in Pacific Grove, California. – for telling me about the artifacts of Chief Red Eagle that are in storage at the museum and were given to them by Lady Kinnoull.

Yolanda Gurries – for allowing the Holy Mass for Lady Kinnoull to be held at her home and for her encouragement and helpful E-mails.

Gino San Felice – for inviting me to Lady Kinnoull's memorial services and for the beautiful pen and ink drawings of the invitations.

Father Francois Laisney – for his wonderful letter describing the day he, Father Finnegan, and Archbishop Lefebvre drove to Carmel to visit Lady Kinnoull.

Anita Roy – for being willing to talk to me about the time she was Lady Kinnoull's assistant. For her terrific sense of humor and great anecdotes and for being such a wonderful neighbor and for the delightful teas we had together. She will be greatly missed.

David, Bob and Louie Roy – for graciously allowing me to include several pictures they had of Lady Kinnoull in the book.

Laurette Barabe - for her fond memories of being Lady Kinnoull's secretary. She will be greatly missed.

Sue McCloud, former Mayor of Carmel-by-the-Sea - for her anecdote regarding Lady Kinnoull and the Sunset Center and her references to others and for her taking the time from her busy schedule to do some inquiries on my behalf.

Jean Nieto - Grew up knowing Lady Kinnoull all her life. Her Aunt and Uncle worked for Lady Kinnoull and traveled with her. Lady Kinnoull would ship her used clothes from Paris to England for Jean when she was a teenager. She graciously provided numerous pictures for the book. She will be greatly missed.

Elisabeth Karr – for her professional reference work in London that uncovered numerous articles and pictures of Countess Kinnoull and for the beautiful photos she provided. Without her help this book would not have been possible.

Sister Francisca – for believing in me and giving me the encouragement to pursue Countess Kinnoull's story and allowing me to interview her. She will be greatly missed.

Sister Mercedes – for being such a delight to interview and for climbing up ladders to get the pictures of the paintings of *The Mysteries of the Rosary* which Countess Kinnoull donated to the Carmelite Monastery and for the lovely gift of the Countess Kinnoull's writing pen and stationary box for which I am very grateful and will forever treasure.

Connie and Ken Hess – the current owners of what use to be called the Kinnoull Estate, for graciously providing several photographs that will be used in the book and for allowing me to tour the estate.

Joy and Wayne Chapman – Wayne for kindly taking time from his trip to Paris to find and photograph Countess Kinnoull's apartment and street where she lived. Joy who always had a smile and words of encouragement, she is dearly missed.

Kathleen Sonntag – for providing Countess Kinnoull's calling card.

Gabe – for loaning me two books on Franco.

Kay Holz and Kathryn Gualtieri– for our many hours of writing discussions and for some great suggestions.

William Neish – The excellent *Story Tailor* whose fine editing and keen insight helped me grow as a writer.

Greg and Cindy Knight – for walking me through every step and feel of flying a double-winged aeroplane, so I would not have to fly in one.

John Ambro, Jr. – for his knowledge of Ancestory.com to locate many useful articles and especially finding the manifest of the ships and airlines that showed Countess Kinnoull, Monsignor Vincent de Moor, Jack (John) and Florence Newbury had been passengers.

Bob Chadwick – for surprising me with the actual program for the 1940 *New York's World Fair*. The descriptions were most helpful.

Grace Gibbons and her daughter, Amy – for helping answer my late night questions with their knowledge of the Catholic religion.

Gloria Valentino – for loaning me a rosary for the book cover.

Bill Akass – for obtaining some last minute information from the London library and for locating a contact for Noel Wills' granddaughter.

Dr. Catherine Wills – for giving me permission to use her grandfather's poem *The Harvest of My Dreams*.

SOURCES

BOOKS

S.J. Watson, *Furnished with Ability, The lives and Times of the Wills Family* – Preface: vii, viii, pages: 32, 69-70, 116-117, 192-194, 210-212, 215-216. 229. 317.

Michael Allaby, *Grasslands* – page: 19.

Bernard Tissier De Mallerais, *The Biography Marcel Lefebvre* – pages: 100-101, 383.

Charles Mosley, editor, *Burke's Peerage, Baronetage & Knightage* – 107th edition,

3 volumes (Wilmington, Delaware, U.S.A.) *Burke's Peerage* (Genealogical Books) ltel, 2003, volume 2 – page 2192.

Ellen Micheletti, *All About Romance: Gambling in Historic England* – pages: 1-2.

Hugo Hinfelaar, *Footsteps on the Sands of Time, A Life of Bishop Jan van Sambeek* – M.Afr. – Rome, Society of Missionaries of Africa 2007 – Missionaries of Africa – History Series No. 8.

Warren Carroll, *The Last Crusade* – pages 23, 39-40, 180.

Gabrielle Ashford Hodges, *A Concise Biography of FRANCO* – pages 105-107, 122, 124-125.

V. De Moor and Claudek, *L'horreur Rouge En Terre D'Espagne.*

L'Edition Universelle, 53 rue Royale, 53 Bruxelles, *La Croisière Bleue et les Missions d'Afrique par L'Équipage de La Croisière Bleue.*

Margery Hamilton Wills, *The Collected Prose, Verse of Noël H. Wills* – page 16 – *The Harvest of My Dreams.*

Monica Hudson, *Images of America – Carmel By-The-Sea* – pages 45, 51, 54.

Daisy Bostick and Dorothea Castelhun, *Carmel at Work and Play* – pages 24, 35-36, 95.

Joan Carroll Cruz, *RELICS* – Chapter 13 Relics of the Saints – pages 218-220.

Jacquelyn Lindsey, *2001 Catholic Family Prayer Book* – OSV Press, page 65

Sharron Lee Hale, *A Tribute to Yesterday* – page 90 – *The Bulletin Board*

Ronald M. and Susan A. James, *Castle In The Sky: George Whittell, Jr. and The Thunderbird Lodge*

Carmelite Nuns of Carmel, CA, *Footprints from Mount Carmel to Carmel by the Sea*

NEWSPAPERS

New York Times – May 21, 1922 – *Widow Pursues Young Earl of Kinnoull*
London Evening News – May 1923 – *Coming Out Party*
London Evening News – August 20, 1923 – *Lord Kinnoull and His Betrothal, Girl Who Writes Poetry*
London Evening News – December 1923 – *Wedding Announcement*
London Times – December 17, 1923 – *Marriage, Earl of Kinnoull and Miss E. Hamilton-Fellows*
The Scotsman – Monday, December 17, 1923, page 7 – *Kinnoull Wedding Picture & Announcement*
The Scotsman – April 26, 1924, page 7
The Scotsman – Monday, May 5, page 4
The Autocar – May 9, 1924, page 15
London Times – November 25, 1924
London Times – January 26, 1925
London Times – March 14, 1925
London Times – April 20, 1925 – *The Estate Market A Ducal Offer*
London Times – June 10, 1925 – *Aeroplane Accident*
Zanesville Times Signal – Sunday, December 12, 1926 – *London – $5,000,000 Wind-Up of the Baby Countess' Love Woes, Fortune Smiles On The Girl Who Impulsively Left Her Bankrupt Earl Flat* – written by Sandown Strachey.
The London Times – Saturday, June 25, 1927 – page 4, *Earl of Kinnoull's affairs. Scheme of Arrangement Opposed*
The Scotsman – Saturday, July 30, 1927 – page 8, *Earl of Kinnoull's Affairs Court Approves Scheme*
The Scotsman – Wednesday, November 2, 1927 – page 8, *Kinnoull Divorce Final*
London Times – September 10, 1927 – *Three Years Disqualification for Motorist*
La Croix Newspaper – *Articles in 1932 Regarding La Croisière Bleue* – March 29, 30, April 1, 2, 3, 5, 6, 7, 9, 10-11, 13, 14, 15,
Catholic Herald – August 10, 1935 – *Films and The Missions Progress of The International Office*
Catholic Herald – August 17, 1935 – *Missionary Work On Films B.I.P.C. Activities*

NEWSPAPERS *(cont.)*

The Times – Monday March 21, 1938 – page 14, *Lord Kinnoull's Obituary*
The New York Times – March 20, 1938 – *Earl of Kinnoull, Labor Peer, Dead*
The Monterey Peninsula Herald – Monday, December 8, 1941 – *Attack on Pearl Harbor*
The Carmel Pine Cone Cymbal – Friday, September 10, 1941, page 1, 4 – *Red Eagle Knew Bad Men of the Early West* by Irene Alexander
The Carmel Pine Cone – Friday, August 22, 1947 – *Red Eagle Ill*
The Monterey Peninsula Herald – October 16, 1947 – *Lady Kinnoull Returns After Trip Abroad*
By Marjory Warren
The Spectator – April 14, 1949 – *Through The North Window by Cashion MacLennan*
The Spectator – June 30, 1949
The Monterey Herald – 1957 – *Carmel's Own Indian Wins Niche in Village History* by Jerry Root
The Monterey Peninsula Herald – January 20, 1973 – *Countess Looks Back On Life of Adventure* by Mary Rodriguez
The Carmel Pine Cone – July 25, 1985 – *Carmel Countess Dies At Age 80*
The Carmel Pine Cone – June 17, 2011 – *In Your Dreams* by Mary Brownfield

NEWSLETTERS

Polish Nobility Association Foundation Newsletter – Spring/Summer 2007, page 10
SPCA Newsletter – Spring 1989 – *A Quality of Heart*
SPCA Newsletter – November/December 1999 – *Horse Rescue & Adoption, Horse Power Now Part of SPCA* page 1, 4
Regina Coeli Repost – April 2010, Number 220
BBC News Africa – *The Reality of Voodoo in Benin*

MAGAZINES

Carmel Magazine – May 1, 2013 – *Animal Instincts* by Renee Brincks

The Monterey Herald Weekend Magazine – May 20, 1970 – *SPCA Sees Dual Role in Serving Community* by Betty Patchin Greene

Peninsula Life – *Forever a Haven For Wildlife* by Anne Germain, Editor

Carmel Magazine – Winter 2015 – *Keeping Pets United with Loving Families* by Catrina Coyle

The Monterey Herald Weekend Magazine – November 5, 1989 – *Caring For Animals In Monterey County* by William Petersen

Mater Dei Magazine – Spring 2007 – *Operation D-Day,* page 2

Edwardian Promenade – *The London Season* by Evangeline, August 31, 2007

The Sketch – A British weekly journal. August 29, 1923, December 16, 1923.

WEBSITES

PastTimesProject.co.uk – 20th Century Review – Flappers

Sampson County Historical Society – http://www.rootsweb.ancestry.com/-ncsampso/hhjun00tm

National Library of New Zealand – newzealand.govt.nz – North Otago Times, Rōrahi XXXI, Putanga 6019, 5 Paengawhàwhà 1886, page 2

St. Paul's Church Knightsbridge – www.spkb.org – The History of St. Paul's

Brooklands Race Track – http://kelvin.leadhoster.com/brooklands/index.htm

Let Frivolity Reign: London's Roaring 1920s: NPR.org

PastTimesProject.co.uk – 20th Century Review – Nightclubs

Mellotone Records: The Rhythm Band – George Fisher & His Kit-Cat Band Playlist

Word-Cross Puzzle – *Invented by Arthur Wynne in 1923 England, later called Cross-Word puzzle*

Seetheholyland.net – Saint Anne Church

www.tripadvisor.co.uk reviews – Church of Saint Anne

The Joseph House website article – Charles de Foucauld

Notre-dame de la Garde – from Wikipedia

www.theancientegyptians.com – *The River Nile* by Adam Ashcroft

www.curuiosity.com – The Discovery Channel – *The Nile River*

www.maristbr.com – *The Marist Brothers*

WEBSITES (cont.)

Feast of Corpus Christi – from Wikipedia
www.medicinenet.com – *Leprosy,* page 5.htm
Lake Tanganyika – from Wikipedia
File: Qanat cross section.svg by Samuel Bailey 2009-12-2 – from Wikipedia
www.wimplonpc.co.uk/CGT PCs01.html#anchor144198 – French Line Mediterranean Services, page 9
www.fisheaters.com/scapulars.html – *Scapulars* – the habit of monks and nuns
Ignacio Zuloaga During and After the Spanish Civil War – from Wikipedia
Nobelprize.org.NobelMediaAB2013.web30Mar2014.http://www.nobelprice.org/nobel_prize/literature/laureates/1911/
Wikipedia.org/wiki/alma_mahler – ALMA: Alma and Lisbon, 1940 Lourdes
www.brainyquote.com/quotes/authors/m/maurice_maeterlinek.html
Sainte-Anne-de-Beaupré – article from Wikipedia
Johnny Roventini, Bellboy from the Wyndham New Yorker Hotel – from Wikipedia
1939-1940 New York's World Fair – from Wikipedia
CriticalPast.com – *The Road of Tomorrow Video*
New York State Route 9B to Rouses Point – from Wikipedia
www.sanctuairesainteanne.org – *Façade and History of Saint Anne*
www.theroadwanderer.net/66illinois/chain.htm – *The Chain of Rocks Bridge*
Menus.nypl.org – *1940 Luncheon Menu*
U.S. Route 66 – from Wikipedia
Fred Harvey Company History – from Wikipedia
www.outpostusa.org – *June 22, 2013 – Route 66 – Canvas Water Bags*
www.desertusatravelguide – *Day Trip #7: Historic Route 66 to Amboy, California*
Ocean Park, Santa Monica, California – from Wikipedia
Mission Santa Barbara – from Wikipedia
www.historynet.com – Weider History – *Japanese Submarines Prowl the U.S. Coastline 1941*
www.serviceofableonlinemedia.com – Friday, September 14, 2007: *For the First Time (or the Last Time) 1947: Last Horse Cab License in London*
www.thefriendshiptrain1947.org/ – *The 1947 Friendship Train* by Dorothy R. Scheele

<u>WEBSITES</u> (cont.)

www.eyewitnesstohistory.com – (2001) *The London Blitz, 1940*
http://en.wololedoa.org/wiki/SecondVatican – article on *The Second Vatican Council*
www.livescience.com – *The Sahara: Facts, Climate and Animals of the Desert* by Kim Ann Zimmerman – *Saharan Love Affair? Article by Jane Atkins, Researcher, deserts and grasslands*
www.thesisonzuloaga.com – *Thesis on Zuloaga* by Dena Crosson (2009), University of Maryland
www.carmelbythesea.com – *Department of Community Planning and Building Historic Survey Evaluation.* Evaluation of the Kinnoull/Watson House, November 10, 1993
Ancestery.com – *Manifest of Alien Passengers for The United States on the S.S. Nea Hellas sailing from Lisbon, Portugal on October 4, 1940. (See page 4 of the Manifest)* and *the S.S. Mauretania Manifest arriving in New York on September 30, 1947* carrying the Newburys and Kinnoull

<u>LETTERS</u>
A letter from Father Laisney – regarding trip with Archbishop Lefebvre to Carmel
The French Consulate letter – San Francisco – Translation of honors awarded
A letter from Countess Kinnoull – to Jean Nieto regarding wedding gift

The Author

Kathleen Ambro

K athleen found a love for writing when encouraged by her fifth grade teacher while living in France. When she returned to the United States she continued her love for writing by becoming a board member of the *California Writer's Club – San Fernando Valley Branch* and wrote articles for *To Life magazine and L.A. Parent magazine* where she was an intern. That experience led her to a position with a local Southern California newspaper, *Valley Life* as a photojournalist with her own weekly column. She is a member of the *Society of Children's Book Writers and Illustrators* and has published three children's books in *The Adventures of Bebe and Poppy* series.

She currently lives in Carmel, California where her writing took a journey of nine years of research into the life of a remarkable woman, Countess Claude Kinnoull who touched the lives of many proving one person can make a difference in a positive way. Kathleen hopes you'll enjoy her first biographical novel. You can contact her at: www.kathleenambro.com.

CPSIA information can be obtained
at www.ICGtesting.com
Printed in the USA
LVHW082118101218
599938LV00037B/1831/P